alfred
HITCHCOCK'S
BORROWERS
OF THE
NIGHT

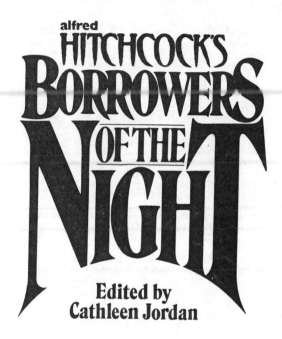

alfred
HITCHCOCK'S
BORROWERS
OF THE
NIGHT

Edited by
Cathleen Jordan

The Dial Press
Davis Publications, Inc.
380 Lexington Avenue, New York, N.Y. 10017

All of the stories in this book were first published in *Alfred Hitchcock's Mystery Magazine*. Grateful acknowledgment is hereby made for permission to reprint the following:

The Souvenir by Donald Olson; copyright © H. S. D. Publications, Inc., 1974; reprinted by permission of Blanche C. Gregory, Inc. *Speak Well for the Dead* by Nancy Schachterle; copyright © H. S. D. Publications, Inc., 1972; reprinted by permission of the author. *The Girl in Gold* by Jonathan Craig; copyright © H. S. D. Publications, Inc., 1970; reprinted by permission of Scott Meredith Literary Agency, Inc. *Four on an Alibi* by Jack Ritchie; copyright © H. S. D. Publications, Inc., 1973; reprinted by permission of Larry Sternig Literary Agency. *The Bag* by Patrick O'Keeffe; copyright © H. S. D. Publications, Inc., 1972; reprinted by permission of Cathleen O'Keeffe. *The Long Curve* by George Grover Kipp; copyright © H. S. D. Publications, Inc., 1969; reprinted by permission of the author. *The Green Fly and the Box* by Waldo Carlton Wright; copyright © H. S. D. Publications, Inc., 1969; reprinted by permission of Roy H. Wright. *Minutes of Terror* by Donald Honig; copyright © H. S. D. Publications, Inc., 1974; reprinted by permission of Raines & Raines. *Long Shot* by Michael Collins; copyright © H. S. D. Publications, Inc., 1972; reprinted by permission of the author. *Puddle* by Arthur Porges; copyright © H. S. D. Publications, Inc., 1972; reprinted by permission of Scott Meredith Literary Agency, Inc. *A Bum Rap* by Marilyn Granbeck; copyright © H. S. D. Publications, Inc., 1973; reprinted by permission of the author. *The Snatch* by Bill Pronzini; copyright © H. S. D. Publications, Inc., 1969; reprinted by permission of the author. *The Right Move* by Al Nussbaum; originally published as "Decisions"; copyright © H. S. D. Publications, Inc., 1973; reprinted by permission of the author. *Night Storm* by Max Van Derveer; copyright © H. S. D. Publications, Inc., 1968; reprinted by permission of Janet Van Derveer. *When This Man Dies* by Lawrence Block; copyright © 1964 by H. S. D. Publications, Inc., reprinted by permission of the author. *Busman's Holiday* by James Holding; copyright © H. S. D. Publications, Inc., 1973; reprinted by permission of Scott Meredith Literary Agency, Inc. *The Feel of the Trigger* by Donald E. Westlake; copyright © 1961 by H. S. D. Publications, Inc.; reprinted by permission of the author. *Public Office* by Elijah Ellis; copyright © 1964 by H. S. D. Publications, Inc.; reprinted by permission of Scott Meredith Literary Agency, Inc. *The Beast Within* by Margaret B. Maron; copyright © H. S. D. Publications, Inc., 1972; reprinted by permission of the author. *Where Have You Been, Ross Ivy?* by Pauline C. Smith; copyright © H. S. D. Publications, Inc., 1972; reprinted by permission of the author. *Bronze Resting* by Arthur Moore; copyright © 1964 by H. S. D. Publications, Inc.; reprinted by permission of the author. *Dead End* by Stephen Wasylyk; copyright © H. S. D. Publications, Inc., 1974; reprinted by permission of the author. *The Trouble Was* by Ron Goulart; copyright © H. S. D. Publications, Inc., 1971; reprinted by permission of the author. *The Grapevine Harvest* by Ed Dumonte; copyright © 1966 by H. S. D. Publications, Inc.; reprinted by permission of Larry Sternig Literary Agency. *Final Acquittal* by Edward Wellen; copyright © H. S. D. Publications, Inc., 1974; reprinted by permission of the author. *Mousetrap* by Edwin P. Hicks; copyright © H. S. D. Publications, Inc., 1968; reprinted by permission of the author. *The Adventure of the Haunted Library* by August Derleth; copyright © 1963 by H. S. D. Publications, Inc.; reprinted by permission of Scott Meredith Literary Agency, Inc.

INTRODUCTION

"**B**orrowers of the night" is a phrase with a particularly ominous ring. In the first place, it comes from *Macbeth*, a play so ringed around with superstitions that—in a long theatrical tradition—actors won't refer to it by name. They call it "the Scottish play" instead.

In the second place, it was a phrase used by Banquo, before he became a ghost. "I must become a borrower of the night/For a brief hour or twain," he tells Macbeth in Act III. Banquo didn't mean anything especially fearsome by that—he was only saying he expected to be out after dark. But unluckily for him, Macbeth saw opportunity in that darkness and sent the First and Second Murderers to do him in, wrapped in its cloak.

The mystery story is, of course, full of those who borrow the night for nefarious purposes. Murderers and burglars have frequently preferred to operate then and have sought its protection (see Donald E. Westlake's "The Feel of the Trigger" in this volume for a story that makes particular use of darkness). But regardless of whether crime and night go together literally, those who commit crimes are borrowers of the night in a metaphorical sense as well—for they must operate clandestinely and hide themselves however they can, and for they have dark purposes in their hearts.

In the stories that follow, many black plans are carried out, or at least attempted. *Alfred Hitchcock's Mystery Magazine* has been specializing in such tales for a long time, and we here present a collection from its pages that takes us from a pleasant small town in America in summer to Solar Pons's London, from the hard world of the police beat to a moonlit night in Lucerne, from a young man being helped by some convicts to a private eye who must track a man down—at peril to them both—in Mexico. There are stories from the point of view of a ghost and from that of a cat; there are eerie tales like Lawrence Block's "When This Man Dies" and Arthur Porges's "Puddle." But whatever the setting and whoever the characters, they are all full of shadowy deeds, cleverly recounted, and—for your reassurance, should you borrow a little night yourself to do some bedtime reading—full of those detectives, professional and amateur, who throw light on the trail.

Cathleen Jordan

CONTENTS

The Souvenir   *Donald Olson* 11
Speak Well for the Dead   *Nancy Schachterle* 21
The Girl in Gold   *Jonathan Craig* 34
Four on an Alibi   *Jack Ritchie* 56
The Bag   *Patrick O'Keeffe* 67
The Long Curve   *George Grover Kipp* 78
The Green Fly and the Box   *Waldo Carlton Wright* 87
Minutes of Terror   *Donald Honig* 96
Long Shot   *Michael Collins* 108
Puddle   *Arthur Porges* 127
A Bum Rap   *Marilyn Granbeck* 131
The Snatch   *Bill Pronzini* 142
Night Storm   *Max Van Derveer* 159
The Right Move   *Al Nussbaum* 170
When This Man Dies   *Lawrence Block* 178
Busman's Holiday   *James Holding* 187
The Feel of the Trigger   *Donald E. Westlake* 203
Public Office   *Elijah Ellis* 224
The Beast Within   *Margaret B. Maron* 236
Where Have You Been, Ross Ivy?   *Pauline C. Smith* 251
Bronze Resting   *Arthur Moore* 264
Dead End   *Stephen Wasylyk* 272
The Trouble Was   *Ron Goulart* 292
The Grapevine Harvest   *Ed Dumonte* 299
Final Acquittal   *Edward Wellen* 309
Mousetrap   *Edwin P. Hicks* 315
The Adventure of the Haunted
    Library   *August Derleth* 330

alfred HITCHCOCK'S BORROWERS OF THE NIGHT

The Souvenir

by Donald Olson

I t was my custom to stay on for a week or two at The Buckeye after the season ended; it was then that I did my best work and in my spare time I would help Margit, my landlady, prepare the ancient rooming house for winter. Her grandmother and aged aunt, with whom she had passed a dull, migratory existence for many years, opening the place in Glen Avon in May, closing it after Labor Day and journeying to St. Petersburg for the winter months, had both died down there within weeks of each other two years before, but Margit still practiced the same ritual; she was like a bird who finds its cage is open at last but can't decide where to go or even if its wings will work.

I happened to be alone in the house, trying to finish the last chapter of my novel and so deeply absorbed I jumped a bit when the bell rang, and when I went down to open the door I found an attractive but doomed-looking woman with blue eyes and cinnamon-colored hair peering through the screen. A foreign sports car was parked at the curb.

"I'm looking for Miss Fanchon. I'm Helen Maier."

The name didn't register at first. I told her Margit had gone for a walk but should be back at any minute.

"I was told the Fillmore—is that its name?—is the only hotel still open. Maybe I ought to go around there and see about a room for the night. I've been driving for hours."

She gave a sudden cry as she followed me into the parlor and I put out my hand, thinking she might have twisted her ankle on the little step-down. Her face was sickly pale and when I saw the direction of her gaze I knew at once who she was.

"Good heavens, how stupid of me! You must be Paul's wife."

She kept staring at that piece of sculpture on the mantel.

"Who's the artist?" she asked faintly.

"Margit—Miss Fanchon." Then, idiotically trying to dispel the awkwardness of the moment, I added, "The head in the middle—that's mine." I always had to tell people because, in truth, it only vaguely

11

resembled me. Margit always said I had the sort of face to which
only Rodin could do justice.

Mrs. Maier's next question was obvious. "And the woman's? Could
that be—her?"

"Juliette Bardo. Yes."

She studied the head with the feigned indifference of a gallery
visitor. "I might have known she'd be stunning." She asked me if
I'd known Paul and I said yes, fairly well, as well as one gets to
know fellow lodgers in a rooming house during a short summer
season.

"Please sit down," I told her. "Or would you rather wait in another
room? I shouldn't have brought you in here."

She was already more composed. "Don't apologize. I'd known for
years that my husband had *feet* of clay. He played first violin in that
orchestra for fifteen years. I played second fiddle in his life for twelve.
This Juliette Bardo person was simply the latest of a long string.
It never bothered me that much, really. I'm not a romantic schoolgirl.
Paul always came back to me when the season ended. He was always
mine for those long winter months." She read my expression and
quickly laughed. "Don't get the wrong idea. I'm not tracking him
down. I've been spending the summer at Lake Placid and on my way
south thought it might be fun to see this place. I never came up
when Paul was with the symphony all those summers. He never
urged me to. Naturally. But I must say I was shocked when I got
his letter. Formal as a letter of resignation—which of course is what
it was. And typewritten at that! Saying he'd fallen in love with this
Juliette Bardo and was going away with her to start a new life. Oh,
it was a masterpiece of cruelty, that letter. Wish now I'd never
burned it. So, I just suddenly took it into my noggin to see the place
where this great romance flowered."

She surveyed the tacky-looking parlor with the sort of disap-
pointed frown one might see on the face of an avid Shakespearean
at his first glimpse of Verona.

She said, in reply to my question, that she hadn't heard a word
from Paul since that letter. "I suppose he was too ashamed. He's
never even tried to claim any of the money. He can't be playing with
any well-known orchestra. I would have heard. But then I suppose
they're living in Love Land, where material worries are unimpor-
tant. You knew her, too, I assume?"

I nodded but didn't feel it necessary to tell her that I'd thought
Juliette Bardo to be a rather sweet young creature. Not innocent—she

was an actress of sorts and had been around—but not tawdry, either. Exactly the sort of girl who would run off with a handsome dark-eyed violinist.

"Were you here when they left?" she wanted to know, and once again I wondered if she were not secretly in pursuit of the pair. Well, I certainly couldn't give her any clues to their destination. Margit had asked me to take some clothes to the dry cleaners in the city for her that day. When I'd got back she'd broken the news to me that the couple had run off.

I told her this, and she looked at her watch with a frown. "I'm hungry and tired. And frankly, this place gives me the willies. I suppose it's the sort of atmosphere only a writer—or musician—could appreciate." She stood up and wrapped her fur stole around her shoulders. "Tell Miss Fanchon I was here, will you? If she doesn't mind, I think I'll drop back later this evening." Then, glancing back, "Maybe I could get her to sell me those heads. Think what a joy it would be to smash them against a brick wall!"

I laughed. "If she thought you'd do that she'd never let you have them. They're the best things she's ever done."

I suppose I owned the worst—that head of the busboy Adonis she'd been working on the first year I knew her—her maiden effort.

Glen Avon, if you've never been there, is rather like Tanglewood or Chautauqua or that place in Vermont where my old college professor used to dry out while lecturing on the metaphysical poets. It has a miniature panorama of the Holy Land, a shaded plaza, an amphitheater where Glenn Miller *and* Toscanini had performed—it was that sort of place, something for everyone, and picturesque enough for the most demanding: quaintly narrow streets of eccentric-looking hotels and rooming houses huddled together in a vast leafy gloom which would abruptly end as you emerged from the shadow of the rambling hotel onto a greensward stretching between the bathing beach and the bell tower, and bordering one of the prettiest lakes in the Adirondacks.

Its eight-week midsummer season was crammed with a potpourri of operas, concerts, plays, lectures, and art classes, and then after Labor Day, when it all came to an end, its population would dwindle to a relative handful. I liked it best then, when its atmosphere was curiously mellow, as if ghostly strains of music still floated upon the quiet air, and a gentle autumnal haze would settle over the lake, and the Westminster chimes from the bell tower would echo among the narrow empty streets with an unearthly resonance, and I would look up from my work with that pleasant feeling of sheltered, isolated cosiness reminiscent of college days on a deserted summer campus.

This place to which I'd been coming for the past four summers was the typical frame rooming house in the center of the grounds, damp and umbrageous, in thickets of lily of the valley and spidery rhododendrons, with a painted sign, *The Buckeye*, nailed over the front door, and a buckeye tree planted beside the porch, because Margit's Auntie Belle and Nanna had come from Ohio in the antediluvian past.

My landlady herself, the spinster survivor of those two formidable dragons, was "an overgrown, clumsy, young-old woman with a plain, intense, kindly face which looked as radiantly sallow as a cloistered Carmelite's, and as ignorant of the more robust emotions,"—which is how I described her in a story I tried to write about her the first season I was here—a story I never finished, incidentally, because its main character seemed to resist my attempts to involve her in any sort of dramatic situation.

While the two female dragons were still alive I would occasionally come upon Margit sitting alone on one of the benches near the bell tower, watching the sailboats or the sunset, and we would exchange the shyest of helloes. Then one day I'd seen her at the Plaza Art Festival where, with others in the beginners' modeling class, she was trying her best to reconstruct in clay on a wire armature the head of a model, but it was pathetically clear to me as I watched her that she would never succeed, not from any specific lack of talent but because she was trying to get more than was there. The handsome youth the class was using as a model was all blue eyes and jawline, whereas Margit was trying to make something spiritual out of him, and I'd felt like stopping behind her and whispering in her ear: "Forget it, my dear. Apollo *has* no soul."

Instead, I'd waited till the rest of the class and spectators had dispersed, leaving her gazing sadly at the result of her wasted efforts, and I'd felt sorry for her and impulsively declared I wanted to buy it. She blinked at me. "Whatever for? It's hideous." I badgered her until she gave in, although she insisted on making me a present of it. It still sits here on my desk. Hideous, yes, but with a singular kind of honesty about it which makes it rather precious to me. In its way, I think it superior to those heads of Paul and Juliette, which seem to me too cheaply attractive, too spiritless.

Helen Maier drove off toward the Fillmore and I returned to Chapter Fifteen. I heard Margit come in about a half hour later and when I went down she was laying out the tea things. Auntie Belle and Nanna had been staunchly British and this habit of afternoon tea was one of their legacies Margit had not abandoned. Her tenants during the season found it rather endearing, and so did I.

My news surprised her. "Paul's *wife*? How very odd. Whatever brought *her* here?"

"She said she was on her way home from Lake Placid and decided to look the place over. Although, between you and me and the buckeye tree, I think it's more of a sentimental pilgrimage than she lets on."

"What do you mean?"

"Or else she's actually trying to track him down. Maybe that's why she wants to see you."

Margit looked scornful. "Well, land sakes, *I* can't tell her anything. If she thinks I played Friar Lawrence to *that* Juliette and her Romeo I'll soon set her straight. I can't tell her a thing she doesn't already know. Her husband was a charming man, but a philandering cheat. That's all I can tell her."

I sat down at the table and she poured the tea. "Your aunt and grandmother were such strict old ladies, I've often wondered why they allowed him to live here."

"Oh, he was smooth as syrup and sweet as honey, you know that. Could worm his way into any woman's good graces—without half trying."

I detected the faintest shadow of a blush and it occurred to me to wonder if Margit herself hadn't had romantic yearnings toward the passionate fiddler. Now, with Auntie Belle and Nanna dead and Paul no doubt far away, I felt bold enough to tease her about it. "I may be wrong, but I seem to recall his flirting with you, as well."

She responded with such a frank and painful blush I quickly backed off. "But then, that was probably my writer's diseased imagination."

She became unexpectedly thoughtful, sipping her tea with a musing, distant look, and then she put the cup down and looked at me with an expression which was brave almost to defiance.

"If you weren't going to Europe next summer I'd be quite willing to have you think so—that it was just your imagination, I mean."

Her face began to shine with an unaccustomed excitement, and once more she blushed.

I was intrigued. "You mean it wasn't only my imagination?"

"Well," this time she was tremulously coy, "not entirely, mabye."

I thought she was going to lose her nerve and pass it off as a joke, but I was wrong.

"You won't ever come back here, will you? I mean, after your summer in Europe. You'll go to other places. You won't ever come back here."

There was no point in lying. "No, I suppose not. But then, who can tell? I'm very fond of this place."

She continued to shake her head. "You won't ever come back. I can tell. The way you look at everything. You're storing it all up, aren't you?"

I admired her perceptiveness. "You should have taken up writing instead of sculpture."

"You said once you'd write a story about Auntie Belle and Nanna. Remember? My, but weren't they flattered? And you listened so patiently to their tales and reminiscences . . . You will write about them someday, won't you?"

"It's very likely."

The next thing she said caught me off guard. "I wish you'd write a story about me someday."

This may not look in print as touchingly wistful as it sounded. She sat across from me, this awkward-looking, soft-eyed, no longer young woman, and she was so painfully sincere it was embarrassing.

"Oh," I said, "I no doubt shall."

She lowered her eyes and shook her head. "No. I'm not the sort of person stories are written about. My life is too dull."

I couldn't help thinking about that story I'd tried to write about her and couldn't. Presently she looked up and gave me a slow, almost provocative smile. "If I tell you something—something I would never in my life tell another soul—will you promise to write a story about me?"

Still thinking of that one paragraph that had led nowhere, and trying not to look as guilty as I felt, I nodded.

"And you must promise never to tell anyone. I mean, in a story, that's different. No one will know it's me. You can change my name and appearance and all that."

"Of course."

She drew her chair in closer to the table. "Well, to tell the truth, Paul did flirt with me. When I'd bring up his towels and things. It was all in fun, of course. I knew he didn't mean anything by it, but how Auntie Belle and Nanna did tease me about it. Then one evening we ran into each other on the plaza and he took me to the Refectory and bought me an ice cream cone. And walked me home. I went to every one of the concerts that season. And the rehearsals. I'd sit way up there in the amphitheater behind the orchestra where he couldn't see me. But he knew I was there. He always knew . . . Want your tea warmed up?" She said this very crisply and I could tell she needed a moment to discharge the emotion in her voice—or to get her story straight in her head. I was almost sure she was making it all up.

"Then one night just a few days before the season ended, after the last concert, I waited for him and he walked home with me. He held my hand and we took a roundabout way along the shore. He kissed me by the bell tower. That night, after everybody was asleep and the house was quiet, he came to my room."

Curiously, she said this without blushing. "I can't believe Auntie Belle and Nanna really found out. They couldn't have. But there was something in the way they looked at me the next morning . . . but they didn't say anything and the season ended and Paul went home. To his wife, I suppose, although none of us knew he even had a wife then. I honestly didn't expect to see him again, you know."

She sipped her tea with a mildly sour expression, as if she found the beverage—or the memory—bitter. "I think I hoped that he wouldn't come back to The Buckeye. But, miracle of miracles, he did. I guess I thought it was a sign from heaven. I behaved foolishly, though I tried to be discreet, of course, and implored him to be. That's why it surprised me now when you said you thought he'd flirted with me. It was a wonderful summer . . . I was older than any of those sweet young things who used to hang around Paul, mooning over his Haydn and Bach; so cool, so resilient. I had no resilience left, and that's why I ought to have known better. But it was now-or-never time for me, and I knew it. Age comes so suddenly when there's been nothing to gauge your progress by. Life is just a landscape without figures. No growing children, no aging husband, no fellow workers, no friends. Auntie Belle and Nanna? Don't be funny. They were always old, far back as I can remember. Walking mummies. Two mummies and a zombie, that was us!"

She emptied her cup and folded her hands in her lap. "But it was all an act. He would have been kinder if he'd broken into the house and—attacked me. Then sneaked off. But the concerts, the after-dark walks along the lake, our special bench behind the bell tower, that funny little tearoom where they were always short of forks, the trip around the lake that night on the *Gadfly,* the mist along the banks and the moonlight on the water. It all meant . . . nothing!

"That winter both Auntie Belle and Nanna died—so unexpectedly. I would have come unraveled if I hadn't had Paul to think about. Paul . . . and the summer to come. I was almost sure he wouldn't return."

The more she said now the uneasier I became, because the conviction kept growing on me that it was all make-believe, wishful thinking.

"But he did come," I was forced to prompt her.

"Oh, he came. Yes, indeed, he came. He was shocked to hear about Auntie Belle and Nanna, and for a while he was nice enough to me. But you remember we had a new roomer that season—dear Juliette. I began to notice how they looked at each other when they thought I wasn't looking. Then as time went on they grew reckless, brazen. Well, I don't have to tell you. You were right here. You remember. Oh, yes, they made no bones about their feelings for each other. You can imagine how *I* felt. People couldn't help remarking how nervous and moody I was—but you all thought it was because of Auntie Belle and Nanna. Well, now you know the truth. Finally, I just couldn't take it any longer. We had it out, Paul and I. And that's when he told me."

She flicked a hanky out of her sleeve and dabbed at her eyes, a gesture that seemed too consciously theatrical. "The reason he'd come back to The Buckeye, you see, after that first season, was that Auntie Belle and Nanna had told him he could stay here *rent free!* As long as he was *nice* to *me!* Yes. God's truth. And that's only part of it. They paid him! Actually gave him *money.* And he'd taken it! That's the kind of man he was. Those two sweet, ridiculous old ninnies had *bribed* him to be nice to me. They were actually going to try to *buy* me a husband."

My astonishment seemed to please her immensely. "There! Isn't that a story for you?"

A story—that is to say, fiction—was what I felt sure it was, but I merely said, "Is that all? That's the end?"

"Ah, well . . . you can supply whatever ending you please. I leave that entirely up to you. They ran away together when the season ended. You can say they lived happily ever after, I don't care."

"Did Juliette know about you and Paul?"

"Of course. I had to tell her. I felt it was my duty. I wanted her to know what sort of wretch she was involved with. But it did no good. She was too moonstruck to care."

I'm not saying that I believed the *entire* story to be a lie. I was sure she was fond of Paul Maier, and I'm sure he did flirt with her in a mild, half-joking manner; and though I supposed it was not inconceivable the two old ladies might have been capable of such a stratagem to get a man for their spinster niece, I couldn't see Paul Maier being a party to it. He hadn't struck me as being that depraved a character. I felt sure that that part, and the part about his going to bed with Margit, was pure fantasy. The story was far more interesting and dramatic the way she told it, of course, but I hadn't a shred of what the courts call "hard evidence" to back it up.

That evening, true to her word, Helen Maier called at The Buckeye again. Margit greeted her warmly. I went to my room and did some more work and when I went back downstairs the visitor was just leaving.

"That head you did of Paul," she was saying to Margit, "may I buy it from you?"

Margit smiled, a very generous smile. "No. But you're welcome to it as a gift."

Helen Maier regarded it dryly, once it was in her hands. "As I told your friend here, I always knew my husband had *feet* of clay. This will be a most appropriate souvenir of our marriage."

"Take the other one, too, if you'd like it."

"No, thanks. I think it's time the lovers were separated."

I believe she half hoped there might be some voodoo-like significance attached to this transaction, that by removing Paul's effigy from the company of his paramour's she was magically effecting some faraway separation of their two bodies.

When she had gone, Margit looked at me with wry satisfaction. "I can see what you're thinking. No, I didn't tell her any of what I told you. That's *our* secret. You can send her a copy of your story—if you ever write it, that is."

The next morning we were standing on the porch of that prim-looking white frame house, the porch that was shaded by morning glories on one side and by the buckeye tree on the other, and we, too, were saying goodbye.

"I ought to have a souvenir, too," I said. "May I have the other head? Juliette's?"

Her eyes twinkled. "Let's trade. Give me back the one I did of you. Don't pretend. You never did like it. And you can have hers."

As we made the exchange she said, "There. Now you own my first and last artistic efforts. As well as my worst and my best."

I never saw her again, and I didn't think I ever would get around to writing that story about her. I suppose I might even have forgotten about Margit altogether if I hadn't had those two heads to remind me of her. The one of the young Adonis, though artistically regrettable, makes a splendid paperweight; Juliette's I used as a bookend, which my friends admired very much, praising the sculptor's superb plastic sense and assuming he must have been someone of renown. I would merely smile and keep the secret to myself.

Then one day as I was reaching for a book I accidentally dislodged the head, which toppled from the shelf and shattered on the hardwood floor. When I knelt to examine it more closely I discovered why it was so nearly perfect a replica of Juliette's head, for the clay was not molded around the conventional armature but instead adhered to an actual human skull—a skull which could only have been Juliette's.

Then I understood why Margit had sent me away on some errand the night Paul and Juliette had "run away together," and why she had said she was going to stay on a while longer than usual at the end of that season, telling me she had some "loose ends that must be tidied up."

As a man, I was quite naturally horrified by this discovery, but as an artist I must admit I couldn't have been more pleased, for now at last I could sit down and finish writing that story about Margit.

I had my hard evidence.

Speak Well for the Dead
by Nancy Schachterle

O'Hara was frustrated, and when Daniel Epstein O'Hara was frustrated, the reverberations were felt for miles around. Harried nurses found themselves cherishing the hope that, since he was obviously not going to leave the hospital soon, he might die inexplicably. Or, desperately, they even weighed the possibility of arranging his untimely demise themselves. At times they considered that their subsequent punishment could never outweigh the relief they would obtain.

Not only was O'Hara confined to a hospital bed, but O'Hara was in traction—and O'Hara in traction was not to be taken lightly.

Aside from his actual detention in hospital, O'Hara was frustrated by the nature of his injury. It was no honorable gunshot wound, taken in the line of duty, but a spiral fracture of the left leg suffered during the last weekend of the skiing season that had him strung up like, he thought privately, a Christmas goose.

The morning bath and its concomitant insults now over, O'Hara, or most of his lean length, lay in a rat's-nest of bed sheets surrounded by sections of the two morning papers. His torso rocked dangerously toward the edge of the bed as he tried to reach for part of the *Clarion-Register* which had slid to the floor, and for a moment it seemed as if he would be suspended from the cast-encased leg strung up to the overhead pulley.

"I'll get it!" Sergeant Giovanni arrived opportunely and dived for the paper before O'Hara could tumble to disaster.

"It's about time," O'Hara growled, over the pronouncements of a newscaster on a television set on the wall opposite him. "The most important murder of the century and I'm left here like a turkey on a spit, trying to scrounge a few facts from the daily papers like any man in the street."

"You're on sick leave," Giovanni reminded him.

"I'll go crazy in this place if I don't have something to keep me busy. My body may be out of action, but my mind isn't."

"I was just supposed to bring some mail that was on your desk," Giovanni said, handing O'Hara several envelopes banded together.

The sufferer barely glanced at them, and shoved them into the drawer of his bedside table. Then he settled back against the pillows, arms firmly folded, his wiry copper-with-gray hair thrust upright by rampaging fingers. "Come on, Giovanni, clue me in."

"Well," Giovanni said, gesturing at the newspapers, "it's pretty much all there."

"Don't give me that, me boyo. There's nothing there. Probyn's dead. That's all that's there. Start at the beginning. How am I to help solve this case if I don't get the facts?"

"Well . . ." Giovanni was hesitant, casting a look at the door. "I guess a few minutes won't make much difference. Deceased was Gerald Probyn," he began, as if reading from a notebook.

"I know that!" O'Hara interjected. "Every schoolchild knows Gerald Probyn. He owns the mines, he owns the mill, and he owns the state senator, if the truth were known. He lives, or used to, at Highgates, an aptly named estate eight miles east of town that is just a little harder to get into than Fort Knox, and somebody bumped him off. Now, are you going to give me the facts, or do I have to hobble down to headquarters and get them myself?"

Giovanni blushed. He was a mild man, short and solid, still a little overwhelmed by O'Hara, but after six months' association becoming almost used to him. He stood at a respectful distance by the window.

"We don't know what time Probyn was shot. It seems he spent most of his spare time in his greenhouse, had been out there since early afternoon. He had a great German shepherd named Vulcan, who prowled the place on his own—more of a pet than a watchdog. A little before five o'clock—she's not quite sure of the exact time—the cook heard Vulcan howling, a real mournful sound, she said, and sent one of the maids off in a hurry to see what was wrong. The maid found Probyn just outside the greenhouse, dead, with the dog howling over him."

O'Hara was leaning forward, listening intently. He threw a murderous glance at the television set, now dripping a fatuous soap opera. "Turn that idiot box off!"

Giovanni studied the set above his head. "You've got the controls," he pointed out reasonably.

O'Hara thrashed among the bed sheets and came up with the remote control. Snowy dead channels flashed intermittently with ancient westerns and cheery game shows as he fumbled the buttons, then finally the set subsided into a black stare. "That's better. And you could come a little closer so I don't have to holler. I'm not infectious, you know."

Giovanni moved to the side of the bed.

"How long had he been dead?" O'Hara asked.

"Well, it was an abdominal wound, and the doc said he could have lasted anywhere from ten minutes to half an hour. He'd dragged himself around—you could follow the trail in the dirt floor—and he'd bled most of the way. I couldn't see much sense in it, the way he went. You see, he was standing at the far end, away from the entrance, when he was shot. My guess is the dog scared off the murderer, or he'd have finished the old man off. Looked like he'd lain there, bleeding, for a little while, then he started off dragging himself. There are three aisles to the place, like this—" Giovanni leaned over the bed, drawing a crude sketch on a corner of the nearest paper with a dull pencil stub. "One aisle leads straight from the door down the center. Probyn was at the back end of that. Now, if he were going for help you'd think he'd head straight to the door, but his tracks are clear as can be, and he swung around the end like this—" A swift jab of the pencil drove through the paper to the bedding. "Then he went halfway down the outside aisle, if that's what they call it. There was a big spread of blood where he'd lain for a minute, then some stains along the upright of the . . . the whatchamacallit—"

"Bench," O'Hara threw in.

"Yeah. Whatever, there was blood on it where he'd reached up, trying to drag himself upright. There was a big bunch of flowers torn out—he still had them in his hand when the maid found him. I guess he fell down, couldn't get up again, so he dragged himself on out the door. But the funny thing—I suppose he must have been pretty much out of his head by then—he didn't go toward the house. He turned the other way, and the maid found him stretched out by a water butt—"

"A what?"

"A water butt. Sort of a cistern affair, but above ground, to catch rainwater. The granddaughter said old Probyn claimed rainwater was best for the plants, more natural nutrients than tap water, or something. Anyway, he was stretched out there, as if he'd been trying to hang onto it. And that's as far as he got." Giovanni's voice dropped with dramatic finality.

"What kind of flowers were they?"

Giovanni shrugged. "The ones in his hand? I dunno. I don't know one from another."

The leg in traction swayed dangerously as O'Hara's torso surged forward. "Well, find out, dammit!"

"Yes, sir!"

The door opened with a muffled swoosh and a heavily built, busty nurse in her middle years bore down on O'Hara.

"Can't you see we're busy?" O'Hara growled.

"Come now, Mr. O'Hara, we mustn't be like that." She slipped a thermometer under his tongue as he opened his mouth to protest, and placed firm fingers along his wrist, her head bent to her watch.

The patient made an urgent *Get on with it!* gesture at Giovanni with his free hand. The latter eyed the pair nervously, cleared his throat, and got on with it.

"The maid found him around five. Probyn'd had a session of intestinal flu most of the day before and all that day, so he wasn't eating regular meals. Hot tea and crackers off and on, whenever he felt up to it, so there was no way of knowing by the stomach contents exactly when he died. The dog, Vulcan, was lying across him, which probably kept him from cooling down normally. Figure how long he lived, and how long till he was found, the doc said he could've been shot anywhere from half an hour to two hours before that."

The nurse drew the thermometer from between O'Hara's lips and held it up to read with a professional turn of the wrist. "Well, Mr. O'Hara," she remarked wryly, "I don't know about poor old Mr. Probyn, but at least *you're* cooling down normally." She made an entry on her records.

O'Hara snapped with a pained air, "Looks like everybody's a comedian around here!"

The nurse bustled out the door, casting a satisfied smile behind as it closed.

"They don't give you any peace in this place," O'Hara said. "But I've got to admit that The Bride of Baal's handy to have around in the wee hours of the morning when the pain's gettin' just a bit too much for a body." He shifted self-consciously among the tangled bedding as if afraid he'd exposed a soft spot, and glowered at Giovanni. "Okay, let's hear the rest. Who've you got for suspects?"

"Nobody firm, yet. First of all there's the household. Besides Probyn himself, there's his sister-in-law, who seems to be some kind of a poor relation, and a granddaughter, Marla . . . Marla . . ."

"Wyman," O'Hara supplied. "I've seen her around town. A darlin' of a colleen, about twenty." O'Hara's one-sixteenth Irish blood was inclined to go to his tongue. "Long black hair, worthy of the sweet Deirdre, and eyes as blue as the River Shannon."

Giovanni wondered privately just how blue the River Shannon might be. "That's her," he went on. "Then there's a butler; a cook, who's his wife; two maids; a chauffeur-handyman type; the old fellow who minds the gate; and his wife. I tell you, O'Hara, nobody gets into that place without old Probyn wants him to."

"Didn't I tell you the place is like Fort Knox? That wall must be eight feet high, solid stone around the whole place, miles of it, and the only gate that isn't locked is guarded day and night."

"Right," Giovanni agreed. "The gatekeeper's wife swears he wasn't gone from his post all day. Unless we can find somebody to swear differently, we can rule him out. And only three people came in after the last time Probyn turned up in the kitchen looking for some tea."

Wrinkles on O'Hara's florid brow tangled as he concentrated his thoughts. "You're sure it was intestinal flu he had, and not a little arsenic or something that somebody slipped into his supper a couple of nights before? The shooting could have been the second try, y'know."

Giovanni perked up like a schoolboy who'd gotten an unexpected A. "That's the first thing I thought of. Doc says he'll be looking out for it when he does the P.M. We'll soon have his report."

"Who's on the case besides us?"

Giovanni hesitated. One of the first things he'd heard on his transfer was: "With O'Hara you never know which way the cat'll jump." Confinement to a hospital bed wouldn't have lessened his sensitive ego.

"Lindstrom and I did the initial investigation."

O'Hara nodded, with a wry twist to his mouth. "He's coming along well. Did a good job on the Masterson case." Giovanni felt a twinge of surprise. O'Hara's previous reference to Lindstrom had labeled him as "a clod in thick boots."

"But remember," O'Hara continued, "I'll be working with you all the way. There's no need to worry. I won't let you down." He wore a gentle smile, as if in contemplation of the comfort this would bring to his colleagues. "Who were the three you said got into Fort Knox?"

Giovanni consulted his notes. "Rupert Kendall clocked in precisely at three o'clock. I've been talking to Probyn's secretary at the plant, and Kendall would be a good man to put your money on. He's been storming around the past couple of weeks claiming the old man stole some milling process he invented."

"Developed."

"Whatever." Giovanni shrugged. "It's supposed to save millions, or thousands anyway, and he's been raising quite a stink. Hawkins, the chauffeur type, was washing one of the cars outside the garage—a four car affair—which is about fifty yards from the greenhouse. He said the two of them were going at it hot and heavy, from what he could hear. Said Kendall called the old man every name he could lay his tongue to."

"Kendall . . ." O'Hara mused. "Seems to me I should know him."

"Early forties, tall and slim, dark, getting a little bald in front. Real intense eyes, look as if they could see right through you."

O'Hara nodded in satisfaction. "I know him. Hawk nose, and a sensitive mouth. Looks like a cross between a poet and a pirate. What does he have to say for himself?"

"He admitted they'd had words," Giovanni said, "but he swore up and down that Probyn was alive when he left."

"Wouldn't you?"

"I suppose so. Anyway, the gatekeeper clocked him out at three twenty. Ten minutes later a fellow called John Locke turned up."

O'Hara nodded. "Him I know. Medium height, in his early fifties? A sarcastic type, used to be married to Probyn's daughter. Not Marla's mother, the other one. She's dead now, and he works for the old man—or did the last I heard."

"That's the guy. An accountant. He went up to the house, the butler told him Probyn was down at the greenhouse, and he headed that way. But he says he changed his mind and decided not to disturb the old man. He didn't check out till three forty-five, though. I asked him what took so long, and he said he'd noticed Marla's Ferrari in the garage, poked around it for a while, checking out the features and wondering if he might ever be able to afford one."

"Wasn't the chauffeur there?"

Giovanni shook his head. "He finished washing the car about the time Kendall left, then came on into town on an errand for the cook. The gatekeeper says he drove out not long after Kendall, and he was seen at the market."

O'Hara leaned across to his bedside table, pulled out one of his letters, and began to make notes on the back of the envelope.

"Locke left at three forty-five?"

Giovanni nodded. "We've got two witnesses to that. Just as he was leaving, the granddaughter's boyfriend, Loren Renaldi, drove up. There's an unsavory type, if you ask me. About twenty-three, I'd guess. He's tall, with a good build, but he's got one of those homely faces, you can't tell if he's a budding genius or verging on moronic. Long, straight hair, down over his collar, and probably none too clean—and his clothes are something else. Of course, old Probyn himself looked as if he'd ridden the rods, in baggy old pants and a jacket that could have been dragged through a stovepipe."

"Millionaires can afford to look like bums," O'Hara remarked. "Did the boyfriend go out to the greenhouse?"

"He says not. Miss Wyman and her aunt both confirm that he spent about twenty minutes with them, and then he took off to hunt the old man out. Renaldi was supposed to be trying to talk Probyn into letting him marry the granddaughter. But he claims he lost his nerve, wandered around the place trying to get it back again, and finally headed out the gate, figuring he could find a better time to tackle the old man than when he was suffering from what Renaldi called 'the gripes.' "

"If the boy married Marla with the old man dead, he'd be married to a nice piece of money. It might seem smarter to marry her first, though, and then knock off the old man, if he's the one who did it." O'Hara cocked his head to one side; bright, birdlike eyes seeming to assess abstracts in the air before him. "It might be even smarter, though, to knock the old man off first. Marla'd get the money either way, and the old man wouldn't be around to object." He swung his gaze back to Giovanni. "How's the pie going to be sliced, now that Probyn's dead?"

"The biggest chunk goes into a foundation, medical research, new library for the city, things like that, with a board controlling it. Marla gets three million outright, in trust till she's twenty-one, and shares in the mill. The aunt, or great-aunt—she's a brother's widow—gets a pension, twenty thousand dollars a year if she lives at Highgates, or thirty-five thousand dollars if for any reason she wants to move. The staff all come in for a nice chunk, except one maid who's fairly new—anywhere from five thousand to fifteen thousand dollars apiece, depending on how long they've been at Highgates. There are a few minor beneficiaries, but nobody who's involved."

O'Hara whistled. "Three million! Nurses and governesses when she was little, the best schools here and in England, a year at the Sorbonne, and now all that money. The luck of some people. But I

don't think my little colleen'd do a thing like that, especially when
she had it so good already. Is she covered?"

"Pretty much. Either her aunt or one or the other of the staff can
testify to her whereabouts except for one period of about twenty
minutes just after the boyfriend left the house. She says she was in
the library making some notes for a report she's working on—she's
a junior at the university—but nobody saw her during that time.
Theoretically, she could have slipped out and shot him, but I'm with
you, I don't think she's the type. She seems pretty much broken up
about the old man's death."

"How about the others?"

"All accounted for. The aunt was in the kitchen with the cook,
going over some new gourmet recipes, while Marla was in the library. The maids were both upstairs. The way they were working,
they cover each other pretty thoroughly, so they're in the clear,
unless they're in it together."

"How about the butler?"

"He was feeling wonky all day, probably the same bug Probyn
had. After Renaldi left, Marla made him go to his quarters and lie
down. One of the maids saw him go up, and she was working in that
area most of the afternoon, said she'd have seen him if he'd come
down."

O'Hara scribbled on the envelope. "So much for the people. Now,
what do we have by way of physical evidence?"

"Not much. He was shot with a .38. There are several guns around
the house, but only one pistol, a .22 in the old man's desk. It hadn't
been fired since the last time it'd been cleaned. Wasn't even loaded."

"Any pertinent fingerprints?"

"The team's working on it, but so far nothing of any use."

"Footprints?"

Giovanni nodded. "One. The greenhouse floor is dirt, pretty hard-
packed, but the chauffeur—he's nurseryman, too—knocked over a
watering can near the doorway a couple of days ago. It had pretty
much dried up, but we've got one partial that looks promising. Hawkins, the chauffeur, said the old man wouldn't let Vulcan in the
greenhouse any more. He was always knocking something over with
his tail. But our partial has one of Vulcan's paw prints over it,
pointing toward the door. That suggests it was made after the dog
interrupted the murderer. Not one of the outsiders had been on the
grounds since the water was spilled, except that afternoon. The
print's real smooth, but there's a sort of scar as if the wearer picked

up a rock that got ground into the sole, and then dropped out. A good clear impression of the hole."

O'Hara's cheeks creased in a wide smile. "Good! We can use something concrete like that. If it is the murderer's, and he doesn't know we've got it, we might match shoes before he gets rid of them."

Giovanni looked at his watch with dismay. "Look, O'Hara, I know you want to hear everything, but I was only supposed to bring your mail and get on with the job. Lindstrom'll be waiting."

"Okay, okay," O'Hara grumbled, "get on your way. But you keep me posted, hear? And don't forget to find out what kind of flowers the old man had in his hand."

Giovanni turned toward the door. "I'll try, and I'll come back tonight, or tomorrow morning at least, and bring you up to date."

"Tonight!" O'Hara called imperiously as the sergeant disappeared. He glowered at the closed door for a moment, then settled back to think.

Out of his frustration, rather than by intention, O'Hara made the second floor staff miserable for the rest of the day. When the shift changed in the afternoon, the most important word passed was not about Mrs. Hurley's violent reaction to the new medication, or Dr. MacCallum's orders to screen Mr. Janeway's visitors for contraband liquor. Rather, the watchword was: "Look out for O'Hara!"

The head nurse at the station drew something like a breath of relief when shortly after supper she saw Sergeant Giovanni ambling down the hall toward 204. Perhaps things would get better soon.

"Well," O'Hara growled when Sergeant Giovanni peered around his door. "You certainly took long enough! Where have you been?"

"I had a lot of work to catch up on, spending so much time here this morning," Giovanni replied, with less of an apologetic air than he would have had a few months earlier. "I found out quite a bit, though."

"Like?"

"For one thing, there was no sign of poison, not even in the small amount that might have made it look like an intestinal upset. No fingerprints in the greenhouse that aren't accounted for in the ordinary way. We've got a nice cast of the one footprint, showing the scar in the sole, and Miss Wyman told me it was gillyflowers the old man had in his hand."

"Gillyflowers?"

"That's what she said. I don't know a thing about flowers."

"Well, what color were they, what did they look like?"

"The old man just caught a handful as he fell. What does it matter?" Giovanni asked with a daring degree of heat.

"Matter! I'll give you *matter,* me boy. You got a look at them, didn't you?"

"The ones in his hand were so wilted by the time we got there you couldn't tell what they were, but the ones on the bench, where he'd grabbed for a hold, were all sorts of colors." He screwed up his eyes and his brow knitted in concentration as he cast his mind's eye back to the greenhouse. "There were some pink ones, and white, and yellow, and some sort of purplish ones—and there were some red ones, too, real pretty. Tall, sort of clustery, real flowery, if you know what I mean."

"I don't know what you mean, if you really want to know," O'Hara complained, "but it's a poor workman that blames his tools."

Giovanni was silent in the face of this apparent *non sequitur.*

"Anything else? Have you found the shoes to fit your cast yet?"

Giovanni shook his head. "Judge Clayton won't issue search warrants for the suspects' houses as things stand. He said if we could come up with something to point to one person, that'd do the trick, but right now there isn't enough evidence to back up a warrant."

"And in the meantime somebody does some figuring and decides it'd be the wise thing to get rid of those shoes. That'd be just our luck. Damn, I wish I were out of this place! I'd find the right shoes, regulations or no."

Giovanni backed a few paces away from the bed. "Well, if you don't need me for anything else I'll . . ."

O'Hara waved him away absently, studying his back-of-the-envelope notes on the case. "Go on. Go on. I'll work with what I've got." The staff at the nurses' station shared apprehensive glances as Giovanni left the floor. The respite had been so brief.

The evening, however, was comparatively quiet. After visiting hours, peace reigned for an unexpected length of time. Charts were brought up to date, shelves were cleaned, nails were polished, and bits of gossip exchanged in hushed voices. Then the sword fell. O'Hara's light went on."Not me!" several nurses declared in unison.

"I'll go myself," the senior nurse offered, and moved briskly and silently down the hall.

"What is it, Mr. O'Hara? Do you need a sleeping pill?"

The room was suitably dark for the sleeping hours, except for the soft glow from a lamp behind the bed. It showed O'Hara teetering on the edge of the bed, his traction equipment straining, one hand braced on the bedside table. The other hand groped ineffectually for the telephone, just out of reach.

"Sleeping pill! I've got to catch a murderer. I don't need a sleeping pill, I need an outside line!"

"Mr. O'Hara please! You'll wake the other patients. Don't you realize it's after two o'clock?"

"Get me an outside line, or I'll not only wake the other patients, I'll wake the dead," he threatened, but in a slightly subdued voice.

"Mr. O'Hara . . ."

"Please?"

This approach was so unexpected that the nurse found herself with the receiver in her hand before she realized what she was doing. "What number do you want?"

O'Hara told her. After a moment she passed him the handset.

"This is O'Hara. Let me talk to Giovanni."

There was a short wait, then a drowsy voice came through the receiver.

"Giovanni, I've got the pointer you need. Roust up Lindstrom, then see if Judge Clayton'll issue a warrant. Get him out of bed, if you have to. Find those shoes, before it's too late."

A crackle of protests and questions from the receiver sounded through the still room. In a series of succinct sentences O'Hara told his sergeant exactly what he'd come up with, and who it pointed to. The nurse standing by, listening eagerly, gave a startled gasp.

"Now get going, and report to me in the morning." O'Hara handed the phone back to the nurse.

"And now, me pretty, I'd be obliged if you'd take yourself out of here. Don't they teach you nowadays that hospital patients are supposed to have plenty of rest?" O'Hara snuggled against the pillow and wormed himself into as comfortable a position as was possible in the circumstances. He directed one long, outrageous wink at the nurse, then closed both eyes and settled himself to sleep.

Orderlies were trundling cartloads of breakfast trays down the hall when Giovanni next entered Room 204. O'Hara greeted him with a smug grin, an effect slightly marred by a mouthful of scrambled eggs. "Find 'em?"

Giovanni nodded. "Judge Clayton said he'd take a chance on your reasoning, and gave us a search warrant. They were at the bottom of a Goodwill collection sack. The pit mark on the sole is clear, and the shoe fits the cast perfectly. And we found a bonus, too." He waited, glowing with pleasure, for O'Hara's reaction. Raised eyebrows and an expectant silence prompted him to go on. "The gun. It'd been cleaned, but we roused the ballistics men, and it was the one that did the job, all right."

O'Hara beamed with satisfaction. "Good work. I figured I'd got the answer before the evidence was gone. Now I'd guess you want to know how I solved the case."

Giovanni hesitated. Had O'Hara forgotten the telephone conversation at two in the morning? Well, he was entitled to his kicks. "I didn't quite catch it all this morning. Your line of reasoning, I mean," he answered finally. "Sounded like a stroke of luck."

O'Hara slapped a triangle of toast back down on the tray. "Stroke of luck! Hardly. It's knowledge of the ways of the world that gave me the answer. That's where those of us who've seen more of life have it over you young fellows. Oh, don't worry, you're bound to catch up, given time and a little more experience. You see, old Probyn's behavior after he was shot was the clue to the whole thing. You spotted it yourself, but didn't follow it up. Why did he drag himself the long way around to the door, and then away from the house? *Away*, mind you, not toward it, where you'd expect him to go for help."

"I can see it now," Giovanni replied. "Before, I thought he was just irrational from pain."

"I've had more time to think than you did," O'Hara admitted. "Probyn didn't grab those flowers while he was falling. No, he deliberately dragged himself up to that bench to *get* those flowers, 'cause he was afraid there wasn't a snowball's chance of him living with a wound like that. Then, with his very lifeblood marking the trail for us, he forced himself to make it to the door and beyond, to seal his killer's death warrant."

"A gutsy old man," Giovanni murmured respectfully.

"Identifying them as gillyflowers almost cancelled out that dying effort, you know."

Giovanni bridled. "I told you I didn't know one flower from the other. Miss Wyman, she's the one said they were gillyflowers. Weren't they?"

"In a manner of speaking." O'Hara paused for effect, while Giovanni shuffled uncomfortably by the bedside. "But you've got to remember, our little Marla had nurses when she was little—English nannies—nothing being too good for the old man to give her. And she went to boarding school in England. So what is it that the English call a gillyflower? What do we call the flower that fits your rather inadequate description? Tall, clusters of flowers, pink, white, yellow, purple? I finally got it. Stock! That's what it is. Stock."

"Never heard of it. But then, I don't know much about flowers."

"Probyn did. He grabbed a handful of stock, then headed out the door, to the water butt, you said."

"That's right."

"Sort of a cistern, you said. Why in the name of all that's good and holy didn't you say, 'Sort of a barrel'?" O'Hara asked peremptorily.

"Anybody knows what a water butt is."

"Not everybody," O'Hara admitted. "But once I thought about it, the whole thing fell into place. All I had to do was ask myself what—or, in this case, who—goes with 'stock' and 'barrel'?"

"Even dragged out of my warm bed, I followed you there," Giovanni remarked. "Locke. And now, if you'll excuse the expression, we've got him under lock and key. When we found the shoes, and showed him the cast of the footprint in the greenhouse he claimed he'd never been in, he hemmed and hawed around, finally admitted he'd gone to see the old man, but swore up and down he'd left him alive. Then we hit him with the dying man's accusation, and he broke down completely. It was the old story. He was a darn sharp accountant, and started doctoring the books. He'd salted away a tidy little sum on the side, but the old man was just a little bit smarter. He found out about it, even though a couple of audits had missed it. I suppose Locke thought that being family, even by marriage, old Probyn wouldn't see him go to jail. But he wasn't much of a judge of millionaires. Out in the greenhouse Probyn told Locke he was going to prosecute, and he'd end up in the pen, so Locke shot him. He had the gun with him, so there won't be any question about lack of premeditation. And now that we have the gun, the case is wrapped up neater than a Christmas present."

"Thanks to old man Probyn," O'Hara declared. "A real present it was, too—handed to you on a silver tray, like the head of the sainted John the Baptist by Salome."

"Yeah," Giovanni said.

"So now," said O'Hara, stroking jam onto a toast triangle, "you can get on with your other work."

"Well, thanks for the help," Giovanni told him, sidling toward the door. "And it was 'to' Salome, not 'by,'" he muttered—but not until the door had shut silently behind him.

The Girl in Gold

by Jonathan Craig

I t was supposed to look like either suicide or accidental death. It was neither. It was murder.

A detective is rarely the first police officer at the scene of a homicide, but this was one of those times. Stan Rayder, my detective partner, and I had been cruising Greenwich Village in an unmarked patrol car, matching faces in the streets against our mental files of wanted criminals, when a small boy had run from the alley behind the hotel, shouting that there was a dead man back there.

The boy had kept on running, and Stan, who was driving, turned into the alley.

Now, at a few minutes past six on as steamy an August evening as I could remember, we stood looking down at the body of a well-dressed, darkhaired young man who had, it would seem, fallen only minutes ago from the open window of the third floor hotel room directly above.

He lay flat on his back, spreadeagled, and in spite of the crushing impact of his body on the concrete there was very little blood. There was a dark swelling across the bridge of his nose and a purplish discoloration of the skin on the left side of his face and on his left hand and wrist.

In New York, detectives aren't supposed to touch a body until the medical examiner has looked at it, but sometimes we cheat a little. I pushed a fingertip against the jaw, and the head moved easily to my touch.

"Any rigor mortis, Pete?" Stan asked.

"No," I said, and slipped the man's wallet from the inside pocket of his jacket. It held eighty-three dollars, some business cards, and an I.D. card that said he was Harry B. Lambert, of 684 East 71st Street. I read the name and address to Stan, put the wallet back, and stood up. We'd make a closer examination, of course, after the M.E. arrived.

"That's quite a bit of postmortem lividity on his left side, there," Stan said. "It'd take about an hour for that much to show up, wouldn't it?"

"About that, yes," I said. Postmortem lividity results from the blood's settling to those parts of the body nearest the floor. In Harry Lambert's case, it meant he had lain on his left side for at least an hour before someone pushed him through that third floor window.

"He'd been boozing a little, it smells like," Stan said, glancing at me with mild surprise.

Stan, who always appears to be mildly surprised about everything, is a tall, wiry young cop with a soft voice, a sprinkling of premature gray in his old fashioned brush cut, and a deceptively mild manner. He also has a black belt, the hardest fists in the department, and an almost complete lack of physical fear.

"You figure that knock he took between the eyes finished him off?" he asked.

"Could be," I said. "Maybe somebody hoped he'd hit the pavement face down. Sort of blot out the evidence, so to speak."

"It just might have worked, too," Stan said. "Well, you're the head man on this one, Pete. What now?"

"Stay here with the body until the M.E. gets here. I'll get on the horn in the hotel and stir things up."

I walked around to the entrance of the Corbin and used one of the phone booths in the lobby to call Lieutenant Barney Fells, Stan's and my superior. Barney would take Stan and me off the duty roster and assign us full time to the homicide. He would also immediately notify the communications bureau. They, in turn, would dispatch an ambulance, and notify the other departments concerned with homicide.

The Corbin was just another small hotel, a little smaller and older and scruffier than most, perhaps, with a minimum of lobby and a bird-cage elevator no larger than a phone booth.

There was no one behind the desk. I tapped the bell a couple of times and waited.

The middle-aged man who finally came out from the room behind the desk was short and slightly built, with a large, almost perfectly round head, thinning strawlike hair, moist gray eyes, and very little chin.

"Yes, sir," he said in a voice much deeper than I would have expected. "May I help you?"

I showed him my badge. "Detective Selby," I said. "You have a Mr. Harry Lambert registered here?"

He nodded. "Yes, sir. He checked in this morning."

"Anyone with him?"

"No."

I got out my notebook. "I'll need your name."

"Dobson. Wayne Dobson."

"Did Mr. Lambert have any visitors?"

"Not that I know of. Why? What's happened?"

"He's dead. Out in the alley behind the hotel. He went out the window."

Dobson sucked in his breath. "A suicide?"

"You know him personally?"

"No. But I . . ." He shook his head slowly. "This is the first time anything like this has ever happened here."

"You only come to the desk when someone rings the bell?"

"Usually, yes."

"What room was Lambert in?"

"Just a moment." He turned to check his file of registration cards. "304."

"He put his home address on there, on the registration card?"

"Yes, sir. It's the law. He put down 684 East 71st."

"What time did he check in?"

"Eleven forty-five."

I put my notebook away. "I'll need a key to his room, Mr. Dobson. And please stay close to the desk. There'll be other police along any minute."

He nodded. "Of course," he said as he handed me a master key on a big loop of heavy wire. "I'll do all I can to help."

I crossed to the elevator, but I had second thoughts. I have a thing about elevators of that size and vintage. I took another look at it, and then walked to the other side of the lobby and started up the stairs.

I might have been in a smaller hotel room at one time or another, but I couldn't remember it; I knew I'd never been in a hotter one. The metal bed and metal dresser seemed to have been painted over with green house paint, and the ratty lounge chair looked to be on the verge of giving way to its own weight.

There were no indications of a struggle, but Harry Lambert appeared to have had at least one visitor, and that one a woman. There was a nearly empty fifth of whisky at one end of the dresser and a couple of hotel glasses at the other, and one of the glasses had a smear of lipstick on the rim.

There was nothing under the bed but dust, and nothing in the closet but more dust and two rusty coat hangers. There was nothing in the bathroom, either.

I went over to search the dresser. There was a handsome black attaché case in the top drawer, nothing at all in the others. I put the case on the bed, handling it carefully to avoid obliterating fingerprints, and opened it.

The case held, among other things, another black case, about ten inches long, six inches wide, and half an inch thick, embossed with Harry Lambert's name in gold, and to which was attached about two feet of gold chain with a clip on the end of it. I'd seen a number of such cases; they are used by diamond salesmen to carry gems and are known as jewelers' wallets. It was empty.

The attaché case also held, in various compartments, a jeweler's loupe, a miniature pair of scales and a set of weights in a clear plastic box, and a large number of the squares of white tissue paper in which diamond salesmen wrap their stones.

I put the case back on the dresser, took off my coat, and began stripping down the bed. I found the tube of lipstick in the space between the pillows.

It was no ordinary lipstick. Even the cheapest ones can look expensive, of course, but this one was the genuine article. It was of heavy gold, with a beautifully engraved floral design along its length and the initials "L.C." in a monogram on the cap.

It was the kind of thing women never buy for themselves. It was also the kind of costly, handcrafted item that just might have a secret jeweler's mark. Headquarters maintains a file of hundreds of such marks, just as it does of laundry marks.

I found the mark with the help of my handkerchief and the loupe from Lambert's attaché case. It was inside the cap, at the top: an anchor surrounded by three concentric circles.

I put the lipstick on the dresser beside the attaché case and finished searching the bed. I was just putting my jacket back on when there was a knock on the door and two techs and a photographer from headquarters came in.

"Hi, Pete," the chief tech said, wiping the sweat from his forehead. "You think it might warm up a little?"

"We can hope," I said. "You finished in the alley?"

"Nothing to do down there. Just the pictures was all. They're done."

"I'd better get a couple of bird's-eye shots from the window," the photographer said, moving off.

"The M.E. show up yet?" I asked.

"He got there just as we left. Doc Chaney."

"Well, it's all yours, Ed," I said, turning to leave. "I want to have a few more words with the desk clerk."

Before I went downstairs, I knocked at the doors at either side of Lambert's and at the one directly across the hall. There was no answer at any of them.

When I reached the lobby, I found that Wayne Dobson had abandoned his desk again. The door behind it was slightly ajar. I went back and opened it the rest of the way.

Dobson was lying on the bed in a room that, except for a portable TV set and the iron bars usually found on first floor windows in New York, was the mirror image of the one I'd just left upstairs. He looked even smaller lying down than he had behind the desk, and his eyes seemed drawn with pain.

"What's wrong?" I asked.

He smiled up at me thinly. "Ulcers. That suicide got me pretty upset."

"Can I do anything for you?"

He shook his head and pushed himself up on the side of the bed. "It'll pass. At least it always has."

"Feel up to talking a little?"

He shrugged. "If I have to, I have to. What do you want to know?"

"Well, first, where are the bellhops? I haven't seen any."

"Joe Moody's on. The trick is to find him."

"Moody go up with Lambert when he checked in?"

"No. Joe wasn't around at the time."

"Lambert had some company," I said. "A woman. You see any women pass through the lobby?"

"I saw one, a beauty. She took the elevator."

"You have any idea who she was?"

"No, but she was something to see; silver blonde, a terrific build, and a gold dress like a second skin. Real bright, shiny gold dress. Must have cost a mint."

"When was this?"

"Oh . . . about four, I'd say. Maybe a little later."

"She the only woman you saw?"

"Yes. Mr. Selby, would you do me a favor, please? There's a shoebox out beneath the desk with a lot of odds and ends in it, stuff people have left in their rooms. I just remembered I put a bottle of antacid tablets in it the other day. Maybe they'd help."

I went out to the desk, dug around in the shoebox until I found the tablets, and took them back to Dobson.

"Thanks," he said. "Don't ever get an ulcer."

"Just one more thing, and I'll let you rest. Do you handle the switchboard?"

"Yes. The desk clerk here does everything but make a living."

"Did Lambert make or receive any calls?"

"Damn!"

"What's wrong?"

"I completely forgot. Yes, he did get a call. And the guy that called him was plenty sore about something. He started right off cussing him. Mr. Lambert kept saying, 'Now, just a minute, Rocky,' and 'Listen, Rocky,' and 'Let me explain,' and things like that."

"All right. But aside from the cussing, what did this man *say*?"

"Nothing. He just kept blessing him out. Then all at once Mr. Lambert hung up."

"The man call back?"

"No."

"When did he call?"

"I can tell you exactly. It was ten minutes of four. As it happened, I'd just set my watch." He suddenly grimaced with pain and lay back on the bed. "Like I told you," he said, "never get yourself an ulcer."

I made a few notes in my book, thanked Dobson for his help, and walked around the hotel to see how Stan Rayder and the M.E. were coming along with their work in the alley.

There were two more police cars and an ambulance there now, and perhaps a hundred or so onlookers.

"Doc Chaney here says he can get a pretty close fix on the time of death, Pete," Stan said, after I'd shouldered my way through the crowd. "He puts it somewhere between four and five P.M."

"That's right," the M.E. said, looking up from where he knelt by the body. "This is the one time in a hundred when I can set fairly tight limits."

"How about that bruise between his eyes, doc?" Stan asked. "You figure it could have killed him?"

"*Could* have, yes. It's likely a depressed fracture. But we'll have to wait till I autopsy him, Stan." He stood up and glanced in the direction of the ambulance. "I'm finished, Pete. If you'll release the body, I can take it back with me."

"You get everything out of his pockets, Stan?" I asked.

"Yes," Stan said, tapping the bulge in the side pocket of his jacket.

"Nothing helpful, though. There was nothing in his billfold but the cards and money."

I had the M.E. sign a receipt for the body. Then Stan and I pushed through the crowd to the car we'd come in and got inside.

"So Lambert was a diamond salesman, eh?" Stan said, after I'd filled him in on my search of the hotel room and my talks with the desk clerk. "What a way to run a railroad. A hundred people could have gone in and out, but the only one we know about for sure is that girl in the gold dress."

"We may pick up some others from the bellhop." I started the engine and began to back the car out of the alley. "I'm going uptown to check at the address on Lambert's I.D. card, Stan. You—"

"Yes, I know," he said wryly. "I get to stay here and boss the operation in that bake-oven upstairs."

"Somebody always has to do the dirty dishes, Stan."

"Sure, but why does it always have to be me?"

"First of all, get hold of that bellhop. Then see if any of the other guests on Lambert's floor saw or heard anything. Also, there's a newsstand across the street. Maybe the man that runs it noticed something."

I turned the corner and pulled up in front of the hotel entrance. "One more thing," I said. "Send somebody over to headquarters with that lipstick. I want a check made on the jeweler's mark."

Stan sighed. "You sure you can't think of any other little things I can do for you?"

"Not offhand," I said. "Still, if I really worked at it . . ."

He grinned. "Never mind," he said, opening the door. "I'll see you at the squad room."

684 East 71st turned out to be a posh-looking converted brownstone. I found a mailbox with a name card that read LAMBERT/MANNING—2A, and pushed the button beneath it. A moment later the buzzer released the inner door of the foyer and I climbed the stairs to the second floor.

A heavyset man with his arms folded across his chest was standing in the open doorway of 2A, frowning at me as I approached. He was about thirty, I judged, with a lot of thick, sand-colored hair, a deep widow's peak, and unusually heavy brows over very small hazel eyes with yellow flecks in them.

"You the one that buzzed 2A?" he asked, giving it a little edge.

I showed him the tin. "Detective Selby," I said. "Are you a friend of Mr. Lambert's?"

"He lives here. We both do. What's up?"

"We could talk a little better inside."

He hesitated for a moment, then shrugged and motioned me into the apartment.

The living room wasn't very large, but the furnishings had cost someone a lot of money. I sat down in a cream leather easy chair and nodded to the sofa across from it.

"Let's see, now," I said as I got out my book. "Your full name is what?"

He glowered at me, but he came over and sat down. "David D. Manning," he said. "And make yourself right at home, Selby."

"Thanks. You and Mr. Lambert pretty close friends?"

"We're roommates," he said. "We get along. Why?"

"I've a little bad news for you, I'm afraid. He's been killed."

He started to say something, then changed his mind and sat looking at me as if he were trying to decide whether I was telling the truth.

I waited.

"How?" Manning asked.

"We're not just sure. Somebody tried to cover it up by pushing him out a window."

"Somebody? Does that mean you don't know who did it?"

"Not yet."

He got up suddenly and walked over to a bar in the corner. "I could use a drink," he said, pouring a couple of inches into a highball glass. "How about some for you?"

"No, thanks."

He took a pull at his drink, walked slowly back to the sofa, and sat down again. "It's hard to believe," he said.

"He married? Separated?"

"No."

"Divorced?"

"No."

"We'll want to notify his next of kin. You know who that might be?"

"No, I don't. He never mentioned any relatives. His parents are dead, I know."

"He have a good income?"

"We averaged about the same, I guess. Twenty thousand one year, twenty-five the next."

"You're a diamond salesman, too, then?"

"Yes."

"Well, the big question is, of course, do you know anyone who'd want him dead?"

Manning smiled sourly. "I can think of two or three who'd like that just fine."

"Who?"

"Well, there's this girl he used to be engaged to, Barbara Nolan. Harry threw her over for another girl. Barbara swore she'd kill him."

"He take her seriously?"

"Not at first. Then he started to. It was beginning to sweat him plenty. I guess she convinced him."

"You know where she lives?"

"It's in the Village. 542 Waverly Place."

"You said there were others."

He took a sip of his drink. "Well, there's a guy named Mel Pearce, another diamond salesman. He thought Harry stole a big sale from him. He had almost an obsession about it. Once I had to get between them to keep them from climbing all over each other."

"You know where I can find him?"

"He lives on Central Park West, I think. I don't know just where."

I turned over to a new page in my notebook. "That's two," I said. "Anyone else?"

"Not that I know of."

"Harry got a tough phone call from somebody named Rocky. That name mean anything to you?"

Manning frowned thoughtfully, then shook his head. "No."

"Was Harry in trouble of any kind? Any dealings with shylocks? Any civil suits? Gambling debts? Anything at all like that?"

"No. At least not so far as I know."

"You said he threw Barbara Nolan over for another girl. What's her name?"

"Elaine Greer." He nodded toward a large color portrait on the coffee table. "That's her picture."

I went over to examine it. The girl was very young, very blonde, and very beautiful, but it was a cold beauty, and the smile that curved her lips had somehow failed to reach her slightly tilted blue eyes.

"I'll want to talk to her," I said. "You know her address?"

"No. She's in the Manhattan book, though, I know."

"Harry pretty much of a ladies' man, was he?"

"No. He practically had to beat them off with a club, but he always stuck pretty much to one girl at a time." He paused. "She must be a very potent proposition, that girl. Elaine, I mean. Harry was practically out of his skull over her. As I said, he and Barbara were going to get married. But when he met Elaine, he forgot all about Barbara. She had Harry so crazy for her he didn't know which way was up."

"You know Elaine yourself, do you?"

"No, I never met her, and I reached the point where I wished Harry hadn't, either. She was all he talked about. He went around mooning over her like a fifteen-year-old kid with his first big crush. You had to see it to believe it."

I shifted my weight around in the chair and ran out a fresh point on my pencil. "Who'd Harry work for?"

"Nobody. He took stones out on memo."

"On memo?"

"On consignment. He might be peddling stones for half a dozen dealers at the same time. A memo is the dealer's record of the stones he gives you. You just sign the memo, and that's it."

"His reputation must have been pretty good, then."

"Better than good. Perfect."

"When was the last time you saw him, Mr. Manning?"

He glanced at me sharply, then raised his glass and finished his drink, watching me over the rim.

"Don't tell me I'm a suspect," he said.

"Just a routine question, Mr. Manning," I said. "But when?"

He put the glass down on the end table beside the sofa. "This morning," he said. "And it was a very strange thing. I didn't know what to make of it."

"What happened?"

"Well, the phone in Harry's room rang early, about six or so. It woke me up. I went out to the kitchen to make coffee, and a few minutes later Harry came in with his attaché case under his arm, all dressed to go out. He looked like something had just scared the hell out of him."

"What did he say to you then?"

"Nothing. I asked him what was wrong, but he walked right past me and grabbed a fifth of whisky out of the cabinet and took a heavy belt straight out of the bottle. I was amazed. It was the first time I'd seen him take a drink in more than a year. He used to have a drinking problem, you see. No tolerance for the stuff at all. And here he was, suddenly gulping it straight out of the bottle."

"He didn't say anything at all?"

"Not a word. I think he was only half aware I was there. I asked him who had called so early, but I don't think he even heard me. He wasn't in the kitchen more than half a minute."

"And he left the apartment right away?"

"Yes."

"Did you overhear any of what he said on the phone?"

"No," Manning said, and got up to pour himself another drink.

I watched him carefully. There was something about Dave Manning that bothered me. He was just too cool for the circumstances; but when he came back and took his seat again, I noticed something that told me the coolness was all on the surface. He sat leaning back comfortably against the cushion, apparently completely relaxed, perhaps even a little bored, but he was gripping his highball glass so tightly that the knuckles of his hand were bone-white.

I thumbed back through my notes, then got to my feet. "Your phone book handy?" I asked.

"Over there, by the bar."

"This diamond salesman you said was feuding with Harry," I said. "Mel Pearce. His first name Melvin?"

"No. Melford."

I located a Melford Pearce at 216 Central Park West. Elaine Greer, the girl for whom Harry had thrown over Barbara Nolan, was listed at 734 East 58th.

"I think that'll do it for this time, Mr. Manning," I said as I crossed to the door. "Thanks very much."

"No trouble at all," Manning said easily. "I wish you luck."

I went down to the street and walked along to where I'd left the car. It was completely dark now, but the soggy air was just as stifling as it had been at noon, and it would be that way all night. There was a lot of heat lightning flickering around the spire of the Empire State Building to the south, and the blare of the boat horns from the East River had that muffled sound they have when an early evening fog has set in.

I worked the car out into the traffic and headed downtown for a talk with Barbara Nolan, the girl whose threat against Harry Lambert's life had caused him considerable concern.

The one room apartment above the curio shop on Waverly Place was small, even by Greenwich Village standards, and the girl who had let me inside was petite and pretty and very angry. She had shoulder-length hair so black that it had blue highlights in it, a small·oval face with skin like fresh cream, and deep brown eyes under sooty lashes so long that at first I'd thought they were false.

"So why come to me about it?" she said, glaring at me from her perch on a hassock. "What am I supposed to do? Throw myself on his funeral pyre or something?"

"Not necessarily," I said. "I'll settle for the answers to a few questions."

She brushed the hair back from her forehead with the back of her hand and crossed her legs the other way.

"You're pretty sure I killed him, aren't you?" she said.

"I didn't say that, Miss Nolan."

"You don't have to. It's written all over your big ugly cop's face."

"We also have a big ugly station house. Would you rather talk there?"

"Well, just for the record, I didn't do it. And also, just for the record, I definitely wish I had."

"And yet, at one time, you were going to marry him."

"Dave Manning certainly gave you a full briefing, didn't he?"

"What do you do for a living, Miss Nolan?"

"I'm a designer. Jewelry, mostly. Also money clips, belt buckles, compacts, lipsticks, perfume bottles, eyeglass frames—et cetera."

"You at work this afternoon? Say, between four and five?"

"Oh, so that's it. That's when he was murdered, wasn't it?" she said.

"Just answer the question, please."

"I work at home. I haven't been out of the place all day."

"You threatened Mr. Lambert's life more than once, I believe."

"I meant it, too." She paused to light a cigarette. "Dave Manning told you about that, too, I suppose?"

"Most girls don't threaten to kill a man just because he changes his mind about getting married."

"Just *because!* You make it sound like nothing at all, like he merely changed his mind about going to a movie or something." She took a short, angry drag on the cigarette and exhaled the smoke through her nostrils. "And besides, I'm not 'most girls.' I'm me. And I just don't take a thing like that."

"And is that all he did to you?"

"Is that all!" Her dark eyes seemed to have tiny fires behind them. "Why, yes, you simple man, that's all he did to me. What more would he have to do? Stake me out on an anthill?"

"You know a girl named Elaine Greer?"

"No. Should I?"

"How about someone named Rocky?"

"No. No Rockys, either."

"You ever been in the Corbin hotel?"

"I've never even *heard* of the Corbin hotel."

"You know anyone who'd have liked to see Lambert dead?"

"Yes. Me. I—"

"Let's cooperate a little here, Miss Nolan. All right?"

She stabbed the cigarette out in a tray on the floor beside the hassock and crossed her legs again. "Just for starters," she said, "How about that fink, Dave Manning? He hated Harry, you know. I mean, *really* hated him."

"Why?"

"Because of me. Harry took me away from him. Did he tell you that? No, of course he didn't." She paused meaningfully. "Dave took it very hard. *Very* hard. It tore him up in little pieces." She raised one eyebrow and smiled at me. "Get the picture?"

"They continued to live together, though."

"What does *that* prove, for heaven's sake?"

I asked Miss Nolan a few more questions, none of which bought me anything, and got up to leave.

"Thanks for your help," I said. "It's possible we'll want to talk to you again, Miss Nolan."

"Oh, no doubt about it," she said. "And thank *you*—for bringing me such good news."

When I reached the squad room at the station house the hands on the big electric clock over the wall speaker stood at nine forty-two. Stan Rayder was at his desk, hammering at his ancient typewriter, a look of faint surprise on his lean face, as if the complaint report in his typewriter were the first one he'd ever seen.

I draped my jacket over the back of my chair and sat down. "How'd it go over at the hotel?" I asked.

"All buttoned up," Stan said. "Police seal on the door and all."

"Come up with anything?"

"Not in the room, no. Somebody'd wiped all the prints off the bottle and the glasses, though. I sent them over to the lab anyhow, along with everything else."

"Good. How about the lipstick? You ask for a check on the jeweler's mark?"

He nodded. "We just had a call on it. They had the mark on file, all right. The engraver lives in Brooklyn. I had them send a man over to see if he can round him up."

"You talk to the bellhop?"

"Yes, for all the good it did. Same goes for the maids. And none of the people in the rooms around Lambert's were in. The newsstand operator across the street saw the girl in the gold dress, though, the one the desk clerk told you about. She went in somewhere around four, he thinks. He didn't notice her come out again."

"Did you get anything else?"

"Yes. We've had a couple of panic calls from diamond dealers. It seems Harry Lambert took out about fifty thousand dollars' worth of stones on consignment this morning." He paused. "Maybe he was murdered for them, maybe not. Maybe he was going to run with them. Maybe a lot of things."

I told Stan what I'd learned from Dave Manning and Barbara Nolan, and then phoned the I.D. bureau to ask for checks on Dave Manning, Barbara Nolan, Elaine Greer, Mel Pearce, and Harry Lambert himself.

A few minutes later they called back to say they had nothing on any of them except Elaine Greer. A cross-reference check had shown that she was the wife of an ex-convict named Ralph Greer, who had been released four days ago from the State Hospital for the Criminal Insane at Matteawan.

Ralph Greer's rap sheet showed bits for grand larceny, aggravated assault, and extortion. His only known criminal associate was another ex-con, Floyd Stoner, now thought to be living at 631 West 74th Street. The present whereabouts of Greer himself were unknown.

"So Lambert's new girlfriend had a husband," Stan said when I relayed the information to him. "And the husband hits the street only four days ago. That sounds pretty good, Pete."

I dialed communications, asked that a pickup order be put out for Ralph Greer, then stood up and reached for my jacket.

"I think Mrs. Greer deserves the pleasure of our company, Stan," I said. "Let's not deny her any longer."

As it happened, Mrs. Greer was to be denied that pleasure, after all. She wasn't home.

We had the same luck when we drove uptown to talk to Floyd Stoner, the man who had once been Ralph Greer's criminal associate. Stoner wasn't home, either.

"We're batting a thousand," Stan said as we walked back down the stairs. "At this rate, we'll wrap things up just in time to put in for our pensions."

I used the wall phone in the first floor hall to ask for pickups on both Elaine Greer and Floyd Stoner, and arranged for plainclothes stakeouts to be stationed at their apartment houses. Then we went out to the car.

"I'll drive," Stan said as he got behind the wheel. "Your driving's too hairy for my nerves. Where to?"

"216 Central Park West."

"Who's there?"

"Mel Pearce, the diamond salesman who thought Lambert cheated him out of a sale."

Stan sighed. "Poor Lambert," he said. "There must be at least one person in this town who wasn't gunning for him. I wonder who it could be?"

Mel Pearce was about fifty, I judged, a graying, slightly stooped man with protuberant eyes behind thick, rimless glasses, abnormally long arms, and very fast answers to every question except the one about his whereabouts between four and five P.M.

He had, he said, spent the time "just walking around the midtown area, mulling over some deals I hoped to make."

As for his troubles with Lambert over the disputed diamond sale, that had all been a misunderstanding. He'd found that he had been in error, had apologized to Lambert, and that had been the end of it.

I called the squad room to see whether there had been any developments. There had.

The stakeout I'd had stationed at Floyd Stoner's apartment house had called to say that a man answering the description of Ralph Greer's former criminal associate had been seen entering the building.

It was a five story house with paper tape across the cracks in the first floor windows, trash in the foyer, and garbage on the stairs. There was no problem getting in; someone had propped the door open with the tattered remains of a phone book in a futile effort to encourage ventilation.

I knocked at the door of 301. There was a faint sound of movement from somewhere inside, but no one came to the door. I knocked again. This time, there was no sound at all.

"Police," I said.

"You're too polite," Stan said. "You got to give it more clout." He stepped close to the door. "It's the law!" he called loudly. "Open up here!"

About fifteen seconds passed.

I drew Stan a little way back from the door. "Stay here," I said. "I'll cover the fire escape. If you hear anything interesting, break in."

I went up to the top floor, climbed the metal ladder to the roof, and eased myself down the fire escape until I was outside the rear window of the apartment.

There was a half inch gap between the bottom of the window shade and the sill. I peered through it into the room beyond. The blonde girl with the slightly tilted eyes who lay trussed and gagged on the bed was the same girl I'd seen in the photograph in Dave Manning's apartment: Elaine Greer. She was struggling against the towels with which she'd been bound, her bright gold dress bunched up around her hips.

I tried the window. It was locked. I stood back and kicked the glass out of the frame. Then I unholstered my gun, jumped inside, and ran toward the bedroom door.

I jerked the door open just as Stan, alerted by the sound of breaking glass, burst through the front door with a crash of splintering wood, gun in hand.

We stood looking at each other across an empty room.

"What the hell?" Stan said. "I heard something in here. So did you."

"There's a girl tied up in the bedroom," I said. "Elaine Greer. What we heard was her trying to get loose."

"Elaine Greer?"

I nodded. "In a shiny gold dress. Just like the girl at the Corbin hotel was wearing."

The noise had brought some of the tenants to investigate, and now they stood gaping at us from the hallway.

"Police business," I said. "Clear the hall, please."

Mrs. Greer was almost hysterical. It was several minutes before she calmed down enough to talk to us. Even then, it took considerable backtracking before we got a coherent story from her.

She had, she said, been an unwilling participant in a phony kidnapping. Her husband, of whom she was terrified, had learned of her affair with Harry Lambert while he was still in the state mental hospital. When he had been released, four days ago, he had looked up his old friend, Floyd Stoner, and together they had worked out a way to make the most of Lambert's feelings for Mrs. Greer.

The two men had taken her to Stoner's apartment, where, under threat of death if she refused, she had been forced to make the early-morning phone call that Lambert's roommate had told us about. She had told Lambert she had been kidnapped, and that she would be killed unless he came up with a ransom of fifty thousand dollars' worth of small, easily sold diamonds. Lambert, whose insurance would cover that amount, was to claim that he had been robbed by two armed men who had forced themselves into his car.

Lambert was to put the gems in a chamois bag, take a room at the Corbin hotel under his own name, and wait for a phone call giving him further instructions. When Ralph Greer had called him there, however, Lambert had not answered the phone. Greer got mad.

"I was half out of my mind," Elaine Greer said. "I knew I had to do something about it. Then I saw a chance to slip out of the apartment, and I did."

"And?" Stan said.

"I'd heard my husband tell Stoner what Harry's room number was at the Corbin. I got a cab and went there. I knocked and knocked, but Harry didn't answer his door. Then I heard someone behind me—and there was my husband, with a gun in his hand. For a minute I thought he was going to kill me right there. I could see it in his eyes. But then he put the gun away and said something about getting the diamonds one way or another. He opened Harry's door with a piece of celluloid. He slipped it between the door and the jamb and—"

"We know the technique," Stan said. "Go on."

"Well, the door opened right up. We went in, and—and Harry was lying there on the bed. He was dead. I must have gasped or something because Ralph slapped me hard and told me to shut up. He looked for the diamonds, but they weren't there. Then he slapped me again and put his jacket over his arm so nobody could see he was holding a gun on me, and brought me back here in a cab."

"Why'd they tie you up?" Stan asked.

"They were going to kill me. I heard Ralph say so. They didn't want me left around to tell what they'd been up to."

"Where are they now?" I asked.

"I don't know. They left about twenty minutes ago." Her eyes suddenly flooded with tears. "They made me do what I did," she said.

"They'd have killed me if I hadn't. They were going to kill me anyway."

Stan and I stood looking at her.

"It's true!" she said. "Everything I've told you is the tɪuth!"

We arranged for additional stakeouts in and around the apartment building, beefed up the pickup order on Greer and Stoner to a thirteen-state alarm, and then took Mrs. Greer down to the station house.

On our way through the squad room to one of the interrogation rooms at the rear, I paused at my desk to see whether there was anything on my call spike or in my IN basket that pertained to the homicide.

There was a lab report saying that the lipstick in the tube I'd found in Lambert's bed and the lipstick on the glass were the same. The smear on the glass, however, had not been left there by a woman's lips; it appeared, rather, to have been put there with the ball of someone's thumb or fingertip. A test had revealed that at the time of his death Lambert's blood had a point five concentration of alcohol.

There was a brief, preliminary report from the medical examiner saying, in essence, that Lambert had died as the result of a blow inflicted by some blunt object to the base of his nose.

There was also a message on my call spike to phone Ed Gault, the detective who had checked out the jeweler's mark in the lipstick I had found in Lambert's room.

"Good news on that lipstick, Pete," Ed said when I got through to him. "I not only found the guy that made it, I even talked to the girl he made it for. It was a gift from a friend of hers, and her name was on the gift certificate."

It had been the wrong thing for Ed to do, since he might have flushed a prime suspect, but I let it go.

"What'd you find out?" I asked.

"Well, the girl's name is Linda Cole. She lives at the Pendleton, and a prettier little liar you won't find, believe me. She finally admitted being at the Corbin hotel, and she even admitted that she might have lost her lipstick there. But she says she was there almost a month ago, and she hasn't been near the place since." He laughed. "Some story."

"Thanks, Ed," I said. "We'll take it from there."

I hung up and sat drumming my fingertips on the desk for a

moment. There had been some lying done, all right, but I had a feeling it hadn't been done by Linda Cole.

I motioned Mrs. Greer to a seat on the chair beside my desk, and then drew Stan away a few paces to tell him about the reports and my talk with Ed Gault.

Stan shook his head, and for once some of the surprise on his face was real. "It looks like somebody ought to get his mouth fixed, doesn't it?" he said. "It just doesn't work right."

"Make sure Mrs. Greer knows her rights and gets a lawyer."

"You're going over there?"

"Yes."

"I'll go with you."

"I don't expect that much trouble, Stan," I said. "Besides, one of us ought to be here in case something breaks on Greer and Stoner."

I went downstairs, checked out a car, and drove the few blocks to the Corbin hotel.

Once again there was no one behind the desk, but there was a light beneath the door of Wayne Dobson's room beyond it, and I could hear someone moving around in there. I went back to the door, turned the knob very slowly, and inched it open.

The desk clerk was moving between his bed and the dresser, packing a suitcase. He was completely dressed for the street, even to a hat, and he was moving quickly, as if he had a lot to do and very little time in which to do it.

"Leaving us, Mr. Dobson?" I said as I stepped inside.

He spun to face me. His jaw sagged for an instant, but he recovered fast. "What's this?" he demanded. "Why didn't you knock?"

"We're old friends by now," I said. "I thought I'd be welcome."

There was an airline envelope on the dresser. I took the ticket out and looked at the name on it. It was made out to "J. Jackson" for a flight to Los Angeles."

"And a one-way ticket, too," I said.

"That belongs to a guest. What's the meaning of this, Selby?"

"And is that suitcase you're packing also a guest's?"

"It's no concern of yours, either way. Is there any law that says I can't go anywhere I want to, *when* I want to?"

"There just might be," I said. "Impeding a homicide investigation is a serious charge."

"Impede? What's the matter with you? Impede in what way?"

"You told me Harry Lambert got a phone call from someone named Rocky at exactly three fifty P.M. You were certain about it."

"So?"

"There wasn't any Rocky, Mr. Dobson. And Lambert didn't do any talking on the phone. He was an ex-alcoholic with no tolerance for liquor at all, but he drank a lot of it in that room, and he died with a point five concentration of alcohol in his blood. At three fifty he wasn't only drunk, he was too drunk even to mumble." I paused, "Why'd you lie?"

"I didn't. I—"

"And there's that fancy tube of lipstick you planted in Lambert's bed. It was lost here a month ago, and you put it in the shoebox under the desk, the one from which you had me get the antacid tablets. What you took for just another jazzy drugstore lipstick was an expensive, hand-engraved—"

"Now I get it," Dobson broke in. "You think you're going to frame me for—"

"And another thing," I said. "You smeared some of the lipstick on a glass to make us think Lambert had company in his room. That puzzles me a little, Mr. Dobson. Why'd you do it?"

"I—" Dobson began, then suddenly compressed his lips and stood there, glaring at me.

I moved to the bed and lifted the top layer of clothing out of the suitcase. It was there, all right—a chamois leather bag, no bigger than the kind that kids keep their marbles in.

I glimpsed the bag in the same instant I felt the stab of Dobson's gun in my back. We stood that way, neither of us moving or speaking, for what must have been a full ten seconds.

Then, "Get into the bathroom," Dobson said. "Take it real slow."

"Why?" I said. "A gunshot will carry just as well from there as it will here."

"Real slow, now," he said. "Get going, Selby."

I shrugged, took one slow step in the direction of the bathroom—and then dropped, clawing for my gun, starting to roll the instant I hit the floor.

Dobson's first shot missed, but his second burned a path across my left bicep. Then my own gun bucked in my hand and I saw Dobson's body jerk back from the impact of a slug in his stomach.

It was like watching a slow-motion film. Dobson's right arm lowered almost inch by inch until the gun fell from his hand, and he folded first one arm and then the other across his middle, stood there swaying back and forth for several seconds. Then, very slowly, he sank to his knees.

I kicked Dobson's gun under the bed, put my own back in its holster, and took two of the clean undershirts from the suitcase.

Dobson had lost interest in everything except the blood seeping from the bullet hole in his abdomen. He watched with dull eyes as I wadded one undershirt beneath his belt to serve as a compress and wrapped the other one around my arm where his slug had furrowed the skin. Then I went out to the switchboard to call an ambulance. The shots had brought several guests to the lobby, but I ignored them.

The ambulance was there in eight minutes. I helped the intern put Dobson's stretcher in the back and took a seat on the bench across from it. The intern climbed in beside me, and a moment later the ambulance lurched away from the curb.

"I'm going to die," Dobson said, almost completely without emotion. "You've killed me, Selby. I'm dying."

There wasn't a chance in a thousand of his dying, of course, and the intern opened his mouth to say so, but I kicked his ankle and he shut his mouth again. When a person is sure he is dying, even though he is not, anything he says has the full legal weight of a "deathbed confession," technically known as a dying declaration. It was my job to get such a declaration if I could.

"I guess there are some things you'd like to say, Mr. Dobson," I said. "Maybe now would be the time."

He lay looking at me unblinkingly while the ambulance traveled the better part of a block. Then his eyes drifted away from mine and he moved his head slowly and sadly from side to side.

"I should never have learned karate," he said quietly, almost as if to himself. "If I hadn't, Lambert would still be alive and I . . . I wouldn't be here dying." His voice was resigned and weak, but steady, with an undertone of irony in it.

"Is that how he died?" I asked softly. "From a karate blow?"

"Yes. When I saw all those diamonds, I . . ." He took a deep breath, held it for a moment, and let it out with a sigh. "I was passing his room. The door was half-open and I could see him in there on the bed with a bottle in his hand. I thought it was just another case of a drunk leaving his door open, and I started to close it for him, but then I saw the diamonds, where he'd spread them out on the bed beside him."

I waited. When he didn't go on, I said, "Too much temptation?"

He nodded. "I knew it would be the only chance I'd ever have to be rich. I've always had to scrounge for every dime. It's been just

one grubby little job after another all my life, and I . . . I don't know,
I thought I could just take them, and who would ever know?"

"And then, Mr. Dobson?" I said.

"I put them in a leather bag that was there, and started to leave,
but Lambert's head moved a little, and I . . . Like I said, I should
never have learned karate. I didn't even think about hitting him;
I just did. I was afraid he was coming to and that he'd see me and . . .
You have to understand. It was suddenly like they were *my* diamonds, not his, and he was about to take them away from me."

"And you thought that by pushing him out the window you might
cover up?"

"Yes. But I didn't think of that till later. Then I went back upstairs
and did it."

He paused, breathing a little more slowly now, his voice a bit
fainter. "All the rest was like you said, the lipstick and the phone
call and all. I was trying to divert suspicion, but I was so nervous
and rattled and sick with my ulcer that I just . . ."

"Go on, Mr. Dobson," I said.

He turned his face away from me. "I've always been a fool," he
said, almost inaudibly, and closed his eyes.

The ambulance was nearing the hospital. I sat watching the neon
streak past through the window beyond Dobson's stretcher, suddenly
tired to the bone. I didn't like the idea of leaving a man, Dobson or
anyone else, under the impression he was going to die any longer
than I had to.

"All right," I said to the intern beside me. "You can tell him the
truth now."

The intern leaned forward, studying Dobson's face. Then he
reached out and raised one of his eyelids.

"He didn't make it," he said. "He's dead."

Four on an Alibi

by Jack Ritchie

I t simply wouldn't do. There lay Uncle Hector, center library rug, in a pool of blood, with a revolver in his right hand.

I had been upstairs in bed, though awake, when I heard the shot. I had immediately slipped into the nether half of my pajamas and gone down to investigate.

On the first floor I opened a number of doors before finally switching on the library lights and finding Uncle Hector so thoroughly dead.

No. It just wouldn't do.

My cousin Clarence and I are co-beneficiaries of my uncle's estate—which I estimate at perhaps two million—and I could foresee no difficulty in that direction.

However, there still remained the question of Uncle Hector's life insurance. Its face value was some four hundred thousand dollars—Clarence and I again co-beneficiaries—but, of course, it would be automatically canceled in the event of suicide.

I sighed. Yes, it must appear that Uncle Hector had been murdered.

He had come downstairs for some reason—let us say that he had heard a noise—and had fallen upon an intruder, who had promptly shot and killed him.

Yes, that ought to do it; neat, clean, simple.

I went to the french windows. Using the corner of a drape, I unlocked one of them and left it slightly ajar. A draft of wind emphasized that it was quite chilly outside.

I removed the revolver from Uncle Hector's right hand and frowned. It was my Smith & Wesson .38. I had used it that very morning for plinking in the woods back of the house.

Usually when I am through shooting, I clean the weapon and return it to the locked gun cabinet in my bedroom. However, I had intended to go out again in the afternoon and so had merely dropped it into one of my bureau drawers. Evidently Uncle Hector had slipped into my dressing room while I was not there and taken it.

I would have to dispose of the gun, of course—throw it into some river or other convenient body of water.

I would do that tomorrow. If I attempted getting one of the cars out of the garage now, it would undoubtedly wake one of the servants quartered in the apartments above.

I surveyed the room again. Everything seemed quite in order.

When I left, I turned off the lights, making certain that any prints on the toggle were thoroughly smudged.

I found a dust cloth in one of the utility closets at the rear of the house and used it to wipe the fingerprints off the gun.

What should I do with the weapon until tomorrow? I thought it precautionary to hide the gun, and as far from my person as possible.

My eyes fell upon the vacuum cleaner in a corner of the closet. Ideal. I slipped the revolver into its bag.

No one else in the house seemed to have heard the shot, or at least bothered to investigate, though Danvers and several other of the servants occupied the third floor.

Should I tell any member of the family what I had just done? No, the fewer people who knew about it, the better.

Besides, Cousin Clarence wasn't even in his rooms. He was out again on one of those all night card games of his.

What about Marian, Clarence's wife? Should I wake her and tell her that Uncle Hector had been murdered?

No. Frankly I preferred for some servant to find the body in the morning and initiate the alarm.

I went upstairs. At my bedroom door I paused to think over the entire situation once more. Then I shrugged and went inside to my bed.

I slept fitfully. In the morning when Danvers came up with some freshly laundered shirts, I waited for a possible announcement, but evidently the body hadn't been discovered yet.

After showering and dressing, I went downstairs and joined Marian at the breakfast table.

"Is Clarence home yet?" I asked.

She nodded. "He staggered in at five or so. Naturally he's asleep now."

Marian is some ten or so years younger than her husband and may be described as being the very antithesis of Twiggy. She possesses an equable nature, a considerable asset when living with someone like Clarence.

She helped herself to bacon. "Uncle Hector seems to be late this morning."

A female scream came piercingly from the hall.

Marian was only mildly startled. "What was *that?*"

I listened to a second and a third scream, the last of a slightly different timbre. "Offhand, I'd say that came from one or more of the maids."

Danvers came into the room bearing the news. "Sir, it seems that one of the maids has just come upon the body of your uncle in the library. He appears to have been the victim of foul play."

I found two maids, white-faced and wide-eyed, just outside the library door. They both pointed urgently.

Yes, Uncle Hector was still in there, though a bit stiffer than when I had seen him last.

I took charge immediately. "Has anyone touched anything?"

"No, sir," one of the maids said swiftly. "I just opened the door and there he lay. I didn't even take one step inside the room."

I nodded approvingly. "Good. We will now close the library door and phone the police."

Marian peered over my shoulder. "How do we know for certain that Uncle Hector is dead? Maybe he could use some first aid?"

"My dear Marian," I said, "I have seen dead men in my time and Uncle Hector is one of them."

I phoned the police.

After six minutes a squad car arrived. The officers appraised the situation and went back to their car radio. In short order a detachment of detectives and a platoon of technical and medical technicians took over.

Marian, Danvers, and I waited in the drawing room until a Lieutenant Spangler, who seemed to be in charge, finally joined us.

He sat down. "Did any one of you hear the shot?"

Marian, Danvers, and I indicated that we had not.

Spangler nodded. "Guns usually don't make as much noise as people think." He opened a notebook. "Now, since your uncle appears to have been murdered, then obviously someone murdered him."

I agreed. "Undoubtedly some intruder. A burglar, or what have you. Poor Uncle Hector heard a noise and went to investigate. The intruder shot him and immediately fled, possibly by way of some open french window."

"Possibly." Spangler rubbed his nose thoughtfully. "How much is your uncle worth?"

I didn't think such a question appropriate in a cut-and-dried case like this one, but I answered. "Somewhere in the neighborhood of two million. My cousin Clarence Hackett and I are the principal heirs."

"Your cousin Clarence?"

"My husband," Marian explained. "Clarence is still upstairs in bed. He isn't feeling too well."

Spangler sympathized, but persisted. "You don't suppose you could wake him?"

Marian sent Danvers up to wake Clarence.

Spangler turned his attention back to me. "Did anyone touch anything in the library?"

"Absolutely nothing. No one even entered the room."

"When was the last time you saw your uncle alive?"

"About eight thirty. I passed by the drawing room and he was in here watching television."

Marian nodded. "I went to bed early—about nine. He was still in here engrossed in a western."

Spangler seemed to consider that for a moment. "I noticed that the light switch controlling the library's central lighting fixture is turned off. Also none of the lamps are on. Would your uncle go to investigate a strange noise in the dark?"

Damn it, why had I turned off the lights when I left the library? Pure habit, of course, but it made things sticky. "He was trying to *surprise* the intruder," I said. "So naturally he wouldn't turn on any lights."

"If he was going to surprise this prowler, why wasn't he armed with some kind of a weapon? A gun, a club? Something. Also, your uncle was drilled neatly through the heart. So, did this intruder first kill your uncle in a lighted room and then thriftily turn off the lights before he left?"

I smiled firmly. "Undoubtedly the intruder carried a flashlight. He used its illumination to shoot my uncle and then departed. By the french window, I suppose."

Spangler regarded me for a moment. "How did you and your uncle get along?"

Actually Uncle Hector and I disliked each other, though not to any serious extent. "We never had any arguments," I said truthfully.

Spangler nodded slowly. "I don't suppose you would mind if one of our people conducted a little test to determine if there might be gunpowder grains embedded in one of your hands?"

Gunpowder grains? Good heavens! Of course there would be gunpowder grains embedded in my hands. After all, I'd been out in the woods behind the house just yesterday morning plinking with that .38.

I laughed lightly. "Actually you *would* find gunpowder grains on my hands. You see, yesterday morning I went plinking in the woods."

"Rather a coincidence," he suggested. "Plinking in the woods on the very day your uncle was murdered?"

"Not at all," I said defensively. "I often plink in the woods."

One of Spangler's assistants came in and whispered into his ear. Spangler excused himself and left the room.

Danvers joined us again. "I succeeded in waking your husband, madam, and elevating him to his feet. I informed him of what has happened and he is now taking a shower.

Spangler returned after fifteen minutes. "One of your maids found a gun in a vacuum cleaner bag she was emptying. I think it might be the murder weapon. Why else would anyone want to hide it there?"

Damn the maid. Why the devil did she have to empty a vacuum cleaner bag when the house was full of police?

"Does anyone in this room own a .38 Smith & Wesson revolver?" Spangler asked.

I hesitated. Since the weapon was registered in my name, it could certainly be traced to me. On the other hand, I had thoroughly wiped off any fingerprints before hiding it, so I could see no point in putting myself closer to the gun than necessary.

I cleared my throat. "I *used* to own a .38 revolver, but I gave it to my Uncle Hector two weeks ago."

Spangler smiled faintly. "I wonder how the intruder got hold of the gun?"

"As I reconstruct the crime," I said helpfully, "Uncle Hector came down here *armed* with the gun. There was a brief struggle—or possibly protracted, for all I know—but anyway, the intruder wrested the gun from Uncle Hector's hand, shot him, and then fled."

Spangler rubbed at the smile. "Shot your uncle? Wiped the fingerprints from the gun? Turned off the lights? Hid the gun in the vacuum cleaner bag? Returned to the library and fled through the french window?"

It did sound a little shaky at that, when it was reiterated.

"When was the last time you fired that revolver?" Spangler asked.

"Two weeks ago, when I gave it to Uncle Hector. I haven't touched it since."

"Did *he* ever fire it?"

"Numerous times. He often went plinking in the woods himself. We are a family of plinkers."

Spangler made himself comfortable in an easy chair. "One of our people found fingerprints."

I frowned. "I thought you just said that the fingerprints had been wiped from the gun?"

"They were. However, we found quite decent prints on the cartridges *inside* the gun chambers. You don't exactly load a revolver with your teeth, you know. Most people use their fingers and fingers leave fingerprints."

I felt that I might actually perspire, something ordinarily too plebeian for me even to consider. Of course my fingerprints would be on the cartridges—particularly the very one which had killed Uncle Hector.

My laugh was slightly high-pitched. "Lieutenant, I haven't *fired* the gun since I gave it to Uncle Hector, but I *did* reload it for him just the other day. You see, he happened to be busy at the moment and so he asked me if I would reload . . ."

No, that was weak.

"Lieutenant," I said. "I have a confession to make."

He got that damn smile again. "I'll get a stenographer."

I held up a hand. "Not *that* kind of a confession."

"What kind are you offering?"

"Actually, Uncle Hector shot himself."

"Is that right?"

"Yes. Suicide." My smile seemed to hurt. "Last night at approximately eleven thirty I heard a shot. I came down here to investigate and found Uncle Hector lying there on the library rug. The gun was in his hand. Obviously he had shot himself."

Spangler smiled patiently.

I was definitely perspiring. "I took the gun away from Uncle Hector, wiped off the fingerprints, and hid the gun."

"Why would you want to do all of that?"

Should I tell him about the insurance? Somehow that would make me appear greedy and that is one thing I am not.

"There is a certain stigma to suicide," I said, a trifle loftily. "I did what I did to protect the family name. I felt it would be much kinder to make the incident seem like murder by an intruder."

"What did you do with the suicide note your uncle wrote?"

"There wasn't any suicide note."

"Why would your uncle want to kill himself?"

"I really haven't the faintest idea."

"Were the lights on when you found him?"

Those damn lights again. What difference did it make? "No," I said, remembering. "I turned them on and there he was."

"So your uncle committed suicide in the dark?"

"Obviously."

Spangler shook his head. "People just don't commit suicide in the dark. Don't ask me why, but they don't. They may close their eyes, but they never turn off the lights."

I wiped my forehead with a handkerchief. "Uncle Hector should have powder grains on one of his hands, shouldn't he? Have you tested for that?"

Spangler decided to give that a fair try. He left the room, apparently to join the technicians in the library and have them perform a test.

Danvers watched me. "Shall I get you a dry handkerchief, sir?"

"Shut up," I said.

After a while, Spangler came back. "There are absolutely no gunpowder grains on your uncle's hands. We checked thoroughly."

I was stunned.

No powder grains? That meant that Uncle Hector really *had* been murdered and his murderer had attempted to make the crime seem like suicide.

Here I stood, powder grains on my hands, my gun as the murder weapon, my fingerprints on the cartridges in that murder weapon, the possessor of an immense motive.

I was lost.

Marian rose. "Lieutenant, at the time of the murder, my cousin Ambrose and I were together."

Good old Marian. Awfully decent of her to put her reputation on the line like that.

Spangler regarded her warily. "I thought you said you went to *bed* at nine?"

She smiled thinly. "I meant to say that I *retired* to the suite my husband and I occupy on the second floor. Ambrose joined me there slightly after nine." She turned to Danvers. "Isn't that right, Danvers? You were there too, and we *all* played bridge."

Danvers rose to the occasion. "Of course, madam. We played bridge until we heard the shot at eleven thirty and that broke up the game."

Spangler's eyes were quite narrow. "You and your cousin played bridge with your butler?" he said.

She drew herself up. "Whatever I am, I am not a snob."

The drawing room door opened and my cousin Clarence was ushered in by one of Spangler's assistants.

Clarence is a rather large, bulky man. His eyes were still a bit bloodshot and he walked with a wince that indicated the did not welcome the day this early, despite a hair of the dog.

Spangler turned on him. "And just where were *you* last night at the time of the murder?"

Clarence took umbrage at the tone of his voice. "Where the hell would I be? I was in bed with my wife."

Why did Clarence have to say that? He had a perfectly good alibi of his own, didn't he? Those people he played cards with all night?

Marian laughed lightly for Spangler's benefit. "My husband means that *after* midnight he and I went to bed. *Prior* to that, until we heard the shot at eleven thirty, all *four* of us were in our suite playing bridge. My husband, my cousin Ambrose, Danvers, and I."

Clarence seemed to chew on his mustache, though he had none. "Ah, yes. We heard the shot at eleven thirty."

I supplied him with more grist. "We heard the shot and all *four* of us went downstairs. We found Uncle Hector apparently a suicide and we decided that for the sake of the family name, we ought to make it appear as though Uncle Hector had been murdered by an intruder."

Clarence swayed slightly. "We certainly did."

I smiled. "Of course our humanitarian gesture did not succeed, and now we are back to the fact that Uncle Hector was truly murdered. Undoubtedly by an intruder."

Clarence went to the liquor cabinet. "I couldn't have put it more succinctly myself."

Spangler and his staff spent the rest of the morning questioning us individually, but as far as I could tell, our story seemed to hold. For the time being, at least.

During a break in the interrogation, I met Clarence upstairs.

"Clarence," I said. "I don't understand why you didn't simply give Spangler the names of the people you played cards with last night. Surely that would have been sufficient to establish your whereabouts at the time Uncle Hector was murdered."

He smiled tolerantly. "One does not drag the names of one's friends into something like this."

"But surely in a case of murder they would understand."

He decided to give me the man-to-man confidential explanation. "Actually, Ambrose, it is not so much *who* I played cards with that I wish to conceal, but *where*. Madam La Fontaine and her charges could get into all sorts of trouble and I certainly wouldn't want that."

Madam La Fontaine? I had heard she had a heart of gold and gave Green Stamps.

I went to my bedroom and lay down on my bed.

So be it. Four on an alibi was better than three, and I needed all the alibi I could get.

I sighed. Surely Uncle Hector *must* have been murdered by an intruder. He had heard the noise downstairs. He had let himself into my dressing room, gotten the revolver from the dresser, and gone downstairs to investigate. In the library he had been overwhelmed by the intruder and shot.

That really did seem the most logical explanation for his death.

On the other hand, how would Uncle Hector have known that I had put the revolver in that particular drawer?

I couldn't see how he would.

Perhaps the intruder himself had found the weapon and taken it downstairs with him?

I went to the dresser and pulled open the top drawer.

I had placed the gun right here beside the tray containing my collection of cuff links, all of them patently expensive; and next to the tray still lay the two jeweled lighters I seldom used and also the engraved cigarette case.

If the intruder had come upon the gun, why hadn't he taken all of these things too? Why just the gun?

No, your typical intruder simply would not leave that much loot undisturbed.

The conclusion was obvious. The gun hadn't been taken by an intruder, nor by Uncle Hector.

Then by whom? Clarence?

No. He also couldn't have known that I had put the gun in that drawer instead of the cabinet as usual.

Marian?

No, but who?

Danvers came into the room. "Lunch is being served, sir."

I stared at him.

Danvers? But of course.

He had been in my room gathering clothes to send off to the dry cleaners when I had returned from plinking. He had *seen* me put the gun away.

I pointed an accusing finger. "Danvers, it was *you* who killed Uncle Hector!"

He regarded me warily. "Really, sir?"

"Of course. Only *you* knew that I had put that revolver in that particular drawer." I smiled grimly. "At this very moment your hands are probably impregnated with thousands of grains of gun powder."

He shook his head. "I doubt that, sir. Before I killed your uncle, I took a long walk on the grounds, brooding upon the necessity and whipping up enough courage for the deed. It was quite chilly, so I wore a topcoat and gloves. Luckily I was still wearing them when I shot your uncle, and since learning about this gunpowder business, I have destroyed both the gloves and the topcoat and thoroughly stirred the ashes, so to speak."

"So it was you who turned off the lights when you left the library?"

"A habit, sir. Automatic, I'm afraid, even under stress."

"Why did you kill him?"

"He had given me notice earlier in the day, sir. Something about a shortage in the household accounts, of which I am totally innocent, sir. However, you know how intransigent your uncle could be. I realized there was no hope for reason or reconciliation."

"You killed him because he fired you? Really, Danvers!"

"Not entirely, sir. However, I knew that in a better day I had been included in his will to the extent of fifteen thousand dollars. It followed that he would immediately cancel that provision and I just couldn't see parting with that much money."

"So you killed Uncle Hector for a lousy fifteen thousand dollars?"

"Sir," he said reproachfully, "in *my* circle fifteen thousand dollars is not at all lousy."

"Danvers," I said, "as a Concerned Citizen, I feel that it is now my duty to inform Lieutenant Spangler that you have confessed to murder."

He smiled faintly. "After I shot your uncle, I hid in the shadows of the hall when I heard a door being opened on the second floor. I looked up, sir, and it was you coming down to investigate."

I stiffened slightly. "You saw me coming out of my bedroom?"

"No, sir. I saw you coming out of *Mrs. Hackett's* suite. Adjusting the nether half of your pajamas, sir." He clucked his tongue re-provingly. "Sir, I do not believe that you and Mrs. Hacket *ever* play cards up there at all."

I rubbed my neck. Unfortunately that was quite true. I actually *had* been in Marian's suite last night, but we had not been playing cards. As a matter of fact, Marian and I *never* waste our time playing cards on those nights when Clarence is off to Madam La Fontaine's or whatever.

"Danvers," I said sternly, "that has absolutely nothing to do with the matter of murder. Absolutely nothing at all."

"Perhaps not, sir, but I do think that if I must confess to murder I ought to tell the lieutenant, and possibly an open court, everything which occurred and was observed on the night in question. That is routine, isn't it, sir?"

We were both silent for a while.

Danvers smiled again. "Do you play bridge at all, sir?"

"I'm afraid not, Danvers. I don't know a thing about the game."

He nodded. "I thought not, sir. And that could be a dangerous flaw in our collective alibi, don't you think, sir?"

He deftly removed a pack of playing cards from the inside pocket of his jacket and proceeded to teach me the fundamentals of the game of bridge.

The Bag

by Patrick O'Keeffe

Unlike Diogenes, Captain Meed didn't go looking for an honest man, but, to his bitter sorrow, he found one, and not with a lantern but with a bag.

It was a small, zippered bag of brown leather and, packed with the usual duty-free bottle of whisky and the Atlantida brand of cigarettes his wife liked, it lay then on the settee as the captain dogged down his cabin ports before leaving for home. As soon as the chief mate came up from the messroom to report that the paying-off of the crew was finished, he'd be on his way.

The captain looked around as footsteps sounded in the passage. He expected to see the chief man, but it was a clean-shaven, dark man of forty or so who appeared in the open doorway, smartly dressed in a cream-colored summer suit with broad yellow tie.

"Remember me, captain—Al Wycka?"

He came in with an aggressive step, a brown straw hat in one hand, the other extended. The captain took the hand limply, trying to hide his annoyance; he was a broad-beamed, dour-looking man of fifty, with a purple-streaked, fleshy face and double chin. Wycka had come north from the Caribbean isle of Atlantida on the *Conte's* previous voyage, and apparently had dropped aboard for a social call.

"You just caught me in time. I'm about to leave for home," said the captain, hoping his former passenger would take the hint.

Wycka shot a glance at the bag and the tweed hat waiting beside it. "I made a special trip over to see you, captain. I'd appreciate it if you'd give me a few minutes." He paused. "What I have to say may be well worth your time to listen to."

Captain Meed frowned. It was midafternoon, and he was tired and anxious to go home and rest. It had been a long, hot day, starting with the moment he was called at four o'clock for the Ambrose pilot, docking the ship throughout the breakfast hour, spending the forenoon around the steamship line's Manhattan offices and at the customhouse, entering the ship. Wycka's urgent tone and manner, however, stirred up enough curiosity to counter weariness. "Sit down."

Wycka looked significantly at the door. The captain stepped over and closed it, and then sat down in his desk chair. Wycka eased himself onto the settee, beside the bag, and came straight to the point.

"Captain, would you be interested in making five thousand dollars in cold cash?"

The captain stared. "In what way?"

"By taking fifty thousand dollars in gold bars aboard your ship to Atlantida."

"You mean unmanifested?"

Wycka nodded. "Hence the five thousand."

Captain Meed's eyes narrowed. "Why did you come to me?"

"For one thing, yours is one of the few ships calling regularly at Atlantida. Another is that during the few days I was aboard, you told me a little about yourself—family obligations, big drop in salary. I wanted to give you first chance to pick up some needed cash."

Captain Meed recalled having told Wycka during a spell of depression that his salary was little more than half of what it would be aboard an American ship. His first command had been with an American company formed during the wartime demand for ships, but the firm had gone under in postwar commercial competition with older and more experienced lines. He'd been glad to get command of the Liberian-registered banana boat *Conte* as the alternative to sailing as third mate of some American flat vessel.

"You figured I was an easy mark for a bribe," he said sourly.

Wycka grimaced. "A commission, captain. I'd be willing to ship the gold in the normal manner, pay freight and insurance, but the gold was obtained from unlicensed sources, so asking for a government permit to export it is out of the question. And then there are the restrictions on importing gold into Atlantida. So I'm offering you a good commission to waive the formalities."

"For breaking the law, is the way I see it."

Wycka smiled deprecatingly. "If that's what troubles you, captain, allow me to point out that all kinds of people are breaking the laws in these times—clergymen, newspapers, university professors—all claiming the right to disobey laws they're opposed to. Some monetary experts don't hold with the gold restrictions. If you side with them and ignore the law, you'll be in good company."

Captain Meed fell silent. Wycka continued persuasively. "You'll simply be using your position as captain for your own advantage, and you'll be in more good company. Public officials, judges, union officials—all use their office to benefit themselves. You read about them almost daily in the newspapers when someone oversteps himself. Men play it smart nowadays and take whatever comes their way. I'm putting something your way, captain. Why not play it smart, too?"

Captain Meed wavered. He'd never yet used his position as captain for his own gain, but then he'd never before been so desperately in need of ready cash. He could use that five thousand. He'd borrowed to the limit on his life insurance. The mortage was due on the new house he'd bought before he lost his old command, stocked with new refrigerator and freezer, washing and drying machines, a raft of appliances and every gadget his wife could think of, color TV console, all on monthly payments. College fees for his two sons were to go up, his daughter to be outfitted for her freshman year, his wife spending money as wildly as though he were still on the old salary. That five thousand could give him a breathing spell.

The captain turned to his desk. Picking up a pencil, he started figuring on a note pad. "Fifty thousand at around forty dollars an ounce—"

"That's the market rate," interrupted Wycka. "It has to be worked out at the official United States rate of thirty-eight dollars a troy ounce."

Captain Meed made hurried calculations. Turning back to Wycka, he said, "It comes to around a hundred and ten pounds. I could hardly stow that under my mattress."

"Surely there must be some way."

The captain hesitated. "What's the gold to be used for? Explosives for the terrorists, buying dope, or what?"

"Captain, to ease your mind on that score, I'll tell you, though if you repeat to others what I'm about to say, I'll deny ever having said it. During my voyage north, I told you I represented a commercial syndicate seeking a certain concession. It was for gambling rights, to open casinos throughout the island. To get the concession, the syndicate must pay fifty thousand dollars to a certain party. He won't take paper money because of a fear he's got about exchange-rate fluctuations, devaluation, the government calling in the old currency and issuing new. He wants the gold in American grade of fineness and in bars of not more than fifty ounces each. I saw you had Atlantida lottery tickets, so I know you've got nothing against gambling."

"I take it you'd have the gold put aboard under wraps, but what about down in Atlantida?"

"Nothing to worry about. That's all been arranged by the party it's going to. It's all ready for shipping aboard, according to whatever instructions you give. If—"

He broke off as someone knocked on the door. It was opened by the chief mate, a thickset, middle-aged man wearing an officer's khaki-topped cap.

"Payoff's all finished, cap'n. No beefs to be settled." Smiling at the captain's visitor, he said, "Hi, Mr. Wycka. Nice to see you again."

"Nice to see you, too, Mr. Moar. I was passing, and thought I'd drop aboard to say hello to Captain Meed."

The chief mate lingered, but the captain didn't invite him in. He withdrew, closing the door.

"You don't seem very friendly toward Mr. Moar," remarked Wycka. "I noticed it during my trip."

"He was chief mate here when old Captain Lund died at sea. He expected to stay in command. He'd sell his soul to get something on me."

"Would he be much of a problem?"

"Enough to make me want more time to think it over."

"How much?"

"Tomorrow morning. Maybe tonight."

Wycka drew a notebook from the inside pocket of his cream-colored jacket and scribbled a number. Tearing off the leaf, he handed it to the captain. "Phone me any time after seven, or before nine in the morning."

Captain Meed slipped the paper inside his wallet and rose. He reached for the bag and his hat lying on the settee. Wycka stood up.

"My car's outside, captain. Could I give you a lift?"

"Up to the bus stop. My wife usually drives down for me, but while I was away on the last voyage, the car didn't pass inspection."

Wycka smiled confidently. "She'll be driving you home in a brand new one next time you come in."

At the pier gate, the uniformed customs guard walked over when he saw the bag, but stepped aside after glancing at the captains's declaration slip, saying, "Okay, cap'n." The bus stop was at the top of the truck-scarred road that wound from the Jersey-side pier across the freight train tracks and up to the highway. Wycka stopped alongside the curb, letting the captain off and handing the bag out to him, and then headed for the Lincoln Tunnel.

Captain Meed walked along to the adjacent telephone booth to let his wife know he was on the way home, but turned back when the bus suddenly hove into sight. As it sped him toward his new home in rural New Jersey, he became so enwrapped in weighing the ins and outs of Wycka's tempting offer that he was almost at his stop before he became aware of the fact. He started for the door without the bag; a woman called him back, but she was an honest woman, not the honest man.

As the captain let himself into the red brick house, his curly-wigged wife came to greet him, wearing a new dress and looking as if she's just come back from adding to the beauty parlor bill.

"We really must get a *new* car and then I can come for you," she said. "And it's such a nuisance shopping at the supermarket and having to carry things home." She relieved him of the bag.

Would she never get it into her extravagant head that with his present salary and bills they'd be lucky if they could afford a *used* car? he asked himself irritably. If he picked up that five thousand, it would never do to let her know, apart from being unable to reveal how he came by it. She'd run through it in a week. Nor would it do to bank it either, in this small, gossipy neighborhood. It should go into a safe-deposit box, to be drawn on as the need arose.

With his thoughts already inclining toward acceptance of Wycka's offer, Captain Meed came to his decision while pretending to read the evening newspaper as his wife prepared dinner. Later in the evening, when his wife was listening to the news broadcast on the color console, he slipped out to the hall telephone and dialed the number on Wycka's slip. Wycka answered after the first ring.

"I'll take the shipment," said the captain.

"Fine!" Wycka sounded immensely gratified.

"Put it into two suitcases, no labels, and locked. That'll make it easy for one man to handle if necessary—me, if I have to. Sailing time is four o'clock tomorrow afternoon. Have them delivered about an hour before then. That's important."

"Will do. And as soon as you've sailed, I'll cable the interested party to be prepared at his end."

"About the commission—"

"I'll bring it aboard as soon as the suitcases are safely on the ship. I'll be parked outside the pier gate, watching."

"What I was going to say is that I want it in small bills—tens, fifties, hundreds, like I get in my pay envelope; nothing larger. Big bills might start talk about shipboard rackets if banked or cashed in my neighborhood."

"That can be arranged."

Toward nine o'clock next morning, Captain Meed returned aboard with the bag, now containing a couple of new khaki uniform shirts and black socks, and odds and ends such as toothpaste and razor blades. He left it on the settee for unpacking later and went over to Manhattan to clear the ship at the customhouse and call on the marine superintendent and other of the line's department heads.

He got back to the ship after the lunch hour. Close to three o'clock he stood at an open porthole of his cabin, which overlooked the foredeck and the gangway. The six passengers booked for Atlantida were aboard, the longshoremen had finished loading general cargo and steamed ashore, and the sailors were topping up the derricks, sweating under the fierce sun. The chief mate was giving some instructions to the carpenter about battening down.

Presently an unmarked van drove down the pier and stopped at the foot of the gangway. The driver jumped off, clutching a delivery sheet. The chief mate intercepted him as he reached the top of the gangway.

"Two suitcases for the *Conte*," the captain heard the driver say.

The chief mate glanced at the delivery sheet and then asked, "Who are they for?"

The driver shook his head. "All I know is, the delivery service I work for told me to run two suitcases over to the *Conte*."

The whine of a winch hauling up a derrick drowned out the chief mate's reply. He beckoned to two sailors and sent them down to the van. Each returned with a large-sized suitcase of black leather and set it down on the deck. The chief mate glanced over them, looking puzzled.

"Wait here," he said to the driver.

The chief mate started toward the ladder to the bridge deck. Captain Meed promptly turned away from the porthole and appeared to be busy at his desk when the chief mate knocked and came in.

"A van just brought a couple of suitcases for us. No names or labels on them. Nor anything on the delivery sheet showing who they're for."

Captain Meed made a gesture as of impatience with himself. "I forgot to tell you. They're for Atlantida. To be treated as over-carried baggage but not manifested. Someone down there will see to landing them."

"Monkey business," grunted the chief mate.

The captain shrugged. "It looks like it. But I do what I'm told by the office and ask no questions. The line has to play ball now and then with some official down in Atlantida wanting a favor done."

"Or else," said the chief mate sardonically. "Where do you want 'em stowed?"

Captain Meed appeared to think "Maybe you'd better stow them in the spare cabin, so they won't get mixed up with the regular baggage and maybe cause a foul-up."

The chief mate went out. Captain Meed returned to the porthole and saw him sign the delivery sheet and heard him tell the sailors to take the two suitcases up to the deck officers' quarters. The spare cabin was two doors along from the captain's, and was used for storing officers' trunks and bags and an occasional piece of special cargo. Captain Meed kept to his cabin while the sailors were bringing up the suitcases and stowing them, and he barely looked around as he acknowledged the chief mate's announcement from the doorway that the job was done.

Captain Meed felt confident that his feigned forgetfulness and indifference to the suitcases would keep the chief mate from suspecting that he had a personal interest in them and trying to find out more about them.

Wycka came aboard about ten minutes later, carrying a brown attaché case, wearing the cream-colored suit but with a pink tie. He laid the attaché case on the settee, moving the captain's bag aside, and opened it while the captain closed the cabin door. Wycka took out a bundle of currency bound with rubber bands.

"Mostly tens, twenties, fifties, with a few hundreds," he said, handing the bundle to the captain.

"Thanks," said the captain avidly. He slipped the money into a desk drawer, his dour face brightening. He turned toward the liquor cabinet. "Feel like a snorter?"

"Thanks, but I must be on my way." Wycka then closed the attaché case and held out four brass keys. "For the suitcases, in case the interested party would like to unlock them instead of breaking them open." Wycka then thrust out a hand. "Good luck, captain. If your ship's in Atlantida when the first casino is opened, you'll be the special guest of the syndicate."

As Captain Meed opened the door to let out his visitor, the chief mate was passing. He stopped on seeing Wycka, looking surprised. "Going south with us?" he asked.

Wycka smiled. "No such luck. I happened to be passing this way again. I didn't realize it was so close to sailing time."

The chief mate walked along the passageway with Wycka, while Captain Meed hooked back the door, biting his lip. This was the second time the chief mate had found Wycka inside his cabin with the door closed—and right after the two suitcases had come aboard. Wycka's remark had made it appear that he'd come aboard by chance again and not by design, but if the chief mate put two and two together, there was no telling what he might make them add up to.

The captain turned to the bag resting on the settee. He unpacked it and stowed it on the floor of the clothes locker. He hoped that when he went home again with it, his worries would be over.

Three weeks later, when the *Conte* arrived back at her Jersey-side pier, there was a plain envelope in the captain's mail, and inside were ten one hundred dollar bills, with a note saying that the shipment had reached the interested party, and that the enclosed was a special bonus for a job well done. The captain tore up the note.

He was not only grateful but relieved. The chief mate seemed to have been not overly curious when two porters, undoubtedly specially assigned, had come for the suitcases in Atlantida and mixed them in with the passenger baggage, obviously to be removed before reaching the customs shed. But sometimes American consuls get wind of things and drop a word in the right quarter. This had evidently not happened. His worries were at an end.

That afternoon, however, as Captain Meed was preparing to leave for home, he underwent a few moments of apprehension. The chief mate had reported the crew payoff finished, and the bag, packed with the usual bottle of whisky and cigarettes, lay on the settee beside his hat. Closing the cabin door, he took the bundle of currency from his safe and dropped it into the bag, together with the envelope containing the extra thousand and letters he had received in the mail that morning.

As he zipped up the bag, it struck him that, with so many robberies and muggings, it was a lot of cash to be carrying around. Recently, more than one crew member leaving or returning to the ship late at night had been held up on the road leading to the pier, and one had been mugged near the bus stop. A purse snatcher might go for his bag.

Captain Meed brushed aside his fears. Those holdups and the mugging had happened at night, not in broad daylight with trucks and cars going in both directions on the pier road. Besides, he might get a ride up to the bus stop.

At the pier gate, the customs guard waved him on after glancing at his declaration slip, but no car was heading up the road and so he started out on foot. Next time, he mused in happy anticipation, his wife would meet him, in a *new* car. The first down payment was right there in the bag, with plenty more besides.

When Captain Meed reached the bus stop, he entered the telephone booth and called his wife. She had just come in from the supermarket, but before she could complain again about the inconvenience of shopping without a car, he told her he'd had a little luck with the Atlantida lottery, and they'd be able to afford a *new* car.

"Goodie goodie!" she said, and then asked how the voyage was. While he was telling her, he saw the bus coming, and hung up and pulled open the folding door.

A man wearing coveralls alighted from the bus. Captain Meed was the only one boarding it. It was only half filled, and he chose a seat to himself toward the middle. It wasn't until he was settled and had been gazing happily through the window for a little while that a sudden thought dismayed him.

His bag!

He glanced around wildly—on the seat beside him, at his feet, in the aisle. He scrambled to his feet and stumbled along to the driver.

"Stop—please let me off!"

The bus had just passed a stop, the second beyond the one at which he had got on. The driver kept his gaze fixed on the road ahead. "Next stop," he growled.

"Now—please now! I left my bag in the telephone booth. There's—there's money in it."

"Next stop," the driver said adamantly.

"Captain Meed eyed him in helpless desperation. The other passengers were staring in his direction. His forehead broke into a sweat not induced by the midafternoon heat. He raged at himself. This was the second time he's forgotten the bag, being so used to dropping it into the back seat of the car and not carrying it.

Three women were waiting at the next stop. Captain Meed startled them by leaping past them from the bus steps and heading down the side of the road. There were only a few pedestrians strung along it. He didn't come in sight of the telephone booth until he rounded a bend in the road, and as he drew nearer to it, he was able to see that it wasn't occupied. He slowed down, out of breath.

A man carrying a briefcase and two young women were at the bus stop. Captain Meed hurried past them to the booth and pushed open the door. The bag was gone.

He walked back to the stop. "Did any of you see anyone use the telephone while you were waiting?" he panted miserably. "I left my bag in the booth."

The man shook his head. One of the young women said, "Not while I've been waiting."

"Much in it?" asked the man sympathetically.

"Quite a bit of money."

"If the bag's got your name and address in it, whoever found it may get in touch with you," said the other young woman.

"I wouldn't count on it," said the man. "I did the same thing once, and I never did hear anything. Nothing in it worth keeping, either."

Captain Meed followed them into the next bus. All the way home he sat staring bleakly through the window. He remembered the workman in coveralls who had got off the last bus. He might have been the one who found the bag. There was plenty of identification in the bag—his name and address inside along with the letters from that morning's mail at the ship. But what workman would pass up an easy six thousand dollars?

Captain Meed rode past his stop and had to walk back. When his wife met him inside the doorway, she asked, "Was the bus delayed?" and then, noticing his empty hands, "Where's your bag?"

"I left it in the telephone booth," he moaned. "I got off and went back, but it was gone."

"It's got your name and address inside, so it may be returned to you. It wouldn't be much of a loss anyway. So don't be upset, dear."

"My lottery winnings are in it," he groaned, "and people play it smart nowadays."

"Oh, dear!" she cried.

During dinner, the telephone in the hallway rang. Captain Meed went out and answered it.

"Captain Meed?" inquired an unfamiliar voice.

"Speaking."

"Captain of the banana boat *Conte?*"

"That's right."

"You left a bag in the telephone booth up by the bus stop?"

"Yes," cried the captain, excited. "This afternoon. You found it?"

"It's right here." There was a pause. "That's quite a bundle you've got in it, cap." There was an insinuating note in the voice. Captain Meed wondered if it was the workman at the other end.

"Yes. I—I never expected to see it again."

"The guy who found it didn't like risking having all that money lying around till he got in touch with you, so he turned it in to us."

"The police?"

"Waterfront precinct station house, close by your ship."

The captain's throat went dry. "I'll—I'll send my wife over to pick it up."

"We'd like you to come yourself and identify the bag and the contents, cap. Any time it's convenient for you."

Captain Meed hung up, shaking. The police wanted to question him. It was to be expected they'd view all that money found in the bag of a man leaving his ship on arrival day as suspiciously like a payoff of some kind. He'd never get away with saying it was lottery winnings, or anything else. They'd tip off the Coast Guard intelligence or the FBI to investigate. It wouldn't take long, once they'd talked to the chief mate with his knowledge of the two unmanifested suitcases and the two closed door meetings with Wycka. Even if they didn't find out what was in them, those two unmanifested suitcases would cost him his captaincy with the line.

He pulled himself together and went back to the table.

"Who was it?" his wife asked.

He swallowed. "The police. The bag was turned in to them."

"You see, dear, you didn't have to worry." She sighed thankfully. "It's so nice to know there are still honest men in the world."

The Long Curve

by George Grover Kipp

S lim Gentry slitted his brown eyes against the brassy heat wafting in from the desert and studied the black sedan churning up dust the length of the main street. Stepping back from the battering heat of the street, Slim leaned his lanky, khaki-covered frame against the shade of an adobe cafe. The man in the car, incongruously clad in a dark suit, emerged from its air-conditioned comfort and ran the gauntlet of heat to the coolness of Ramon's cantina. As Slim moved forward to scan the car's license plate, sunlight shattered brilliantly against the star on his shirt. With the number tucked in the back of his head, he moved back up the street in long, purposeful strides until he came to the sheriff's office. Inside the small room, shuttered and cool and dark, he fired his Stetson at an ancient hall tree and flopped into a chair facing an elaborate radio setup.

The answer to his message came in from Tucson before he had finished a leisurely beer from the small refrigerator in the corner of the office. A Tucson agency had rented the car, a Buick, to an A. K. James that very morning. James, from Chicago, had presented himself as a tracer of lost and missing persons. Returning the speaker to its bracket, Slim digested the information slowly.

When A. K. James left the cantina and headed directly across the street toward the hotel, Slim moved through the side door of the saloon. "Save that bottle, *amigo*," he called to the Mexican behind the mahogany.

Ramon grinned widely, teeth gleaming whitely in his dusky face. "Sure, Slim. I think I save you all the bottles and glasses from now on. That's all you do any more; follow strangers in here and carry away their fingerprints. How many does this make? Four? Five? By the way, where did you go last night? The party was just getting started when you left."

Slim shook his head gently, as if something were loose. "I didn't feel good. Not enough to eat . . . too much tequila . . . too much bourbon . . ." He wondered fleetingly how a man of thirty-five could get so stupid in such a short time. From the taste in his mouth he still wasn't sure he hadn't eaten supper with a coyote. With his little finger hooked inside the neck of the beer bottle, he returned to the office. Lifting the fingerprints, he slipped them into an envelope, then summoned a stout Mexican from his dozing place in the shade of the barber shop next door. "Take my jeep and get this to Tucson, Angel. *Muy pronto.* Send it registered airmail. Vamoose." As the jeep roared away in a cloud of dust, Slim clomped along the wooden sidewalk toward the hotel.

A. K. James was seated in the lobby studying a telephone directory. He was fortyish, given a bit to flab, and his eyes were cold and hard. "Nice little town you've got here, sheriff," he said affably. He smiled readily; a bit too readily. "Just finding this town was something of a surprise. After all those miles of chuckholes and chuck wallas, I expected Chaco Wells to be just a watering place for burros."

Slim had heard the same words, or variations thereof, too often, and they had sounded stupid even when he didn't have a big head. "That's exactly what Chaco Wells used to be," he replied honestly. "We leave the road unpaved because we don't believe in encouraging the hotrod set. Besides, unpaved streets and wooden walks lend a touch of authenticity to the town, which is almost exactly as it was a hundred years ago. We have a theatre with gaslights, Woo Toy's hand laundry, a blacksmith shop, a livery stable, a town hall; the whole frontier works. And every building is made of adobe. Matter of fact, a town ordinance prohibits any other type of construction. We're quite a tourist attraction in the winter. Not much action here in the summer, which brings me around to you. Anything in particular bring you to Chaco Wells?"

James fished a card from his shirt pocket. It read: TRACKDOWN, INC. LOCATORS OF LOST AND MISSING PERSONS. "I'm looking for a Jason Connors, supposedly living in Chaco Wells. He's about your age and height, but he weighs a touch over three hundred pounds and is probably bald."

"Probably?" Slim asked quizzically, returning the card. "Don't you have a picture of him?"

A.K. tucked a cigarette between his lips and reached for a match. "His hair was thinning rapidly seven years ago, which was about the time he disappeared from Chicago. You see, his uncle, Zachary Trieste, died a few months ago, intestate as they say. Which means his nephews, his only living relatives, Bart Morritz of Chicago and Jason Connors, supposedly of Chaco Wells, are to share equally in a three hundred thousand dollar estate."

Slim emitted a long, low whistle. *"Mucho dinero."*

James batted his cold eyes. *"Mucho dinero?"*

"Lots of long green," Slim explained. "But what makes you so sure Connors is in Chaco Wells? And you still haven't explained why you don't have a picture of him."

James expelled a cloud of smoke. "For your first question—a friend of Morritz's sent him a postcard from Tucson some time ago saying he had seen a man he was certain was Connors right here in Chaco Wells. Unfortunately, the man who sent the postcard was killed in a traffic accident the same day, making further information unavailable. For your second question—I don't have a picture of Connors because the last one taken of him was in 1940, when he was six years old."

Slim slouched down lazily on the lobby divan, furrows of doubt ridging his brow, his hat low over his right eye. "I'm afraid you're wasting your time here. I've been around a long time and I can't think of *anybody* who weighs anywhere near three hundred pounds. Your man, this . . . this . . ."

"Connors."

"This Connors could have been here, but if so, he was probably passing through, maybe stopping for an hour or so. But don't take my word for it. There are four hundred people in Chaco Wells and on an average Saturday night you can find three hundred and ninety of them at one fiesta or another around town. The other ten will be in the calaboose for overindulging or fighting. This being Saturday, you can start looking most any time after the sun goes down."

Shortly after the sun had gone into the cholla-covered western hills and the balmy night breezes were drawing the day's heat from the adobe buildings, Slim lounged in the heavy shadows surrounding Ramon's cantina and watched the hotel. When A. K. James finally appeared, he studied the street to the left and then the right, undecided, then turned to his left and headed toward the sounds of distant revelry.

Crossing the street, Slim unlocked the rental car with a special key. Among the items he found of more than passing interest were a high-powered rifle with a telescopic sight and a folding stock, a .38 caliber revolver fitted with a silencer, and a minutely detailed description of Jason Connors on a slip of paper in the pocket of a soiled shirt. A magnetic tray on the top of the dash yielded a handful of book matches from the Palm Club in Chicago. Slim recorded the serial numbers of the two weapons, relocked the car, and began ambling casually along the street on his first round of the night.

He encountered A. K. James viewing the festivities at a large fiesta on the edge of town. "Any luck?" Slim asked sociably.

James had exchanged the suit for a sport shirt and slacks, but he still looked out of place. "Nothing yet. But the night's young; I'll keep on looking." He waved a hand to encompass the crowd around the barbecue pit, the strolling musicians, the swirling dancers. "Who are all these people? Where do they come from and what do they do?"

Slim's booted foot was keeping time with a snappy fandango. "Prospectors, ranch hands, miners, waitresses, housewives, businessmen and business women. Swedes and Mexicans, Indians and Negroes, Chinese and Irish. We've got the whole package here in Chaco Wells. Our best Spanish guitar player is a Jewish boy from Tel Aviv, and our best western barbecue man is an Italian from Jersey City. Not to mention about thirty retired couples who've spent most of their lives in the fields of science, medicine, construction, agriculture, music and the theatre."

"Connors would go for this," James asserted adamantly. "He's got to be here."

Slim's foot kept tapping out the rhythm. "He could be. But in case you don't locate him, drop by the office in the morning anyway."

James was in the office the next morning, early. "Nothing," he said in response to Slim's unasked question. "Nothing at all."

Slim yawned widely and ran his hand through his thick brown mane. "I was pretty sure you were just wasting your time, James."

"But the man who sent Morritz the postcard knew Connors well at one time," James insisted doggedly. "He's here somewhere, on a ranch, in a mine. I can feel it in my bones."

"Wait a minute," Slim said suddenly. "I forgot about the art colony."

Interest gleamed in James's glacial eyes. "Art colony?"

"It's up in the mountains south of here," Slim explained. "The only way to get there is by walking or on horseback. The residents are dropouts from civilization. They hate smog, taxes, the war in Viet Nam, sit-ins, the Beatles, motor scooters and Communism, to name a few of their peeves. They sell some paintings from time to time and manage to get by. Must be a hundred or so of them up there. In case you're interested I can fix you up with a saddle horse and a guide. It takes a full day to get there. Then you can spend tomorrow looking the place over and come back the next day."

James licked his lips. "It sounds like a good hiding place."

Slim's brow lifted perceptibly. "You didn't say Connors was hiding . . ."

"Not really hiding," James hedged. "But he's the type who would go to extreme lengths to get away from it all. He hated Chicago . . . the crowds . . . the traffic jams . . ."

Slim leaned back lazily in the ancient swivel chair and draped his long legs across the corner of his desk. "It is a good hiding place. Matter of fact, I've never seen a better one."

"I'll be ready to go in half an hour," James said abruptly. "Soon's I get some breakfast and pack a few things."

James had no more departed the office than Slim crossed the room to stand in the open door. When a lone Papago came along the dusty street, Slim motioned him into the office. He explained his desires and handed the man a twenty dollar bill.

A short while later he watched silently as the Indian rode up the street, followed by James. The city man was having a time of it, hanging onto his suitcase and keeping his equilibrium on what was undoubtedly the first horse he had ever straddled. As soon as they were out of sight, Slim meandered down the street to the Buick. Both the rifle and the revolver were gone. Nor were they in James's room in the hotel. Returning to the office, Slim waited until his deputy showed up, then headed for his bachelor's pad behind Woo Toy's, for some much-needed sleep.

At mid-morning, four federal agents descended on Chaco Wells from Tucson with a warrant for the arrest of Al Fenelli, alias A.K. James, wanted on a half dozen charges, including murder and extortion in New York. When Slim informed them Fenelli was *not* in custody, the agent in charge had come dangerously near a coronary. He shook his head in utter despair. "You mean you just stood to the side and let this vicious hood go merrily on his way, Gentry? Why, man, why? You must have suspected something or you wouldn't have sent his prints to Washington in the first place."

Slim nodded solemnly. "You're right. I did suspect something. And in order to check out my suspicions I had to let him go. I needed time, I could have arrested him for illicit interstate transportation of firearms, but he'd have sworn he bought the guns in Arizona. Any shyster lawyer in the county would have had him back on the street inside an hour. And with his prints on the way to Washington do you really think he'd have stuck around waiting for the report to come back?"

"Which way did he go?" the agent snapped angrily. "The bureau's been after him too long to let him get away now."

Slim shook his head slowly from side to side. "Simmer down, boys. Fenelli will be back about sundown. But before you get him, he's all mine for half an hour. Okay?"

The chief agent's jaw sagged stupidly. "He'll be back about sundown? You gotta be kiddin', Gentry. Fenelli is noted for his unmitigated nerve, but for a man on the 'Ten Most Wanted' list to come in on his own . . ." Realization gleamed suddenly in the agent's eyes. "Fenelli doesn't know you're onto him, does he?"

"Not yet," Slim replied honestly.

"And you don't really want Fenelli," the agent said slowly, sifting the matter through his mind. "Or else you'd have him in jail now."

Slim scratched the day old stubble on his chin. "You're right. I don't want Fenelli. He just happens to be the lever with which I pry a rat out of his hole."

"He must be *quite* a rat," the agent hazarded gently.

"Hollywood doesn't build them any slimier," Slim said, a faraway look in his somber brown eyes.

The desert sun had cooked Fenelli's pale skin to a lobster red, the saddle had chafed his hide raw from his ankles to his groin, and the relentless barbs of the cholla and saguaro had left him pain-ridden and limping. The Papago guide had done his job well, taking the hoodlum on an arduous, roundabout, thirty mile ordeal instead of the usual ten mile jaunt straight over the mountains. Fenelli was angered and frustrated, and fire leaped from his cold eyes as he glared up at the five lawmen surrounding him. "I don't say a word unless my lawyer is present," he snapped angrily. "I know my rights."

"We're fully aware of your rights," Slim said absently as he poked through a sheaf of papers on his desk. "We're also aware of a few other things. We know that Bart Morritz of the Palm Club in Chicago made a deal with you to find Connors. But not so he would get one hundred and fifty thousand dollars from the Trieste estate. Your job was to kill Jason Connors. Then you and Morritz were to cut up Connors' share of the estate."

"You're outta your skull," Fenelli snarled.

Slim grinned with the confidence that comes from having secret knowledge. "You want more, Fenelli? Morritz gave us the whole story. Zachary Trieste was an old-line member of the Mafia, which was the cause of his beef with Connors seven years ago. When Connors found out about his uncle's underworld connections, he tried to talk the old boy back onto the straight and narrow. But Trieste liked the easy money and refused to quit the rackets. Connors slapped the old boy all over his posh apartment.

"For Connors it wasn't much of a chore, him being a big boy well over three hundred pounds. He didn't know that the real Mafia punk was Morritz; that Morritz had forced Connors' uncle into an alliance with the organization, as a front man for Morritz and his cutthroat schemes. After that, Connors took a powder. That would have been the end of it, but when Trieste died, Morritz let his greed get the upper hand on his better judgment. He wanted Connors' share of the estate so badly he sent you out here to gun Connors. Now Morritz has told the Chicago police that when *you* suggested doing Connors in for a piece of his share in the estate, he thought you were kidding. According to Morritz, the whole caper was *your* idea."

Fenelli sagged weakly in his chair, his eyes on the scope-mounted rifle and the .38 on Slim's desk. He opened his mouth to utter a final protest, but Slim was on his feet, leaning far over the desk, his dark eyes flashing fire. "Can the garbage," he snarled disgustedly. "Only two people knew about this deal; you and Bart Morritz. And the *only* way I could have gotten all this information was for one of you to blow the whistle on the other. Morritz sang a beautiful song when the law dragged him out of . . . of . . ." Slim ran a finger down one of the pages on his desk. "Of the Palm Club. They knew he would try something like this, and they'd been watching him since the night Zachary Trieste died." Fenelli looked up at the grim triumph on Slim's suntanned features, and around to the four federal men, their faces cold and expressionless. Then he leaned forward slowly and buried his face in his hands.

Two hours later, as three of the federal men took a chained and subdued Fenelli out to the waiting car, the agent in charge, brow a furrow, eyed Slim Gentry closely. "I still don't know how you did it. It was all so neat, so . . . so prewrapped. We've really got Fenelli sewed up now. You made him fold like a wet dishrag, taking Morritz and a half dozen others down with him. Mind telling me *how* you did it?"

"A lot of it was shooting in the dark," Slim confessed soberly. "The barber next door used to clip hair in the Windy City. He still takes a Chicago paper, and passes it on to me. I read some time ago where

Zachary Trieste had passed away. Being a top echelon member of the Mafia, he made the front page. The article mentioned his estate and the heirs, Bart Morritz of Chicago, and Jason Connors, whereabouts unknown. Morritz is notoriously greedy and it figured he wasn't going to settle for half the Trieste estate if he could pull a string and get the whole package."

"You *knew* Morritz?" the agent asked skeptically.

Slim left his desk and crossed the room to the small refrigerator in the corner. When he extracted two beers, the agent raised a hand in refusal. Replacing one of the bottles, Slim returned to his desk.

"Didn't I tell you I used to live in Chicago? I did. Right in the same neighborhood as Bart Morritz. I got fed up with the big city bit years ago and migrated out here. I knew the Morritz-Trieste setup about as well as anybody. When Trieste gave up the ghost, I knew Morritz would be out to find Connors and do him in for his share of the estate. When I saw another hood, a boyhood friend of Morritz's, run a red light in Tucson and get himself killed, I had a flash of true genius. I sent Morritz a card telling him I was certain I'd soon his cousin, the missing Connors, in Chaco Wells, and I signed the name of the dead hood. That way there was no chance for Morritz to check back and determine if the hood had really sent him the card. With one hundred and fifty thousand dollars hanging in the balance I doubt that he even tried. He finally located a top torpedo, Fenelli, and sent him out here to kill Connors. From there on, you know as much about the situation as I do."

The agent had been eyeing Slim shrewdly. "You really hated Morritz." It wasn't a question, but a statement.

"There's no other way to say it," Slim said candidly. "I knew him well. Too well, perhaps."

"And your *only* interest in this matter was to tag Morritz, and possibly the gun he sent after Connors?" the agent continued relentlessly.

Slim let a swallow of cold beer soothe his hot pipes. "Is that bad? We got Morritz cold and a member of the 'Top Ten' to boot. Who's gonna complain about a deal like that?"

"But the three hundred grand," the agent inquired warily. "What happens to it?"

Slim tipped the bottle up again. "It was stolen from the people in the beginning, and with nobody to claim it, it'll undoubtedly go back to the people in one form or another."

The agent had seen more than his share of vice and corruption and greed. "Suppose *you* had a good clean shot at that kind of money?"

Slim stretched luxuriously. "I've got a good job. I even manage to bank a few dollars every month; life here is loaded with fine food, good drinks, and pretty women. Besides which, the worst 'criminal' in town is an old desert rat who gets drunk and goes to sleep on somebody's lawn. If I had a chance to trade all this for twice three hundred thousand dollars I'd say, 'No deal.' "

A light was beginning to glow in the deep recesses of the federal man's brain. "You say you came out here years ago, Gentry. About seven years ago?"

Slim nodded. "More or less." He swept the rich brown hairpiece from his head to reveal a shiny, slightly suntanned pate, and dropped it on the desk. "The rug has nothing to do with vanity. I lost my hat out in the desert once and let me tell you, that sun is murder on a bald head. The rug is strictly for protection."

"You lost any weight since coming to Chaco Wells?" the agent inquired, humorous wrinkles appearing around his eyes.

"Not too much," Slim replied. "About a hundred and twenty lousy pounds. I met a retired doctor who was an expert on weight problems right after I got here. He took me under his wing and peeled the lard off me by the layer. And for free, too. Chaco Wells is that kind of place. Which reminds me . . ." Slim took a small brown bottle from a desk drawer and washed down a thyroid pill with a swallow of beer.

"Have you been in touch with Chicago at all?" the agent asked.

Slim failed to suppress a grin. "Uh-uh. Like I said, I was shooting in the dark; playing it by ear. I sent Fenelli on the goose chase to the art colony strictly to put the time element on my side. Three days would have been plenty of time for me to get all my information from Chicago. Luckily, Fenelli bought it. I wonder what dear old cousin Bart will think when the law walks into the club and lowers the boom on him cold turkey."

"The law's gain was baseball's loss," the federal man said in open admiration. "With the kind of curves you throw, you'd have been a cinch for the major leagues." He crossed the room to the door, then halted and turned. "What do you suppose ever happened to Jason Connors?"

"Jason Connors?" Slim repeated blankly. "I don't believe I've ever heard of the man . . ."

The Green Fly and the Box
by Waldo Carlton Wright

A fly buzzed under the edge of the blue blind. It sounded like a plane diving toward the woods, at once near and then far away down the valley. Hanford lay without breathing, knowing if he did it would hurt deep down in his ribs, the way the pain had flared up with the blast of the shotgun.

There had been an accident. Of that Hanford was sure. Just where or how was still back there, in the blackout; but now he felt fully awake and light enough to float.

Cautiously he tried to open one eye, to watch the fly, knowing it sat on the windowsill preening its wings. It had come to lay nits in his insides, hasten the decomposition of the body he had dragged around the fields and barn. His body had served him well, making a living of a sort on the old farm, finding joy in being alive but never becoming a capable farmer.

The morning light carried the same urgency that disturbs a seed buried in the ground. He was too young to be lying idle in this box with the white satin lining. His son Shean needed a guiding hand; and Betty was still young enough to marry again. It hurt just to think of that.

Now over the edge of the box he could see the fly. It was a female, large and green. Her wings glistened in the wedge of sunshine under the blind, near enough to swat. He reached out swiftly.

The motion lifted him clear of the box and he found himself floating. It was a bit awkward at first, moving like a cloud. It was smoother than using a crutch, the way he had hobbled around after he broke his leg when his first tractor turned over on the side hill.

He was drifting toward the wall and closed his eyes, expecting a bump. Instead he passed through it, just as if there were nothing there. Outdoors in the sunshine he circled the catalpa tree, riding a merry-go-round of nothingness.

The second time around he saw the couple drawing up in a large sedan, parking by the garden gate. Now he realized it was the purring of their car on the hill that had wakened him. He swung back under the fretwork of the porch to see who they were.

Then from the henhouse his son Shean appeared, carrying two buckets of eggs. Hanford must remember to caution his son to clear the nests at least twice a day in this heat.

By rolling on his side, still hearing the blowfly buzzing inside against the glass, Hanford recognized the visitors, his wife's sister, Elizabeth, and her husband, Matt Burr. Coming to the wake, no less.

"Mother's expecting you, Aunt Bess, in the living room," Shean said, setting down the buckets of eggs. Hanford noted the yellow seal on the back of Shean's blue sweatshirt: Future Farmers of America.

The woman spread her arms to embrace the boy. "What a horrible thing to happen," she said.

The lad pulled away, pushed back his stubborn mop of red hair, and motioned the woman toward the kitchen door.

Elizabeth's husband covered the embarrassment by reaching for one of the buckets of eggs. "Let me help you put these in the refrigerator," he said.

"I can do it, Uncle Matt." Hanford's son picked up both buckets and headed for the cellar.

"I'd like to see how the apple trees are coming along, the ones you set out the last year you were in high school," Elizabeth's husband called after him.

As Elizabeth opened the side door and passed inside, a gust of air blew Hanford from under the porch so that he hung, light as the fluff of a milkweed pod, over the woodshed.

Elizabeth's husband, waiting for Shean to come out of the cellar, reminded Hanford of the centurion who had told Jesus he was accustomed to ordering men around. Born in a Brooklyn ghetto, he had learned to climb over other men's backs, until he was head of his own Somerset mills; master of all, except in his own home.

Shean came out of the entry carrying Hanford's shotgun in the crook of his arm. Shep, the collie, uncoiled from under the lilac bush, his tail wagging like the metronome Betty kept on the top of the parlor organ. Shean led the way, up the path by the blighted cherry tree, toward the leaning silo and the old red barn, and Hanford wondered why neither of them looked up to see him hanging in the air, right smack over the weather vane.

The sheep dog turned his nose skyward and sniffed. Then, to show his disdain of men who floated around instead of walking like normal critters, the dog raised his leg and watered a patch of dandelions.

At the barnyard, Shean's heifer moved out from under the straw stack to lean her muzzle over the rail for the boy's caress, and Shean said, "She's due to freshen any day now, Uncle Matt."

Matthew Burr reached out to pat the heifer's neck but she drew back, shaking her head and watching them. Floating around the stack, Hanford chuckled to himself about the heifer drawing away instinctively from Elizabeth's husband.

"But why a Jersey?" Burr was asking.

"You sound like my old man," Shean said. "Don't you know it pays to raise the butterfat over four percent?"

"Well, now, that makes sense," Elizabeth's husband said. "What have you done to modernize the barn?"

"Come and I'll show you the surge milker and the stainless steel storage tanks," Shean said.

They passed under the overhang, into the stalls. Hanford preferred not to try to wedge in, to hear what Burr would say about the new stanchions and the water cups. His son had bought these against his advice, going deeper and deeper in debt, and somehow Hanford no longer felt a part of all this.

He began to get the hang of floating in air. The trick was wishing to be someplace, hard enough, and resting in space, doing nothing, like floating on your back when swimming. Up here he could hear anything they said.

"My old man felt he could strip the cow's udders better by hand, more cream, the way his folks had done in Ireland all their lives." Shean's voice bounced out the entry and slithered soft-toned off the stone wall by the watering trough.

"But your mother—she was on your side, wasn't she?" Burr's voice was prodding, researching, firming up the facts, to lay them one-two-three on the intercom. You standardize this, you automate that. So, the Problem stands resolved.

They were outside again, walking right under him past the watering trough, heading for the orchard. There the old trees had died out, and Hanford had sawed them down singly with a one-man crosscut, for firewood. His son had laid out the new orchard on the same west side of the ridge, as a 4-H project, with the help of the county agent.

Hanford had been against the project. Milk was a money crop, and cows returned strength to the soil. The new orchard would have to be sprayed with all those new poisons that killed the curculio and leafrollers and checked the powdery mildew. Poisons soaked into the soil and in time would seep into the well and creep into the home vegetables. Science can go too far, his Scanlon grandfather had told him as a boy, when they went up Sunday afternoons to salt the sheep.

"My old man loved this place, just as it was; just as his father and grandfather had struggled here," Shean was saying. He walked in long high-stepping strides, the way a farm boy learns to clear the furrows left by the spring plowing, carrying this stride with him all his life.

"It's just as if he were out of step with life," Burr said, the way he would explain why it was necessary to let one of his accountants go, now the employee was over fifty and wages were handled by one machine, even the check writing.

Elizabeth had written to Betty about these time savers her husband had made at the Somerset mill, but his wife had never complained to Hanford or even hinted he was out of step with this thing called progress. That was why he had kept on believing in her, loving her, feeling her warmth smother some wildness in his heart, nights on the old farm.

Below him, the boy and man walked down the center row of the young trees. Every now and then his son would stop to examine the fruit, rubbing a green Rome Beauty with the sleeve of his blue shirt.

"They're beginning to show color," he told his uncle.

"How often do you have to spray them?" Burr asked.

Hanford couldn't catch the number of times Shean mentioned. Sliding along above the tops of the trees, brushing his stomach on the soft green leaves, he could feel the chalky coating rub off on him, the way powdered lime sifts right through your shirt, smarting your chest.

Up here, higher than the ridge, it looked like a toy farm, with its old log house, red barn, and the black and white specks of the Holstein herd grazing along the creek. The clover held back the soil from washing into the valley. The cows enriched the land, giving back measure for measure to maintain the balance. It was a slicker accounting with time than any of Burr's data processing machines could attain. Life here was simpler, mocking all the furor of pouring more steel, shaping it into pistons and gears, refrigerators and cars, speeding up the looms, sealing more packages, capping more bottles. The nonsense of it made Hanford laugh out loud.

At the rumble of Hanford's voice, Shean glanced up between the trees. For a moment he thought his son saw him floating there.

"The thunderheads are building," he told Burr. "We'd better take a shortcut to the house."

"I distinctly heard something," Burr said, frowning up at Hanford as if ordering him to come down from his perch and be a man again. Burr had often told him, "You'd make more in a year working for me than you will on this old farm the rest of your life."

No, no, you tried that before, dangled other offers through my wife's sister. Now you'll try to lure my son away—unless he's got some of my Irish rebel blood in his gizzard.

"I can get you a good job at the mill, you know." Burr was taking quick military strides down the field, half stumbling over the cross contour lines left by the plow, trying to keep up with the boy.

Shean walked ahead, the shotgun bobbing in the crook of his arm. From across the field came shrill barking. A rabbit jumped clear of the pine woods, headed toward them. The boy brought the gun to his shoulder. At the blast, dust spurted almost in the rabbit's nose. It swung down the field, leaping high to clear the clumps of clover, disappeared into the woods. The sheep dog came running from the woods toward the gun, his tongue lolling, expectant of picking up a limp rabbit.

"You missed," Burr was criticizing his son, just as he would the first time Shean let a faulty gadget slide by him on the inspection line.

Hanford knew better. Shean had purposely missed the rabbit, merely wanted to scare it out of the clover. He gets that hate of killing wild things from his mother.

Hanford watched Shean break open the barrel, ejecting the red plastic shell. Then he blew through the breech, the way he had been taught. You don't have to explain twice to an Irishman to keep your gun at the ready.

They had come to the stake and rider fence that separated the clover from the cornfield. Hanford banked lower on the current of hot air that flowed down the ridge, to hear what would be said. This was the spot where he last remembered carrying the gun. Was it yesterday or a week ago? Or beyond time? But it was here. He was almost sure.

"This is where I found him yesterday," Shean said, as if that were on his mind when he aimed in front of the rabbit.

"Right at this spot?" Burr asked, staring at the brown spot near the rails. He would have to know the facts exactly.

"It wasn't as if he didn't know how to crawl over a fence." Shean handed the gun to Elizabeth's husband. "Hold this while I take down a rail."

"Do you suppose the trigger caught?" Burr asked.

It seemed terribly important to Hanford to hear what his son would say, but just as Shean crawled over the rail, lightning struck a tree in the woods. The blast pushed Hanford aside, sent him tumbling down the hill on a current of hot tangy air. When he recovered himself, floating over the Holsteins, Hanford bounced upward, fluttering the bulges that were his arms, like wings. By now the rain was falling through him, and Shean and the man were running past the vegetable garden, toward the fan doorway of the farmhouse.

Hanford floated after them, finding it breathless to keep up, feeling something was being washed out of him, the way water leaches the salts out of the soil, eroding it, leaving it fallow.

They had gone in ahead of him and closed the door. He knew they were gathered in the parlor and that his wife Betty would have raised the blind only after she was sure the lid was on the coffin.

Hanford slid noiselessly through the plaster chinks, between the old logs that his grandfather had laid up when he first settled here a hundred and fifty years ago, retreating from the potato famine in Ireland.

Elizabeth sat in the rocker by the window, facing Betty, who stood by the door as if keeping watch over the coffin. Burr had slid into Hanford's captain's chair, an heirloom of a Scanlon. Burr's feet were stretched out to relax after the climb around the old place. Shean wasn't in the room. He must have gone up to the barn to see whether the Jersey heifer had dropped her calf.

Instead of sliding back into the coffin through the black lid, Hanford rested on a strand of cobweb along the ceiling above the mantel. The strand was soft and springy and from here he could watch them all, even hear their breathing. From the way Elizabeth's finger knocked the ashes from her long cigarette into the blue jardiniere, he knew his wife's sister had something that had to be said before the lad came in, now her husband was there to witness.

"Matthew will buy the place," she said, and then looked up quickly at the corner of the room, as if she had seen Hanford lying there on the cobweb. She shrugged as if she felt a chill, then brushed her hand over her eyes to fan away the puff of smoke coming from her nose.

Betty sat down quickly, the way the legs of a calf sag when the butcher hits it with a sledgehammer between the eyes. He had seen her collapse that way once before, when lightning struck the old barn just after haying. Grain and hay, even the herd, everything but the house, had gone up in flames. It was the summer she had been carrying Shean.

Hanford eased his leg over the cobweb to relax. He suddenly felt tired to death, wanting to stretch out in the chair where Burr lolled. The man was waiting for Betty's reaction to his offer to buy the farm. Betty and the boy would move into the city. Shean could have a job on the inspection line, the way he had offered it back there at the fence, holding the gun that had somehow been part of this meeting, while the lad crawled over.

"The way of the world is change," Burr was saying. "The trick is to move ahead of the changes."

That must be how he thinks, that change is everything, always for the better. Hanford shook his head but knew they would not look up to him for guidance. He was just an old fashioned farmer, proud of his acres. However lean, the land had still supported him, his wife and son. Until the accident, that was.

The female blowfly was again zooming around the room, dipping and buzzing, protesting at being shut out of the coffin. She sounded heavy with eggs, the nits that would assure Hanford's decomposition.

"You'll be better off living in a small house in Somerset." Elizabeth snuffed out her cigarette on the edge of the blue jar and dropped the butt among the dried pussy willows, to indicate it was all agreed, settled.

The door swung open and Shean stood outlined like a backcountry *Blue Boy* in a frame. Raindrops trickled off the mop of red hair and his face was splotched with mud.

"Ma, Betsy's had her calf. Isn't that great?" Still grinning, he turned to Elizabeth's husband. "You must come up and see it."

"No, thanks. We've got to be going shortly," Burr said, sitting up straight, the way he brought a meeting of his board of directors around to a decision.

Elizabeth reacted to her husband's cue, first glancing at the coffin and then turning to face the lad. "Matthew will see that you get ahead at the mill. It might even be yours some day."

Hanford rolled over on his side on the cobweb, to watch his son's face. Shean seemed unable to grasp what was being spread out before him by his rich uncle.

The collie, wedged by Shean, turned once, then stretched out at

Betty's feet. The gesture seemed to ask, and what about me? Who'll feed me?

"I wouldn't like working in your mill," Shean said. "This is my farm. This is where I belong."

"For shame, Shean," Betty said. "Matthew only wants to help us, not take the farm."

"The farm is not for sale." His son's eyes seemed fixed on the black lid of the long box in the corner, as if he were making a vow.

"Well, think it over and if you change your mind . . . " Elizabeth's husband stood up. His head bobbed into Hanford's ribs. Then the visitor brushed a cobweb from his bald head and strode decisively through the door.

Goodbye, goodbye. Hanford almost fell off the cobweb laughing for joy. His son was every inch an independent Irishman.

Betty lingered behind for a moment. She stroked the lid of the box lightly, then drew the blue blind down to the windowsill like a curtain falling on the last act.

When she had gone, Hanford listened for the revving of the car motor. Its departure rattled the windowpanes like the rumble of distant thunder. The green fly took up its frustrated hum, reminding him of its urgency.

Hanford could feel the open spaces, cleansed by the rain, like a cool draft when he opened the door of the egg refrigerator. He could still hear the priest kneeling beside him, mumbling the words of the last rites. Then he remembered his own mumbling, his thick tongue, his smoldering fire. He had been drinking all day in the barn, not even bothering to milk the cows. He had spent the egg money for a little fun, to forget with a jug of Irish whisky, the best.

Just as it was getting dark, Shean had driven in. The lad had wasted the whole day at a meeting of the county apple growers association down in Bedford. He had insisted Hanford go with him, right then, up the ridge where the new orchard would be. What angered Hanford most was the crazy fool buying a thousand more four-year-old red Delicious on bank credit, through the word of the county agent, putting him deeper in debt. It didn't make sense to Hanford.

As they walked they quarreled. At the stake and rider fence, his anger mixed with the whisky. He clouted his son across the mouth, knocked him into the corn stubble. Flames of rebellion to a changed way of life, all he had worked for, roared through his mind, licked out at the cause of all his frustration. He remembered aiming the gun at Shean's chest. The lad grabbed the barrel and hung on, pleading. There had been this yellow blast and Hanford felt his ribs cave in, the way they had done when the tractor fell on him.

Somehow he had expected to wake up in hell. Or maybe, if he had been absolved, crowned and alone, sitting on the ridge of a cloud, wearing a white robe, sipping stale beer from a golden mug, his blunt fingers trying to pick out "Londonderry Air" on an Irish harp. Instead, this heaven was more like an extension of memory, linking him with the living, forever near those he loved on this old farm.

World weariness seeped through him into the open spaces left by the rain. He was falling into a bottomless sleep. Feet first, drawn out like a wisp of smoke, he slid slowly into the long black box, feeling the satin brush his cheek like Betty's hand in the night: *Now go to sleep, Hanford my love, my Irish prince.*

Just before oblivion, he remembered to push up the edge of the lid with one toe. That way the female blowfly could wedge in, lay her nits, assure the return of his body to the soil that had formed him.

Minutes of Terror

by Donald Honig

Mel Gifford's house was the last one on the dirt road, which ran nearly a mile in from the highway before becoming a dead end. There were only two other houses along the road and then Gifford's, and beyond that nothing but the pine forest, slowly elevating itself along the mountain slope, rising higher and higher, cresting at two thousand feet. There were ski trails on the other side of the mountain and when the Vermont winter drained the sky of color and spilled its snows, the area became a bustling ski resort.

Now it was November, one of the two transitional seasons (the other occurred in April); the fall foliage was gone and the snows had not yet come. Gifford called it the quiet season. There were no tourists on the roads or in the woods, and things were quieter in town too. Certainly there were fewer people coming into the bank. Many of the local businessmen took their vacations this time of year, just before the onset of the ski season.

"I wish my business were seasonal," Gifford said that morning after the alarm had brought him jarringly awake. He sat up in bed and with dull eyes faced the dim gray morning. Helen had barely moved. He looked at her inert bulk under the covers. No one ever looked graceful lying under covers.

"I said—" he began again.

"I heard you," she said, talking into her pillow.

"I wouldn't mind a month's vacation right now. Hadley left for Florida yesterday, for a month."

Hadley owned the next house down the road. The third house, the one nearest the road, had been rented as a ski lodge for the winter; the owners had already vacated and the new people had not arrived yet. So both houses were empty.

"A whole month," Gifford said, yawning. "He was in the bank the other day to say goodbye. Said he was going to turn off the gas, the electricity, the phone and pack up and go. The lucky stiff."

"You'd better get up," Helen said, "and wake the kids."

Gifford got out of bed and stood by the window. He gazed listlessly for a moment and then, as he turned away, he thought he saw something move among the pine trees. He turned back and stood at the window again, squinting.

"I think I saw a deer," he said.

"Must be a crazy one," Helen said drearily. "Doesn't know the hunting season's started, I guess."

He continued to peer out at the woods, hoping to catch sight of whatever it was that had moved, but all he saw was the extraordinary stillness of the pine in the windless gray light. After several minutes, he said, "I think I saw a deer."

"Mel," his wife said, still talking into her pillow, "please wake up the kids. You've got to take them to school."

"And open up the bank and sit behind my desk and smile at everybody. Look, I think I saw a deer and if I did, then it's the most exciting thing that's happened to me in six months."

"Don't be bitter, darling."

"Who's bitter?" he muttered leaving the window.

He put on his bathrobe and walked across the hall, first to Jennifer's room. He opened her door and paused, listening to the seven-year-old snoring lightly. Then he walked to the bed, gazed for a moment at the sleeping face, the dark hair sprawled over the pillow. Gently he put his hand on her shoulder and shook her. A querulous look crossed her sleeping face as she began to turn.

"Good morning, Jennifer," he said.

Her eyes opened, searched sleepily for a moment, then found him standing there by her bed.

"Get up, sweetheart," he whispered.

She stretched and yawned.

"Okay?" he asked.

"Okay."

Then he went to Billy's room. The towheaded eight-year-old was already up.

"I was dreaming, Dad," he said when Gifford walked in.

"Tell me about it later. First, get dressed."

Gifford returned to the bedroom window and peered out again, a puzzled frown on his face. Helen was fully awake now, lying in bed watching him.

"I thought I saw a deer," Gifford said, studying the pine forest with gravely thoughtful eyes. The night shadows seemed to be lingering among the poised, graceful trees. Nothing was moving.

"Maybe it was a hunter," Helen said.

"The woods are posted."

"Since when has that stopped them?"

"Well," Gifford said, "they'd better keep away from here."

After he had washed and shaved and dressed, he sat down to breakfast with his family. Billy and Jennifer yawned, and toyed uninterestedly with their food. Gifford noted it but said nothing; there was a general ennui in the house this morning which was catching.

While Helen helped the children into their coats, Gifford stood at the hall mirror, gazing at himself in a rather detached way. He was thirty-eight and he supposed he looked it. His brown hair had begun to thin. Soft, passive lines were appearing around his mouth. His brown eyes were cool, unreadable, good eyes for a banker to have; good eyes for listening. He thought he was getting a bit flabby, thought he did not really want to admit it. He'd ski again this winter, maybe do some hiking. Tone up those muscles.

He put on his topcoat, opened the door and went outside. He stood on the porch feeling the cool, fresh morning air on his face, then headed for the garage, hoping he wouldn't have any trouble starting the car this morning.

As he approached the garage—the door was open—he turned and looked over his shoulder one more time at the pine forest. Had he seen a deer or not? So he was not looking at the garage and did not see the man step from inside it and stand in the doorway. When Gifford finally did turn back and found himself being confronted by the stranger, they were about ten feet apart. He stopped dead in his tracks.

The man was much younger than Gifford, perhaps in his mid-twenties, but there was a lot of hard experience etched into his face, into the calculating steadiness of his gaze, and in the almost contemptuous nonchalance with which he stood. He was wearing a plaid jacket which was two-thirds unzipped, and one hand was concealed inside, at once calmly and menacingly.

"Who are you?" Gifford asked. "What are you doing in there?"

"Just relax, Mr. Gifford," the man said, the tone of his voice suggesting he was giving some very good advice. "You just keep your head and do as you're asked and nobody is going to get hurt."

"I want to know what you were doing in my garage."

"We were waiting for you."

"We?" Gifford said.

The second man appeared then, stepping out of the garage. This one was older, perhaps Gifford's age, with that same steady gaze that wasn't necessarily hostile or threatening, that was simply there to be observed, noted. He was wearing a trenchcoat and a small felt fedora and he looked almost European. He was holding a small revolver in his hand, pointed at Gifford.

"Get into the house," he ordered.

"Why?" Gifford asked, making a conscious effort not to look at the gun, as if refusing to acknowledge it, its primacy.

"Because I tell you to," the older man said impatiently.

"My family is in there."

"We know that. And the best way you can help them is to do exactly as we say, with a minimum of fuss and talk."

"There isn't much money in the house," Gifford said. "But whatever there is, you're welcome to."

"Just get in the house," the older one repeated, putting the gun in his coat pocket but keeping his hand on it.   Gifford turned and, followed by the two men, walked back to the house. The door was still open. He could hear Helen talking to the children.

When she heard his footsteps on the porch, she said, "Don't tell me the car won't start."

When he walked inside, followed by the two men, Helen took one look and moved the children around behind her. She didn't have to be told that this was trouble. It was written on her husband's face.

"It's all right, Helen," Gifford said. "They haven't explained themselves yet, but it's all right."

Helen turned to the children and said, "These are friends of your Daddy's. Say hello to them."

Shyly, the children nodded to the men.

"Now take off your coats and go upstairs to your rooms," Helen told them. "We'll call you when it's time to go."

Slowly, uncertainly, with backward looks, the children went upstairs. The two men smiled pleasantly at them.

When the children were gone, the older one said, "Well, done, Mrs. Gifford. Now, if this kind of cooperation is maintained everything is going to be just fine."

"What do you want?" Helen asked.

"Sit down, both of you," the older one ordered. "It's very simple, really. All cut and dried, from point A to point Z."

The Giffords sat down on the living room sofa. While the younger man lounged in the doorway, his hand still inside his jacket, an expressionless, uncompromising look on his face, the older one stood before the Giffords.

"I'm going to drive into town with you, Mr. Gifford," he said. "My partner is going to remain here, to oversee your wife and children, as a sort of guarantee for your cooperation until our return."

"You mean you're going to hold them hostage," Gifford said angrily.

"Well, yes. I know you don't like it, but it's the best way, all around, believe me. Now, here's what's going to happen. Instead of opening your bank at nine o'clock, as you normally do, you're going to open a bit earlier today, before your staff gets in."

"And you're going to clean it out," Gifford said, "Well, you've overlooked one thing: there's a time lock on the vault. It doesn't open until nine o'clock and there's not a damn thing I can do about it."

The gunman stared sternly at Gifford for a moment, then began to laugh softly. "We know that, Mr. Gifford," he said. "Look, if it makes you feel any better, we're not amateurs. We know about these things. We've been studying you and your bank and the habits and procedures of all concerned. We've been here nearly a week, and the fact that you haven't noticed us tells you something about our expertise."

"You're not perfect," Gifford said. "I saw you in there yesterday at closing time."

The gunman laughed again, a short, mirthless chuckle. "So we're not perfect," he said, "but don't let that reduce your confidence in us. There's nothing like a smalltown bank. You're very trusting people here. You don't lock up all of your cash at night. Your tellers leave their cash drawers full. That's what we want."

Gifford looked at the floor. The man was right. It was not recommended practice, but out of old habits the tellers did leave their cash in their drawers overnight as crime was virtually nonexistent here. Bank robbers or other serious criminals all seemed so remote.

When Gifford looked up at the gunman there was resentment in his eyes, as if his trust had been betrayed.

"Now," the older man said, looking at his watch, "it's exactly seven thirty. The drive into town is forty minutes, which means we arrive at the bank at eight ten. It shouldn't take us more than fifteen minutes to do what we have to do. So it's then eight twenty-five. With the drive back, we should be returning here at a few minutes after nine."

"That's if he doesn't make trouble," the other gunman added.

"Don't worry, Alf," the older one said, smiling at Gifford. "He won't make any trouble. He knows what's at stake, don't you, Mr. Gifford?"

Gifford said nothing.

"Because," the gunman went on, "if we're not back here on time, and let's allow a few minutes for delays, then his family will be in deep trouble. If we're not back by, say, nine twenty, Alf will safely assume that someone tried to upset our plans."

"And then what?" Gifford asked. "What happens then?"

The gunman smiled, shrugged, and said, "Who can tell—with Alf's temper?"

The implied threat infuriated Gifford; the very idea that anyone would think of harming his family almost deranged his thinking for a moment and he had to suppress the impulse to leap at these men.

"All right," the older gunman said curtly, "let's get moving. For you and your family, Mr. Gifford, the clock has begun to tick."

Gifford did not, would not, get up until the revolver had reappeared. Gesturing with it, the gunman brought Gifford to his feet and followed him outside.

"We'll take your car, Mr. Gifford," the man said as they went down the porch steps.

So for the second time that morning, Gifford headed for his garage. This time he went in with his companion, got into his car, and backed out. As he turned to head down the driveway Gifford took a last, longing look back at his house. It suddenly had an aspect of closed, cold inaccessibility. It provoked in Gifford one single, driving resolve: to get this over as quickly as possible and get back to his family. He had no intention of trying to play the hero. They could take the money and be damned.

As he drove toward the highway he passed the two empty houses and for the first time realized how isolated he was back there. He passed the gunmen's car along the side of the road and knew that no one would see it, no one would pass who might be curious enough to question its presence.

When they got to the highway, Gifford pressed down hard on the accelerator and headed for town.

"Please observe the speed limit, Mr. Gifford," the gunman said. "We don't want to break the law," he added with a sardonic chuckle.

They drove in silence after that. Occasionally they exchanged glances and when they did, the gunman nodded politely and showed a faint, whimsical smile.

As they neared town, Gifford broke the silence. "Won't it look strange to people," he said, "you walking into the bank with me?"

"No, the people here don't have suspicious minds. No reason for them to."

"Suppose some of my staff show up early?"

"Have they ever?"

"No," Gifford said glumly. "But what happens when they arrive and the bank is closed?"

"I can tell you what will happen. They'll call your home, where your wife, with Alf standing right next to her, will tell them you overslept and are on your way in."

"But if someone has already seen me there, entering and leaving . . ."

"We'll let them puzzle it out, Mr. Gifford. By the time they begin to become overly-curious, it won't matter any more. Alf and I will be well on our way."

When they reached the bank, Gifford was told to park in the alley adjacent. They got out of the car and, without being seen by anyone, entered the bank. The blinds were drawn, concealing the bank's interior from the street.

"Eight ten on the button," the gunman said with a note of quiet satisfaction in his voice.

Gifford suddenly whirled and confronted him and, in an unnaturally loud voice, asked, "What happens to my family if we don't get back there on time?"

As if annoyed or perhaps alarmed by this sudden belligerence, the gunman drew his revolver.

"I'm asking you a question, damn you!" Gifford shouted, taking a step toward the other, and as he did the gunman lifted the revolver to eye level and pointed it coldly and directly at Gifford.

"Get on with it, Mr. Gifford," he said testily. "If you have your family's well-being at heart you won't tempt the fates by wasting time. Now, you have the keys to those cash drawers, so get on with it."

Gifford got his keys and began unlocking the drawers. The gunman went with him to the tellers' stations, holding a canvas bag which he had pulled from his pocket, and watched Gifford go from drawer to drawer filling it. The gunman had figured fifteen minutes in the bank; it took less than ten.

"All right, Mr. Gifford," the gunman said when all the drawers had been emptied, "now comes the delicate part—walking out of here carrying an obviously stuffed bag. I might add that with the money now in my possession my outlook on things becomes a bit obsessed. The idea of a large sum of money is one thing, the possession of it is another. If anyone challenges us I'm prepared to use this gun—on you or them. Do you understand?"

"I understand," Gifford said.

"So give me your cay keys. In the event I have to shoot you dead I'll have to leave in your car."

Frightened now, Gifford handed him the keys. The gunman seemed tense, even angry, as if the mere thought of having to relinquish the money was intolerable.

They opened the door and walked outside. The sidewalk was empty, for which Gifford was grateful, for he had taken quite seriously the man's threats. They walked around to the alley and got into the car, Gifford in the driver's seat. The keys were returned to him.

"Now head back."

"What time is it?" Gifford asked, then looked at his watch. It was eight twenty.

"This is no problem, Mr. Gifford. Just get moving."

Gifford backed out of the alley. Several people passing on the sidewalk seemed to take no notice. In this small, insular New England town they were so conditioned to minding their business that they seemed to feel it was an intrusion even to glance at someone. Gifford damned their aloofness now. If any one of them had any brains they would notice that something was amiss here and call the police—except that the police in this town consisted of two middle-aged men who were totally inadequate to cope with a situation like this.

As they drove back along the highway, Gifford began having some disturbing thoughts. What would happen after they returned? Would the two gunmen simply take the money and leave? The more Gifford thought about it the more his doubts began to grow. At best, they would tie up the family, so as to have ample time in which to get away; and the worst—but Gifford didn't want to think about that.

Grimly silent, Gifford sped along the highway, anxious to get back, to be with his family, to face together whatever happened.

They passed few cars on the highway; there was only the constant passing on either side of the road of the endless evergreen. Between the monotony of the drive and the consuming depths of his thoughts, Gifford was paying only mechanical attention to what he was doing, to the extent that it was the gunman who had to point out that they were nearing the side road.

"The turnoff is coming up," he said, noting that there had been no deceleration to allow for the turn.

His voice barely penetrated Gifford's reverie and, with an uncomprehending expression, he turned his head to look at the man.

"The turn is coming," the gunman yelled, pointing ahead with his finger.

Instinctively, without thinking, without braking or even decompressing the accelerator, Gifford suddenly swung the wheel, but the car was going too fast, the angle too sharp. There was a shuddering and a skidding as the car bounded off the highway onto the dirt road; the trees seemed to be flashing through every window, swooping and abrupt, as if doing some wild dance around the car. Unable to make its turn, the car made a screeching sound and plunged off the dirt road. It bolted furiously through the roadside brush, ran over some scrub pine and came suddenly and barbarously to a stop with a sickening thud against an enormous boulder that had been cast from the mountaintop in another age.

Gifford remembered his head hitting against the window. He thought he had been knocked unconscious then, yet he remembered the car flattening the scrub pine and then the boulder looming up like something rising from the undersea. He also remembered the jolting and unceremonious stop to which they had come, but it was all vague and unreal, ill-recorded by memory.

He was lying against the door, aware of a dull aching in his head, his thoughts unable for the moment to emerge coherently from under the pain. He blinked several times before he was able to understand what it was he was seeing. The hood had been thrown into the air by the impact of the crash and hung now like the open jaw of some voracious bird of prey. He could not immediately remember where he was, what had happened. Then he turned and saw his companion, and he remembered.

The gunman looked as though he had been hurled against the door with great fury; he seemed crushed and crumpled. His face, in profile, wore an expression of shocked anger, made the more furious by a copious flow of blood. His hat was gone and his hair looked as though it had been about to leave his head and then stopped.

Gifford gazed at him with simple, uncomplicated curiosity, until the realization had set fully in—the man was dead.

Then Gifford remembered all the rest of it and a shock of terror rushed through him. He looked at his watch: it was ten minutes after nine. He turned around and stared with building panic at the road, then undid his seat belt and opened the door and got out. He walked around behind the smashed and seething car to the other door and opened it. The gunman, who had not been using his seat belt, tumbled softly to the ground. Gifford reached down and took the revolver out of the man's pocket.

He glanced again at his watch. There was still time. Alf was expecting them back at nine twenty and there would surely be allowed some margin for delay, but how much? He thought about the possibility of going back to the highway and hailing a car but that would consume time.

Another thought occurred: take the bag of money to the house, tell Alf what had happened, and perhaps he would go. The idea was appealing, except that Alf might suspect a trick, might suspect that Gifford was trying to trap him, and in that situation there was no telling what the man might do.

Then, under the pressure of elapsing time, with the determination to help his family, Gifford disdained all further thought and speculation and began to run toward his house, revolver in hand. He passed his neighbors' empty houses. A fleeting thought to break in and telephone the state police had to be rejected; the telephones in both houses had been disconnected.

What am I going to do? Gifford kept asking himself. He couldn't simply burst in there, gun or no gun. There was no telling what Alf's frame of mind was, nor what it would become. Doubtless an awful tension had been building in that house during the past hour. The young gunman had to be getting more and more concerned and nervous, and consequently unpredictable and dangerous.

Gifford stopped in the middle of the road, panting. He lifted his hand and covered his eyes for a moment. Get out of the road, he told himself. Alf would almost certainly be watching the road.

So he began approaching the house in a roundabout way, through the pine forest, moving slowly, cautiously. When the side of the house came into view he lay down on the pine needles, trying to formulate some plan, some kind of assault that held a reasonable chance of success. *Think,* he told himself. *Think. Think.*

He could enter through a basement window, carefully and quietly, and work his way upstairs and take Alf by surprise—but the least sound, with his wife and children sitting in front of a gun . . . He closed his eyes for a moment. Were the basement windows locked? He hadn't checked them in months; there was never reason to, in this "crime-free" environment. If they were locked, how could he get in without breaking one? There was no telling what the least sound might provoke in Alf's mind.

He should have gone back to the highway and summoned help, he realized now. This was foolhardy. He had no experience at this sort of thing. He was jeopardizing his family.

Then, as he lay there agonizing over his situation, a shot suddenly rang out, shattering the pristine silence of the pine forest. Gifford instinctively pressed himself tensely to the ground, his eyes glaring. He looked at his watch: ten minutes after nine.

Only ten minutes after nine?

With his eyes widening in terror he studied the face of the watch. The sweep hand was still. The watch had stopped, probably during the accident. But when? How long ago? How long had he been unconscious in the car?

Now the echo of the shot began to reverberate through him. What was happening in the house?

Without waiting to shape another thought, suddenly seized and impelled by an uncontrollable terror, he got to his feet and began running at breakneck speed for the house, pointing the gun out ahead of him. He crashed through the underbrush and out onto the road, running faster and faster, driven forward by the single, maniacal thought of getting the man who was inside the house, unmindful of his own safety, unencumbered by any idea of stealth or strategy. That was all gone now, replaced by the primitive urge to protect his family.

He ran across the front lawn, took the porch steps in two bounds and burst through the front door. He ran through the front door. He ran through the hallway—and was suddenly confronted by Alf. The gunman was in the act of running from the living room to the hallway, his gun swung out from his body.

Without stopping, Gifford fired, his finger suddenly frozen on the trigger. The revolver's recoil made him shudder and stagger as a fury of motion was enacted before him. The running Alf was struck several times in mid-flight and now his animation became spastic and grotesque as one after the other the bullets struck him. He slammed into the wall, then arched back, spun in a half circle and dropped to the floor.

Gifford raced into the living room where he found his startled wife standing, her clasped hands covering her mouth.

"Where are the children?" Gifford demanded.

Helen gasped, her fixed eyes upon the smoking revolver in her husband's hand.

"Where are they?" Gifford shouted.

"Upstairs," she said in a small, strained voice that sounded like a gasp.

"Are they all right? Are you all right?"

"Yes-yes-yes," Helen said, trembling.

Then she ran to him as Gifford let the gun fall to the floor and he threw his arms around her.

"I heard a shot . . . " he said, wracked by unspent tension.

"He was getting more and more restless and nervous," Helen said. "It was terrible."

"He didn't harm any of you, did he?"

"No."

"But what was he shooting at?" Gifford asked.

"He said he saw something moving in the trees. He thought it was the police. But I saw it. It was only a deer . . . but he didn't believe me."

She looked once at Alf's inert, bloody, bullet-torn body, then closed her eyes and pressed her forehead against Gifford's chest.

"A deer?" Gifford said softly. "That's what he shot at?"

"What happened?" Helen asked. "Are you all right? Are you all right?"

Gifford sighed and shook his head. "Not yet. Give me a little time," he said, closing his eyes as he heard his children calling from upstairs.

Long Shot

by Michael Collins

Around the Chelsea slums of New York they tell the story of an immigrant who came here with only the clothes on his back and a dream of opening his own restaurant. He knew that hard work and saving his money was the way to get his dream, so he worked day and night as a waiter, and after ten years he had $312.27 in the bank. He thought about it a while, then took the $312.27 to Belmont Park and put it on a hundred to one shot. The horse came in, and that's how the immigrant got his restaurant.

Frank Marno knew that story as well as anyone.

It was hot the day Frank came into my office. He was twenty-five, busy, and eager. "You'll handle a job for me tonight, Dan?"

"What kind of job?" I asked. I'd known Frank Marno most of his life. His father had been Sal Marno—chair number two at Cassel's Barber Shop. Sal had left Frank that chair as his legacy, but Frank had other ideas.

"Same as usual," Frank said. "You deliver the package out to Kennedy International tonight. Negotiable bonds, so take your gun, okay? The client likes to see a gun."

Frank had no education beyond cutting hair, but he had imagination and energy. He started by picking up whatever he could sell for a profit. He hustled pool, gambled when he had a stake. He ran messages for bookies, and worked up to taking small bets. Then he got a franchise from the top men for his own book, started his legitimate messenger service, handled a few actions I didn't want to know about, and finally bought a share of a good liquor store. At twenty-five he was doing fine.

A long time ago, when Frank had been just a kid, his father, Sal Marno, had saved my life by hiding me out when some unpleasant types wanted me dead. Sal had stood up to the muscle and the cops, had taken more than one beating, but had not revealed where I was hiding. I got out of the country on a ship; the ones who were out to get me ended up dead themselves, and I hadn't forgotten what I owed Sal Marno.

When Frank started his messenger service he wasn't flush, and he knew the principle of holding down the overhead, so he kept his staff low. When he needed a bonded man, he hired me. I remembered Sal, and detective work in Chelsea doesn't make a man rich, so I took the work.

This time I picked up the package at Frank's store. That was unusual, as normally I got the package straight from the client. I didn't think much about it then, which shows how careless a man can be when dealing with friends. Frank himself gave me the package and the instructions.

"Get to the hangar at eight o'clock, Dan. Not before, the client says, and don't be late. Okay?"

"Pay me, and I fly," I said.

He paid me, and I went to eat some dinner. I had time for a few good Irish whiskies with Joe Harris, and then I caught the airport bus from the East Side Terminal. Frank Marno didn't pay enough to waste my money on a taxi.

At the airport I got directions to the right hangar, and finally found it just two minutes before eight o'clock. I went in with my big cannon displayed to impress the client. There was a small private jet all warmed up in front of the hangar.

Two people waited inside the hangar. One was a really beautiful girl.

The other was Frank Marno.

Frank had a gun in his pocket. He let me see it once. "Hand over the package, Dan."

I gave it to him. "Why, Frank?"

He grinned at me. "You mean why do it like this? I couldn't carry it around, Dan. Too dangerous. I had to cover myself."

"Cover what?"

"Why my delivery was late. I covered it okay, but it would've looked funny if I was carrying a big package. He might have wanted to know what was in it, or maybe why I took a package on a date."

"Who might have wanted to know?"

"Mr. Krupp," Frank said. "I had to pick up Angela, and make it look like just a regular date."

I wasn't following him all the way, but enough to have a cold feeling—cold and hard like ice. The girl came up then, and she was maybe nineteen. She held Frank's arm and looked up at him. Every man should have a woman look at him like that once in his life; with adoration, love, and a fierce kind of possession. Frank Marno was a lucky man. He was also insane; I recognized the girl now—Angela Krupp.

She smiled a defiant smile. "Hello, Mr. Fortune. Don't blame Frank, he couldn't tell you. You might—"

"I might have gone to your father," I said. "Maybe I would have. I like living."

Angela Krupp, the only daughter of Mr. Wally Krupp. The apple of Mr. Krupp's eye, guarded from the harsh world like a vestal virgin. She wasn't in an airport hangar with Frank Marno with the blessing of Wally Krupp. Never.

Krupp had been Krupanski once. I don't think Wally Krupp ever realized the symbolism of his changed name—he wasn't a man given to thinking much about symbolism. But Wally Krupp lived by the gun as much as his famous namesakes had—the gun, the numbers, the dope, and the terror. Second only to Andy Pappas himself in New York, he was polite to Pappas, but to no one else. Racket boss number two, and trying hard.

Frank Marno said, "You didn't know I've been working for Mr. Krupp for over a year now? My own operation in the liquor store? A big take, Dan, and I met Angela. Bingo! That was it for both of us, me and Angela."

"You and Angela and a jet plane, Frank?"

"We're in love, we got a right. I ain't losing her!"

Angela said, "My father hates all men who look at me."

I said, "You're married, Frank."

"To a tramp I dropped a year ago! I'll get a divorce down south, and if I can't, hell. We're in love. You got to grab in this world to get your share."

"What's in the package, Frank?" I asked.

His face was set. "You got to have money, too, Dan. That's what's in the package. One hundred thousand cash. A month's take. I worked it all out. We're going to live a good life."

I stared. "Krupp's money, too? You are crazy."

"My money!" Frank snarled. "I worked for it, I conned for it, I muscled for it. It's mine, and Angela's mine!"

When you're young, death is far away. The bigger the risk, the sweeter the triumph. Frank would be rich, and loved, and outlast the whole world.

I'm not young any more. "Krupp'll get you, Frank."

"I can handle myself," he said, proud and tough. "I'll take care of Mr. Wally Krupp, and anyone he sends. I can shoot, I know judo,

I fly my own plane, and I'm smarter than any illiterate like Wally
Krupp."

"One man you can beat, but there won't be only one. Remember
all the hired hands who never held any tool except a gun."

"Maybe a year," Frank said, "and he'll quit looking. I got it
planned. What's a lousy hundred grand to somebody named Wally
Krupp?"

"He can't let you get away with it, not one of his own men double-
crossing him. And there's Angela—no punk was ever going to touch
his daughter. She was going to marry respectable; maybe a prince.
You can't marry her even if he'd let you. He's a moral family man,
Krupp is."

"If he won't quit, I'll get him. I mean it, Dan."

"You can't get him. He's invulnerable, and you know it. Behind
his hired guns and shyster lawyers he can't be reached. He snaps
his fingers, you die, and you can't fight back."

For that one instant I think I got to him. One glimpse of doubt
in his eyes, maybe fear. Angela Krupp squeezed his arm.

He said, "I've got it planned good, Dan."

Then he was gone—with his package, his woman, and his gun. I
didn't wait for the plane to take off. I didn't want to be around if
Wally Krupp happened to show up. I didn't ever want to see Frank
Marno again.

You don't always get what you want.

Six months passed. Word gets around in Chelsea; a private detective hears whispers he doesn't always want to hear.

If it had been only money, Wally Krupp might not have looked
so hard. Or if it had been only Angela. Money and daughter were
too much—a slap in the face of Mr. Wally Krupp, and face and
reputation are important to a racket boss. They were laughing at
Krupp—silently. Only Frank Marno's blood would help.

I heard only bits and pieces, but they added up to a story.

A blonde cried in her beer one night only two months after Frank
had run. Her man had been shot in Veracruz; he had been one of
Wally Krupp's gunmen.

An old woman asked the D.A. if he could help her son and another
man who were in jail in Caracas. They, too, worked for Wally Krupp.
Krupp wasn't helping them much now.

Lieutenant Marx from the precinct came around to ask if I knew
why Rico Stein had been in Peru. I'd known Rico pretty well at one

time. Rico had just fallen off a cliff near Cuzco; rumor said he had
been hired recently by Wally Krupp.

Chelsea lowered the odds against Frank Marno. He was proving
to have sharp teeth, it looked like, and maybe he would beat Wally
Krupp after all. At least maybe Krupp would give up. How many
men could he lose before the troops rebelled? Frank could be the
winner.

I knew better. Frank might be winning some skirmishes, but the
pressure had to be taking a toll, the roses had to be all gone by now.
Frank and Angela weren't getting much of the good life—they were
running faster and faster, looking over their shoulders, jumping at
shadows. They were sleeping with crushed newspaper on the floor
and the windows locked, no matter how hot it was where they were.

I knew the law of averages.

The averages ran out for Frank and Angela in a place called Rio
Arriba down in Central America. Captain Roy from the D.A.'s squad
told me. The D.A. was interested.

"Two of Krupp's best men caught them in Rio Arriba," Roy said.
"One of the gunmen ended in the bay, the other's in jail down there
on a murder charge. Frank Marno got away, Angela Krupp didn't.
They found her in the bay, too."

It was a cold day, but not as cold as Wally Krupp's heart. His
Angela was dead, killed by Frank Marno, of course. Wally Krupp
wouldn't blame himself. No, he would tell himself that Frank Marno
killed her by eloping with her, by stealing the money, by not protecting her.

"Krupp'll never quit now," I said to Captain Roy. "Not if it takes
twenty years. Frank's a walking dead man."

"He always was, Fortune. No one escapes Wally Krupp, not this
side of the grave. The D.A. knows you talked to Marno that last day,
and—"

"How do you know?"

"Don't panic, Krupp doesn't know. What the D.A. wants to know
is how much Marno really liked the Krupp girl."

"I don't know, captain. He's young. Who can say?"

"Enough to want Krupp dead? To want that bad?"

"Maybe."

"Enough to come back here to get Krupp?"

"No one can reach Wally Krupp."

Roy sighed. "I guess you're right, Fortune. The D.A.'s just kind of eager. Marno kills Krupp, and we're rid of Krupp. Krupp maybe kills Marno *here*, and we get Krupp."

"Or they kill each other," I said. "That'd be nice."

"Why not?" Captain Roy said, and left my office.

They brought Angela's body back. Krupp buried her in the biggest funeral Chelsea ever saw. I didn't go, but I got some of the news that came out of the funeral. Wally Krupp had the word out; no one was to touch Frank Marno. No one was even to bruise Frank—just find him, and report back to Krupp.

It figured, now Wally Krupp would handle Frank Marno personally. It had to be, when I thought about it. A family thing now, personal as well as business, a vendetta. Krupp would kill Frank with his own hands, if not tomorrow, then the next day—or next year.

Six more months went by. I was feeling better, until I got the letter from Frank Marno.

The letter was in a cheap envelope, with no date, no return address, and a New York postmark. Frank had given the note to someone to mail for him in New York, a note with his name scrawled, and just three words: *Find me, please!* So scared he couldn't risk telling even me where he was. Trust no one. Even if he trusted me, Krupp could be watching me by now, and Krupp could get to anyone.

Find me, please!

How long ago had the letter been written? Maybe months. What did Frank want—someone to hold his hand? Was his nerve gone now that he was alone, without Angela, the real reason he'd crossed Krupp in the first place?

What could I do for Frank? What could anyone do, even if I could find him?

Nothing—but that didn't matter. I owed Sal Marno's son, as I always had, and in Chelsea word gets around when you owe and don't pay. No, I had to go, if I wanted to live and work further in Chelsea.

Rio Arriba was a typical small Latin American capital city with wide streets, marble government buildings on scrubbed green squares, the shacks of the poor hanging on muddy hillsides.

The Ministry of Justice was a skyscraper with a lot of statues. I asked for Captain Guzman—that much the New York D.A. had told me—the name of the officer who had handled the shooting.

Captain Guzman was a tall, *hidalgo* type in a military uniform complete with medals and polished boots. "Señor Fortune," he said, bowing me to a chair. "You wish to speak of the Angela Krupp murder?"

"I'm looking for Frank Marno, captain."

Guzman nodded. "A tragic young man. Foolish, I think, but strong also. The señorita was most beautiful. His grief was great, but he was a man, a *caballero, sí*? I watch, I see he has a stone in him—he will exact retribution."

"Do you know where he is?"

Guzman shook his head. "We investigated closely, of course, but it was clear that the two *pistoleros* had come to kill Marno and Miss Krupp. The weapons were lost in the bay, but the surviving *pistolero* confessed all to us. Marno acted in self-defense, and we released him. Where he went, I do not know."

"Can you tell me where he lived at the time?"

"Of course."

Five minutes later I walked out with Frank Marno's address, where he had lived after his release over six months ago. It wasn't encouraging: The Hotel San Martin.

The clerk was polite. "No, señor, he left us soon after the tragedy. Alas, I should have known that there was trouble—the señorita was so silent, so afraid, yes. The assassins actually came here!"

"It happened near the hotel?"

"Oh, no. In the slums, at the docks. So terrible."

"He left no forwarding address?"

"No, señor."

Stupid question. Frank wouldn't leave an address.

"I'll take a room," I said. I slipped him a twenty. "Pass it around that I'll pay for any information."

I waited around the hotel for three days. No one came near me, so I went out to try the usual routine.

A man must eat, sleep, have some fun. He can change almost everything except his habits. He can even try to change those, but he has to do *something* with the days and hours, and sooner or later he will slip. If you can look deep enough, he'll eventually give himself away.

I had a photograph. I tried the movie houses, theaters, jai alai fronton, racetrack, restaurants, and bars. Everywhere I passed out word that I would pay. I drew a blank. There were bartenders and waiters who recognized Frank's picture, but they hadn't seen him for months. It looked hopeless, until one waiter remembered one small incident.

"*Sí*, they sit in my corner many day," the waiter said. "The pretty señorita is very unhappy, the man he is angry."

"You never saw him alone later?"

"I think two, three times. He talks with Carmen."

I found Carmen at the bar of another cafe later that night; she was alone, drinking tequila. She shrugged at my question.

"I see many Americano men."

"I'll pay for information about this one."

"What information, hombre?"

"About where I can find him. He needs help."

I showed Carmen the letter; she blinked at it. She looked at me for a time, carefully. "Buy me a whisky, scotch."

I bought her a scotch. She drank with a deep sigh.

"Sometimes, I dream of the scotch whisky," she said. She drank again. "This Marno was a sad man; he had lost his woman. He did not talk much. He say sometimes he don't feel so good; he say he will not long be alone."

"You know where he is now?"

"You are his friend?"

"Maybe the only friend he has."

I signaled for another scotch. She stared at it when it came. She drank.

"The last time I am with Marno, he take me to where he live. I show you."

We went through the back streets of the city far from the wide boulevards and scrubbed public squares. The place she took me to was a cheap, dirty rooming house. Frank Marno had not been there for many months. The manageress didn't know where he had gone, and she didn't care.

"He is drunk, always alone. Who can care?" she said.

As I started to leave, an enormous fat man came out of the manager's rooms. "Hey, yanqui. Come with me."

The manageress turned on the fat man, spat something in gutter Spanish. The fat man grew red, and snarled at her. She shrank from his anger, walked away.

He nodded to me. "Come inside."

His eyes were sunk in layers of flesh—cunning eyes that were counting my money through my clothes and wallet. He sat down inside the filthy back room. He grinned at me. "You wear fine suit. You are a rich man?"

"No," I said, "but I'll pay to find Frank Marno."

"Of course you will pay. But how much, eh?"

"Fifty dollars."

He sighed, and the whole great mound of his body shook. I could smell the greed. Men like him are what make it so hard for another man to vanish.

"Señor Marno is generous," he said. "He pay more so I not tell where he go. How can I tell for so little?"

"You're a man of principle," I said.

He shrugged. "A man must live. I sell him to you, but I will not sell cheap, *sí*? I am honest man."

"Like a saint. How much?"

"Five hundred American."

"Goodbye. I like a man to stay honest."

"Four hundred."

"I'll find him some other way."

Under the rolling layers of fat his muscles tensed. His reaction was a surprise, he was anxious, nervous.

"Two hundred fifty, *sí*?

"One fifty. Final offer."

"Okay, okay. You are hard man. Pay me."

"Tell me," I said.

He mopped his face. "I do not know where Señor Marno is now, but I know how you find him. Before he leave he go many days to hospital—they will know where he is."

"The hospital?"

"The big hospital for the rich, and the Americano."

I paid him.

The hospital was large, modern, and in the best section of Rio Arriba. The nurse at the night desk said that Frank Marno had been a patient of Dr. Paul Kolcheck, the senior resident. I found Kolcheck in his office, a thin, mousy man who looked self-important and hungry.

"Frank Marno? Why, yes, I remember him well. A tourist from Chicago. Nothing serious; stomach trouble, but it was mostly nerves."

Nerves I could believe for Frank Marno. "Where can I find him now?"

"I have no idea."

"Can I look at his chart? It might have an address."

"No, you . . . " His voice rose sharply; he tried to calm it again. "I'm sorry, but his chart was lost."

"Lost?" I watched his face.

"Yes, in a fire. We had a small fire here."

There was a wariness all over him now. I wondered if he happened to be a plastic surgeon, a little side practice? It was something Frank Marno would have considered very fully, I was sure.

I said, "He made many trips here, doc, I know. You're sure it was nothing serious? You don't know where he went?"

"Quite sure on both counts. Now, if you'll excuse me."

I left on the cue, but I didn't go far. I hid where I could watch Kolcheck's office door. When he came out, he looked around, then hurried along the corridor without looking back. I followed him straight to the Record Room.

When he came out of the Record Room he had a manila folder. I tailed him to the living quarters. He hurried into a room, and came out again empty-handed. I ducked into a room to let him pass, then headed for my hotel to get my picklock.

Back at the hospital I didn't go in the front way. I slipped along corridors to the room in the living quarters. When I was sure I was alone, and that the room was empty, I picked the lock.

It took me five minutes to find the manila folder, and read it. It was Frank Marno's chart, and I knew why he had wanted a friend, and where to look for him next.

In the morning I took the noon train for the fishing resort of Lake Anacapa up the coast. An ancient taxi took me to the hospital. There they said they had never heard of Frank Marno. I told them about Frank's chart. "It lists letters between the Rio Arriba hospital and the hospital here—letters from Dr. Jesus Rosas, Chief."

"Rosas?" the administrator of the Lake Anacapa hospital said. "An American would never go to Rosas' hospital."

"There's another hospital here?"

He nodded. "For the natives; a pesthole that's been here a hundred years. Rosas is half veterinarian. A crime, really, but the peons trust him. He's head doctor there, and the only licensed doctor. No American in his right mind would—"

I didn't wait to hear more. Frank Marno was in his right mind, and it was just where he would go. He had—three times within the last three months.

Dr. Rosas shook his head sadly. "What can one do? Such a case

I see only once before. The last time he stayed here two weeks, then I sent him home. I do not expect him back again, señor."

"Where is home?"

"Santa Ynez. It is inland near the desert and the Sierra Negra. Some go to hunt; there is nothing else there."

"How do I get there?"

Dr. Rosas shrugged. "A car. It takes many hours."

Santa Ynez was a dusty misery of a village, a ruin before it began, and never known enough to have been forgotten. A few hundred Indians, two cantinas, one hotel for hunters, and the desert vast and empty to the distant mountains of the Sierra Negra.

As I drove into the silent town, the only signs of life were the vultures riding thermals above the scorching red hills of the desert. The police consisted of a *jefe* and two cartridge-draped Indians. They recognized the picture of Señor Marno.

"I think yes," the chief said. "He is much different."

"Where do I find him?"

The chief consulted the stars. "He lives here, there. You must look in the cantinas, *sí?*"

I didn't find Frank Marno in either cantina. There was nowhere else to look until morning. I took a room at the one hotel, and, after staring at the bed, decided to sleep on the floor. I'm as antiseptic as the next American.

In the morning I looked into the hotel cantina and found Frank Marno. He was alone at a table. The sun wasn't above the huts yet, but he had a bottle of mescal.

I sat down. "Hello, Frank."

He didn't smile or frown, just reached for the mescal. I stared at the changes in him. The assurance was gone; the eagerness, the youth—and fifty pounds. His dull eyes were sunk into an emaciated face. His ragged clothes were filthy, his hands shook, and he looked sixty.

His voice was a croak. "Six months, Dan, nothing to do except sit in the dust. After Angela, and the—"

I knew what he had been going to say—after the hospital—but he stopped, drank, and looked out the open cantina door at the wall of heat that hung over the dusty street.

"Angela's dead, did you know?" he said. "I'm alone in this hole. I—" He looked at me from his wasted face. "I'm scared, Dan. Booze and pills; pills and booze. I don't want to die, but Krupp—you can't beat Krupp."

I said, "I read the hospital report in Rio Arriba, Frank."

"You read it? Kolcheck promised he wouldn't show it to —"

"I know how to find things, Frank."

He nodded slowly. "You know, what gets you here is the sameness. Not even a cloud, just those vultures. They're waiting, like me. Only they're waiting *for* me, right? Just me. Everyone else here was born dead."

"How long, Frank? A year? You've got a year, maybe?"

For a moment he didn't seem to hear me, then he looked straight at my face. "Go away, Dan. I'm dead. Can't you see that now?"

"You sent for me."

He drank a long drink. "That was a long time ago. Angela was just . . . Go back, Dan, I was wrong. Go home."

"I came too far, Frank."

He drank again, and began to giggle. "To help a corpse, yeah. A corpse, Dan, one way or the other! A laugh!" He giggled, drank, and collapsed on the table. It wasn't even ten o'clock yet.

The bartender came to the table "He do it all the time now," he said in careful English. "Very fast. Sick. I take him to room. I am Ortega, his friend."

Ortega picked Frank up like a feather and carried him out. I followed to a windless hovel where Ortega laid Frank on a pile of rags. He lay as if already dead, and I went out to walk in the sun and dust. Indians watched me from a distance.

Frank woke up in three hours. It began again: the cantinas, the mescal, the babbling talk, the telling me to go home, until he passed out once more.

On the third day I sobered him enough to make him shave, and find the one suit he had worn when he arrived at Santa Ynez. I told him I had a car, and the train left from Lake Anacapa. Then I lost him again. He screamed I was fingering him for Wally Krupp. He grabbed the bottle, and ended in a stupor by dark.

After a week I had him sober for almost a day—sober, silent, and nervous. He had agreed at least to go back to Rio Arriba. We were settling it in the hotel cantina, with Ortega hiding the mescal bottle, when I heard the car, a big car out in the late afternoon dust and heat.

Frank Marno heard it, too. The only car in Santa Ynez was the chief's Land Rover. This wasn't a Land Rover. Frank's head jerked up, sober, to look fearfully at Ortega. The bartender hurried toward the rear door.

A man in a dark city suit came in through the rear door. He only glanced at Ortega hurrying out. It was a hundred in the shade, but the newcomer wore his suit buttoned, and his tie knotted. He just stood there, empty-faced.

Wally Krupp came in the front way.

Krupp's fleshy face sweated in rivers, not used to such heat. His eyes were cool. Two more dark suits followed him in and stood where they could see the whole room. Krupp sat down at a separate table.

"You're a long way from home, Fortune," he said.

I felt a little sick. He wasn't surprised to see me. He knew I'd be here. I'd led him to Frank Marno!

Now he looked at Frank and said, "Hello, Frankie."

"What took so long?" Frank Marno said in that croak.

Krupp nodded. "You always were smart, Frankie. You could have gone a long way with me. Too bad."

"Go to hell, Krupp," Frank said, his voice all at once a lot stronger. "I took your money and your daughter; she wanted me, not a prince. My woman, you hear? You killed her."

Krupp's face darkened. "I know what killed her, punk."

"Do you?" Frank said. "What does it matter? If she couldn't have me, she wanted to be dead anyway. You came to kill me, get it over with, then."

Wally Krupp smiled at Frank Marno. "You want to die, Marno?" he said softly.

Frank's sunken eyes were dark. "Why not? You killed *my* Angela. The money's all gone. Why not?"

"Gone? A hundred grand in a year? Not here, Marno."

"I found ways to spend it. You get nothing—no money, no daughter. Go on and kill me. You're the loser."

"I get the fun of it, Marno," Krupp said.

"Not even that," Frank croaked. "Angela's dead, the money's gone, back home who cares? Kill me for nothing, Krupp."

I watched Frank Marno. Something had changed. He was goading Krupp, asking to be killed. Did he think he could trick Wally Krupp into letting him live by asking to die? A crazy hope to risk his life on—and mine. I had no illusions about my fate. I had to figure my own way out, if there were one.

"So," Krupp said, "you got it all figured out, punk."

I never saw his signal. One of the gunmen was behind him. I had no chance to reach for my gun; the gunman lifted it from me. The second gunman searched Frank Marno; Frank had no gun.

Wally Krupp stood up. "The car. Watch the local cops."

We went out into the wall of heat on the lone street of Santa Ynez. The chief lounged in the shade across the street, mildly interested in us. It was all unreal, as if we were playing a scene in a bad movie. The dusty village, the silent Indians, the comic opera chief in his cartridge belts . . .

"Krupp," I said. "Listen, I—"

"In the car, Fortune," he said. "You did me a service leading me here, but you shouldn't have tried to help Marno. Bad luck."

I got into the car, and it was then I got the hunch—a crazy hunch. Krupp had followed me here. How had he known to follow me? It had not been that hard to find Frank Marno, not really. A hunch—or was it only a straw to clutch at?

The big car was cool inside, and silent; air-conditioned and solid. We drove, and there was nothing to measure distance by in the desolate land—or time.

We drove along the one macadam road, then off across dirt roads through the low red hills. A thick cloud of red dust hung in the heat behind us. Beyond the dust rising, nothing moved in that desert, nothing existed. Finally we stopped.

"Out," Krupp said.

We were at the edge of a small box canyon among jagged sand hills. Our own dust cloud still hung in the air behind us; beyond it I saw only the empty desolation. Or—was there another dust cloud? Very close?

"Walk, Fortune," Krupp said.

We walked deeper into the box canyon, in silence. I listened, but I heard nothing beyond the steady crunch of our feet in the red sand. We walked for almost five minutes, the canyon curving deeper into the jagged hills, deserted and almost soundless.

"All right," Krupp said.

He had stopped behind us. We turned. His gunmen stood behind him, alert.

Krupp looked at Frank Marno. "You killed my Angela. Maybe you loved her, but you killed her. You got anything to tell me?"

"No," Frank croaked. His hands were shaking. "Go ahead and shoot. Go on!"

Krupp said, "Maybe I should stake you out, tie you down in the sun and let you die slow."

Frank licked his lips. "You'd never be sure."

"That's right. I have to shoot you to be sure."

"Yes," Frank croaked, then shouted, "Shoot me!"

His words echoed and bounced loud in the canyon. Krupp's smile was cruel.

Then I saw them, up on the rim of the canyon, not a hundred yards away, rifles in their hands; the chief and his two bandits. My wild hunch had been true!

"Krupp," I said, "it's a trap! He wants you to kill him." I told him about the hospital chart. "He's got maybe a year to live. The local cops are in the hills. You shoot us, they'll kill you, or take you. This is their country—you'd be helpless down here with a murder charge against you. He's dying already, Krupp! He wants to take you with him."

Frank cried, "He's crazy! Why would I—"

Krupp's laugh was cold, nasty, cruel. "I know all about it, Fortune," he said. He turned to Frank Marno. "Smart boy, the money's gone, and maybe a year you got to live. So you think you'll get even with Wally Krupp, take me with you. Why not? I'd do the same myself if I had the same reason and chance."

He looked up at the hills.

"You think you trap Wally Krupp so easy? That bartender at the cantina, I figured you sent him to the cops. I let him go so I could watch you sweat. I know what it means—Hodgkin's disease—you'll go slow and hard, right? Always cold, the book says, even down here. In the end you'll crawl in the dirt, too weak to walk. Look at you already! Why should I kill a dead man?"

His dark eyes glittered in the setting sun. He was enjoying the vision of how Frank Marno was going to die; cold and alone.

He said, "I'm going home, Frankie. I leave a man to watch, to keep you here. Try to leave, you die faster. When my man tells me you're dead, I'll give a party! Now you can walk back; maybe the walk helps you die faster." He walked away up the canyon, his gunmen followed. They hadn't said one word all the way; maybe they didn't know how.

When they were gone, Frank Marno's legs gave out. He slumped to the dust and began to cry.

Ten minutes later the chief picked us up. No one spoke all the way to Santa Ynez.

I packed in my hotel room, then went down to the cantina. For once, Frank wasn't there. I found him sitting on the floor of his hovel, his sunken eyes glittering.

"Just to make Krupp die, too?" I said. "You sent me that note—and you sent another note to tip Krupp to follow me! You wanted me to lead Krupp to you, but you had to make it look hard."

"He wouldn't have fallen for it if it was easy."

"Get him here, trap him into murdering a dying man!"

"He killed Angela. I had to get him before—" He didn't finish. He didn't have to.

"A slim chance," I said, "A long shot all the way."

"I've played longer. Damn it, it should have worked. Doc Kolcheck was supposed to lead you here, but hide the chart."

"You knew I'd found out when I came."

"I tried to make you go."

"Because you wanted to save me?" I said. "No! You were just hoping Krupp hadn't found out about your disease, and you were afraid I would tell him."

He shrugged in that dismal room. I didn't matter.

I said, "You owe me expenses."

"The money's gone, Dan. You heard me tell it."

"Yeah," I said, "and you need what you have for mescal. You might live over a year."

I walked out. It was almost dark, but I didn't care about the dangers of driving in the dark through the desert. I had a drink in the cantina, got my car, heaved my bag in, and started out of the village. As I drove past Frank Marno's hovel, I saw the chief come out with a fat manila envelope; he whistled as he walked away. I didn't see Frank Marno.

I drove to Lake Anacapa. In the morning I took the train to Rio Arriba, and caught the first jet home. All I wanted to do now was forget about Frank Marno and his desperate long shot to "get" Wally Krupp. I tried hard, but I couldn't forget Frank.

Wally Krupp told the story, and in Chelsea they all buried Frank Marno—a dead man was empty space in a busy world. Not to me. I lay awake thinking about it for a whole month. I thought about how close Krupp had come to murdering a dying man; about the chief whistling coming out of that hovel; about almost a hundred thousand dollars spent in a year on the run; about Frank Marno waiting alone to die.

I took the jet back to Rio Arriba a month later. I went to Captain Guzman and told him the whole story, then I took a room in the Hotel San Martin to wait.

I didn't think the wait would be too long.

Six weeks later, Captain Guzman called me. "Marno is dead; in the hospital in Lake Anacapa. The notice is in the newspapers. He will be buried in Lake Anacapa."

Guzman drove me up himself. They took Frank from the hospital to the pauper's cemetery in a ten dollar pine coffin. The *jefe* of Santa Ynez came, Dr. Jesus Rosas, Guzman and I, a man who had to be Wally Krupp's watcher, and no one else.

"He did not want to live, took no care, drank too much, refused the medicine," Dr. Rosas said at the grave. "The end was quick, he did not suffer too much." In the coffin, Frank Marno had shrunk to an old man. His sunken eyes were closed, his face the color of sand under the heavy makeup of the local embalmer. Dr. Rosas said a few words, and the coffin was closed and buried.

Captain Guzman left with the fawning chief of Santa Ynez, I hired another car and drove alone to Santa Ynez. Once more I arrived just at dusk. I went to the hovel; it was dark, no one was there. A few pieces of Frank Marno's useless life, nothing more. I went back outside and crouched in the shadow of a low mud wall. I shivered as the night grew colder, but I never took my eyes off the shadowy hovel. It was a mistake.

He was behind me before I heard a sound, the gun against my back. "Turn around, sit down, hands on the ground."

I could see him by the starlight. He had a pale beard, blond hair, glasses, a large nose and wore a light tropical suit. He carried a leather bag, and his gun was aimed at me. I would never have known him. "The money wasn't in the hut," I said.

"Safer out here," he said. "I watched the funeral. No one examined the body."

"On purpose, Frank, so as not to tip you we knew."

"How?" Frank Marno said from his new face. "How did you figure it, Dan? It had to be you, damn you!"

"I saw the chief leave your place with an envelope. He was whistling. I asked myself: what made the chief happy? A payoff? But you said you had no money, and why would you pay him if your scheme had failed? It made me wonder. I went on home, but a question stuck in my mind: how could you have thought Krupp wouldn't find the chart about your disease?"

I waited for an answer. He only watched me in the night.

"You knew Krupp, he couldn't have missed that chart," I went on. "Your plan wasn't to trap him into killing you, it was to make him *think* you were trapping him! You didn't have any fatal disease. The whole thing was fake, to make him come here, and go away leaving you alive! You played us all like fish—especially me. I was the convincer."

He smiled. "A good act, eh, Dan? I didn't eat much or sleep much for months, I never washed, and I watered the mescal. I looked dead even to you—I had to test it on you first."

"Good act," I said. "Krupp might have shot you anyway. It was a million-to-one shot."

"Sooner or later he would've gotten me if I kept running. One big risk to be rid of him was better," he said. "The odds weren't that bad. I know Krupp; it was a 'plan' he'd believe. All I had to do was make him dig it out, and add you for scenery to make it real. He believed because he'd have done it himself."

A long shot, sure, but played on knowledge. Frank had used Krupp's own cunning against him—Krupp's kind of trick.

The old confidence was back in Frank's voice. "Down here I can buy anything. Those people in Rio Arriba; Doc Kolcheck to fake the chart; Doc Rosas in Lake Anacapa; the chief; Ortega the barman to fake the drinking and dying; the undertaker to get a body and slip on a mask of my face. New papers, Dan, a new face, a new life—with fifty grand still left—I'm free of Krupp, rich, and no one hurt."

I said, "And Angela?"

"Angela? What about Angela?"

I said, "I made Guzman look closer at the case, Frank. He doesn't have the same gun, but he has the bullets. Angela, it seems, was shot with the same gun that killed Krupp's gunman that night. The gunman in jail says it wasn't one of their guns—wrong caliber. Is that the gun you've still got on me?"

"They can't prove anything now!"

"They're simple people," I said. "They won't believe your scheme. They'll ask themselves: *What better way for a killer to escape than by pretending to die?* They'll convict you."

His eyes were steel, the eyes of the boy who wouldn't settle for the barber shop where his father had lived and died. "She turned on me, Dan. She was going back to Daddy! She said I didn't have a chance this side of the grave. That gave me the whole idea, but I couldn't do it if I let her go. She'd have known it was a fake. I guess we hated each other by then." He looked straight at me. "And I had to make Krupp hate me enough to come after me himself."

Kill Angela to make Krupp hate him enough. It worked.

He said, "Take half the money. I don't want to kill you."

"You won't. Guzman is watching the front of your hut; a shot brings him. Hit me, I'll yell. Where can you go?"

He shrugged. "The desert. The Sierra Negra."

"You couldn't make it. No chance."

"There's always a chance," he said.

"The long shot again?"

Another shrug. "When you're born poor in a rich world, all you've got are long shots. Give me a half hour, Dan?"

"No."

He nodded. "You know, I'm sorry about Angela, I mean that. I pulled it all to have her. Kids in love. It didn't work, Dan, pressure changes people. She got to hate me, and I had to stay alive any way I could. That changes a man, too—the thinking of nothing except staying alive. You change." I said nothing. What was there to say?

He went on, "Maybe Krupp really did kill her. If he'd let us go, who knows? We started in love, but he didn't let us go, and we broke, and I pulled the trigger. It happened like that. Who knows how it would've been if it had happened some other way?"

He was gone, fast and silent in the cold night. I didn't move. Simple caution. I heard a car engine start out in the desert. I was safe, but I still didn't move. Why? Maybe because some of what he said was true—he had done it all, but not alone. Others had a share of the guilt, even Angela herself in a way, and even the world that had taught Frank Marno how to survive.

Or maybe because he'd lived his short life on the illusion of long shots. He had no chance in that desert, but he'd try. Maybe I wanted him to have that much to the end—the hope that the long shot would come in. I waited half an hour, then I went and told Guzman.

He nodded. "We will look tomorrow. No hurry, Señor Fortune. Out there is only heat, empty mountains, no water, hungry Indians and animals. His car will not go far, and no man has ever reached our border on foot."

They found the car, but not Frank. Guzman blocked all roads and sealed the borders, just in case. He rounded up the bribe-takers. After two weeks I went home.

It was two years before I got the letter from Captain Guzman. They had found Frank Marno's bones—in the mountains, not in the desert. The money was beside the bones.

Captain Guzman was impressed that an American had gotten so far alone.

Puddle

by Arthur Porges

A great poet promised to show us fear in a handful of dust. If ever I doubted that such a thing were possible, I know better now. In the past few weeks a vague, terrible memory of my childhood suddenly came into sharp focus after staying tantalizingly just beyond the edge of recall for decades. Perhaps the high fever from a recent virus attack opened some blocked pathways in my brain, but whatever the explanation, I have come to understand for the first time why I see fear not in dust, but water.

It must seem quite absurd: fear in a shallow puddle made by rain; but think about it for a moment. Haven't you ever, as a child, gazed down at such a little pool on the street, seen the reflected sky, and experienced the illusion, very strongly, so that it brought a shudder, of endless depth a mere step away—a chasm extending downward somehow to the heavens? A single stride to the center of the glassy puddle, and you would fall right through. Down? Up? The direction was indefinable, a weird blend of both. There were clouds beneath your feet, and nothing but that shining surface between. Did you dare to take that critical step and shatter the illusion? Not I. Now that memory has returned, I recall being far too scared of the consequences. I carefully skirted such wet patches, no matter how casually my playmates splashed through.

Most of my acquaintances tolerated this weakness in me. After all, I was a sturdy, active child, and held my own in the games we played. It was only after Joe Carma appeared in town that my own little hell materialized, and I lost status.

He was three years older than I, and much stronger; thickset, muscular, dark—and perpetually surly. He was never known to smile in any joyous way, but only to laugh with a kind of *schadenfreude,* the German word for mirth provoked by another's misfortunes. Few could stand up to him when he hunched his blocky frame and bored in with big fists flailing, and I wasn't one of the elect; he terrified me as much by his demeanor as his physical power.

Looking back now, I discern something grim and evil about the boy, fatherless, with a weak and querulous mother. What he did was not the thoughtless, basically merry mischief of the other kids, but full of malice and cruelty. Where Shorty Dugan would cheerfully snowball a tomcat, or let the air out of old man Gruber's tires, Carma preferred to torture a kitten—rumor said he'd been seen burning one alive—or take a hammer to a car's headlights.

Somehow Joe Carma learned of my phobia about puddles, and my torment began. On several occasions he meant to go so far as to collar me, hold my writhing body over one of the bigger pools, and pretend to drop me through—into that terribly distant sky beyond the sidewalk.

Each time I was saved at the last moment, nearly hysterical with fright, by Larry Dumont, who was taller than the bully, at least as strong, and thought to be more agile. They were bound to clash eventually, but so far Carma had sheered off, hoping, perhaps, to find and exploit some weakness in his opponent that would give him an edge. Not that he was a coward but just coldly careful; one who always played the odds.

As for Larry, he was good-natured, and not likely to fight at all unless pushed into it. By grabbing Carma with his lean, wiry fingers that could bend thick nails, and half-jokingly arguing with him, Dumont would bring about my release without forcing a showdown. Then they might scuffle a bit, with Larry smiling and Joe darkly sullen as ever, only to separate, newly respectful of each other's strength.

One day, after a heavy rain, Carma caught me near a giant puddle—almost a pond—that had appeared behind the Johnson barn at the north end of town. It was a lonely spot, the hour was rather early, and ordinarily Joe would not have been about, as he liked to sleep late on weekends. If I had suspected he might be around, that was the last place in the world I'd have picked to visit alone.

Fear and fascination often go together. I stood by the huge puddle, but well away from the edge, peering down at the blue sky, quite cloudless and so far beneath the ground where it should not have been at all; and for the thousandth time tried to gather enough nerve to step in. I *knew* there had to be solid land below—jabs with a stick had proved this much before in similar cases—yet I simply could not make my feet move.

At that instant brawny arms seized me, lifted my body into the air, and tilted it so that my contorted face was parallel to the pool and right over the glittering surface.

"Gonna count to ten, and then drop you right through!" a rasping

voice taunted me. "You been right all along: it's a long way down.
You're gonna fall and fall, with the wind whistling past your ears;
turning, tumbling, faster and faster. You'll be gone for good, kid,
just sailing down forever. You're gonna scream like crazy all the
way, and it'll get fainter and fainter. Here we go: one! two! three!—"

I tried to scream but my throat was sealed. I just made husky
noises while squirming desperately, but Carma held me fast. I could
feel the heavy muscles in his arms all knotted with the effort.

"—four! five! Won't be long now. Six! seven!—"

A thin, whimpering sound broke from my lips, and he laughed.
My vision was blurring; I was going into shock, it seems to me now,
years later.

Then help came, swift and effective. Carma was jerked back, away
from the water, and I fell free. Larry Dumont stood there, white
with fury.

"You're a dirty skunk, Joe!" he gritted angrily. "You need a lesson,
your own kind."

Then he did an amazing thing. Although Carma was heavier than
he, if shorter, Larry whipped those lean arms around the bully,
snatched him clear of the ground and with a single magnificent
heave threw him fully six feet into the middle of the water.

Now I wonder about my memory; I have to. Did I actually see
what I now recall so clearly? It's quite impossible, but the vision
persists. Carma fell full-length, face down, in the puddle, and surely
the water could not have been more than a few inches deep. But he
went on through! I saw his body twisting, turning, and shrinking
in size as it dropped away into that cloudless sky. He screamed, and
it was exactly as he had described it to me moments earlier. The
terrible, shrill cries grew fainter, as if dying away in the distance;
the flailing figure became first a tiny doll, and then a mere dot; an
unforgettable thing, surely, yet only a dream-memory for so long.

I looked at Larry; he was gaping, his face drained of all blood. His
long fingers were still hooked and tense from that mighty toss.

That's how I remember it. Perhaps we probed the puddle; I'm not
sure, but if we did, surely it was inches deep.

On recovering from my illness three weeks ago, I hired a good
private detective to make a check. The files of the local paper are
unfortunately not complete, but one item for August 20, 1937, when
I was eight, begins:

NO CLUES ON DISAPPEARANCE OF CARMA BOY
After ten days of police investigation, no trace has been

found of Joe Carma, who vanished completely on the ninth of this month. It is not even known how he left town, if he did, since there is no evidence that he went by either bus or train. Martin's Pond, the only deep water within many miles, was dragged, but without any result.

The detective assures me that Joe Carma never returned to town, and that the name is unlisted in army records, with the FBI, or indeed any national roster from 1937 to date.

These days, I skin dive, sail my own little sloop, and have even shot some of the worst Colorado River rapids in a rubber boat. Yet it still takes almost more courage than I have to slosh through a shallow puddle that mirrors the sky.

A Bum Rap

by Marilyn Granbeck

A guy getting out of prison figures he needs two things right away: a drink and a dame. I'd made that mistake the last time I walked out the gate. This time I had it figured.

I was already thirty-eight and had been in prison more than half those years, from reform school to the state penitentiary. The parole board would take an unfavorable attitude if I came back again. Besides, my last fall was a bum rap.

I'd been in a bar and Chicago Harry, who's done time in five states, offered me a ride home. I was drunk enough not to notice how drunk he was. I fell asleep as soon as I climbed into the car and didn't come to until sirens were screaming around us. Harry had stopped and held up a gas station, the attendant set off a hidden alarm, and we were caught before we got six blocks. At the trial the kid swore I was in the car with the motor running while Harry pulled the job. I got two-to-ten.

When I got out, I wanted to stay out. I was getting too old to keep starting over at the bottom. If I went back to my old life it would only be a matter of time. I figured if I stayed away from drinking and women, I'd have a chance. So I came up with my plan.

Rule one was no drinking in bars. I'd buy a pint and have a few when I got home from the lousy job my parole officer had lined up for me. With only a pint I couldn't get into any trouble.

By staying away from bars, I also would not meet any broads to lead me to more booze and more trouble. This only half solved the problem, since I didn't really want to stay away from women. That's where the second part of my plan came in. I ran an ad in the personal column of the newspaper. I spent a long time getting it just right:

Middle-aged male, wrongfully convicted, just released after five years, desires to meet liberal-minded female with mean $$$$. Contact by phone. 777-3214. Ask for Big John.

When the paper came out, the hall phone in the boarding house rang twice. The first time, the dame was young, drunk, and sounded like trouble even over a few miles of wire. I got rid of her fast.

The second call was from Bunco Bill, who wanted to know what

I was up to, how much the take would be, what his share was, and when I'd gotten out—in that order. He laughed when I said I was going legit. We'd known each other twenty years. Bill knew more about me than the police blotter, and his information could put me away where the parole board would never find me, but Bill played the percentages and kept his eye and hand out for the easy buck. The fact that his hand was always in someone else's bag showed his shrewdness. He didn't risk his neck or freedom by pulling jobs. He was content with his cut for brainwork.

I still owed him a bundle for his help on a job I pulled twelve years ago. He wasn't happy when I got picked up before I could pay off and he was even less happy when the take vanished with the broad in whose apartment I had hidden it. Bill's memory was long when it came to money, and the five years I'd just done hadn't dimmed it. I stalled him by promising to stop by in a couple of days.

It was almost noon when the phone rang again.

"Hello?" I was gruffer than I'd meant to be. I was edgy from waiting.

"Hello. Is Big John there?"

"Who wants to know?"

"Amy Valdish."

I felt a stir of excitement. My tone softened. "This is him."

"I'm calling . . . I saw your ad in the personals."

Phase two of my plan called for a slow and easy buildup. Amy Valdish . . . she sounded middle-aged and lonely.

"I'd like to talk to you," she said.

I reviewed the steps of phase two. "Do you want to talk on the phone, Miss Valdish, or should we meet someplace?"

"I think we should meet." She didn't correct my use of Miss.

"How about the Armand Hotel coffee shop? You pick a time. Then if you change your mind you don't have to show."

"I wouldn't do that." She sounded very sure of herself. "Is two o'clock too soon?"

"It's fine."

"How will I know you?"

"I'll tell the hostess I'm waiting for you. She can point me out and you can make up your mind. I'll wait until two thirty."

"I'll be there at two," she said.

At the Armand, I sat by the window with my back to the door. She'd see my best angle first. No one had ever accused me of being handsome, but I had a rugged quality that seemed to appeal to women. I'd picked up fifteen extra pounds sitting in a cell, but the cut of the blue sport coat hid them. My angular face could be called strong instead of tough, and the streaks of gray the last five years had given my hair added a touch of dignity. At least I like to think so.

I studied the reflections in the glass. I made out the doorway and the girl in yellow who was seating people. A gray blur joined her and I concentrated on it as they came toward me. The hostess pulled out the other chair. I looked up.

The gray suit was perfectly tailored, no rack job. The sparkling pin on her lapel was real diamonds. She wore a sheer scarf at her throat, but under it I could see the wrinkles time had drawn. She was past forty and probably had been pretty once. She still wasn't bad, but her face was set in hard lines. Her hair was gray enough to look frosty; her eyes were lavender in the reflected light from the street, or maybe it was the scarf.

I smiled. She sat, putting her hands on the table palms down, like a teacher waiting for the class to come to attention. Her fingers were long and thin and the huge diamond ring looked top-heavy. She seemed unaware of it or my quick appraisal.

"Miss Valdish?"

"Yes. I told you I would come."

"I'm glad you did." I kept my voice low. "My name is John Collins."

"How do you do?"

I laughed softly at her automatic politeness and it got a twitch of a smile from her. I began to feel a little confident, but not enough to forget phase two. "You're wondering what my ad is all about, aren't you?"

She looked right at me. "Yes."

I waited while the girl poured her coffee and refilled my cup. Amy shook her head when the waitress offered a menu.

"I'll explain," I said. "Don't say anything until I finish."

She sat back and waited. Slowly, in a voice that didn't carry past the table, I told her my story. When I finished, I lifted my hands in a gesture of defeat. "I got two-to-ten and served five years in the state pen." I glanced out the window and then back at her. "I'm going to level with you. I have the feeling you're the kind of woman who appreciates complete honesty. This wasn't my first rap."

She never even blinked.

"I did six years, three months, and eighteen days on a burglary rap twelve years ago." I frowned. "That's why I didn't have a chance this time. A guy can prove he was someplace else and have ten witnesses to back his story, but it doesn't cut ice with a judge or jury. Once you have a record, you're guilty, no matter what."

The diamond on her finger sent arrows of light across the table. "You were with the holdup man," she said.

I nodded. "But I wasn't in on the job. I told the truth at the trial, for all the good it did."

"Didn't the other man tell the police you were innocent?"

"The word of an ex-con caught redhanded in a heist?" I laughed. "I was violating my parole just being with him." I traced a pattern on the tablecloth. "That's the hard part of getting out. You're not supposed to have anything to do with other ex-cons, but the straight Johns on the street won't have anything to do with you." I looked up. "That's why I put the ad in the paper."

"To meet someone who is not an ex-convict?"

"Right. I can make a few bucks as a dishwasher or dock loader, but that's not how I want to spend the rest of my life. Last time I got out I worked at the crummy jobs people are willing to give ex-cons, and all I met were other ex-cons." I shrugged. "How could I meet anyone else? When I went up for parole this time, I knew if I went back to slopping dishes I'd be in trouble before I knew it." My voice dropped. "I can't take being locked up again."

She leaned forward. "Why did you advertise for a woman of means?" The words were little chips of ice floating in the silence. At least she didn't beat around the bush.

I didn't, either. "I want a woman who can help me financially until I get on my feet." We both weighed the statement and each other. "In return I'll escort her wherever she wants to go, be on call for anything she needs. When I make it, I'll pay back every penny she's invested in me—with interest." I paused. "I just need someone to believe in me."

She looked at me. "I believe in you, Mr. Collins."

I smiled. "It was lucky for me you saw my ad, Miss Valdish . . . Amy. But I don't want you to make a hasty decision. Think about it."

She set down her cup. "I already have. I wouldn't have called otherwise. Everyone is entitled to a second chance. To make mistakes is human, John. I've made some, too, and as a result I'm lonely." Her gaze didn't waver. "I was married for a short time, but it didn't work out. Since then I've had companions and housekeepers, but they were very dull. The company of a man, an escort, should be far more satisfactory."

It seemed odd that she had to buy friends, but I wasn't going to argue. She was exactly what I'd described in my ad.

The next day I moved into the huge house two miles outside of town. It was a relic, full of crystal and silver, Oriental rugs and antiques. Except for a woman who came in every day but Thursday to cook and clean, we were alone. If Amy worried about gossip, it didn't show.

It took a while to settle into the new life I'd found. At first I kept being surprised by Amy's easy acceptance of things I'd only dreamed existed. We ate in the long dining room by candlelight, using sterling silver and bone china. After dinner, we sat in front of the fireplace drinking brandy from snifters the size of flowerpots. I smoked hand-rolled cigars she bought me, wore the brocaded smoking jacket she'd chosen. When she decided, we went upstairs; and when she said so, I spent an hour or two in her room before I went to sleep in my own. It was as if she had waited a long time for me. She was a demanding lover, but I didn't object. At forty-odd, she wasn't bad; and at thirty-eight, I finally had it made.

Amy may have been lonely before I came along, but it didn't take me long to realize that she wasn't weak. She knew what she wanted and she got it. She organized my life completely, filling the hours with the things she wanted to do. She didn't refer to my past. The question of finding me a job never came up, and I didn't mention it.

I drove her to town in the sleek black sedan a couple of times a week. She shopped often and she wasn't stingy. She bought me suits, coats, and shoes to fill a closet. She watched my diet, and my waistline began to slim down. We went to concerts, art shows, the Garden Club meetings. She really liked having me near her. She had a way of curling her fingers on my arm as though I were part of her. Once I pulled away and the quick flash of anger in her eyes showed me she didn't like it. Her fingers seemed tighter after that but I never pulled away again. Living with Amy was a lot better than a cell or that lousy boarding house. I could put up with her possessiveness in exchange for my new role as gentleman of leisure.

The only work I did was to putter in the garden or greenhouse. Amy was proud of her flowers and very fussy about them. A regular gardening service came in once a week and kept everything in top shape, but I liked to breathe the fresh air and feel the sun on my back. Also, it was the only time I ever got away from Amy for more than a minute or two.

I'd been there about two months when Bunco Bill called. Amy

handed me the receiver with a scowl. Nobody had phoned me before, and she didn't like the change in the pattern.

"Hello?"

"Long time no see, Big John. How's it going?" Bunco's gravelly voice was cool but firm.

I glanced through the archway to the living room to make sure Amy was out of earshot. "Okay, Bill. What can I do for you?" As if I had to ask.

"There's a little matter we should talk over," he said.

"I don't think that's a good idea," I answered quickly.

He laughed. "I do. I was thinking maybe I should come over and introduce myself to your lady friend. From what I hear, she's got quite a place there, and you ain't hurting none."

I lowered my voice to a whisper. "It's not what you think, Bill. I'm playing it straight."

He snorted. "So am I, Big John. I want my dough and I want it now."

"I can't—"

"Think about it, Big John. With your smarts, you'll find a way. Suppose I come out there to see you—let's say tomorrow morning about ten?"

"I can't do anything that fast!"

"Find a way," he said coldly, "or I'll find it for you." The phone clicked.

It was several minutes before I replaced the receiver and returned to the living room. I avoided Amy's eyes.

"Who was that?" she demanded.

I had trouble getting the words out. "A guy I know."

"Obviously. What 'guy,' as you so crudely put it?"

I poured the brandy and handed her a glass. My hand shook a little and my brain was on overtime trying to come up with an answer that would satisfy her without cutting my own throat. "He helped me out once, and I owe him some money."

The silence was harder than her look. I tried again. "I'm sorry, Amy, but it's the truth. I didn't make any excuses for the kind of life I led before I met you. Bunco Bill was part of that life, and he thinks I should pay off my debt."

"You have a new life now, John. I won't tolerate any ties with your old one.

I frowned. "Bill sees things differently."

Her eyes glittered. "How much do you owe him?"

I sipped the brandy, swirling the glass slowly between my palms.
"He figures ten grand." I kept my gaze on the dark liquid in my
glass. I heard her soft, indrawn breath and waited.

"And how do you figure?" There was a tight band of anger in her
tone.

I looked up and shrugged. "In cash, he only put up a couple of
hundred bucks. But he considered it an investment—one that should
have paid off. It wasn't his fault the deal fell through."

A log fell in the grate and a shower of sparks flared against the
fire screen. The tiny lights reflected in her eyes. She stared at me
for a long time. Then she put the brandy glass on the table and went
to the desk. She took out the steel box where she kept the household
money, unlocked it, and came back to me with some bills.

"I assume your 'friend' made some arrangements to collect his
money. Give him this." She fanned the money and I saw there were
five century notes. "Tell him it pays your actual debt and some
interest. It's all he's going to get. He'd better be satisfied with it.
Make sure he knows this is the *only* payoff. I want him to leave you
alone. He's not to call or contact you again in any way. You have
no ties at all with your past any more. See that he understands it."
She dropped the bills in my lap and walked out. She paused in the
doorway and looked over her shoulder."I'll wait for you upstairs."

I pocketed the dough. I was surprised at how easily she'd given
it to me. Maybe her idea would work; maybe Bill would settle for
the cash. It was a long shot, but it was worth a try. Besides, I didn't
have any choice. I finished my brandy and poked the logs to the
back of the fireplace before I turned out the lights and went up to
her.

In the morning I was up early. I watched at the front window,
hoping Amy wouldn't come down before Bill got there. I spotted him
walking up the drive and went out to intercept him. He looked a
little surprised when I steered him into the greenhouse. He kept
looking over my shoulder toward the kitchen door.

"You got my ten G's?" he asked.

I shook my head. "There's no way, Bill. You're asking the impossible."

His experienced eye took in the rows of plants, the air-conditioning
unit in the corner, the garden beyond the glass walls. He was adding
their value to that of the house and the cost of its upkeep. I wasn't
conning him. He'd probably checked and knew more about Amy's
bank account than I did.

I tried to fast-talk my way out. "Look, Bill, all my life I've wanted a sweet spot like this. Hell, for the first time I'm on easy street." I dug into my pocket and pulled out the five hundreds and waved them under his nose. "Here, take this. There's no way I can come up with the dough that stupid broad ran off with. She's got that spent long ago. And I ain't pulling any more jobs and risking more time." I avoided his cold glance. "I like the setup here, but if you push too hard, I'll have to move on."

"I'll find you wherever you go, Big John."

I tried to look unconcerned. "What good will it do if I'm broke? I haven't got the dough, and there's no way I can get it."

Bill's eyes swept around the layout. I knew what he was thinking.

"That won't work, either," I said quickly. "When she gave me the five hundred, she said that was it."

He looked at the expensive slacks and the monogrammed sport shirt I was wearing.

"She handles all the money," I added.

He reached for a cigar from his pocket and spat the end toward a shelf of seedlings. "Listen, Big John, and listen good. You have found yourself a gold mine and you'd better start working it. I'll be back in two weeks for the next installment. You should be able to come across with a grand every couple of weeks."

"Two weeks! I can't do anything that fast!"

"You'll think of something," he said with a cold smile. "Your lady friend has plenty of jewelry. She wouldn't miss a few pieces. Otherwise, the cops may uncover a few facts they've overlooked before and you could wind up back in the joint." He clamped the cigar between his teeth and his hand snaked out for the five hundred. "I'll be back two weeks from Monday." He walked out.

I watched numbly until he was out of sight beyond the high hedge. I jerked at a small sound behind me, but there was nothing. The kitchen door was closed tight and the garden was empty. My nerves were jumpy.

They didn't get any better the next two weeks. Every time I walked past the silver coffee service on the buffet, my palms began to sweat. When Amy dressed to go out, I could hardly take my eyes off the diamond earrings and rings she put on; but there was no way I could meet Bill's demand. Amy had been just as positive in hers, and I was caught between them. Even if I had found the nerve to try to take something from the house, I was never alone long enough to try it.

Amy didn't mention Bill again. It was as though the matter were settled and wiped from her mind. However, she watched me with a new kind of possessiveness that made me uneasy.

Then the deadline Bill had set passed and I began to relax a little. He hadn't phoned or come back. Maybe I had convinced him after all. Maybe the long shot was paying off.

On Thursday I was whistling as I walked into the greenhouse. Amy was standing at the sink washing her hands, Her gloves and a basket of pink and white peonies lay on the counter. She looked up. "I thought some flowers would brighten the house."

"I'd have cut them if you'd asked."

"It's such a lovely morning, I wanted some fresh air. By the way I saw some aphids on the roses. We'd better not wait for the gardener. You'll have to spray the bushes right away." She turned to inspect a shelf of cans and bottles. "Yes, I knew I still had it. There," she pointed, "use that. The directions are on the label."

I lifted down the can with the poison warning under the skull and crossbones. She picked up her basket and started for the house. "Do a good job, John. The roses are coming along so beautifully, I'd hate to lose them."

By the time I finished spraying, the sun was overhead and the day had grown hot. I left my dirty shoes by the door and walked stocking-footed across the kitchen. I heard a low murmur of voices, and when I walked into the living room I stopped in my tracks. Sitting across from Amy, looking very comfortable in the gold velvet chair, was Bunco Bill.

Bill grinned and lifted his coffee cup with his little finger stuck straight out. "Hello, Big John. Nice to see you again."

I stared. I knew then that he had phoned, but Amy had taken the call. I looked at her.

"We've been having a chat," she said carefully. "Go change those gardening clothes and join us."

I was back in less than ten minutes.

"Anyone who's done time knows the problems a man faces when he gets out," Bill was saying.

Amy frowned but looked interested. "And you think a halfway house is the solution?"

Bill lifted his shoulders. "There's no quick cure, but if the men have a place where people understand them, they have a better chance. They need time to get on their feet and find work. If they're broke and lonely, they drift right back into crime."

"And you think ten thousand dollars is enough to set up the program?"

So that was it! He was trying to con her out of the money I owed him. He didn't trust me to get it! For a minute I was mad, then the tension eased. If he got the dough, maybe he'd leave me alone—and Amy had plenty more. Maybe it was a way out. I couldn't be responsible for what Bill did with the money once he left.

Bill sipped his coffee before he answered. "For a start."

Then I knew this was only the beginning. I could hear the wheels turning in his skull, counting the dollars he could milk from Amy. He'd never be content with a slice if he could grab the loaf.

Amy lifted a plate of iced cakes and held them out to him. "Try one of these. I made them myself." She glanced at me. "None for you, John. We don't want to spoil your diet, now that you're doing so well on it."

I felt Bill's quick glance of amusement, but he let it go. He bit off half the cake in one bite.

"What do you think about a halfway house, John?" Amy asked.

I hid behind my coffee cup and tried to think. I was still thinking hard when Bill's cup clattered from his hand and a dark stain of coffee trailed down the front of his coat. His face twisted horribly behind the flecks of cake crumbs clinging to his lips. He tried to get up but his body jerked forward and he fell to the floor. He doubled up and each breath squeezed from his lungs in a painful gasp. His eyes searched mine for a second, then closed. He twitched and was still.

Amy looked at me. "He won't bother us any more, John."

I was still looking at Bill.

"I think it would be wise to bury him in the garden. Near the roses, perhaps."

My mouth opened but no sound came out.

"Don't dig too close to the Crimson Glories. They're doing so well now." She glanced at my clothes. "You'll have to change again."

I couldn't move. She had murdered Bill in cold blood for a lousy ten grand! I stared at her. No, not for ten grand! To keep me! She'd heard Bill and me in the greenhouse that morning, and she wasn't taking any chances on letting me slip away.

If I buried Bill I would be an accomplice to murder. A film of sweat coated my neck. Suddenly the easy life didn't seem worth it. Robbery is one thing, but murder—

Amy's eyes were like amethysts, hard and cold. "Do as I say, John. We wouldn't want the police."

I wasn't so sure.

"It might be difficult to explain how your friend died, especially with your fingerprints on the can of poison." Her mouth carved a smile across her face. "Go now, but don't be long. We're due at the Garden Club at two." Her eyes held mine. "A pity he didn't believe you really have a whole new life."

In the greenhouse, I saw the can of poison was gone. I wondered about the Crimson Glories and Amy's husband who hadn't been around very long. I got a shovel from the tool shed and dragged Bill between the rows of potted plants. The sun slanting through the frames of the roof was as cold as it had ever been through steel bars.

The Snatch

by Bill Pronzini

I was introduced to Louis Martinetti in the austere, walnut-paneled study of his home in Hillsborough, on the Peninsula fifteen miles south of San Franciso. He was sitting behind a dark, oblong desk set in front of heavily draped windows, both hands resting flat on the desk's polished surface, when we came in. As we approached the desk, he took his eyes from the telephone at which he had been staring and looked up.

Jack Lerner, a special investigator with the district attorney's office of San Mateo County, made the introductions. I sat down and studied Martinetti across the desk. He was a tall man, granite-hewn, hair and eyes the color of steel, nose strong and wise and Gothic, the nostrils in a perpetual flare. It was all there, just as the newspaper photographs pictured him. He looked dynamic and overpowering, and most of the other superlatives the papers like to bestow on him, but there were cracks beginning to etch the granite.

There was a gauntness to his face, a gray-shadowed hollowness to the eyes, and a tic on the left side of his face, high on the cheekbone. His full, expressive mouth was quirked oddly because of it.

Abruptly, Martinetti got to his feet and walked silently across the study to a portable bar recessed into a small alcove. He paused there, turning slightly, exposing his profile. It was very impressive.

He said to me, "Would you care for a drink?"

"No, thank you," I answered.

"Allan?"

Allan Channing, who was sitting on the leather couch across from me, shook his blond head. "Not just now, Lou." He uncrossed his legs and sat with his hands on his knees.

He was a big man, Channing, not fat, tanned in that remarkable bronzed way blond people somehow manage to achieve. His eyes were wide and blue and innocent; almost guileless. Those eyes had fooled a lot of people. That was why Allan Channing was worth something like four or five million dollars at the last estimate.

They made a pretty awesome pair, Channing and Martinetti. They were speculators, angle boys. If you live in California you know the type; it's a breeding ground for them. They are the buyers and sellers, the finaglers and cajolers, the liars and cheaters. They invariably get what they set after, and these two stood head and shoulders above the rest.

Martinetti had made and lost a million dollars three or four times over the past twenty-odd years. Channing, however, was conservative. He played it close to the vest, didn't take the wild gambles Martinetti did. He'd never come out on the short end. That was the difference between the two of them. Those who had tried to stand in the way of either man had been trampled.

Martinetti made his drink and returned to the desk. When he was seated, he looked up to where Jack Lerner and the other investigator, Ken Vlasek, were standing respectfully.

Martinetti said, "Have you told him all of it?" He rolled his eyes to me.

"No," Lerner said. "Just a sketch."

Martinetti nodded, still looking at me. "They tell me you are a very thorough man. I presume you would like to have all the details."

I had no idea why he wanted a private investigator in on this. He had Lerner and Vlasek, and they were pretty good men. Jack hadn't told me, and I had let it ride. I said, "Whatever you want to give me."

Martinetti made a pyramid with his fingers and rested his head against it. "At ten o'clock this morning, a man dressed in a dark blue business suit and carrying a briefcase entered the headmaster's office at Smithfield Military Academy in Burlingame. He introduced himself as a Mr. Edmonds, a member of my legal staff, and showed a note written on my personal stationery to Mr. Young, the headmaster. The note said that Young was to release my son, Gary, to this Edmonds on a matter of the gravest personal importance. The note was ostensibly signed by me."

Martinetti paused. It was very quiet in the dark room.

"Mr. Young summoned Gary from his class," he went on, "and he and the man then left Smithfield in a light blue 1967 Pontiac station wagon."

"How do you know about the car?" I asked.

"This Young was watching from the window of his office when they pulled away," Jack put in.

"Did he get the license number?"

Vlasek shook his head. "Didn't have any reason to. As far as he was concerned, it was on the up and up."

I looked at Martinetti. "How old is your son?"

"Eight."

"Are you in the habit of summoning him from school in this manner?"

"No," he said, meeting my eyes, "I'm not."

"Why didn't Young confirm the note with you?"

"We talked to him about that," Jack said. "He didn't think it was necessary at the time. The note was written on Mr. Martinetti's personal stationery, and the signature looked all right. Besides, Young said this bird was a smooth talker, a charmer."

"Did you get the note?" I asked.

"We got it," Jack said. "Nothing there so far. We lifted a few prints and sent them out, but you can bet we won't turn anything on them. It's a nice job, the way he pulled it off. He'd be too smart to let fingerprints trip him."

"Do you have any idea how he got your personal stationery?" I asked Martinetti.

He wagged his head faintly. "None," he said. "I suppose he could have gained access to it at my office somehow. I keep a quantity there for business purposes."

"What about a description?" I asked Lerner.

He shrugged, spreading his hands. "Tall, brown hair, medium complexion, no visible scars or deformities."

I lit a cigarette and looked around for an ashtray. There were none. I put the match in my coat pocket. "All right," I said. "Did you get the call yet?"

"At five o'clock," Martinetti said. "Allan and I had played a round of golf this afternoon, and we'd just gotten back when it came."

"How much do they want?"

Martinetti took a deep breath, releasing it slowly. "Two hundred and fifty thousand dollars," he said.

I tapped some ash into the palm of my hand. The silence seemed to build in the room. Martinetti took a long swallow from his drink.

I said, "Are you going to pay it?"

"What choice do I have?" Martinetti said. "The man on the phone made it very plain that if I didn't, the police could look for Gary in the Bay."

"Did they let you talk to him?"

"Just for a moment, yes."

"Did he seem all right?"

"Yes, considering. He was frightened, of course."

"What kind of arrangements did they give you?"

"The bills are to be in small denominations, nothing larger than a hundred. I suppose that's standard procedure."

"It's the way they usually work it," Vlasek said.

"I'm to put the money into a plain briefcase. Then I'm to wait for further instructions."

"Did they say when?"

"Sometime tomorrow. That was all the man said. Except that I . . . wasn't to call the police."

"Be thankful that you did," I said. "The police are the best friends you can have on something like this."

"Yes," Martinetti said. "Yes."

I went to the large fireplace near the desk, threw my cigarette in there and dusted the ash off my hands. Then I turned face Martinetti. "Suppose you tell me why I'm here? You've got the police in on it, and there isn't anything I can do they can't."

"They want a third party to handle the exchange," Jack said. "Nobody directly involved. I guess they figure there's too much chance of a slipup otherwise."

"You've got plenty of men available for that," I said.

"Sure, but you can figure them to spot a cop two miles off. If they tab one of my men, there's no telling what might happen."

"What about Mr. Channing here?"

"I'm sorry," Channing said from the couch. "My name was mentioned, but I'm afraid I couldn't do it. I wouldn't want to take the responsibility."

No, I thought, *but it's all right if I take it.*

I said to Martinetti, "One of your people?"

"To be perfectly honest," he answered, "there is no one I would care to trust with that kind of money."

"What makes you think you can trust me?"

Martinetti looked at Lerner. Jack said, "I stuck myself out on a limb. We've known each other a long time. When they put it to me, you were the first person I thought of."

"Yeah," I said.

"Will you do it?" Martinetti asked.

I wet my lips. I didn't like it. If I made a mistake, and something happened to the kid, I was jammed right into the middle of it. They were all watching me. I sat down again.

Martinetti said, "I'll pay you very well, of course."

"Sure," I said.

"All you have to do is make the drop" Vlasek said. "Then you're out of it."

"What about you?"

"How do you mean?"

"Will you put a tail on me? Stake out the drop area?"

Jack glanced briefly at Martinetti, "No tail," he said. "And no stakeout."

"I want my son back," Martinetti said. For the first time, there seemed to be a trace of emotion in his voice. "My son's safety is imperative above all else. I want nothing done to jeopardize him."

I thought it over. Somebody had to do it, and I wasn't in any position to back out gracefully. "All right," I said. "I'll make the drop."

Riding in Jack Lerner's car down the dark, winding roads of Hillsborough, I said, "What do you think, Jack?"

"I don't know," he answered. "It's a ticklish situation. If I stick a tail on you, or put a stakeout on the area, and something goes wrong, it's my neck."

"The same way it'll be mine if something fouls up on my end."

He was silent for a moment. Then he said, "Listen, I'm sorry to drag you into this. But there was nobody else."

"I suppose I should appreciate the confidence."

He wiped one large, red hand wearily across his face. "This is a rotten business," he said. "There's something unnatural about kidnapping. You know?"

"Yeah," I said. "I know."

I lit a cigarette, staring out at the road and the fine, affluent homes lining both sides. I asked, "Any chance of your making the guy or the car?"

"Doesn't seem to be. We had the headmaster, Young, going over mug books all afternoon and he didn't turn up a thing. Chances are our boy never did any time."

"Nothing likely on the car, either," Vlasek said from the back seat. "You can figure it to turn up stolen."

"Doesn't leave you with much, does it?"

"Nothing at all," Jack said. "Our hands are tied until after the drop is made and they release the kid."

"If they do release him," I said.

"I don't want to consider that possibility," Jack said. "Martinetti's an important man. He's got enough influence to crucify half the officials in this county if anything happens. No matter what we do."

We came down out of Hillsborough and onto El Camino Real. Jack turned south and after a few miles we went over and got onto the Bayshore Freeway, down toward Redwood City.

I broke the silence by saying, "Martinetti seems to be taking the thing pretty well."

"He doesn't shake too easily," Jack agreed. "He didn't get where he is now by yielding to pressures."

"No," I said. "I guess he didn't."

"His wife took it badly, though. She broke down when they told her, and they had to put her in the hospital. She's under heavy sedation."

I couldn't think of anything else to say, and we rode the rest of the way to Redwood City in silence. Lerner and Vlasek and I had some coffee in a restaurant near City Hall, and then I told them I'd get down sometime in the morning to wait it out. There was no telling when the second call would be made to Martinetti, though sometime later in the day seemed the best bet. Jack told me the phone company was on a twenty-four hour standby for tracing purposes, just in case.

I picked up my car and drove up Bayshore to San Francisco. I had picked up a king-sized headache somewhere along the line, and I slept very badly that night.

I was in my office at eight thirty the next morning to catch up on a few things before I left. I was punching out a report for an insurance company I had done a job for when the telephone rang.

It was a secretary to Allan Channing. She wanted to know if it would be possible for me to come by his office in San Mateo later on in the morning. I said it would.

I wondered why Channing wanted to see me. I put in a call to Jack Lerner.

"Anything come up?" I asked.

"Not much," he said. "I just talked to the man out at Martinetti's and everything's quiet there. We found the car abandoned on a side street in Belmont. At least we think it's the one."

"Stolen?"

"Early yesterday morning from the commuter parking lot at Southern Pacific. Owner works in San Francisco, and he didn't discover the theft until he came in on the train last night."

"Find anything in the car?"

"A few prints. They're still going over it. We turned up a negative

on the ones we sent out yesterday. Whoever our boy is, he doesn't
have a record and he's never been in military service."

"Have you talked to Martinetti?"

"No. Our man says he locked himself in the study all night, going
over his books or something. Channing was with him."

"Okay," I said. "I'll be down pretty soon."

I had a tasteless breakfast at a cafeteria near my office, then drove
south. I stopped for gas, and asked directions to the address Allan
Channing's secretary had given me on the phone earlier.

The building turned out to be a sprawling, ranch-style combine
in San Mateo. I parked in the adjacent lot and went inside.

Channing's secretary was a dumpy woman in her mid forties, with
pinched cheeks and efficient manner. Channing was apparently a
no-nonsense boy when it came to business.

I gave the secretary my name. She went into a private office, came
out after a moment and told me I could go in.

Channing was standing by the window, peering out through the
slats in the Venetian blinds. Sunlight slanted in across his face, and
I could see deep, purplish circles beneath his eyes.

We exchanged greetings and a perfunctory handshake, and then
I asked him what I could do for him.

He went to his desk and sank tiredly into his chair. He pressed
thumbs to his eyes. "I'd like your opinion," he said.

"Opinion on what?"

"This thing with Lou's son. You seem to know about these matters."

"Not much," I said.

"Well," Channing said, rubbing the back of his neck, "what I'd
like to know, after the ransom is paid, is the victim usually released?"

I frowned, puzzled by his question. "You can't tell beforehand,"
I said. "It takes a certain kind of individual to pull a kidnapping,
and you never know how he'll react."

"Would you say the chances were likely?"

"I wouldn't say."

"All right," he said. "I don't want to pin you down." He took a
cigar from a humidor on his desk and began to unwrap it carefully.
"What are the odds on the police catching the kidnapper? After the
ransom's been paid?"

What was he getting at? I said, "Sometimes they catch him, and

somethimes they don't. It depends on circumstance. It's not something you can predict."

"I see," Channing said. He flicked a lighter and put flame to his
cigar. After a time he said, "I suppose I should be frank with you."

"That would be nice."

"Last night, Lou Martinetti and I made a careful check of his
negotiable assets."

"And?"

"He doesn't have two hundred and fifty thousand dollars," Channing said. I hadn't expected that. I said, "He's asked you for the
ransom money, is that it?"

Channing nodded. "Yes. A loan. I'm not in the habit of loaning
money, not even to personal friends, and the sum he wants is quite
a lot of money. On the other hand, if the ransom isn't paid, and his
son is . . ." He couldn't bring himself to say it. "If that were to
happen, it would be on my conscience, mine alone. I couldn't bear
a cross like that."

"Are you going to give him the money?"

"I don't really have a choice, do I? I suppose, when I asked you
here, I just wanted some reassurance that I would get my money
back. Not that Martinetti wouldn't repay it. He would, certainly, as
soon as he was able."

"And you wouldn't like to have your money not producing any
returns."

"I'm not a hard man," Channing said defensively. "Oh, I've stepped
on a few people in my life, but those incidents were unavoidable, if
unfortunate. I'm not a driving force, the way Martinetti is."

"That's your concern," I said. I didn't want to listen to him ra-
tionalizing.

"Yes," he said. "I suppose it is." He got to his feet, extending his
hand. I took it. "Are you going out to Lou's?"

"Shortly," I answered.

"I'll be there later this afternoon," Channing said. "It will take
some time to gather the money together."

I said I would see him there, and then I left. There was something
about the man that rubbed me the wrong way.

Jack Lerner was on the phone when I got to his office in Redwood
City. He looked a little haggard, and I guessed he had been up most
of the night, too. A cup of cold, neglected coffee stood at his elbow.

He motioned me to sit down, then finished his call, hung up the receiver, and ran a hand through his thinning red hair. "That was Martinetti," he said. "No call yet."

"How does he sound?"

"Exhausted. Who isn't?"

"Yeah."

"I've had the reporters sniffing around all morning," he said. "They can smell it when something's up. We're having a hard time keeping the whole thing quiet."

I nodded. After a moment, I said, "I just left Allan Channing's office." I told him about our talk.

"I can't say that I'm greatly surprised," Jack said. "Martinetti has lost a few fortunes in his time. But Channing is as tight-fisted as they come. What made him agree to the loan?"

"He's afraid if he doesn't, and something happens to the kid, he'll have to shoulder the blame."

Jack nodded. "It would take something like that to make Channing put out."

Ken Vlasek came in. Lerner looked at him. "Anything?"

Vlasek shook his head. "They went over the car from top to bottom. Nothing there."

"Still negative on the prints?"

"Not a thing."

"Well," Jack said, getting to his feet, "I suppose we'd better head out to Martinetti's. It's nothing to wait out alone." He glanced at me. "You eaten anything today?"

"Some soggy eggs for breakfast," I told him.

"Want a sandwich before we go?"

"Not particularly," I said, "but I could use some coffee."

We went to the same restaurant as the night before, and I had coffee while Lerner and Vlasek ate. Then we climbed into Jack's car and drove up to Hillsborough.

Martinetti looked terrible. He had bags under his eyes the size of lemons, and he'd been on the bottle. He wasn't drunk, but you could smell it on his breath. He was sitting on the leather couch, staring at a point high on the opposite wall.

"Not yet?" Jack asked him when we went in.

"No," Martinetti answered. "Not yet."

"Have you talked with the hospital?"

"Yes. They're keeping Laura under sedation. They're afraid of a breakdown."

"You ought to get some sleep," Jack said. "We'll watch the phone."

"No, I'm all right," he protested.

"Whatever you say."

Martinetti asked Lerner if he'd turned up anything new, and Jack said that he hadn't, and after that there wasn't much more to be said. We sat down for the wait.

We waited mostly in silence. Martinetti got up periodically to refill his glass from the bar. He was putting a lot of it down, but he seemed to be holding it well. I went through a pack of cigarettes, thinking about anything and nothing. Jack fell asleep in his chair. He snapped awake after an hour and apologized for it, but Martinetti waved his hand. He was still staring at the spot high on the wall opposite the couch.

The call came at ten minutes past five.

The sound of the bell seemed to explode in the strained silence of the room. Martinetti came off the couch in a convulsive jump, and stood trembling in front of the desk. Jack went immediately to the extension phone in the hallway and put his hand on the receiver. I sat tensely on the edge of my chair.

"All right," Jack said from the hallway, motioning for Martinetti to answer the call. They caught up the receivers at the same time.

Martinetti said, "Hello?" in a hoarse voice.

He did not say anything else, but held the receiver to his ear for perhaps a minute, his hand white and rigid around the instrument. Then he put it down slowly, mechanically.

I looked at Jack, and he was jiggling the button violently on the hallway extension. When he got the operator, he snapped, "Did you have enough time?"

He listened for a moment, and then he replaced the receiver. The slump of his shoulders told me all I needed to know.

He came back into the study. "They couldn't trace it," he said.

Martinetti had returned to the couch. He sat there with his hands held between his knees. He looked drained.

I got to my feet. "Well?" I said to Lerner.

"Nine o'clock tonight," he said. "There's a dirt road leading off Old Southridge Road, up in the hills back of San Bruno. You're to drive in there exactly one mile. You'll leave your car in a turnaround there and walk down the embankment at the left side of the road until you reach a flat sandstone rock. You put the money on top of the rock and return to your car. Then you'll turn your car around and go back the way you came."

"Sounds kind of isolated," I said. "He's leaving himself wide open."

"Not really," Jack said. "There's another road at the bottom of the embankment. My guess is he'll be waiting down there. When he sees you make the drop and return to your car, he'll pick up the money and drive off down the lower road. There are a dozen streets he can slip into from there."

"Was there anything else he said?" I asked.

Martinetti looked up from the couch. "A warning," he said softly. "No police, and no tricks. If he's picked up, and doesn't return to a certain place at a certain time, there is someone with Gary who has instructions to . . ." He broke off, unable to continue. He buried his face in his hands.

Jack said, "When he's got the money, we'll get a call telling us where to find the boy. That's all of it."

I took a breath. "Have you got a map of the drop area? I'd like to see where I'm going."

"There's one in the car," Lerner said. He nodded to Vlasek, who left the room.

Martinetti went to the portable bar, made himself another drink, and put it away in one swallow. Jack and I looked at each other, but neither of us spoke. Vlasek came back with the map, and we spread it open on Martinetti's desk. Jack pointed out the area, and the spot the drop was to be made. When I had familiarized myself with it, and with the route I would take to get there, we folded the map and I stuck it in my pocket.

Shortly before six, Allan Channing came in somberly carrying a large brown briefcase. He spoke softly to Martinetti. Lerner, Vlasek and I left the study.

From the phone in the hallway, Jack put in a call to his office and told one of his men to pick up my car and bring it out. While he was relaying the details of the call Martinetti had received, Vlasek went to find the houseman. Presently, the two of them came back with cups of black coffee. Jack was just hanging up.

I accepted the coffee gratefully. "What time do you think I ought to leave?" I asked Lerner.

He thought about it for a moment. "Say eight twenty," he said. "That ought to be about right."

I nodded. I was beginning to feel a certain tension. The weight of the affair was settling on my shoulders now; the others were assuming passive roles. If anything went wrong tonight . . .

Well, all right, I told myself. All you have to do is follow the instructions. No games and no heroics. That's simple enough, isn't it?

The door to the study opened and Allan Channing came out. He shut the door quietly behind him. He appeared nervous.

"Lou asked to be left alone for a while," he said to us.

"You give him the money?" Jack asked.

Channing glanced at me. The look said I had betrayed a confidence. "Yes. Yes, I gave him the money. All of it."

"Did he tell you about the instructions?"

"He did, yes," Channing said, then to me, "I wouldn't want to be in your shoes tonight."

I did not say anything. Jack gave him a sharp look. Channing flushed slightly, looking away.

"I'm going out for some air, if you should want me," Channing said. He moved off abruptly toward the front door.

Jack said to me, "That one—he's more concerned about his money than the safety of Martinetti's kid."

"Yeah," I said. I put my coffee down. It had suddenly grown tasteless.

Time crawled like a slug. Seconds became lifetimes, and minutes became miniature eternities. The waiting before had been bad, but this was something else again. You could feel the pressure building, like a tangible entity through the dark and silent house.

At ten minutes until seven, the man from Jack's office showed up with my car. Channing came back from his walk a little while later, glanced briefly at us, and disappeared into another part of the house. Martinetti still had not come out of his study.

I had been chain-smoking, something I rarely do, and my throat grew raw and sore. I went to the kitchen and drank a glass of water. I had picked up another headache, and it was a parasitic pounding in my temples and in back of my eyes.

When I came back into the hallway, Lerner and Vlasek were gone, but the study door was open. I went in there, and they were standing in front of the desk with Martinetti. Channing had reappeared and was there, too. On the polished surface of the desk was the brown briefcase he had brought with him.

Martinetti, oddly, looked much better than he had before. He was still drawn and a little haggard, but the granite jaw had set and his features were controlled. His hands were steady.

He turned slightly as I approached the desk, looking at me. I could read his eyes plainly enough.

He said, "It's seven forty."

I nodded.

"You know exactly what you are supposed to do?"

I said I knew.

He was completely in command of the situation now. "I want you to know that I have complete faith in you," he said. "I am certain you will do exactly as instructed. In light of that, I hope you will not misunderstand the fact that I have locked and sealed the briefcase containing the ransom money."

I glanced at the case on the desk top. Sealing wax had been placed over the catch. I brought my eyes back to Martinetti.

"In a situation like this," I said, choosing my words carefully, "the wisest thing to do is take all the precautions available."

His smile was tired and faint, almost imperceptible. "You are an astute man," he said. "And I am very grateful for all you've done."

I did not think I wanted to say anything else. I went to the chair I had occupied earlier and sat down. Jack Lerner came over and put his hand on my shoulder reassuringly.

We did the rest of the waiting in silence.

At eight fifteen, Martinetti took the briefcase and the five of us went out through the house to where my car was parked. He gave me the case there, and I put it on the seat beside me.

Jack murmured, "Luck."

"Thanks," I said, and got the car going.

When I reached the front gate, I looked up at my rear view mirror. They were all standing there on the graveled drive, silhouettes against the twilight sky, watching me.

I drove north, slowly, both hands on the wheel, concentrating on the darkening pavement, trying to keep my mind on what lay ahead, but there was something bothering me. I couldn't place the feeling, and it made me uncomfortable. It seemed to be nagging just out of reach.

I drove through Millbrae and into San Bruno. At Sneath Lane I turned left and followed it up into the hills. It was totally dark by then, and the fog floating in across Pacifica from the ocean gave an eerie, disembodied quality to the lights of the Peninsula behind and below me. The sound of the wind was a low and mournful soul song at the windows of the car.

I found Old Southridge Road without difficulty, and the dirt road leading off of it. I slowed there, just as I made the turn into it, and pulled to the side. I looked at my watch. It was ten minutes to nine.

I lit a cigarette, checked the odometer, and then pulled out onto the road again.

I drove along the dirt road exactly one mile. There was the turnaround to my right, a flat space beneath several tall, aromatic eucalyptus trees. I stopped the car there and shut off the engine and the headlights.

It was very dark, and the night sounds were muted and directionless, distorted by the trailing vapors of fog. The luminescent dial of my watch showed that it was three minutes until nine.

All right, I thought. *Here we go.*

I caught up the briefcase and stepped out of the car. A cold breath of wind touched my face and neck, and I shivered involuntarily.

I crossed the dark and empty road and stood on the embankment at the opposite side. I could not see the road below; the fog had formed an impenetrable pocket there. I could make out shadowed forms on the surface of the bank, but they were unidentifiable through the mist. I knew he couldn't see me, either, but he knew I was here. He'd have heard the car.

I took a firmer grip on the briefcase, hefting it in my hand, and started down the embankment—and then I stopped. I stopped cold. A dark thing moved up along my back and settled between my shoulder blades, prickling the skin with viscid fingers.

I raised the briefcase in front of my eyes and held it there with both hands, and I knew what it was that had been bothering me—the case had no weight. That stopped me.

I had first noticed it, but attached no significance to the fact, when Martinetti handed it to me at my car earlier. Money is heavy. Two hundred and fifty thousand dollars in small bills was sure to be heavy, but this case felt airy, light, almost as if it contained nothing but . . .

The dark thing moved higher onto my back. A thought began to pound at my brain, growing in magnitude, fusing into a possibility I did not want to accept, but could not deny.

I knew there was only one way I could find out for sure. I had to look inside that briefcase. My fingers jumped to the locked and sealed catch—and froze there.

There wasn't time. There was a man down there, hidden in the fog and darkness, I knew that for certain. He might become frightened by the delay, and panic and run. What would happen to Gary Martinetti if I were wrong? And I could be, I knew that. I could be dead wrong.

My throat was dry and parched. I tried to work saliva into my mouth. I had to make a decision, and I had to make it quickly. If I hesitated too long . . .

The sound of a twig cracking, a thin report, drifted up to me from somewhere beneath the blanket of fog, and I knew in that instant that there was only one thing I could do; I did not have the right to do anything else.

Once again, I started down the embankment. I had gone a few yards, making my way through the tangled grasp of unseen growth, when I saw the flat rock. I went directly to it, keeping my eyes fixed there. I placed the briefcase on its top, just as I had been instructed, and then I turned and went back up the embankment, and across the road, and into my car.

I started it and made the turn before I switched on the headlights. I drove back the way I had come, slowly. I was thinking of the briefcase, the light and airy briefcase; and I was thinking of the possibility that still burned itself into my brain, the terrible possibility that could not be proved now, perhaps could not ever be proved.

They were waiting for me when I got back to Martinetti's home in Hillsborough, their faces tired and impassioned and drawn. I listened to their questions, and gave them the answers. I did not say anything of the thoughts rotating in my mind, but I could not bring myself to meet Martinetti's eyes.

Twenty-five minutes after I had returned, at ten fifteen, the telephone rang.

Martinetti sprang to his desk, and Jack Lerner to the hallway extension, and they lifted the receivers simultaneously. I watched the cathartic relief ebb and flow across the granite features of Martinetti's face, and the glistening drops of wetness form at his eyes, and I thought, *Can he be acting? Is it possible for him to have been acting all this time?*

When the conversation ended, Martinetti let the receiver slide from his fingers to bang on his desk. He sank against the wood, his entire being giving the appearance of emotional draining. "They've got the money," he said in a barely audible voice. "They said Gary had been released, and that we can look for him in the parking lot of the shopping center. They said he's all right, and he knows we're coming."

I turned away as Vlasek and Channing went to Martinetti's side, and looked at Lerner talking animatedly into the hallway extension, ordering the closest patrol unit to the Hillsdale shopping center in

San Mateo. Then I stood and went to the study window, lifting aside the heavy drapes there, and looked out at the winking lights of the Peninsula.

I did not trust myself to think.

Ten minutes later, Lerner's office called to say Gary Martinetti had been found, unharmed and in good spirits, and was being taken to the San Mateo police station.

Two months have passed now, since it happened. The police have not caught the kidnapper yet. When they questioned the boy, he was unable to add anything to the original description Mr. Young and Smithfield Military Academy had given them. The man had been very nice, the boy told them, and had allowed him everything he asked for. He did not know where he had been kept prisoner, except that it was in a nice house somewhere, and Lerner and his men had not located it. The boy said that there was only one man, and that when the man went out he was locked in one of the bedrooms. He hadn't minded that too much, he said; there were lots of books for him to read, some of his favorites.

A week after the boy was found, Martinetti sent me a check in the mail for five thousand dollars. I returned it to him with a polite note saying that I did not feel I could accept the money. He tried to call me after that, but I refused to talk to him. He spoke to Jack Lerner, and Jack called me to ask what was the matter. I put him off with vagaries; there was no purpose to be served in bringing my possibility out into the open, not without corroboration.

Perhaps I'll never know the real answer behind the kidnapping of Gary Martinetti, but the other morning I read in the newspaper that Louis Martinetti had made what amounted to a fortune on some kind of large scale real estate deal in Southern California.

I called a friend of mine who works at the *Chronicle*.

"I don't know the whole story," he told me. "It's very hush-hush. But Martinetti and a couple of others put up a sizeable chunk to buy this property down there."

"How much of a chunk?" I asked.

"Three, four hundred thousand apiece, would be my guess," my friend said. "Cash money. Martinetti engineered the deal, a real stab in the dark that paid off, and there were a few heads that rolled because of it. He's ruthless, you know."

"Yeah," I said, and I was thinking about what Allan Channing had told me. Martinetti had not been too far removed from bankruptcy.

I thought about a lot of other things, then, just as I had the night on the dirt road. I thought about the note written to the headmaster at Smithfield, the note written on Martinetti's personal stationery and carrying a signature that wasn't questioned. I thought about Channing's reluctance to lend money, even to a personal friend and especially on some wildcat deal, and how Jack Lerner had said it would take something like a kidnapping to make him part with it. I thought about how Martinetti was alone in his study for a considerable length of time after Channing had given him the money, and how it would have been so very simple for him to have taken the money out and hidden it somewhere, and then to refill the briefcase with newspaper.

I thought about that briefcase, and how light and airy it felt. I thought about how it was locked and sealed, and how the reason for that could have been Martinetti's fear that I would open it to check on the contents.

I thought about the man who had kidnapped Gary Martinetti, the single man, the man who had treated him so well and provided him with books to read, his favorite books.

I thought about all those things, and when I was finished thinking, I still did not know the answer. The circumstantial evidence was full and complete, but there was not a shred of concrete proof. When I placed the briefcase on that rock, unopened, it is conceivable that I helped Louis Martinetti achieve a perfect and unpunishable crime.

Because I don't know, and because my mind refuses to accept the existence of a man so merciless, so cruel, as to arrange the kidnapping of his own son for personal gain, I am not sorry I did it that way.

Night Storm

by Max Van Derveer

Ed Adams had been murdered. His body had been found by his wife Maude in the wind-tilted red barn. A pitchfork stuck up from his back. Now, anyone in his right mind can tell you a man doesn't take his own life by ramming a pitchfork between his shoulder blades.

The Midwest sun was hot, the sky was blue, the air was dry. It was a good day for a funeral, too good, actually, for the man we were burying, and certainly better than the night he had been killed. There had been a summer storm that night, one of those noisy storms with lightning flashing and thunder a constant rumble. Sheriff Malone had already theorized the storm had helped the killer. The noise of the thunder had undoubtedly covered Ed Adams' scream when the fork had been shoved into him. Nobody on the Adams farm had heard Ed cry out; not Maude nor their daughter Elsie Lou, who were in the main house, nor Abe and Maryanne Carter, who were in the tenant house.

At least, that's what they had told Sheriff Malone.

I stood in the intersection of the main corner in the business district, blocking traffic from three directions so the car procession could travel uninterrupted from Jeff Brown's funeral parlor out to the cemetery on the east city limit. Malone was at the cemetery entrance. If you want to be technical, neither of us had to be at these posts. Funeral processions are under the jurisdiction of the town's two-man police department, but Nestor is a small county-seat town and Malone and I always give a helping hand if we aren't busy with county business.

I kept the long procession moving with a constant waving of my arm. No doubt about it, this was the biggest funeral we'd had in Nestor since we buried old Avon Henry, the son of the man who had founded Henry County. Actually, the turnout of folks was kinda amazing.

It was Maude and Elsie Lou, of course. Folks were paying their respects, all right, but not to Ed Adams. Ed wasn't our kind. He had been arrogant, an egotist, and downright mean. He hadn't liked people and people hadn't liked him. That kind of attitude probably had helped him amass his fortune, all right, but it hadn't earned him any badges for congeniality.

Maude and Elsie Lou were different. Folks liked them although nobody understood how Maude had put up with Ed for twenty-nine years, and everyone was sure that someday Elsie Lou would tell her father where he could go. You just can't totally dominate two people without something's snapping sooner or later. Well, it had snapped for Ed, okay. Folks weren't actually saying it was Maude or Elsie Lou—or maybe the two of them together—who had shoved the fork into Ed's back, but there was plenty of over-the-fence speculation.

They finished burying Ed by three thirty that afternoon. From my vantage on the slatted bench in the shadow of the ancient courthouse, I watched the cars return to the business district from the cemetery while I waited for Malone, and I knew the feeling of a necessary task's having been completed. Well, almost completed; there was the investigation yet. Malone and I were going to have to determine just who had killed Ed. Malone had thought it best to delay the prying until after the funeral out of respect to Maude and Elsie Lou, but now the funeral was over so . . .

I watched Malone brake the county sedan in a long tree shadow at the curb. He joined me on the bench. He was perspiring freely as he jackknifed his long, weathered frame beside me with a sigh of relief and lit a cigarette. Then he reflected, "It's been eighteen years since we've had a murder in Henry County. I'd been sheriff almost seven years when old Bob Morgenthaw took a shotgun to Rudy Paine. You didn't know Bob or Rudy, did you, Thad?"

"No."

He wagged his head. "There was no mystery there. Old Bob was a pretty big cattleman in these parts and he caught Rudy short-weighting some of his stock at the sale barn and that was it. Old Bob drove out to his place, got the gun, came back into town, and blasted Rudy. He didn't even bother to kite out, but just sat there at the barn with the gun cradled, waiting for me to come and get him."

"Sounds like this Rudy was due a killin'."

"Yeah, maybe."

"Ed Adams was due a killin', Barry. You can't argue that."

"Uh-huh," he said thoughtfully.

"You know what I mean," I said, instantly defensive.

He smoked, silently.

"He killed my wife. As sure as we're sittin' here, Barry, he murdered—"

"No," Malone interrupted. "It wasn't murder, Thad. He struck Velda with his car, true. He'd had a drink, true. But he wasn't drunk. The tests proved that. And Velda *did* step from between two parked cars into Ed's path. People saw that much."

"He ran over her just like he ran over everyone he ever knew," I said sourly.

"And he paid."

"Paid? A suspended sentence! Fined! Is that how much value you put on a human life, Barry?"

Malone looked at me, his deep blue eyes narrow under shaggy brows. "I've never heard you talk like this, fella."

"You've never seen me roll around in that empty bed at night, either."

"You've stored up a lot of hate."

"So it's spilling over," I said bitterly.

"Enough?"

I measured his look. "For what?"

"To kill Ed Adams? You were off duty that night."

I continued to measure him, then said, "What do you think?"

He was quiet for a long time. Then he dropped the cigarette and twisted it against the cracked sidewalk with a toe of his shoe. "You could have, but I don't think you did." Then he stood up and was at ease again. Towering over me, he allowed a crooked grin. "So let's find out who did. Maude corralled me at the cemetery. She wants us to drive out to the farm."

"Now?"

"She'n Elsie Lou were goin' home alone. She turned thumbs down on folks goin' with 'em. She wants to talk to us."

"So maybe we don't know Maude Adams like we thought we did, huh?"

"How's that?"

"She sounds mighty cold-blooded to me."

"Could be." He shrugged.

The Adams place was on the highway east of town, about a mile out. One thing about Ed Adams, he had been a neat man and his place reflected it. The buildings had been kept up and the thick-grassed, deeply-shaded yards in front of the large, white frame main house to the left of the only red shale drive in all of Henry County, and the smaller, yellow-tinted tenant house to the right of the drive looked manicured. Adams land stretched out in every direction from the two houses, was tautly fenced, and sprouted crops that appeared laid down by a slide rule. Straight ahead when Malone turned the county sedan into the drive was the red barn, the death scene. It had been tilted slightly by an early spring windstorm and now looked a bit incongruous with the other buildings. If Ed had lived, the barn would have been straightened by summer's end.

Maude and Elsie Lou were in webbed chairs in the front yard of the main house. They stood as Malone braked the sedan under a large oak at the edge of the turnaround. They had changed clothing, Maude forsaking the simple black dress she'd worn to the funeral for a bright cotton; Elsie Lou, bare-legged, tanned and healthy looking at nineteen, wearing a white blouse, pink skirt, and scuffed moccasins, her golden hair catching arrows of sunlight that pierced the tree leaves.

Maude was stony-faced when she greeted us. On Elsie Lou's oval face you could see a strange mixture of suppressed feelings deep in her green-flecked eyes. The shock of her father's death—*how* he had died—was still there, and there was the strain of the past few days; but far back, if you looked hard, you could also find relief. More important, I thought, was what you *couldn't* find in those eyes: grief.

Maude put us in chairs. "Barry," she said in a firm voice, "you have questions to ask. I thank you for waiting until now, but I see no reason for further delay."

"You're standin' up well, Maude," Malone said.

I knew he was stalling, organizing in his mind, putting his questions for her and Elsie Lou in proper order. He was that kind of man. Actually, I was more interested in Elsie Lou.

I didn't hold it against her for not grieving. I didn't know all of the trials an attractive, nineteen-year-old girl had endured while being reared by a man the likes of Ed Adams, but enough were common gossip in Nestor to understand why this girl might find a certain amount of solace in his passing. Ed Adams had ruled his daughter with an iron hand. She hadn't lacked the necessities, of course, but she had missed out on most of the frills and fun of blossoming into the teens, the most important gap being boys. Ed Adams had been a passionately displeased man when it came to Elsie Lou and boys. No young feller in all Henry County would go near Elsie Lou Adams if he was interested in self-preservation because Ed would've had his head for breakfast.

On the other hand, there was Fred Tole, whose father owned the only hardware store in Nestor. Fred was Elsie Lou's age, a first-year college boy now home for the summer vacation and different from most of the young'uns around the county. He was a good lad, easygoing most of the time, seldom in any kind of trouble, and found a laugh in most things. Folks, me included, liked Fred Tole, but the boy had a polite, defiant streak in him, too. If he felt he was correct, if he felt he was being properly respectful, he stuck by his guns in any controversy. He wouldn't be pushed. It had been like that with him and Elsie Lou. He was interested in the girl, had coveted her with proper respect, politeness, and kindness and, in this, he had firmly defied Ed Adams. I'm not sure that Fred Tole had ever actually told Ed to take his nineteenth century inhibitions and plumb go fly a kite, but the boy had that kind of gall in him.

Attach to this a liking by Elsie Lou Adams for Fred Tole and his ways, and then mix in a generous amount of turnabout when it came to Ed Adams, satisfying his own lusts with Maryanne Carter, who lived in the yellow tenant house, and you could see where Elsie Lou might find it difficult to summon grief over her father's demise.

It also made you wonder about Maude Adams. The woman was not stupid. She was not constructed of stone. She had to be aware of her husband's passion, and somewhere behind the carefully controlled outer shell there had to be emotions.

I sat in the chair listening to Malone's questions and Maude's answers, and attempted to inventory both Maude and Elsie Lou without being obvious. Maude was blunt, completely resigned to the necessity of the investigation. Elsie Lou sat quietly, listening intently, I thought. Occasionally, I'd catch her sliding an oblique glance toward me. A quick, uncertain smile would twitch across her faintly painted lips and then she would again concentrate on the words between her mother and Malone.

I started to pay attention to those words, too. Malone was finally getting down to the meat of things.

"All right, Maude," he said, "this is what we know. Ed left the house about eight o'clock. He didn't say where he was going. He—"

"You knew my husband, Barry," Maude put in. "He wasn't one for words."

Malone continued as if he had not been interrupted. "The storm came up about nine. Elsie Lou went to bed. She doesn't like storms. But you sat in the front room watching television. Then along about eleven you heard a car turn in. You thought it was your husband returning home, but when Ed didn't come into the house a few minutes later, you became curious and went to a window and looked out. You saw Abe Carter's car over by the tenant house. It was Abe you had heard drive in, not Ed. I understand Abe attended an American Legion meeting in town that night."

"Yes," Maude nodded to all of it.

"Were there lights on in the tenant house?"

"Yes," Maude said firmly and then she turned to her daughter. "Elsie Lou, bring a pitcher of iced tea."

"I'll pass, Maude," Malone said.

"Me, too," I echoed.

"Then fetch me a glass, Elsie Lou."

The girl's face was blank as she left us to enter the house, but I had a strong suspicion she knew why she was being sent on the errand.

Malone took quick advantage of her absence. "The morning after Ed was killed, Maude, his car was found parked in a lane only a half mile down the road from here."

"I know," she said without expression.

"He left the house around eight. He could've walked back and then Abe could've come home from the Legion meeting sooner than was expected."

"It wasn't Abe, Barry."

"Why are you protecting him?"

"A woman learns to put up with a lot of things in life, Barry Malone. Maybe I've put up with more than most women should, Elsie Lou bein' the main reason. A nineteen-year-old girl needs a home, no matter what. On the other hand, I never would protect the man who killed my own husband. It wasn't Abe Carter."

"I wish I could be as sure, Maude."

"I saw the man run from the barn."

"You're standin' at the window, you're lookin' over at the Carter place, and you see this man run from the barn."

"It was raining buckets, Barry, but there was so much lightning it was almost as if the world was lighted."

"But you didn't recognize the man."

"I know it was a man, that's all."

"And not Abe?"

"No, I don't think it was Abe."

"A moment ago you were positive."

"The man who came from the barn didn't run to the tenant house. He ran off toward town."

"Which doesn't necessarily eliminate Abe Carter."

"Well, no, but—"

"Was he built physically like Abe?"

"No . . ."

"Was he young, middle-aged or—"

"Barry, I just don't know!"

"Could it have been the Tole boy?"

"Fred Tole?" Maude looked startled.

"Ed's thinking about Elsie Lou and boys wasn't exactly a secret, Maude," Malone said flatly, "and we all know Fred Tole. The boy has a defiant streak in him a mile wide."

"It could have been Fred," Maude said slowly, "but I don't think it was."

Malone switched his line of questioning suddenly. "Maude, why did you go down to the barn?" he asked. "I mean, it was raining hard, it was—"

"It was a hunch, Barry. A . . . " she shrugged " . . . feeling. I saw a man running and I knew something wasn't right."

"You didn't kill your husband, did you?"

"No!" she denied emphatically

"You didn't hear Abe drive in, go to the window, watch Abe enter the yellow house over there, then see your husband sneaking out the back door and bolting for the barn?"

"It could've happened that way," she admitted, "but it didn't."

Malone seemed to ponder her answer, and then he stood suddenly, just as Elsie Lou came out of the house carrying two glasses of iced tea. "Okay, Maude," he said. "Guess we'll chat with the Carters for a few minutes. I see their car over there."

"They're home," she said. "They drove in from the funeral just ahead of us. They're going to be leaving in a couple of weeks. I've given Abe notice. We both agree it will be much better if he and Maryanne leave the county now. I'll find someone else to work the land."

Barry and I crossed the shale drive, and the rear door of the small tenant house opened as we approached. Abe Carter, large, rawboned, balding at thirty, necktie pulled down, white shirt collar opened, pushed the screen door open for us and said, "Come in, come in, sheriff. We saw you comin'."

His wife sat at the kitchen table. She had changed into shorts and a blouse, filling them both well. Her long, bare legs were crossed, the top foot was cocked under the table, and a brown loafer hung loose from her toes. Her red smile for the both of us was generous; then she lifted a cigarette to those lips, inhaled deeply.

"We can offer you a beer," she said.

"No," Malone refused.

I remained silent.

Maryanne Carter's dark eyes laughed at me; her lips looked swollen and sensuous as she pulled on the cigarette. Drat her! She disturbed me—she'd disturb any man—she knew, and she was laughing at me.

"Well, I'm going to have one," she said. She left the table, took a can from a small refrigerator and snapped a pop top.

Her husband was at a small sink opposite us. I concentrated on him. There was a window over the sink, but the cotton curtains were closed against the late afternoon sun. I watched him part the curtains, look out toward the drive and the main house, then turn to us. When he found me surveying him, his face reddened slightly.

"Habit is strong, I guess," he said with a sheepish grin. He came to the table, scooped up the beer can quickly, and drank. "This is nasty business, huh, sheriff?" he asked Malone. "Tough on Mrs. Adams and that girl over there."

"Yeah," Malone agreed. Then he hit Abe between the eyes. "Maude tells us you folks are pushin' on."

Abe reddened again and fidgeted. "Tha's right."

Did I detect an edge of animosity?

"Know where you're goin'?"

"No."

"But you know *why* you're goin'," Malone said significantly.

These hardnose tactics surprised me. This wasn't the Malone I knew. Normally his questions were pointed but gentle. I shot a look at him. He appeared grim, determined.

Abe said, "Well, we have our reasons, naturally." The words were clipped.

"So I've heard."

Abe was abruptly defiant. "What does that mean?"

Malone looked down at Maryanne. "Ed Adams just didn't happen to be over here the night he was killed, did he?"

She arched a finely penciled brow. "Sheriff, I think you have a dirty mind."

"Your husband, I understand, was in town, at a Legion meeting."

"So?"

"You tell me, Mrs. Carter."

"There's nothin' to tell!" Abe cried out, his face now fiery red. "Look, these stories about Ed Adams and Maryanne are . . . are distorted. They—"

"Ed Adams was an *old* man, sheriff," Maryanne put in. She looked smug, chuckled, drew on the cigarette. "Man, if I wanted to dip around, do you think I'd pick on the ancient? I'd . . . well, I'd be a helluva lot more inclined to go along with some guy like your deputy here."

I felt on fire as she chuckled again. I wished I was somewhere else—anywhere. The scent of her was suddenly heavy in the tiny kitchen.

Malone came to the rescue. He said stonily, "You had reason to kill him, Abe."

Abe wailed, "No more than anyone else!"

"Like whom?" Malone snapped.

"Well . . . " Abe hesitated, shuffled his feet. "What about Mrs. Adams?" he said quickly. "That story of hers about a man runnin' in and out of the barn could be . . . could be a lotta hogwash. Mrs. Adams had plenty of reason to want Ed Adams dead! She inherits this place, doesn't she?"

"And if she does?"

"Well, a section of land ain't to be sneered at."

"Do you really think it happened that way, Abe?" Malone paused. "And for that reason?"

Abe fidgeted again, suddenly was silent.

"I'd rather talk about a man who wrote a check about a year ago and used Ed Adams' signature," Malone said.

Abe stiffened. "That's finished!"

"Was it?" Malone shot a glance at Maryanne again. "Or was Ed usin' it as a club to get somethin' he wanted?"

"No! It wasn't like that a-tall!"

"I'm afraid it was, Abe. Ed Adams wasn't the kind of man to let another fella beat him out of anything. With Ed Adams, the other fella *always* paid. I knew somethin' was up the day he came to me and wanted to press charges against you, and then came back later and said to forget the whole thing. I didn't know what Ed had in mind then, but it became obvious later. Both you and Maryanne have been payin' a steep price for that check."

"Not me, sheriff," she said from the table, a flicker of a smile playing at the corners of her red mouth. "Ed Adams never was *that* much trouble—for me," she said.

She hit me hard. I'd never known her kind of woman. You hear about them, you read about them, but I'd never known one.

She jarred Malone, too. He didn't look it, but I knew that inside he was caught up in loathing distaste.

He turned suddenly and went out of the house, but we were in the sedan and heading back to Nestor before he finally exploded, "Damn, why do they make that kind of women, Thad?"

I didn't have an answer.

"That check! That damned check!"

"Ed Adams had a hold," I admitted.

"On Abe maybe! Not on that woman! She just doesn't give a damn! She could have filed a complaint with me!"

"Abe," I pressed.

"Yeah," Malone said. "He probably snapped. Finally. But how are we gonna prove it?"

Nestor was quiet in five o'clock heat.

"You want me to drive you home?" Malone asked.

I shot him a look. "I thought we might be gonna talk to the Tole boy now. Change your mind?"

"I've already talked to his father. The two of them, Fred and Leonard Tole, were in Des Moines the night Ed was killed."

"Oh?" I digested that, then: "Well, if we're finished for the day I'll buy you a drink in my kitchen."

His grunt was acceptance.

He braked the county sedan in the drive beside the small bungalow I once had shared with a wife but now occupied alone. We went around to the shaded back yard.

"Park," I told him. "The house will be hot."

He sat on the third step going up to the cluttered back stoop. The stoop needed cleaning. I'd have to get to that chore some day soon—along with a lot of other domestic chores. It seemed that ever since Velda had been killed things had piled up around the house.

An old broom had fallen across the screened door and my runabout galoshes were in the way. I set the broom aside and kicked the galoshes out of my path.

Malone talked to me through the screen door while I dug out ice cubes and mixed the bourbon and tap water. "You got any definite ideas about the killin', Thad?"

"Sure. Abe Carter."

"He was at the Legion meeting. I've checked."

"Sure, but Maude said she saw this guy runnin' from the barn *after* Abe got home."

"And then again maybe someone else was lurking 'round the place."

"Huh?"

"Maybe someone else saw Abe going into the Legion Hall that night. Maybe someone else had a yen for Maryanne Carter. Maybe someone else went out to the Adams place, found Maryanne busy, became caught up in jealousy, desire—and revenge—chased Ed Adams into his barn, killed him   "

With a drink in each hand, I kicked open the screen door. Barry Malone couldn't prove a thing—except that he sat there on my back porch steps and he was picking red shale chips from the dried mud caked on the shoe scraper on the bottom step.

He twisted and looked up at me. "I only know of one driveway in the entire county that's shaled," he said.

I stood frozen.

"You know," he went on, "a man ain't had occasion to wear galoshes since the night Ed was killed. That's the last time it rained. I'd like to see your galoshes, Thad. Now!"

I didn't attempt to run—not from *this* Malone.

The Right Move

by Al Nussbaum

Jeff Cranston crouched in the telephone booth, peering out through the dirty glass at the bus station waiting room. There had been a price on his head for a month, but this was the first time he'd felt even a twinge of fear. He had been certain no hired killer was ever going to put a bullet into his head. Now he wasn't so sure.

He'd just missed being seen by Willie the Finger. If Cranston hadn't seen him the instant Willie stepped through the entrance, there was no telling how long he could have expected to live. Or, if the waiting room had a row of wall-mounted phones instead of the ancient booths, he'd have had no place to duck from sight. It was luck, pure blind luck, that had saved him; and, for Cranston, being saved by luck was almost as bad as not being saved at all.

He prided himself on always making the right decision. He saw himself as a man who could size up a situation instantly, ignore all the irrelevant data and arrive at the best course of action without hesitation. When Nick Foley had given him the package to deliver and let it slip that the package contained money, Jeff Cranston hadn't paused an instant before deciding to keep it for himself. The package had weighed fifty pounds. Even if it had been full of one-dollar bills, it would have been worth the risk of crossing Foley.

As it turned out, the package had been stuffed with twenty-dollar bills, but it wasn't until Cranston had spent a few dozen of them that he noticed they all had the same serial number.

It was too late to get back the counterfeit bills he'd spent, so Cranston did the next best thing. He replaced the missing bills with mint-fresh, genuine notes. He then resealed the package and delivered it, explaining away his lateness with a story about car trouble. There hadn't been much risk. No one was likely to count phony money as carefully as the real thing; and no matter how good the real money might look, the people to whom he had taken it believed all of it was homemade. The substitution wouldn't be discovered.

Cranston had been right. Weeks went by and nothing happened. Then, all on the same weekend, fifty-eight people were picked up in ten different cities for passing counterfeit twenty-dollar bills. When Nick Foley heard about it, he swore imaginatively and sent Jeff Cranston out to buy the early editions of the newspapers.

When Cranston saw the papers, he pointed his car toward the city limits and kept going. That had seemed like the right move.

The newspapers told how the Treasury Department had been expecting a big push of near-perfect counterfeit. Weeks before, several bills were detected by Chicago banks. Because they were from a new series and of the highest quality, the police knew it was just a matter of time before the bills showed up again in huge quantities. They distributed fliers describing the bills' few flaws and listing their serial number. After that, they had lain in wait and simply scooped up anyone who tried to pass one of the bills.

Jeff Cranston realized that the bills he had passed prematurely destroyed the surprise of Nick Foley's push. Instead of having an entire weekend to dump the phony money undetected, all of Foley's pushers had been busted. Cranston knew that all the protesting in the world wouldn't do him any good. This fiasco cost Foley a fortune and was going to cost him another one in legal fees. He wouldn't wait until he was certain he had his leak. Everyone who had handled that package was going to take a one-way trip to the cemetery. If a few innocent heads rolled, that wouldn't bother Foley.

Cranston hadn't stopped driving until he'd put a thousand miles between himself and his former employer. After that, he sold his car, bought a plane ticket and kept right on traveling. A month passed, a month during which Cranston had been in almost constant motion. Then, just as he was beginning to feel he could never be traced, and was thinking of looking for a place to stop, Willie the Finger somehow caught up with him.

Not that Willie the Finger was, by himself, an especially formidable enemy. He wasn't. At five foot two, he was two hundred pounds of soft, yielding flab, about as unimpressive as a man could be. However, Willie knew Cranston by sight and it was well known that Willie was the finger man for the most successful assassin in the business. The Exterminator was the only hired gun who never defaulted on a contract. He always got his man. During the ten years he had been operating he'd never failed.

Part of the killer's success was due to his talent for his profession, the rest was the result of his total anonymity. He had to be cold-blooded and possess lightning-like reflexes, judging from the long list of victims he had dispatched with his .45 caliber handgun; and no one knew who he was. It was Willie who accepted or rejected all contracts offered. Willie was the one who pointed out the victims. Willie was the one who collected the fees. It was like something out of a comic book, but it was real.

Now, Jeff Cranston hid from Willie the Finger because he knew The Exterminator, and the .45 that was his trademark, had to be close by. If Willie saw him, he would give some secret signal to the killer, and from then on Cranston would have to fear every unfamiliar face in a world full of strangers. It had been bad enough knowing there was surely a price on his head that every hood in the country would be trying to collect, but knowing The Exterminator had taken up the hunt was worse.

The fact of Willie's presence carried a frightening implication. Chicago was far behind, but for some unknown reason they had expected Cranston to be here. They must know him better than he knew himself, because his route had been completely aimless. Or maybe he was unconsciously conforming to some pattern they had noticed in the behavior of previous fugitives.

Jeff Cranston watched Willie the Finger move slowly back and forth across the waiting room. He kept the door of the phone booth slightly ajar so the dome light would remain dark, and he would have a better chance of remaining undetected. If the booth looked unoccupied, Willie might not even give it a glance.

The fat man turned suddenly and headed directly toward the line of telephone booths. Cranston wrapped his fingers around the butt of the snub-nosed .38 he carried in a belt holster. He resolved to blow the fat man's head off if he were seen. If the fat man spotted him, Cranston would have nothing to lose, and he wasn't going to die cheaply.

Willie the Finger never quite reached the booth where Cranston waited. He turned sharply when he was almost there and struggled into the vacant booth next to it. Cranston heard the sound of a coin being dropped into the phone slot, followed by the clicks of a rapidly-spinning dial.

Willie had an exceptionally resonant voice, which penetrated the thin partition between the booths as clearly as though there were no wall. "It's me—Willie," he announced. "I'm at the bus station. I looked aroun' real good, but he ain't here."

There was a pause while Willie gave the person on the other end a chance to talk, then he said, "Yeah, I know this's where he should be startin' t' feel a pinch, but maybe he pulled a score somewhere and picked up more money. That's possible."

That explained how they'd known where to look for him. It had been no big trick to find his flashy sports car and learn how much he had received for it. That told them approximately how much money he had. From there it had taken only simple mathematics to figure out when the money would be so low he'd be reduced to riding buses. They must've had people watching for anyone with his description. If someone had reported seeing him in this area, that's all it would have taken to bring them to the bus station in force. Luckily, Cranston had been careful about having his picture taken. A description is never as good as a photograph.

"Three of Nelson's boys are here. They know what he looks like—a sharp dresser, thirty-five, medium height, longish black hair, mustache, travelin' alone."

Cranston touched his bare lip where his mustache had been, but he didn't feel much better. He fit the description in every other way, and it would be expected that he had probably shaved off the mustache.

"Right! I'll come back now and wait with you. Nelson's boys will stay here an' keep an eye out for Cranston. If they see him, they'll stick with him an' call me." Another pause, shorter this time, followed by, "If he's aroun', they'll spot him." There was the sound of the handset being dropped into its cradle, then Willie the Finger struggled out of the booth and waddled away.

Cranston didn't know who Nelson was, and hoped he never found out. Foley had connections all across the country, though, so it wasn't a surprise that he had been able to borrow Nelson's "boys."

He peeked out at the waiting room, trying to spot the watchers. He couldn't; they were good. Whoever they were, they had managed to blend with the normal scene. Perhaps the cabdriver loitering near the front entrance was one of them, or the old guy having his shoes shined near the magazine stand. Cranston couldn't be sure.

There were three long benches in the waiting room; each was about sixty feet long, holding a scattered assortment of travelers. There were old men, women with children, teenagers, and one young man in a Marine Corps uniform who was probably on his way home. Several of them could have been there to watch for Cranston.

Cranston wished it were earlier. It was after midnight, and the crowd was sure to thin out more than it had already. As it was, there was no one else in the place who fit his description. Soon, however, one of the watchers was sure to become restless and check the phone booths. The longer he waited, the less chance there was that he'd be able to make the right move. Time was on the side of the watchers.

Then Cranston saw the cop. He was moving along the line of the nearest bench, stopping to speak to the least prosperous-appearing of the generally down-at-the-heels group. The way a few groped in their pockets for tickets to display, while others got up and left the terminal, made it plain he was rousting the derelicts.

There was a woman sitting opposite Cranston's booth. She appeared to be in her late twenties or early thirties and had no luggage. There was a large shoulder bag on the seat beside her, but that was all. Her straight, shoulder-length hair was a dull, mousy brown. The light blue cotton suit she wore was years out of style and wrinkled badly, and her shoes were scuffed and worn.

The closer the cop approached, the more agitated the woman became. She picked up her oversized bag and put it on her lap, then returned it to her side. She bit her lip and glanced around the room as though seeking a means of escape. Cranston knew the feeling. He shared it.

He examined the woman more closely. She was plain, but not ugly, and she seemed to have a good figure. He noted a tightness around her eyes that comes from lack of sleep. He didn't think she was a hustler. Hustlers usually dressed better, and they never had to sleep in bus station waiting rooms. She was just one of life's losers, nearing the end of the line.

The cop had almost reached the woman when Jeff Cranston threw open the door of the booth and stepped out. He walked over to her and held out his hand. "Sorry to keep you waiting, honey," he said, "We can go now."

The woman looked from him to the approaching cop and back at him again. Finally, she stood and took his arm. The top of her head barely reached his shoulder.

"Where are we going?" she asked softly. Her voice had a husky note that Cranston liked immediately.

"Hungry?"

"Yes," she said.

"Me, too. Let's get something to eat."

Cranston had a small overnight case in one of the coin-operated lockers along the far wall. He mentally kissed it goodbye. Perhaps he'd be able to send the woman back to pick it up for him later, but he wasn't going to count on it.

There was an all night restaurant two blocks away. They walked to it in silence. Cranston glanced back over his shoulder a few times; no one seemed to be following them. So far, so good. They were looking for a man alone, and he wasn't alone any more.

"I was scared to death the policeman would arrest me for vagrancy or something when he found out I had no money. Why did you help me?" the woman asked. They were seated at the lunch counter in the restaurant. Cranston smiled with relief at having been smart enough to have outfoxed the watchers at the bus station.

"It seemed like the right move," he said.

She took a rumpled cigarette package from the pocket of her little jacket and offered it to him.

He waved it away. "I don't have any bad habits," he said, believing it.

"You're lucky."

"Yes," he agreed. "I am."

They each had a sandwich and coffee; and when the woman asked if she could have a slice of pie, too, he nodded. He had less than two hundred dollars left, but by comparison to the woman he felt rich.

Out on the street again, he tried to decide what to do next.

The woman must have sensed his indecision. She clutched her huge purse to her side. "Take me with you?"

"You don't know where I'm headed." He didn't add that he didn't, either.

"It doesn't matter. I've been alone too long."

"You don't even know my name."

"That doesn't matter, either."

"Okay." He started walking down the street in the direction away from the bus station. They passed the brightly-lighted show windows of the downtown stores. "We'll find someplace to stay, but first I have something to do."

"Something to do?" she echoed in a tired voice.

"I want to find out if I'm being followed."

There was an outdoor telephone mounted on the side of a closed service station. Cranston led the way up to it. He took a small notebook from his pocket, then went through the motions of making a phone call. After hanging up the handset, he made some cryptic markings in the notebook and tore out that page. He crumpled it into a ball and threw it to the asphalt with an angry gesture that could be seen a block away.

Taking the woman's arm, he began walking rapidly, pulling her along. None of the people on the street at that hour seemed to be paying attention to them, and the cars all sped past without slowing. The woman walked as though she were exhausted, as if each step were painful. They turned right at the first corner, walked past the empty stalls and stacked crates of an outdoor market, then made two more right turns and were back at the gas station again.

"Is someone after you?" the woman asked, frowning.

The crumpled paper was still on the asphalt where he'd thrown it. If he were being followed, the tail wouldn't have been able to resist picking it up, he decided. "No, no one's after me," he said.

He took her arm again and started around the block a second time. When they were in front of the outdoor market, Cranston looked both ways and found the street was deserted.

"Come on," he said, guiding her between the stacks of empty crates and mounds of refuse that were waiting to be collected. Far back from the street he located an unlocked stall that had a couple of crates they could use for seats.

The woman sat down with a sigh, leaning back against the bare wooden wall and thrusting her legs out in front of her. "I was locked out of my room two days ago for not paying my rent. I've been out of work for over a month," she said. She dug the cigarette package from her pocket and placed a badly bent cigarette between her lips. Before lighting a match, she looked at Cranston and showed him the matchbook.

"Go ahead," he said. "We're too far back from the street for anyone to see the light." He took out his pistol and cocked the hammer while the match flared. It was a couple of minutes before the woman's eyes readjusted to the dim light and she reacted to the snub-nosed .38. Her eyes grew wider, and the cigarette slipped from her fingers. She sat up straight and clutched her purse protectively.

"Wha—what are you going to do with that?"

"Shoot you, probably," he answered, matter-of-factly.

"But why? I haven't harmed you."

"Only because I didn't give you the chance, baby."

Her tongue darted out and touched her upper lip. She seemed to shrink in size, and she placed her left hand flat against her chest in a gesture of innocence and bewilderment. "Why would I want to hurt you?"

"Because you're The Exterminator. All the while I was hiding in that phone booth, thinking I was ducking Willie the Finger, he'd already spotted me. He spent all that time pretending to look for me to give you time to get into position on the bench. His phone call was a phony, and that cop probably was too. It was all staged to get me to pick you up so you could do a job on me with your .45."

"My .45?" The woman's eyes were showing a lot of white as she stared at the revolver in Cranston's hand.

"That's right—your .45. That big purse of yours is just what you'd need to carry it around. A .45 like yours is a big pistol. If you have a silencer on it, the whole weapon must be at least a foot and a half long. No one could carry it in a pocket."

"You're wrong—really you are. I have no pistol. I'm not plotting to hurt you."

Cranston continued as if she hadn't spoken.

"You and Willie made a mistake. You let me give him the slip too easily. It was just too good to be true. Once he was that close to me, it didn't make sense that I could get away with so little effort."

"Please, mister, don't hurt me. Let me go. You've got me wrong, I'm not trying to hurt you. I'm lonely and I need someone, and I hoped . . . I thought you did, too." Her tone rang with sincerity, and a tear left a shiny trail down her cheek. Cranston felt a surge of doubt, and he allowed the barrel of his pistol to point at the floor.

The woman moved her hands nervously and took the cigarette package from her pocket. It was empty. She tossed it aside, and with a completely natural motion thrust her hand into the opening in her purse.

Without hesitation, Cranston reached out with his revolver and shot her in the head. They were less than six feet apart, so it was more a case of pointing the weapon than of aiming it.

The woman was thrown back against the wall and then slid sideways to the floor. She ended up lying on her side next to the empty crate with her hand still deep inside her purse.

Cranston gazed down at her. She looked very peaceful, not at all like a loser. He bent and started to reach for her bag, but stopped. He took a deep breath and let the air out very slowly. Then he stood up and walked away without touching the purse.

It didn't matter whether she was The Exterminator or not. If he'd been wrong about her, he would know it soon enough. All things considered, he was satisfied he'd made the right move.

When This Man Dies

by Lawrence Block

The night before the first letter came, he had Speckled Band in the feature at Saratoga. The horse went off at nine-to-two from the number one pole and Edgar Kraft had two hundred dollars on him, half to win and half to place. Speckled Band went to the front and stayed there. The odds-on favorite, a four-year-old named Sheila's Kid, challenged around the clubhouse turn and got hung up on the outside. Kraft was counting his money. In the stretch, Speckled Band broke stride, galloped home madly, was summarily disqualified, and placed fourth. Kraft tore up his tickets and went home.

So he was in no mood for jokes that morning. He opened five of the six letters that came in the morning mail, and all five were bills, none of which he had any prospect of paying in the immediate future. He put them in a drawer in his desk. There were already several bills in that drawer. He opened the final letter and was at first relieved to discover that it was not a bill, not a notice of payment due, not a threat to repossess car or furniture. It was, instead, a very simple message typed in the center of a large sheet of plain typing paper.

First a name:

Mr. Joseph H. Neimann

And, below that:

When this man dies
You will receive
Five hundred dollars.

He was in no mood for jokes. Trotters that lead all the way, and then break in the stretch, do not contribute to a man's sense of humor. He looked at the sheet of paper, turned it over to see if there was anything further on its reverse, turned it over again to read the message once more, picked up the envelope, saw nothing on it but his own name and a local postmark, said something unprintable about some idiots and their idea of a joke, and tore everything up and threw it away, message and envelope and all.

In the course of the next week he thought about the letter once,

178

maybe twice. No more than that. He had problems of his own. He had never heard of anyone named Joseph H. Neimann and entertained no hopes of receiving five hundred dollars in the event of the man's death. He did not mention the cryptic message to his wife. When the man from Superior Finance called to ask him if he had any hopes of meeting his note on time, he did not say anything about the legacy that Mr. Neimann meant to leave him.

He went on doing his work from one day to the next, working with the quiet desperation of a man who knows his income, while better than nothing, will never quite get around to equalling his expenditures. He went to the track twice, won thirty dollars one night, lost twenty-three the next. He came quite close to forgetting entirely about Mr. Joseph H. Neimann and the mysterious correspondent.

Then the second letter came. He opened it mechanically, unfolded a large sheet of plain white paper. Ten fresh fifty dollar bills fluttered down upon the top of his desk. In the center of the sheet of paper someone had typed:

Thank You

Edgar Kraft did not make the connection immediately. He tried to think what he might have done that would merit anyone's thanks, not to mention anyone's five hundred dollars. It took him a moment, and then he recalled that other letter and rushed out of his office and down the street to a drugstore. He bought a morning paper, turned to the obituaries. Joseph Henry Neimann, 67, of 413 Park Place, had died the previous afternoon in County Hospital after an illness of several months' duration. He left a widow, three children, and four grandchildren. Funeral services would be private, flowers were please to be omitted.

He put three hundred dollars in his checking account and two hundred dollars in his wallet. He made his payment on the car, paid his rent, cleared up a handful of small bills. The mess in his desk drawer was substantially less baleful, although by no means completely cleared up. He still owed money, but he owed less now than before the timely death of Joseph Henry Neimann. The man from Superior Finance had been appeased by a partial payment; he would stop making a nuisance of himself, at least for the time being.

That night, Kraft took his wife to the track. He even let her make a couple impossible hunch bets. He lost forty dollars and it hardly bothered him at all.

When the next letter came he did not tear it up. He recognized the typing on the envelope, and he turned it over in his hands for a few moments before opening it, like a child with a wrapped present. He was somewhat more apprehensive than child with present, however; he couldn't help feeling that the mysterious benefactor would want something in return for his five hundred dollars.

He opened the letter. No demands, however. Just the usual sheet of plain paper, with another name typed in its center:

Mr. Raymond Andersen

And, below that:

When this man dies
You will receive
Seven hundred fifty dollars.

For the next few days he kept telling himself that he did not wish anything unpleasant for Mr. Raymond Andersen. He didn't know the man, he had never heard of him, and he was not the sort to wish death upon some total stranger. And yet—

Each morning he bought a paper and turned at once to the death notices, searching almost against his will for the name of Mr. Raymond Andersen. *I don't wish him harm,* he would think each time. But seven hundred fifty dollars was a happy sum. If something were going to happen to Mr. Raymond Andersen, he might as well profit by it. It wasn't as though he was doing anything to cause Andersen's death. He was even unwilling to wish for it. But if something happened . . .

Something happened. Five days after the letter came, he found Andersen's obituary in the morning paper. Andersen was an old man, a very old man, and he had died in his bed at a home for the aged after a long illness. His heart jumped when he read the notice with a combination of excitement and guilt. But what was there to feel guilty about? He hadn't done anything. And death, for a sick old man like Raymond Andersen, was more a cause for relief than grief, more a blessing than a tragedy.

But why would anyone want to pay him seven hundred fifty dollars?

Nevertheless, someone did.

The letter came the following morning, after a wretched night during which Kraft tossed and turned and batted two possibilities back and forth—that the letter would come and that it would not. It did come, and it brought the promised seven hundred fifty dollars in fifties and hundreds. And the same message:

Thank You

For what? He had not the slightest idea. But he looked at the two-word message again before putting it carefully away.

You're welcome, he thought. *You're entirely welcome.*

For two weeks no letter came. He kept waiting for the mail, kept hoping for another windfall like the two that had come so far. There were times when he would sit at his desk for twenty or thirty minutes at a time, staring off into space and thinking about the letters and the money. He would have done better keeping his mind on his work, but this was not easy. His job brought him five thousand dollars a year, and for that sum he had to work forty to fifty hours a week. His anonymous pen pal had thus far brought him a quarter as much as he earned in a year, and he had done nothing at all for the money.

The seven fifty had helped, but he was still in hot water. On a sudden female whim his wife had had the living room recarpeted. The rent was due. There was another payment due on the car. He had one very good night at the track, but a few other visits took back his winnings and more.

And then the letter came, along with a circular inviting him to buy a dehumidifier for his basement and an appeal for funds from some dubious charity. He swept circular and appeal into his waste-basket and tore open the plain white envelope. The message was the usual sort:

Mr. Claude Pierce

And, below the name:

> *When this man dies*
> *You will receive*
> *One thousand dollars.*

Kraft's hands were shaking slightly as he put the envelope and letter away in his desk. One thousand dollars—the price had gone up again, this time to a fairly staggering figure. Mr. Claude Pierce. Did he know anyone named Claude Pierce? He did not. Was Claude Pierce sick? Was he a lonely old man, dying somewhere of a terminal illness?

Kraft hoped so. He hated himself for the wish, but he could not smother it.

He hoped Claude Pierce was dying.

This time he did a little research. He thumbed through the phone book until he found a listing for a Claude Pierce on Honeydale Drive. He closed the book then and tried to put the whole business out of his mind, an enterprise foredoomed to failure. Finally he gave up, looked up the listing once more, looked at the man's name and thought that this man was going to die. It was inevitable, wasn't it? They sent him some man's name in the mail, and then the man died, and then Edgar Kraft was paid. Obviously, Claude Pierce was a doomed man.

He called Pierce's number. A woman answered, and Kraft asked if Mr. Pierce was in.

"Mr. Pierce is in the hospital," the woman said. "Who's calling, please?"

"Thank you," Kraft said.

Of course, he thought. They, whoever they were, simply found people in hospitals who were about to die, and they paid money to Edgar Kraft when the inevitable occurred, and that was all. The why of it was impenetrable. But so few things made sense in Kraft's life that he did not want to question the whole affair too closely. Perhaps his unknown correspondent was like that lunatic on television who gave away a million dollars every week. If someone wanted to give Kraft money, Kraft wouldn't argue with him.

That afternoon he called the hospital. Claude Pierce had been admitted two days ago for major surgery, a nurse told Kraft. His condition was listed as *good.*

Well, he would have a relapse, Kraft thought. He was doomed—the letterwriter had ordained his death. He felt momentarily sorry for Claude Pierce, and then he turned his attention to the entries at Saratoga. There was a horse named Orange Pips which Kraft had been watching for some time. The horse had a good post now, and if he was ever going to win, this was the time.

Kraft went to the track. Orange Pips ran out of the money. In the morning Kraft failed to find Pierce's obituary. When he called the hospital, the nurse told him that Pierce was recovering very nicely.

Impossible, Kraft thought.

For three weeks Claude Pierce lay in his hospital bed, and for three weeks Edgar Kraft followed his condition with more interest than Pierce's doctor could have displayed. Once Pierce took a turn for the worse and slipped into a coma. The nurse's voice was grave over the phone, and Kraft bowed his head, resigned to the inevitable. A day later Pierce had rallied remarkably. The nurse sounded positively cheerful, and Kraft fought off a sudden wave of rage that threatened to overwhelm him.

From that point on, Pierce improved steadily. He was released, finally, a whole man again, and Kraft could not understand quite what had happened. Something had gone wrong. When Pierce died, he was to receive a thousand dollars. Pierce had been sick, Pierce had been close to death, and then, inexplicably, Pierce had been snatched from the very jaws of death, with a thousand dollars simultaneously snatched from Edgar Kraft.

He waited for another letter. No letter came.

With the rent two weeks overdue, with a payment on the car past due, with the man from Superior Finance calling him far too often, Kraft's mind began to work against him. *When this man dies,* the letter had said. There had been no strings attached, no time limit on Pierce's death. After all, Pierce could not live forever. No one did. And whenever Pierce did happen to draw his last breath, he would get that thousand dollars.

Suppose something happened to Pierce—

He thought it over against his own will. It would not be hard, he kept telling himself. No one knew that he had any interest whatsoever in Claude Pierce. If he picked his time well, if he did the dirty business and got it done with and hurried off into the night, no one would know. The police would never think of him in the same breath with Claude Pierce, if police were in the habit of thinking in breaths. He did not know Pierce, he had no obvious motive for killing Pierce, and—

He couldn't do it, he told himself. He simply could not do it. He was no killer. And something as senseless as this, something so thoroughly absurd, was unthinkable.

He would manage without the thousand dollars. Somehow, he would live without the money. True, he had already spent it a dozen times over in his mind. True, he had been counting and recounting it when Pierce lay in a coma. But he would get along without it. What else could he do?

The next morning headlines shrieked Pierce's name at Edgar Kraft. The previous night someone had broken into the Pierce home on Honeydale Drive and had knifed Claude Pierce in his bed. The murderer had escaped unseen. No possible motive for the slaying of Pierce could be established. The police were baffled.

Kraft got slightly sick to his stomach as he read the story. His first reaction was a pure and simple onrush of unbearable guilt, as though he had been the man with the knife, as though he himself had broken in during the night to stab silently and flee promptly, mission accomplished. He could not shake this guilt away. He knew well enough that he had done nothing, that he had killed no one.

But he had conceived of the act, he had willed that it be done, and he could not escape the feeling that he was a murderer, at heart if not in fact.

His blood money came on schedule. One thousand dollars, ten fresh hundreds this time. And the message. *Thank you.*

Don't thank me, he thought, holding the bills in his hand, holding them tenderly. Don't thank me!

> *Mr. Leon Dennison*
> *When this man dies*
> *You will receive*
> *Fifteen hundred dollars.*

Kraft did not keep the letter. He was breathing heavily when he read it, his heart pounding. He read it twice through, and then he took it and the envelope it had come in, and all the other letters and envelopes that he had so carefully saved, and he tore them all into little bits and flushed them down the toilet.

He had a headache. He took aspirin, but it did not help his headache at all. He sat at his desk and did no work until lunchtime. He went to the luncheonette around the corner and ate lunch without tasting his food. During the afternoon he found that, for the first time, he could not make head or tails out of the list of entries at Saratoga. He couldn't concentrate on a thing, and he left the office early and took a long walk.

Mr. Leon Dennison.

Dennison lived in an apartment on Cadbury Avenue. No one answered his phone. Dennison was an attorney, and he had an office listing. When Kraft called it a secretary answered and told him that Mr. Dennison was in conference. Would he care to leave his name?

When this man dies.

But Dennison would not die, he thought. Not in a hospital bed, at any rate. Dennison was perfectly all right, he was at work, and the person who had written all those letters knew very well that Dennison was all right, that he was not sick.

Fifteen hundred dollars.

But how, he wondered. He did not own a gun and had not the slightest idea how to get one. A knife? Someone had used a knife on Claude Pierce, he remembered. And a knife would probably not be hard to get his hands on. But a knife seemed somehow unnatural to him.

How, then? By automobile? He could do it that way, he could lie in wait for Dennison and run him down in his car. It would not be difficult, and it would probably be certain enough. Still, the police were supposed to be able to find hit and run drivers fairly easily. There was something about paint scrapings, or blood on your own bumper, or something. He didn't know the details, but they always did seem to catch hit and run drivers.

Forget it, he told himself. You are not a killer.

He didn't forget it. For two days he tried to think of other things and failed miserably. He thought about Dennison, and he thought about fifteen hundred dollars, and he thought about murder.

When this man dies

One time he got up early in the morning and drove to Cadbury Avenue. He watched Leon Dennison's apartment, and he saw Dennison emerge, and when Dennison crossed the street toward his parked car Kraft settled his own foot on the accelerator and ached to put the pedal on the floor and send the car hurtling toward Leon Dennison. But he didn't do it. He waited.

So clever. Suppose he were caught in the act? Nothing linked him with the person who wrote him the letters. He hadn't even kept the letters, but even if he had, they were untraceable.

Fifteen hundred dollars—

On a Thursday afternoon he called his wife and told her he was going directly to Saratoga. She complained mechanically before bowing to the inevitable. He drove to Cadbury Avenue and parked his car. When the doorman slipped down to the corner for a cup of coffee, Kraft ducked into the building and found Leon Dennison's apartment. The door was locked, but he managed to spring the lock with the blade of a pen knife. He was sweating freely as he worked on the lock, expecting every moment someone to come up behind him and lay a hand on his shoulder. The lock gave, and he went inside and closed it after him.

But something happened the moment he entered the apartment. All the fear, all the anxiety, all of this suddenly left Edgar Kraft. He was mysteriously calm now. Everything was prearranged, he told himself. Joseph H. Neimann had been doomed, and Raymond Andersen had been doomed, and Claude Pierce had been doomed, and each of them had died. Now Leon Dennison was similarly doomed, and he too would die.

It seemed very simple. And Edgar Kraft himself was nothing but a part of this grand design, nothing but a cog in a gigantic machine. He would do his part without worrying about it. Everything could only go according to plan.

Everything did. He waited three hours for Leon Dennison to come home, waited in calm silence. When a key turned in the lock, he stepped swiftly and noiselessly to the side of the door, a fireplace andiron held high overhead. The door opened and Leon Dennison entered, quite alone.

The andiron descended.

Leon Dennison fell without a murmur. He collapsed, lay still. The andiron rose and fell twice more, just for insurance, and Leon Dennison never moved and never uttered a sound. Kraft had only to wipe off the andiron and a few other surfaces to eliminate any fingerprints he might have left behind. He left the building by the service entrance. No one saw him.

He waited all that night for the rush of guilt. He was surprised when it failed to come. But he had already been a murderer—by wishing for Andersen's death, by planning Pierce's murder. The simple translation of his impulses from thought to deed was no impetus for further guilt.

There was no letter the next day. The following morning the usual envelope was waiting for him. It was quite bulky; it was filled with fifteen hundred dollar bills.

The note was different. It said *Thank You,* of course. But beneath that there was another line:

How do you like your new job?

Busman's Holiday

by James Holding

How do you recognize an answer to a prayer?

I recognized Paul St. Clair, who seemed to be calling himself René Vincent now, by the way he splayed his right foot when he walked. He had shaved off the mustache and imperial that Carl had described to me, but the toed-out foot gave him away.

He arrived at eight twenty-eight P.M. on the train from Basel, and when he came through Exit Gate 7 into the station proper, I was waiting for him beside the gate. Before he caught sight of the hotel name on the visor of my cap, I had a moment to look him over.

He was slight in stature, yet carried himself with an air. He wore a dark topcoat over conservatively-cut clothes. I was astounded to note that his gaze, searching the crowd outside the gate, was direct and candid, even naïve.

It was hard for me to believe that he was what Carl said he was; but then, the answer to a prayer is frequently misleading.

I stood quietly, giving no sign of recognition until he spotted my cap and made his way toward me. Then I moved forward quickly. "For Hotel Minerva?" I said. "Monsieur Vincent? I was told to meet a Monsieur Vincent."

When he nodded, I said, "Welcome to Lucerne." I relieved him of his two bags. "The hotel car is parked outside. Will you follow me, please?" I spoke in French.

He hustled along beside me, his head barely even with my chin. "Whew!" he said. "That's a long train ride from Paris. And do you know, there seem not to be any porters in your Swiss stations? When I changed trains at Basel, I had to handle my luggage myself. And here, too." He obviously wasn't used to that. "I'm exhausted!"

"You'll be ready for dinner, then," I suggested respectfully. "We serve until nine."

"Good. Am I the only passenger for the Minerva?"

"The only one. It is September. The season is all but ended here."

"That suits me. I'm principally in search of rest and quiet." As he said "rest and quiet," I thought I saw his lips curve slightly in a secret smile. That was a good sign, I felt.

I put his bags in the car and held the door for him while he climbed into the back seat. "Rest and quiet are specialties of the Minerva, you might say, sir." I got behind the wheel.

We left the *bahnhof* and crossed the Seebrücke over the River Reuss. To our left, Chapel Bridge with its water tower angled across the river, only partially revealed by the city lights and the three-quarter moon rising over the walls of the old city. Above it, the towers of Hotel Chateau Gütsch gleamed in their floodlights like a Walt Disney castle.

As I took the turn into Adligenswilerstrasse, Monsieur Vincent leaned back against the cushions. "After those damned trains, this is sheer luxury," he said. "What a comfortable car!"

The hotel car is American-made, a black seven-passenger sedan and a pleasure to drive. I like it far better than the ones used by other deluxe hotels in Lucerne. I said over my shoulder, "Thank you. If you plan to take any sightseeing excursions while you're here, sir. I can drive you in this car, if you like. It's a hotel service. Goes right on your hotel bill. Far more satisfactory, guests tell me, than taking the crowded bus tours."

"I'll keep it in mind," Monsieur Vincent said.

"Very good, sir. You can make arrangements with the concierge at the hotel if you want me." I thought I'd let that decision be his. At least, to begin with—until I'd had the chance to observe him more closely.

As it turned out, my luck was in. The next day, Herr Grüber, our concierge, called me and told me Herr Vincent, the guest in Room 424, wanted to take a little drive in the hotel car, with me to drive him shortly after luncheon.

I felt my spirits lift. "Any particular excusions?" I asked Grüber.

"I thought Axenstrasse would be a good one to begin with. Give him the Wilhelm Tell treatment." Grüber laughed. "The French and the Americans love that. They're so romantic."

"Axenstrasse it is," I said.

I took the hotel car out and got it filled with petrol and was waiting for Monsieur Vincent at the foot of the Minerva's funicular at two o'clock when he came out.

"Good afternoon, Kreutz," he greeted me. "I'm taking your advice, you see. Shall we start?"

We set out. He lounged in the back seat of the car in lonely grandeur. Our route led along the lake shore through Meggen and Küssnacht. Monsieur Vincent showed faint traces of interest when we passed Queen Astrid's Chapel, but when I made a stop at Tell's Chapel near the Hollow Lane, where William Tell lay in wait for Gessler with his bow and arrow, Vincent didn't even bother to get out of the car. "Let's go on," he said. "I want to see this Axenstrasse your concierge was so enthusiastic about."

We skirted the Lake of Zug, Mount Rigi looming above us, and drove to Brunnen, where the Axenstrasse begins. The Axenstrasse is a narrow road along the edge of the cliffs bordering the lake, tunneled in some places through the solid rock. I gave all my attention to driving until we came to Altdorf.

There, I showed Monsieur Vincent the William Tell monument in the public square and gave him my lecture number three about our national hero. He listened courteously.

At the end, I suggested we repair to the Swan Inn and have cakes and hot chocolate before we undertook the return trip. It was a beautiful clear day, not too chilly, so we sat outdoors under a gilded wrought-iron sign displaying a mother swan and two cygnets.

Afterward, at the car, Monsieur Vincent decided that he would sit in the front seat with me, if I didn't mind. He felt like a fool, he said, lording it alone in the enormous tonneau. I made no objection, of course. His changed position in the car did not change his attitude toward me, however—that of the well-heeled master toward the faithful but humble chauffeur.

As we entered the village of Vitznau on our way back to Lucerne, I said, "I hope you have found the trip interesting, sir."

"Very," he answered. He lit a cigarette with a gold lighter, his graceful, small-boned hands making the simple action a thing of beauty. "Why?"

"Because," I said, "meaning no disrespect, I think you've been bored stiff the whole time."

He laughed. "What makes you think that, Kreutz?"

"Your lack of the standard enthusiasm, sir. I think you admired the scenery, as who would not? But I suspect you found my lecture on the Axenstrasse and William Tell very dull, indeed. Not so?"

He blew smoke at the windshield. "Since you tax me with it, yes. No fault of yours, though, Kreutz. I heard all that twaddle about William Tell before I was five, of course. And the road along Lake Garda in Italy impressed me far more than your Axenstrasse. I'm sorry."

I shrugged. "Each one to his own taste," I murmured philosophically. Then, with the air of a man trying his best to please a dis-

tinguished patron, I said, "Now that I know what your taste is, sir,
I think I can promise you an excursion that you will find infinitely
more interesting than this one."

"Oh? And what excursion would that be, Kreutz?"

"To Liechtenstein," I said. "To Vaduz, where the Prince of Liechtenstein's superb art collection may be seen upon request."

Vincent suddenly went very still in the seat beside me. His hand,
lifting his cigarette to his mouth, made a split-second pause before
continuing its smooth progress.

"Vaduz? An art collection? I care nothing for art, my friend." He
was very casual. Too casual?

"Perhaps not," I said, keeping my eyes on the road. "Yet I believe
you care a great deal for the money famous art works can bring
you."

His body jerked as though an insect had stung him between the
shoulder blades. "That is an impertinence, Kreutz," he said coldly.
"Stop the car, please, I wish to return to the back seat."

I hastened to apologize. "I have no wish to offend you, Monsieur
St. Clair."

No wince, this time. No sudden stillness. Just a glare of chilly
lightning out of his innocent-seeming eyes.

"St. Clair?" he asked. "What name is that?"

"It is yours, sir."

"Ridiculous!"

I didn't stop the car. Significantly, he did not repeat his order for
me to do so. I knew now that I was on firm ground.

"With all respect, sir," I said as humbly as I could, "I happen to
know that you are Paul St. Clair, the eminent art dealer from Paris,
vacationing in Lucerne incognito."

He sucked on his cigarette until it glowed red for half an inch.
"How do you know my name?"

I said, without emphasis, "My cousin in Paris telephoned me you
were coming here."

"Your cousin?"

"The travel agent through whom you booked your accommoda-
tions."

"He was a stranger. He didn't know me. Why would he telephone
you?" He spoke with heat, remembering, I was sure, that my cousin
in Paris had recommended the Hotel Minerva to him.

"Why did he telephone me? Because he thought you were the right
man to help us with a project we contemplate," I said.

"What does that mean?"

"He recognized you."

"How could he do that?"

"He saw your photograph in the papers."

"Me? He saw *my* photograph in the papers? He was wrong, I assure you. This is all a mistake, Kreutz."

"No, sir," I said. "He remembered the picture very well. You still had your mustache and imperial then. You were being questioned by the police in the matter of an art theft. A very valuable painting, stolen from the Jeu de Paume. Everybody thought you were guilty, apparently, including my cousin. But nothing could be proved."

"You're damned right it couldn't!" St. Clair, touched in his vanity, spoke with pride. "I'm not completely stupid, even though a Frenchman!"

I said, "You are a skillful thief, sir, that's what you are." I took my hands from the wheel for a moment to spread them in a gesture of apology for this blunt statement. "And you decided to leave France until things cooled off a bit. My cousin guessed that, which is why he telephoned me."

"*Alors*, I have stolen no works of art in Switzerland, anyway," he said nastily. "You know that."

"Of course. And that is exactly what I have to offer you, sir. The opportunity to help us—my cousin and me—bring off a truly memorable art theft here."

St. Clair pressed out his cigarette in his ashtray. He said nothing for a moment, yet he seemed vaguely more at ease. Perhaps he was reassured to find he was talking to another thief—would-be thief, rather. "What, if you do not mind my asking, could be worth stealing in this benighted city? You have no art here worthy of the name. A few landscape daubs of the eighteenth and nineteenth centuries in your Kunsthall. Nothing else."

I said, "I mentioned the art gallery in Vaduz, sir. *There*, you will admit, are some paintings worth stealing."

He shrugged. "What paintings?" he asked noncommittally.

"A hundred," I answered seriously. "However, our project contemplates the theft of only two."

"From the prince's collection?" He knew all about it, of course.

"Yes." Then I was silent, letting him sniff the carrot.

At last he asked, "Which ones?"

"The two Meissoniers. You know them?"

"Who does not?" His tone was wistful. "They are known all over the world. Too well known. You could never sell them."

"My cousin and I have given a great deal of thought to that," I said. "It's another reason why we believe you can be enormously helpful to us."

"You flatter me."

"Not at all. When the Meissoniers are in our hands, you will smuggle them out of Switzerland, do you see? And with due caution, you will sell them to a customer or customers of yours. For cash—a great deal of cash. I am sure you know collectors who will not ask embarrassing questions if presented with the chance to acquire an original Meissonier?"

"I have a few connections, yes," St. Clair admitted cautiously.

A few connections! I thought. He has at least one connection who is willing to buy from him a painting stolen from the Jeu de Paume and ask no questions!

Thinking about the Prince of Liechtenstein's two Meissoniers, St. Clair flushed slightly, his quickened blood coursing strongly through the little veins just below the surface of his skin. "What are your Meissoniers worth, may I ask?"

"The *prince's* Meissoniers," I said. "They are not yet ours. They are insured for a million and a half Swiss francs." I allowed this succulent figure to hang in the air between us for a moment before I went on. "And you, with your connections, can probably realize twice that amount."

"To be divided up three ways, eh? You, your cousin and me?"

"Two ways," I said. "Half for you. Half for us. After all, you will do most of the work."

"I begin to realize that."

"Does it sound attractive to you?" I asked.

"It has definite possibilities. I must know more, of course."

"Of course." I overtook a six-wheeled lorry on the outskirts of Weggis, and pulled out to pass. When we were on our own side of the road again, I said, "I happen to know that the prince's two Meissoniers were removed last week from their places in the art gallery in Vaduz for a periodic cleaning by Herr Gustav Mizner. Herr Mizner's shop, where he cleans and restores the prince's art treasures when needful, is a hundred yards away from the gallery on a side street. Herr Mizner is a dedicated craftsman. He is also, thank heavens, a simple and trusting man. When he closes up shop for the night, he locks up whatever valuable paintings he may be working on in his old fashioned safe, and blithely departs. There are no guards."

"Not even burglar alarms?" asked St. Clair.

"There are alarms, yes. A complicated series of them—of American manufacture, I believe—arranged to alert the police a block away, and Herr Mizner himself at his home, should any attempt be made to force entry into his shop." I paused. "That is mainly why we need you, sir. You must have had wide experience with such electronic devices?"

He smiled for the first time. "I know something of them, it is true."

"And of safecracking?"

"That, too."

"My cousin and I were confident you would."

"But," said St. Clair, "I'll want to examine the situation before we try anything, you understand."

"Perfectly. That's why I think you will find an excursion to Vaduz tomorrow most interesting. You will have a chance to look over the ground. If circumstances seem favorable, we will stay overnight in Vaduz, and you will relieve Herr Mizner of the two Meissoniers during the small hours. We'll be back in Lucerne the following day in time for luncheon at the Minerva."

"You go too fast, my friend," St. Clair said, waving a slender hand in the air between us. "You tell me I'm to smuggle the paintings from Switzerland into France and sell them to one or another of my clients. Then I send you your share of the money. Is that right?"

"Or turn over our share to my cousin in Paris, if you prefer," I said.

"You trust me to take the paintings out, and send you half the proceeds of their sale?"

"We must trust you, sir. It is all we can do. We cannot overcome the electronic alarms of Herr Mizner's shop without you. Even if we could, we could not dispose of the pictures profitably in Switzerland. They are known here, as you point out. The announcement of their theft will alert every art dealer and collector in Switzerland. So we *must* trust you. You see?"

"What makes you think I won't keep the whole amount for myself?"

"There is honor among thieves, is there not?" I pointed out.

He gave me a surprised look.

I went on. "When my cousin Carl dealt with you in Paris, he judged you to be not only a skillful thief, sir, but a man who would abide honorably by a contract made with a colleague. After spending an afternoon with you, I concur in that judgment. If we are wrong, there is nothing to be done about it."

St. Clair nodded. "You are not wrong, Kreutz. On the contrary you are more perceptive than most. I thank you. Yet let us not stoop to sentimentality." He hesitated, reluctant to reveal his curiosity. Then he asked, "What about you and your cousin, Kreutz? Why this attempt to get into the dangerous business of art theft? You are men of education and intelligence. You both have good jobs—"

I interrupted him. "Good jobs? A hotel chauffeur and an underling in a travel agency? For men with master's degrees from the University of Zurich? For men who can speak four languages fluently? Pardon me, sir, but we do not consider our present employment worthy of our talents. It is as simple as that. We mean to remedy our condition as quickly as possible. Three hundred and seventy-five thousand francs apiece should accomplish that for us."

"Well, well. I understand and sympathize, Kreutz. Say no more." He lit another cigarette and this time he offered me one. I took it and for a few moments we smoked in companionable silence. At last St. Clair said, "These two Meissoniers. Tell me about them."

"You know what they are, do you not?"

"Of course, *Napoleon's Retreat from Moscow* and *Marshall Ney Addresses the Troops.* But what are the dimensions of these paintings? That is what signifies at this moment. I fear we'll never be able to get them out of Switzerland, once we have them. Or out of Liechtenstein, for that matter."

"Don't worry about Liechtenstein," I said. "Switzerland and Liechtenstein have had a customs and monetary union since 1924."

"Oh? Well, paintings are not the easiest things in the world to smuggle across *any* border."

"I know. There should be no difficulty, however. These paintings, like most of Meissonier's works, are quite small. Twelve by eighteen inches—plus the frames, of course. And we can discard the frames, once we have the paintings."

"Still," said St. Clair, "even small oil paintings present a knotty smuggling problem . . . " His voice trailed off.

"Rest easy, sir," I reassured him. "I have another skill besides driving an automobile. As a hobby, I also work in leather. And I promise you that with the valise I shall supply to replace your present one, you will acquire a foolproof hiding place for the Meissonier paintings."

"I do not understand."

"A suitcase of top-grain leather. Leather lined, hand sewn. Between the outer and inner leather skins, who is to know there lie two priceless Meissonier canvases protected by sheets of lamb's wool? I have already completed this suitcase, sir—in anticipation that we should work together—save for the final edge seams. When we return from Vaduz with the paintings, they shall be sewn into the suitcase walls. I guarantee they will be undetectable by even the most suspicious customs agent."

"Clever," St. Clair said. "That should do nicely. Tell me now about the prince's art gallery in Vaduz, Herr Mizner's shop, and whatever you know about the American burglar alarms that protect it."

I told him with a sense of exhilaration.

In Vaduz, everything went smoothly.

We left the Minerva at nine the next morning and drove in leisurely fashion to Liechtenstein by way of Zug, the Herzel Pass, Rapperswill and the Ricken Pass. White clouds sailed majestically over the high peaks. Bright sunshine warmed the cool September air. We stopped en route at Wedenburg to see the picturesque fourteenth century houses, still sound, still very much lived in today.

We had luncheon in Vaduz. From the restaurant window we could see the prince's castle, perched on a high rock overlooking the town and the beautiful vineyards surrounding it.

Afterward, I drove St. Clair to the art gallery and waited outside with the car while he toured this display of extravagantly valuable art works. When he came out, I drove him the few yards to Herr Mizner's shop which, in addition to restoring and cleaning art treasures for the prince, dealt in the sale of antiquities to tourists as well.

After half an hour, St. Clair emerged from the shop wearing a rather smug smile. He carried an Austrian cross of carved wood he had bought from Herr Mizner.

"Well?" I asked, my voice thin from nervous strain.

"Child's play," he declared, clambering into the back seat of the car while I held the door for him. "We are favored by the gods, Kreutz. The complicated American alarm systems you described are, in reality, obsolete jokes. Laughable. Not even a decent challenge to my abilities."

I released my breath in a sign of relief. "And the safe? Did you manage to catch a glimpse of it?"

"Even more obsolete than the alarms," he replied complacently.

"You can leave the rest of this little adventure to me, Kreutz." He lit a cigarette. "Let us now check into the hotel. I wish to take a nap before dinner."

I was, of course, enormously encouraged by his cavalier attitude toward the undertaking that lay before him. He was an experienced man, aware of all the difficulties involved. If he regarded them lightly, I could do no less. We checked into the leading hotel in Vaduz—St. Clair into a suite, as befitted a prosperous French tourist—I into a basement sweatbox, as befitted a hotel chauffeur.

After dinner, St. Clair told me airily, "Go to bed, Kreutz, and rest easy. I shall not need you. However, give me the keys to your car."

I gave him the keys and went to bed, after agreeing to meet him for breakfast at six the following morning in order to get an early start back to Lucerne.

"Hopefully," he said, smiling, "before Herr Mizner opens his shop and discovers he has been robbed."

At breakfast, he was in high spirits. "You slept well, Kreutz?" he quipped.

I hadn't. "And you?" I said, accompanying the query with a smile.

He returned it. "Exceptionally well, thank you. I wakened about four and could not get back to sleep for an hour or so. But all in all, it was a very rewarding night."

I had to be satisfied with that until we were out of Liechtenstein and bowling along the road to Walenstadt. We had decided to return to Lucerne by a different route so that St. Clair, like the avid sightseer he pretended to be, could visit Einsiedeln on the way home.

The skies, with the unexpectedness of mountain weather, suddenly became overcast, turned leaden gray, and opened wide to pour torrents of cold rain upon the countryside through which we drove. The weather, however, could do nothing to dampen our spirits. Once out of Liechtenstein, I stopped the car on a deserted stretch of road and, with St. Clair beaming over my shoulder, looked my fill at the two Meissoniers, resting in their elaborate gold-leaf frames in the dusty trunk of the car.

"You *did* get them, didn't you!" I said.

"What did you expect? Of course I got them!"

I said from my heart, "You are an answer to prayer, Monsieur St. Clair!"

He preened himself slightly, although he probably would have thought it vulgar to gloat.

I took the paintings from their frames and buried the frames in the drainage ditch nearby while St. Clair kept watch for approaching cars.

At Einsiedeln, I began facetiously to give my lecture about the monastery being founded in 835 by St. Meinrad, and the baroque eighteenth century church, visited by two hundred thousand pilgrims a year, being especially notable for its black marble columns.

St. Clair stopped me. "Please do not joke about serious matters," he told me firmly. "This shrine is an architectural marvel worthy of our honest admiration."

This was a side of him I had not suspected. Yet he was an art dealer, after all, I reminded myself, albeit a dishonest one. I lapsed into silence and waited in the car while he entered the church, bare head reverently bowed, rivulets of rain running down his cheeks.

True to my promise, we were back in Lucerne in time for luncheon. I let St. Clair out of the car at the Minerva's street entrance, holding the door for him once again. "The suitcase?" he asked me softly as he descended from the car.

"Three o'clock tomorrow morning in your room," I answered. "After the hotel staff has retired."

He nodded and disappeared into the hotel, hugging the two Meissoniers flat against his side under his wet topcoat. It was still raining.

The hotel was like a tomb, fifteen hours later, when I came down the stairs from my sixth floor cubicle to the fourth floor room of Monsieur Paul St. Clair. I had the leather valise in my hand.

There was no need to knock—his door was unlocked. I turned the knob and slipped into the room. A single lamp burned on his bedside table. He was sitting beside it, fully dressed, reading the evening newspaper.

He raised his eyes at my entrance, put down the paper and stood up. His eyes went to the suitcase I carried. "Good!" he said with satisfaction. He went to his closet and secured the two Meissonier canvases from their temporary hiding place under the spare blankets on his shelf. "Let's get started, then," he said, handing the paintings to me.

I put my suitcase on the bed, wrapped one of the paintings in a thin sheet of lamb's wool, and slid it into the open seam at one side of the case, between outer leather and inner leather lining. Then I sewed up the seam with the cobbler's thread I had brought with me. The leather was tough, the work went slowly, but when the seam was at length closed, no one without X-ray eyes could have guessed what lay within.

"Can I help?" St. Clair asked, watching with interest.

"No, thanks, sir," I answered without raising my head. I snipped off the thread at the end of the sewn seam. He handed me the second painting and I repeated the procedure. When I finished, I put my leather punch, needle, and the remaining thread into my trousers pocket and stood erect, stretching the kinks out of my back.

"Finished," I said. "Are you satisfied with my 'smuggler's friend'?"

"Brilliant, Kreutz," he said. "Both concept and workmanship. I think at this point, we both deserve a drink." He poured champagne from a full bottle he had been cooling in his small refrigerator. "Come out to the balcony, Kreutz."

I followed him through the open french doors onto his small balcony. His was one of the Minerva's deluxe rooms. His balcony overlooked the lake. It held a tiny metal table and two straight chairs.

We didn't sit down. He raised his champagne glass, silently toasting me, and drank deeply. I returned the gesture.

"I shall not soon forget Lucerne," he murmured softly. The rain had almost ceased now and the moon drew a silver path across the placid surface ot the Vierwaldstattersee far below us. The view was spectacular. To our right, the twinkling night lights of the city formed a sleepy cluster where the River Reuss emptied into the lake. Directly across the lake, and three thousand feet above it, the lights of Burgenstock's three hotels were like three new constellations floating low in the southern sky. To the east, the head of Rigi was a blunt silhouette against the sky. Overall, the moonlight made a glory of the distant snow peaks on the horizon.

St. Clair put down his glass on the table with a brittle sound. "I owe you, Kreutz, and Lucerne, a great debt," he said in a whisper. "I want you to know that."

He had a strange way of showing his appreciation; for when I turned my head and looked at him, he was pointing a gun, fitted with a silencer, at my heart.

"Sir!" I said in surprise. "Monsieur St. Clair! What is this? We are colleagues, partners in an enterprise . . . " I ran out of words. I could see his innocent-appearing eyes glinting with amusement in the moonlight.

"Past tense," he corrected me gently. "We *were* partners. But, as the young people say, who needs you now, Kreutz?"

I looked over my shoulder toward the safety of his room and the corridor outside his door. I looked over the balcony rail at the long drop to the dining room terrace, four floors below.

"Too late," St. Clair said, not without sympathy. "You understand why I have to kill you, do you not?"

"No," I said, as calmly as I could. "You could get to France and merely keep all the proceeds from the paintings for yourself. Why kill me?"

"I no longer need your amateur help, Kreutz. I am a professional, you see. And no true professional leaves behind him an eyewitness to his crime. Even an amateur like you should know that." His lips curved in that secret smile I had noticed the night he arrived in Lucerne.

I simply stared at him.

"Give me the keys to your hotel car, Kreutz."

Slowly I handed them over, realizing that he had planned this from the beginning.

"If you shoot me," I argued weakly, "someone will hear you."

"The hotel is asleep. There are no occupants in the rooms immediately around mine. I took pains to find that out. The end of the season, remember? No one will hear me. Especially with this." He touched the silencer on his pistol barrel.

"My cousin in Paris will know you killed me."

"I'll take that chance. You don't think I'm going back to Paris with the paintings, anyway, do you? I'm not welcome there right now, as you know." He nodded at me, pitying my innocence.

"You promised me you would take the Meissoniers to Paris," I said. "And send me our share of the proceeds."

"Ah, yes. Honor among thieves, wasn't that it? Well, I'm driving your hotel car to Zurich presently, and tomorrow I am flying from there to New York. I have even more connections in New York than in Paris, Kreutz. No one will know you are dead until the chambermaid finally decides, several days from now, to defy the *Do Not Disturb* sign I shall leave on my door. Do you understand?"

"I understand," I said. "For the first time, I truly understand you, monsieur."

"I warned you that art theft is a dangerous business, you know." He glanced at his wristwatch. "I should say that I can reach Zurich comfortably by dawn, shouldn't you? In your excellent car?"

His finger tightened on the trigger of the pistol. I could see his knuckle go white in the moonlight. I stood like a statue.

"Goodbye, Kreutz," he said. "No hard feelings, you know." He pulled the trigger.

I leaned over, quite slowly, and set my champagne glass on the table beside his. "You have made a fatal error," I said.

He scarcely heard me. He was looking accusingly, incredulously, at the gun in his hand. I saw genuine shock in his eyes. *"Sacré!"* he swore. He pointed the gun at me once more and pulled the trigger rapidly six times. The clicks of the hammer falling on empty chambers were like the clicks a child makes with his tongue when playing a desperado.

"Three nights ago," I said, "when I met you at the station, you went into the dining room to have dinner immediately upon registering at the hotel. Remember? While I put your luggage in your room? Knowing that I might have dealings with you later, I confess I glanced inside your bags and found your pistol. I removed the cartridges . . . just in case." I gave him a smile. "It seems I was wise to do so, eh?"

He said, "Very wise," still staring down at his pistol. "I called you an amateur just now, Kreutz. I apologize. You are a professional. I salute you. So now we start over, is that it?"

"Not quite. As you so admirably phrased it, who needs *you* now?" I paused deliberately. "You have finished your work. Those burglar alarm systems—and the safe. To my shame, I know nothing about electricity or safecracking. But now that the Meissoniers are in my hands, you can see that your usefulness ends, sir."

"You can't dispose of the paintings without my help, Kreutz. You said yourself it would be impossible in Switzerland or Liechtenstein."

"That is so."

"Therefore," he said, trying to sound more confident than he felt, "you'll still be needing me to sell the paintings through my connections, Kreutz. Is this not so?"

"I never intended to sell the paintings," I said.

"What? Then why all this elaborate pretense with the handsewn suitcase?"

I grinned. "Merely a homely touch to assure you of my good faith."

"Good faith, indeed!" St. Clair laughed, with a note of hysteria in it. "Honor among thieves!"

I inclined my head, relishing the irony of the thing.

He said, "I suppose your cousin is a myth, too?"

"Not at all. He is my real cousin. And I, instead of you, shall be taking the paintings in my suitcase to Paris on the eleven twenty plane from Zurich tomorrow."

"You can't sell them for half their value!"

"I told you. We don't intend to sell them."

He looked at me. "Then why did you steal them?"

"My cousin in Paris," I said, "is also the son of my uncle who works in the claims department of the French insurance company which insures the art treasures of Prince Franz Joseph II of Liechtenstein."

St. Clair's shoulders slumped.

"When any of the prince's paintings are reported stolen," I went on, "the insurance company in Paris generously offers a reward of ten percent for their safe return, with no questions asked, I happen to know that, since my uncle's firm paid that amount on a previous occasion."

"You mean pictures have been stolen from the Vaduz gallery before?"

"Once before. I arranged that theft, also."

"You collected the reward before?"

"I and my cousin," I said. "It was on the Pieter Bruegel painting you saw in the prince's collection yesterday."

"And you will collect the reward on these two Meissoniers?"

"Yes. Seventy-five thousand francs apiece for my cousin and me."

St. Clair nodded judiciously. "Very neat, indeed," he murmured in the tone of one expert to another.

I said, "My cousin does the difficult part—selecting professional help for us from among the tourists he sends here—as he selected you, Monsieur St. Clair. Of course, we must pay a small percentage to my uncle for his cooperation."

"I am afraid I underestimated you, Kreutz," said St. Clair.

"Yes. But take comfort. You will die gazing at the most beautiful view in all of Switzerland."

"Die!"

"What else did you expect? You yourself explained that it is unprofessional to leave a living witness behind you."

St. Clair reversed the empty gun in his fragile, graceful hand and drew back his arm for a savage blow, intending to use the weapon as a bludgeon. I reached out and took it from him. As I have said, he was slight of stature; physically a child, compared with me.

I put his gun into my jacket pocket with one hand, while with the other, I drew his slight form so tightly against my chest that he had no breath for crying out. I began to lift him upward then, using both hands, onto the wrought iron rail of the balcony.

I said, "You will be a suicide, my friend. Did you know that for the past three days, as I drove you sightseeing, you have been telling me with despair of an unrequited love in Paris? The first and only great love of your life? Did you know *that* is why you came to Lucerne? To try to get over your foolish passion for another man's wife? Anyway, that is what I have been gossiping about to the hotel staff, sir . . . even to the *herr* director of the Minerva himself.

"So no one will think it unlikely that when you gazed at the ineffable beauty of this moonlit scene tonight, realizing your passion was hopeless, you did what many another lover has done . . . leaped to welcome death from your hotel balcony."

I forced him to look downward at the stone-flagged terrace of the dining room. "Your body will be found there tomorrow morning," I said, holding his struggling, breathless body on the balcony rail with one hand while I dipped the other into his pocket for my car keys. "I bid you goodbye, monsieur," and brought the edge of my free hand, stiffened to a rigid blade, against his Adam's apple, choking off the shout for help that was at last bubbling in his throat.

Then I pushed him off the balcony rail.

As I watched his body pinwheeling downward toward the stone terrace, it occurred to me that Paul St. Clair, as befitted an answer to a prayer, at that moment actually seemed to be dropping from heaven.

The Feel of the Trigger

by Donald E. Westlake

braham Levine, detective of Brooklyn's Forty-third Precinct, sat at a desk in the squad room and worriedly listened to his heart skip every eighth beat. It was two o'clock on Sunday morning, and he had the sports section of the Sunday Times open on the desk, but he wasn't reading it. He hadn't been reading it for about ten minutes now. Instead, he'd been listening to his heart.

A few months ago, he'd discovered the way to listen to his heart without anybody knowing he was doing it. He'd put his right elbow on the desk and press the heel of his right hand to his ear, hard enough to cut out all outside sound. At first it would sound like underwater that way, and then gradually he would become aware of a regular clicking sound. It wasn't a beating or a thumping or anything like that, it was a click-click-click-click—click-click-

There it was again. Nine beats before the skip that time. It fluctuated between every eighth beat and every twelfth beat. The doctor had told him not to worry about that, lots of people had it, but that didn't exactly reassure him. Lots of people died of heart attacks, too. Lots of people around the age of fifty-three.

"Abe? Don't you feel good?"

Levine guiltily lowered his hand. He looked over at his shift partner, Jack Crawley, sitting with the Times crossword puzzle at another desk. "No, I'm okay," he said. "I was just thinking."

"About your heart?"

Levine wanted to say no, but he couldn't. Jack knew him too well.

Crawley got to his feet, stretching, a big bulky harness bull. "You're a hypochondriac, Abe," he said. "You're a good guy, but you got an obsession."

"You're right." He grinned sheepishly. "I almost wish the phone would ring."

Crawley mangled a cigarette out of the pack. "You went to the doctor, didn't you? A couple of months ago. And what did he tell you?"

"He said I had nothing to worry about," Levine admitted. "My

203

blood pressure is a little high, that's all." He didn't want to talk about the skipping.

"So there you are," said Crawley reasonably. "You're still on duty, aren't you? If you had a bum heart, they'd retire you, right?"

"Right."

"So relax. And don't hope for the phone to ring. This is a quiet Saturday night. I've been waiting for this one for years."

The Saturday night graveyard shift—Sunday morning, acutally, midnight till eight—was usually the busiest shift in the week. Saturday night was the time when normal people got violent, and violent people got murderous, the time when precinct plainclothesmen were usually kept on the jump.

Tonight was unusual. Here it was, after two o'clock and only one call so far, a bar hold-up over on 23rd. Rizzo and McFarlane were still out on that one, leaving Crawley and Levine to mind the store and read the Times.

Crawley now went back to the crossword puzzle, and Levine made an honest effort to read the sports section. Levine was a short and stocky man, fifty-three years of age. In his plain brown baggy suit he looked chunky, flabbier than he really was. His face was round and soft, with mild eyes and a formless nose and a broad sensitive mouth, all bracketed by faint fine lines like a pencil sketch.

They read in silence for ten minutes, and then the phone rang on Crawley's desk. Crawley scooped the receiver up to his ear, announced himself, and listened.

The conversation was brief. Crawley's end of it was limited to yesses and got-its, and Levine waited, watching his wrestler's face, trying to read there what the call was about.

Then Crawley broke the connection by depressing the cradle buttons, and said, over his shoulder, "Holdup. Grocery store at Green and Tanahee. Owner shot. That was the beat cop, Wills."

Levine got heavily to his feet and crossed the squadroom to the coatrack, while Crawley dialed a number and said, "Emergency, please."

Levine shrugged into his coat, purposely not listening to Crawley's half of the conversation. It was brief enough, anyway. When Crawley came over to get his own coat, he said, "DOA. Four bullets in him. One of these trigger-happy amateurs."

"Any witnesses?"

"Wife. The beat man—Wills—says she thinks she recognized the guy."

"Widow," said Levine.

Crawley said, "What?"

Widow. Not wife any more, widow. "Nothing," said Levine.

If you're a man fifty-three years of age, there's a statistical chance your heart will stop this year. But there's no sense getting worried about it. There's an even better statistical chance that it *won't* stop this year. So, if you go to the doctor and he says don't worry, then you shouldn't worry. Don't think morbid thoughts. Don't think about death all the time, think about life. Think about your work, for instance.

But what if it so happens that your work, as often as not, is death? What if you're a precinct detective, the one the wife calls when her husband just keeled over at the breakfast table, the one the hotel calls for the guest who never woke up this morning? What if the short end of the statistics is the end you most often see?

Levine sat in the squad car next to Crawley, who was driving, and looked out at the Brooklyn streets, trying to distract his mind. At two A.M. Brooklyn is dull, with red neon signs and grimy windows in narrow streets. Levine wished he'd taken the wheel.

They reached the intersection of Tanahee and Green, and Crawley parked in a bus stop zone. They got out of the car.

The store wasn't exactly on the corner. It was two doors down Green, on the southeast side, occupying the ground floor of a red brick tenement building. The plate glass window was filthy, filled with show-boxes of Kellogg's Pep, and Tide and Premium Saltines. Inevitably, the letters SALADA were curved across the glass. The flap of the rolled-up green awning above the window had lettering on it, too: *Fine Tailoring.*

There were two slate steps up, and then the store. The glass in the door was so covered with cigarette and soft drink decals it was almost impossible to see inside. On the reverse, they all said, "Thank you—call again."

The door was closed now, and locked. Levine caught a glimpse of blue uniform through the decals, and rapped softly on the door. The young patrolman, Wills, recognized him and pulled the door open. "Stanton's with her," he said. "In back." He meant the patrolman from the prowl car parked now out front.

Crawley said, "You got any details yet?"

"On what happened," said Wills, "yes."

Levine closed and locked the door again, and turned to listen. This was their method, his and Crawley's, and it made them a good team. Crawley asked the questions, and Levine listened to the answers.

"There weren't any customers," Wills was saying. "The store stays open till three in the morning, weekends. Midnight during the week. It was just the old couple—Kosofsky, Nathan and Emma—they take turns, and they both work when it's busy. The husband—Nathan—he was out here, and his wife was in back, making a pot of tea. She heard the bell over the door—"

"Bell?" Levine turned and looked up at the top of the door. There hadn't been any bell sound when they'd come in just now.

"The guy ripped it off the wall on his way out."

Levine nodded. He could see the exposed wood where screws had been dragged out. Somebody tall, then, over six foot. Somebody strong, and nervous, too.

"She heard the bell," said Wills, "and then, a couple minutes later, she heard the shots. So she came running out, and saw this guy at the cash register—"

"She saw him," said Crawley.

"Yeah, sure. But I'll get to that in a minute. Anyway, he took a shot at her, too, but he missed. And she fell flat on her face, expecting the next bullet to get her, but he didn't fire again."

"He thought the first one did it," said Crawley.

"I don't know," said Wills. "He wasted four on the old guy."

"He hadn't expected both of them," said Levine. "She rattled him. Did he clean the register?"

"All the bills and a handful of quarters. She figures about sixty-two bucks."

"What about identification?" asked Crawley. "She saw him, right?"

"Right. But you know this kind of neighborhood. At first, she said she recognized him. Then she thought it over, and now she says she was mistaken."

Crawley made a sour sound and said, "Does she know the old man is dead?"

Wills looked surprised. "I didn't know it myself. He was alive when the ambulance got him."

"Died on the way to the hospital. Okay, let's go talk to her."

Oh, God, thought Levine. We've got to be the ones to tell her.

Don't think morbid thoughts. Think about life. Think about your work.

Wills stayed in front, by the door. Crawley led the way back. It was a typical slum neighborhood grocery. The store area was too narrow to begin with, both sides lined with shelves. A glass-faced enamel-sided cooler, full of cold cuts and potato salad and quarter pound bricks of butter, ran parallel to the side shelves down the middle of the store. At one end there was a small ragged-wood counter holding the cash register and candy jars and a tilted stack of English muffin packages. Beyond this counter were the bread and pastry shelves and, at the far end, a small frozen food chest. This row gave enough room on the customer's side for a man to turn around, if he did so carefully, and just enough room on the owner's side for a man to sidle along sideways.

Crawley led the way down the length of the store and through the dim doorway at the rear. They went through a tiny dark stock area and another doorway to the smallest and most overcrowded living room Levine had ever seen.

Mohair and tassels and gilt and lion's legs, that was the living room. Chubby hassocks and overstuffed chairs and amber lamp-shades and tiny intricate doilies on every flat surface. The carpet design was twists and corkscrews, in muted dark faded colors. The wallpaper was somber, with a curling ensnarled vine pattern writh-ing on it. The ceiling was low. This wasn't a room, it was a warm crowded den, a little hole in the ground for frightened gray mice.

The woman sat deep within one of the overstuffed chairs. She was short and very stout, dressed in dark clothing nearly the same dull hue as the chair, so that only her pale frightened face was at first noticeable, and then the heavy pale hands twisting in her lap.

Stanton, the other uniformed patrolman, rose from the sofa, saying to the woman, "These men are detectives. They'll want to talk to you a little. Try to remember about the boy, will you? You know we won't let anything happen to you."

Crawley asked him, "The lab been here yet?"

"No, sir, not yet."

"You and Wills stick around up front till they show."

"Right." He excused himself as he edged around Levine and left.

Crawley took Stanton's former place on the sofa, and Levine worked his way among the hassocks and drum tables to the chair most distant from the light, off to the woman's left.

Crawley said, "Mrs. Kosofsky, we want to get the man who did this. We don't want to let him do it again, to somebody else."

The woman didn't move, didn't speak. Her gaze remained fixed on Crawley's lips.

Crawley said, "You told the patrolman you could identify the man who did it."

After a long second of silence, the woman trembled, shivered as though suddenly cold. She shook her head heavily from side to side, saying, "No. No, I was wrong. It was very fast, too fast. I couldn't see him good."

Levine sighed and shifted position. He knew it was useless. She wouldn't tell them anything, she would only withdraw deeper and deeper into the burrow, wanting no revenge, no return, nothing but to be left alone.

"You saw him," said Crawley, his voice loud and harsh. "You're afraid he'll get you if you talk to us, is that it?"

The woman's head was shaking again, and she repeated, "No. No. No."

"He shot a gun at you," Crawley reminded her. "Don't you want us to get him for that?"

"No. No."

"Don't you want us to get your money back?"

"No. No." She wasn't listening to Crawley, she was merely shaking her head and repeating the one word over and over again.

"Don't you want us to get the man who killed your husband?"

Levine started. He'd known that was what Crawley was leading up to, but it still shocked him. The viciousness of it cut into him, but he knew it was the only way they'd get any information from her, to hit her with the death of her husband just as hard as they could.

The woman continued to shake her head a few seconds longer, and then stopped abruptly, staring full at Crawley for the first time. "What you say?"

"The man who murdered your husband," said Crawley. "Don't you want us to get him for murdering your husband?"

"Nathan?"

"He's dead."

"No," she said, more forcefully than before, and half-rose from the chair.

"He died in the ambulance," said Crawley doggedly, "died before he got to the hospital."

Then they waited. Levine bit down hard on his lower lip, hard enough to bring blood. He knew Crawley was right, it was the only possible way. But Levine couldn't have done it. To think of death was terrible enough. To *use* death—to use the fact of it as a weapon—no, that he could never do.

The woman fell back into the seat, and her face was suddenly stark and clear in every detail. Rounded brow and narrow nose and prominent cheekbones and small chin, all covered by skin as white as candle wax, stretched taut across the skull.

Crawley took a deep breath. "He murdered your husband," he said. "Do you want him to go free?"

In the silence now they could hear vague distant sounds, people walking, talking to one another, listening to the radio or watching television, far away in another world.

At last, she spoke. "Brodek," she said. Her voice was flat. She stared at the opposite wall. "Danny Brodek. From the next block down."

"A boy?"

"Sixteen, seventeen."

Crawley would have asked more, but Levine got to his feet and said, "Thank you, Mrs. Kosofsky."

She closed her eyes.

In the phone book in the front of the store they found one Brodek—Harry R—listed with an address on Tanahee. They went out to the car and drove slowly down the next block to the building they wanted. A taxi passed them, its vacancy light lit. Nothing else moved.

This block, like the one before it and the one after it, was lined on both sides with red brick tenements, five stories high. The building they were looking for was two-thirds of the way down the block. They left the car and went inside.

In the hall, there was the smell of food. The hall was amber tile, and the doors were dark green, with metal numbers. The stairs led up abruptly to the left, midway down the hall. Opposite them were the mailboxes, warped from too much rifling.

They found the name, shakily capital-lettered on an odd scrap of paper and stuck into the mailbox marked 4D.

Above the first floor, the walls were plaster, painted a green slightly darker than the doors. Sounds of television filtered through most of the doors. Crawley waited at the fourth floor landing for Levine to catch up. Levine climbed stairs slowly, afraid of being short of breath. When he was short of breath, the skipped heartbeats became more frequent.

Crawley rapped on the door marked 4D. Television sounds came through this one, too. After a minute, the door opened a crack, as far as it would go with the chain attached. A woman glared out at them. "What you want?"

"Police," said Crawley. "Open the door."

"What you want?" she asked again.

"Open up," said Crawley impatiently.

Levine took out his wallet, flipped it open to show the badge pinned to the ID label. "We want to talk to you for a minute," he said, trying to make his voice as gentle as possible.

The woman hesitated, then shut the door and they heard the clinking of the chain being removed. She opened the door again, releasing into the hall a smell of beer and vegetable soup. She said, "All right. Come." Turning away, she waddled down an unlit corridor toward the living room.

This room was furnished much like the den behind the grocery store, but the effect was different. It was a somewhat larger room, dominated by a blue plastic television set with a bulging screen. An automobile chase was careening across the screen, pre-war Fords and Mercuries, accompanied by frantic music.

A short heavy man in T-shirt and work pants and slippers sat on the sofa, holding a can of beer, and watching the television set. Beyond him, a taller, younger version of himself, in khaki slacks and flannel shirt with the collar turned up, was watching, with a cold and wary eye, the entrance of the two policemen.

The man turned sourly, and his wife said, "They're police. They want to talk to us."

Crawley walked across the room and stood in front of the boy. "You Danny Brodek?"

"So what?"

"Get on your feet."

"Why should I?"

Before Crawley could answer, Mrs. Brodek stepped between him and her son, saying rapidly, "What you want Danny for? He ain't done nothing. He's been right here all night long."

Levine, who had waited by the corridor doorway, shook his head grimly. This was going to be just as bad as the scene with Mrs. Kosofsky. Maybe worse.

Crawley said, "He told you to say that? Did he tell you why? Did he tell you what he did tonight?"

It was the father who answered. "He didn't do nothing. You make a federal case out of everything, you cops. Kids maybe steal a hubcap, knock out a streetlight, what the hell? They're kids."

Over Mrs. Brodek's shoulder, Crawley said to the boy, "Didn't you tell them, Danny?"

"Tell them what?"

"Do you want me to tell them?"

"I don't know what you're talking about."

On the television screen, the automobile chase was finished. A snarling character said, "I don't know what you're talking about." Another character said back, "You know what I'm talking about, Kid."

Crawley turned to Mr. Brodek. "Your boy didn't steal any hubcap tonight," he said. "He held up the grocery store in the next block. Kosofsky's."

The boy said, "You're nuts."

Mrs. Brodek said, "Not Danny. Danny wouldn't do nothing like that."

"He shot the old man," said Crawley heavily. "Shot him four times."

"Shot him!" cried Brodek. "How? Where's he going to get a gun? Answer me that, where's a young kid like that going to get a gun?"

Levine spoke up for the first time. "We don't know where they get them, Mr. Brodek," he said. "All we know is they get them. And then they use them."

"I'll tell you where when he tells us," said Crawley.

Mrs. Brodek said again, "Danny wouldn't do nothing like that. You've got it wrong."

Levine said, "Wait, Jack," to his partner. To Mrs. Brodek, he said, "Danny did it. There isn't any question. If there was a question, we wouldn't arrest him."

"The hell with that!" cried Brodek. "I know about you cops, you get these arrest quotas. You got to look good, you got to make a lot of arrests."

"If we make a lot of wrong arrests," Levine told him, trying to be patient for the sake of what this would do to Brodek when he finally had to admit the truth, "we embarrass the police department. If we make a lot of wrong arrests, we don't stay on the force."

Crawley said, angrily, "Danny, you aren't doing yourself any favors. And you aren't doing your parents any favors either. You want them charged with accessory? The old man died!"

In the silence, Levine said softly, "We have a witness, Mrs. Brodek,

Mr. Brodek. The wife, the old man's wife. She was in the apartment behind the store and heard the shots. She ran out to the front and saw Danny at the cash register. She'll make a positive identification."

"Sure she will," said the boy.

Levine looked at him. "You killed her husband, boy. She'll identify you."

"So why didn't I bump her while I was at it?"

"You tried," said Crawley. "You fired one shot, saw her fall, and then you ran."

The boy grinned. "Yeah, that's a dandy. Think it'll hold up in court? An excitable old woman, she only saw this guy for a couple of seconds, while he's shooting at her, and then he ran out. Some positive identification."

"They teach bad law on television, boy," said Levine. "It'll hold up."

"Not if I was here all night, and I was. Wasn't I, Mom?"

Defiantly, Mrs. Brodek said, "Danny didn't leave this room for a minute tonight. Not a minute."

Levine said, "Mrs. Brodek, he *killed*. Your son took a man's life. He was seen."

"She could have been mistaken. It all happened so fast, I bet she could have been mistaken. She only thought it was Danny."

"If it happened to your husband, Mrs. Brodek, would *you* make a mistake?"

Mr. Brodek said, "You don't make me believe that. I know my son. You got this wrong somewhere."

Crawley said, "Hidden in his bedroom, or hidden somewhere nearby, there's sixty-two dollars, most of it in bills, three or four dollars in quarters. And the gun's probably with it."

"That's what he committed murder for, Mr. Brodek," said Levine. "Sixty-two dollars."

"I'm going to go get it," said Crawley, turning toward the door on the other side of the living room.

Brodek jumped up, shouting, "The hell you are! Let's see your warrant! I got that much law from television, mister, you don't just come busting in here and make a search. You got to have a warrant."

Crawley looked at Levine in disgust and frustration, and Levine knew what he was thinking. The simple thing to do would be to go ahead and make the arrest and leave the Brodeks still telling their lie. That would be the simple thing to do, but it would also be the wrong thing to do. If the Brodeks were still maintaining the lie once Crawley and Levine left, they would be stuck with it. They wouldn't dare admit the truth after that, not even if they could be made to believe it.

They must be wondering already, but could not admit their doubts. If they were left alone now, they would make the search themselves that they had just kept Crawley from making, and they would find the money and the gun. The money and the gun would be somewhere in Danny Brodek's bedroom. The money stuffed into the toe of a shoe in the closet, maybe. The gun under the mattress or at the bottom of a full wastebasket.

If the Brodeks found the money and the gun, and believed that they didn't dare change their story, they would get rid of the evidence. The paper money ripped up and flushed down the toilet. The quarters spent, or thrown out the window. The gun dropped down a sewer.

Without the money, without the gun, without breaking Danny Brodek's alibi, he had a better than even chance of getting away scotfree. In all probability, the grand jury wouldn't even return an indictment. The unsupported statement of an old woman, who only had a few hectic seconds for identification, against a total lack of evidence and a rock solid alibi by the boy's parents, and the case was foredoomed.

But Danny Brodek had *killed*. He had taken life, and he couldn't get away with it. Nothing else in the world, so far as Levine was concerned, was as heinous, as vicious, as *evil*, as the untimely taking of life.

Couldn't the boy himself understand what he'd done? Nathan Kosofsky was dead. He didn't exist any more. He didn't breathe, he didn't see or hear or taste or touch or smell. The pit that yawned so widely in Levine's fears had been opened for Nathan Kosofsky and he had tumbled in. Never to live, ever again.

If the boy couldn't understand the enormity of what he'd done, if he was too young, if life to him was still too natural and inevitable a gift, then surely his parents were old enough to understand. Did Mr. Brodek never lie awake in bed and wonder at the frail and transient sound of his own heart pumping the life through his veins? Had Mrs. Brodek not felt the cringing closeness of the fear of death when she was about to give birth to her son? They knew, they had to know, what murder really meant.

He wanted to ask them, or to remind them, but the awful truths swirling in his brain wouldn't solidify into words and sentences. There is no real way to phrase an emotion.

Crawley, across the room, sighed heavily and said, "Okay. You'll set your own parents up for the bad one. That's okay. We've got the eyewitness. And there'll be more; a fingerprint on the cash register, somebody who saw you run out of the store—"

No one had seen Danny Brodek run from the store. Looking at the smug young face, Levine knew there would be no fingerprints on the cash register. It's just as easy to knuckle the No Sale key to open the cash drawer.

He said, to the boy's father, "On the way out of the store, Danny was mad and scared and nervous. He pulled the door open, and the bell over it rang. He took out his anger and his nervousness on it, yanking the bell down. We'll find that somewhere between here and the store, and there may be prints on it. There also may be scratches on his hand, from yanking the bell mechanism off the door frame."

Quickly, Danny said, "Lots of people got scratches on their hands. I was playing with a cat this afternoon, coming home from school. He give me a couple scratches. See?" He held out his right hand, with three pink ragged tears across the surface of the palm.

Crawley said, "I've played with cats, too, kid. I always got my scratches on the back of my hand."

The boy shrugged. The statement needed no answer.

Crawley went on, "You played with this cat a long while, huh? Long enough to get three scratches, is that it?"

"That's it. Prove different."

"Let's see the scratches on your left hand."

The boy allowed tension to show for just an instant, before he said, "I don't have any on my left hand. Just the right. So what?"

Crawley turned to the father. "Does that sound right to you?"

"Why not?" demanded Brodek defensively. "You play with a cat, maybe you only use one hand. You trying to railroad my son because of some cat scratches?"

This wasn't the way to do it, and Levine knew it. Little corroborative proofs, they weren't enough. They could add weight to an already-held conviction, that's all they could do. They couldn't change an opposite conviction.

The Brodeks had to be reminded, some way, of the enormity of what their son had done. Levine wished he could open his brain for them like a book, so they could look in and read it there. They must know, they must at their ages have some inkling of the monstrousness of death. But they had to be reminded.

There was one way to do it. Levine knew the way, and shrank from it. It was as necessary as Crawley's brutality with the old woman in the back of the store. Just as necessary. But more brutal. And he had flinched away from that earlier, lesser brutality, telling himself *he* could never do such a thing.

He looked over at his partner, hoping Crawley would think of the way, hoping Crawley would take the action from Levine. But Crawley was still parading his little corroborative proofs, before an audience not yet prepared to accept them.

Levine shook his head, and took a deep breath, and stepped forward an additional pace into the room. He said, "May I use your phone?"

They all looked at him, Crawley puzzled, the boy wary, the parents hostile. The father finally shrugged and said, "Why not? On the stand there, by the TV."

"May I turn the volume down?"

"Turn the damn thing off if you want, who can pay any attention to it?"

"Thank you."

Levine switched off the television set, then searched in the phone book and found the number of Kosofsky's grocery. He dialed, and a male voice answered on the first ring, saying, "Kosofsky's. Hello?"

"Is this Stanton?"

"No, Wills. Who's this?"

"Detective Levine. I was down there a little while ago."

"Oh, sure. What can I do for you, sir?"

"How's Mrs. Kosofsky now?"

"How is she? I don't know. I mean, she isn't hysterical or anything. She's just sitting there."

"Is she capable of going for a walk?"

Wills's, "I guess so," was drowned out by Mr. Brodek's shouted, "What the hell are you up to?"

Into the phone, Levine said, "Hold on a second." He cupped his hand over the mouthpiece, and looked at the angry father. "I want you to understand," he told him, "just what it was your son did tonight. I want to make sure you understand. So I'm going to have Mrs. Kosofsky come up here. For her to look at Danny again. And for you to look at her while she's looking at him."

Brodek paled slightly, and an uncertain look came into his eyes.

He glanced quickly at his son, then even more quickly back at Levine. "The hell with you," he said defiantly. "Danny was here all night. Do whatever the hell you want."

Mrs. Brodek started to speak, but cut it off at the outset, making only a tiny sound in her throat. But it was enough to make the rest swivel their heads and look at her. Her eyes were wide. Strain lines had deepened around her mouth, and one hand trembled at the base of her throat. She stared in mute appeal at Levine, her eyes clearly saying, *Don't make me know.*

Levine forced himself to turn away, say into the phone, "I'm at the Brodeks. Bring Mrs. Kosofsky up here, will you? It's the next block down to your right, 1342, apartment 4D."

It was a long, silent wait. No one spoke at all from the time Levine hung up the telephone till the time Wills arrived with Mrs. Kosofsky. The five of them sat in the drab living room, avoiding one another's eyes. From another room, deeper in the apartment, a clock that had before been unnoticeable now ticked loudly. The ticks were very fast, but the minutes they clocked off crept slowly by.

When the rapping finally came at the hall door, they all jumped. Mrs. Brodek turned her hopeless eyes toward Levine again, but he looked away, at his partner. Crawley lumbered to his feet and out of the room, down the corridor to the front door. Those in the room heard him open the door, heard the murmur of male voices, and then the clear frightened voice of the old woman: "Who lives here? Who lives in this place?"

Levine looked up and saw that Danny Brodek was watching him, eyes hard and cold, face set in lines of bitter hatred. Levine held his gaze, pitying him, until Danny looked away, mouth twisting in an expression of scorn that didn't quite come off.

Then Crawley came back into the room, stepping aside for the old woman to follow him in. Beyond her could be seen the pale young face of the patrolman, Wills.

She saw Levine first. Her eyes were frightened and bewildered. Her fingers plucked at a button of the long black coat she now wore over her dress. In the brighter light of this room, she looked older, weaker, more helpless.

She looked second at Mrs. Brodek, whose expression was as terrified as her own, and then she saw Danny.

She cried out, a high-pitched failing whimper, and turned hurriedly away, pushing against Wills, jabbering, "Away! Away! I go away!"

Levine's voice sounded over her hysteria: "It's okay, Wills. Help her back to the store." He couldn't keep the bitter rage from his voice. The others might have thought it was rage against Danny Brodek, but they would have been wrong. It was rage against himself. What good would it do to convict Danny Brodek, to jail him for twenty or thirty years? Would it undo what he had done? Would it restore her husband to Mrs. Kosofsky? It wouldn't. But nothing less could excuse the vicious thing he had just done to her.

Faltering, nearly whispering, Mrs. Brodek said, "I want to talk to Danny. I want to talk to my son."

Her husband glared warningly at her. "Esther, he was here all—"

"I want to talk to my son!"

Levine said, "All right." Down the corridor, the door snicked shut behind Wills and the old woman.

Mrs. Brodek said, "Alone. In his bedroom."

Levine looked at Crawley, who shrugged and said, "Three minutes. Then we come in."

The boy said, "Mom, what's there to talk about?"

"I want to talk to you," she told him icily. "Now."

She led the way from the room, Danny Brodek following her reluctantly, pausing to throw back one poisonous glance at Levine before shutting the connecting door.

Brodek cleared his throat, looking uncertainly at the two detectives. "Well," he said. "Well. She really—she really thinks it was him, don't she?"

"She sure does," said Crawley.

Brodek shook his head slowly. "Not Danny," he said, but he was talking to himself.

Then they heard Mrs. Brodek cry out from the bedroom, and a muffled thump. All three men dashed across the living room, Crawley reaching the door first and throwing it open, leading the way down the short hall to the second door and running inside. Levine followed him, and Brodek, grunting, "My God. Oh, my God," came in third.

Mrs. Brodek sat hunched on the floor of the tiny bedroom, arms folded on the seat of an unpainted kitchen chair. A bright colored shirt was hung askew on the back of the chair.

She looked up as they ran in, and her face was a blank, drained of all emotion and all life and all personality. In a voice as toneless and blank as her face, she told them, "He went up the fire escape. He got the gun, from under his mattress. He went up the fire escape."

Brodek started toward the open window, but Crawley pulled him back, saying, "He might be waiting up there. He'll fire at the first head he sees."

Levine had found a comic book and a small gray cap on the dresser-top. He twisted the comic book in a large cylinder, stuck the cap on top of it, held it slowly and cautiously out the window. From above, silhouetted, it would look like a head and neck.

The shot rang loud from above, and the comic book was jerked from Levine's hand. He pulled his hand back, and Crawley said, "The stairs."

Levine followed his partner back out of the bedroom. The last he saw in there, Mr. Brodek was reaching down, with an awkward shyness, to touch his wife's cheek.

This was the top floor of the building. After this, the staircase went up one more flight, ending at a metal-faced door which opened onto the roof. Crawley led the way, his small flat pistol now in his hand, and Levine climbed more slowly after him.

He got midway up the flight before Crawley pushed open the door, stepped cautiously out onto the roof, and the single shot snapped out. Crawley doubled suddenly, stepping involuntarily back, and would have fallen backward down the stairs if Levine hadn't reached him in time and struggled him to a half-sitting position, wedged between the top step and the wall.

Crawley's face was gray, his mouth strained white. "From the right," he said, his voice low and bitter. "Down low. I saw the flash."

"Where?" Levine asked him. "Where did he get you?"

"Leg. Right leg, high up. Just the fat, I think."

From outside, they could hear a man's voice braying, "Danny! Danny! For God's sake, Danny!" It was Mr. Brodek, shouting up from the bedroom window.

"Get the light," whispered Crawley.

Not until then had Levine realized how rattled he'd been just now. Twenty-four years on the force. When did you become a professional? How?

He straightened up, reaching up to the bare bulb in its socket high on the wall near the door. The bulb burned his fingers, but it took only the one turn to put it out.

Light still filtered up from the floor below, but no longer enough to keep him from making out shapes on the roof. He crouched over Crawley, blinking until his eyes got used to the darkness.

To the right, curving over the top of the knee-high wall around the roof, were the top bars of the fire escape. Black shadow at the base of the wall, all around. The boy was low, lying prone against the wall in the darkness, where he couldn't be seen.

"I can see the fire escape from here," muttered Crawley. "I've got him boxed. Go on down to the car and call for help."

"Right," said Levine.

He had just turned away when Crawley grabbed his arm. "No. Listen!"

He listened. Soft scrapings, outside and to the right. A sudden flurry of footsteps, running, receding.

"Over the roofs!" cried Crawley. *Damn* this leg! Go after him!"

"Ambulance," said Levine.

"Go *after* him! *They* can make the call." He motioned at the foot of the stairs, and Levine, turning, saw down there anxious, frightened, bewildered faces peering up, bodies clothed in robes and slippers.

"Go on!" cried Crawley.

Levine moved, jumping out onto the roof in a half-crouch, ducking away to the right. The revolver was in his hand, his eyes were staring into the darkness.

Three rooftops away, he saw the flash of white, the boy's shirt. Levine ran after him.

Across the first roof, he ran with mouth open, but his throat dried and constricted, and across the second roof he ran with his mouth shut, trying to swallow. But he couldn't get enough air in through his nostrils, and after that he alternated, mouth open and mouth closed, looking like a frantic fish, running like a comic fat man, clambering over the intervening knee-high walls with painful slowness.

There were seven rooftops to the corner, and the corner building was only three stories high. The boy hesitated, dashed one way and then the other, and Levine was catching up. Then the boy turned, fired wildly at him, and raced to the fire escape. He was young and lithe, slender. His legs went over the side, his body slid down; the last thing Levine saw of him was the white face.

Two more roofs. Levine stumbled across them, and he no longer needed the heel of his hand to his ear in order to hear his heart. He could hear it plainly, over the rush of his breathing, a brushlike throb—throb—throb—throb—throb—

Every six or seven beats.

He got to the fire escape, winded, and looked over. Five flights down, a long dizzying way, to the blackness of the bottom. He saw a flash of the boy in motion, two flights down. "Stop!" he cried, knowing it was useless.

He climbed over onto the rungs, heavy and cumbersome. His revolver clanged against the top rung as he descended and, as if in answer, the boy's gun clanged against metal down below.

The first flight down was a metal ladder, and after that, narrow steep metal staircases with a landing at every floor. He plummeted down, never quite on balance, the boy always two flights ahead.

At the second floor, he paused, looked over the side, saw the boy drop lightly to the ground, turn back toward the building, heard the grate of door hinges not used to opening.

The basement. And the flashlight was in the glove compartment of the squad car. Crawley had a pencil flash, six buildings and three floors away. Levine moved again, hurrying as fast as before. At the bottom, there was a jump. He hung by his hands, the revolver digging into his palm, and dropped, feeling it hard in his ankles.

The back of the building was dark, with a darker rectangle in it, and fire flashed in that rectangle. Something tugged at Levine's sleeve, at the elbow. He ducked to the right, ran forward, and was in the basement.

Ahead of him, something toppled over with a wooden crash, and the boy cursed. Levine used the noise to move deeper into the basement, to the right, so he couldn't be outlined against the doorway, which was a gray hole now in a world suddenly black. He came up against a wall, rough brick and bits of plaster, and stopped, breathing hard, trying to breathe silently and to listen.

He wanted to listen for sounds of the boy, but the rhythmic pounding of his heart was too loud, too pervasive. He had to hear it out first, to count it, and to know that now it was skipping every sixth beat. His breath burned in his lungs, a metal band was constricted about his chest, his head felt hot and heavy and fuzzy. There were blue sparks at the corners of his vision.

There was another clatter from deeper inside the basement, to the left, and the faint sound of a doorknob being turned, turned back, turned again.

Levine cleared his throat. When he spoke, he expected his voice to be high-pitched, but it wasn't. It was as deep and as strong as normal, maybe even a little deeper and a little louder. "It's locked, Danny," he said. "Give it up. Throw the gun out the doorway."

The reply was another fire-flash, and an echoing thunderclap, too loud for the small bare-walled room they were in. And, after it, the whining ricochet as the bullet went wide.

That's the third time, thought Levine. *The third time he's given me a target, and I haven't shot at him. I could have shot at the flash, this time or the last. I could have shot at him on the roof, when he stood still just before going down the fire escape.*

Aloud, he said, "That won't do you any good, Danny. You can't hit a voice. Give it up, prowl cars are converging here from all over Brooklyn."

"I'll be long gone," said the sudden voice, and it was surprisingly close, surprisingly loud.

"You can't get out the door without me seeing you," Levine told him. "Give it up."

"I can see you, cop," said the young voice. "You can't see me, but I can see you."

Levine knew it was a lie. Otherwise, the boy would have shot him down before this. He said, "It won't go so bad for you, Danny, if you give up now. You're young, you'll get a lighter sentence. How old are you? Sixteen, isn't it?"

"I'm going to gun you down, cop," said the boy's voice. It seemed to be closer, moving to Levine's right. The boy was trying to get behind him, get Levine between himself and the doorway, so he'd have a silhouette to aim at.

Levine slid cautiously along the wall, feeling his way. "You aren't going to gun anybody down," he said into the darkness. "Not anybody else."

Another flash, another thunderclap, and the shatter of glass behind him. The voice said, "You don't even have a gun on you."

"I don't shoot at shadows, Danny. Or old men."

"I do, old man."

How old is he? wondered Levine. *Sixteen, probably. Thirty-seven years younger than me.*

"You're afraid," taunted the voice, weaving closer. "You ought to run, cop, but you're afraid."

I am, thought Levine. *I am, but not for the reason you think.*

It was true. From the minute he'd ducked into this basement room, Levine had stopped being afraid of his own death at the hands of this boy. He was fifty-three years of age. If anything was going to get him tonight it was going to be that heart of his, skipping now on number five. It wasn't going to be the boy, except indirectly, because of the heart.

But he *was* afraid. He was afraid of the revolver in his own hand, the feel of the trigger, and the knowledge that he had let three chances go by. He was afraid of his job, because his job said he was supposed to bring this boy down. Kill him or wound him, but bring him down.

Thirty-seven years. That was what separated them, thirty-seven years of life. Why should it be up to *him* to steal those thirty-seven years from this boy? Why should *he* have to be the one?

"You're a goner, cop," said the voice. "You're a dead man. I'm coming in on you."

It didn't matter what Danny Brodek had done. It didn't matter about Nathan Kosofsky, who was dead. An eye for an eye, a life for a life. No! A destroyed life could not be restored by more destruction of life. *I can't do it,* Levine thought. *I can't do it to him.*

He said, "Danny, you're wrong. Listen to me, for God's sake, you're wrong."

"You better run, cop," crooned the voice. "You better hurry."

Levine heard the boy, soft slow sounds closer to his left, weaving slowly nearer. "I don't *want* to kill you, Danny!" he cried. "Can't you understand that? I don't *want* to kill you!"

"I want to kill *you,* cop," whispered the voice.

"Don't you know what dying is?" pleaded Levine. He had his hand out now in a begging gesture, though the boy couldn't see him. "Don't you know what it means to die? To stop, like a watch. Never to see anything any more, never to hear or touch or know anything any more. Never to *be* any more."

"That's the way it's going to be, cop," soothed the young voice. Very close now, very close.

He was too young. Levine knew it, knew the boy was too young to *feel* what death really is. He was too young to know what he wanted to take from Levine, what Levine didn't want to take from him.

Every fourth beat. *Thirty-seven years.*

"You're a dead man, cop," breathed the young voice, directly in front of him.

And light dazzled them both.

It all happened so fast. One second, they were doing their dance of death here together, alone, just the two of them in all the world. The next second, the flashlight beam hit them both, the clumsy uniformed patrolman was standing in the doorway, saying, "Hey!" Making himself a target, and the boy, slender, turning like a snake, his eyes glinting in the light, the gun swinging around at the light and the figure behind the light.

Levine's heart stopped, one beat.

And every muscle, every nerve, every *bone* in his body tensed and tightened and drew in on itself, squeezing him shut, and the sound of the revolver going off slammed into him, pounding his stomach.

The boy screamed, hurtling down out of the light, the gun clattering away from his fingers.

"Jesus God have mercy!" breathed the patrolman. It was Wills. He came on in, unsteadily, the flashlight trembling in his hand as he pointed its beam at the boy crumpled on the floor.

Levine looked down at himself and saw the thin trail of blue-gray smoke rising up from the barrel of his revolver. Saw his hands still tensed shut into claws, into fists, the first finger of his right hand still squeezing the trigger back against its guard.

He willed his hands open, and the revolver fell to the floor.

Wills went down on one knee beside the boy. After a minute, he straightened, saying, "Dead. Right through the heart, I guess."

Levine sagged against the wall. His mouth hung open. He couldn't seem to close it.

Wills said, "What's the matter? You okay?"

With an effort, Levine nodded his head. "I'm okay," he said. "Call in. Go on, call in."

"Well. I'll be right back."

Wills left, and Levine looked down at the new young death. His eyes saw the colors of the floor, the walls, the clothing on the corpse. His shoulders felt the weight of his overcoat. His ears heard the receding footsteps of the young patrolman. His nose smelled the sharp tang of recent gunfire. His mouth tasted the briny after-effect of fear.

"I'm sorry," he whispered.

Public Office

by Elijah Ellis

O n any Saturday afternoon, the ancient courthouse in Monroe
is a lonely place. All the county offices, except for the sheriff's
office down on the ground floor, close at noon. By one o'clock
or so, the ugly old pile of stone and marble and worm-eaten wood
is about as lively as a mausoleum.

This particular Saturday was raw and rainy, much too wet and
dismal for golf. So I'd decided to stay on at my office on the third
floor and catch up on my paperwork. By two o'clock I was regretting
my decision. I leaned back in my chair, lit a cigarette, and sourly
eyed the heap of work yet to do. Then the phone rang. Eagerly I
picked it up. "Yes?"

"This the county attorney's office?" The voice was curiously muffled. "County Attorney Gates?"

"Yes, this is Lon Gates speaking. Can I help you?"

"Go look in the dome."

I took the receiver away from my ear, frowned at it, then replaced
it. "Go do what?"

"Go look in the courthouse dome. And I hope it makes you happy.
You dirty rat."

Click. My caller hung up quickly.

Slowly I cradled my phone. "Now what?" I asked the empty office.
I swiveled my chair around to stare out the tall, narrow windows
in the far wall. Beyond them, the sky was a smear of cold gray-
black. Rain fell steadily, speeded on its way by occasional jabs of
lightning, followed by sullen booms of thunder. A lousy day.

Look in the dome?

Well, why not? It'd give me a few minutes away from this mass
of paperwork. And besides, I'd never been up there, even though it
was a famous place in Pokochobee County folklore. About seventy-
five years ago, a disgraced county official had hanged himself from
one of the beams that supported the dome.

Lightning streaked across the stormy sky. Thunder crashed.

Yes, this was surely the day to inspect the famous dome. I laughed,
but I didn't enjoy it much. I was remembering the cold venom in

that voice on the phone. ". . . I hope it makes you happy. You dirty rat."

I got up, left the office, and went along the dim, echoing corridor. Between the county courtroom and the court clerk's office, I found an unmarked door. I pulled it open with a creak of hinges. I stepped inside. It was a small narrow room, crowded with junk. At the far end was the beginning of a spiral iron staircase leading upwards.

Everything—the floor, the walls, the staircase—was furred with inch-thick dust. Squinting through the thick, musty gloom, I saw a trail of scuffed footprints, leading to the iron stairs. I followed them up the corkscrew of the staircase. I was halfway up before I realized that there wàs no sign of footprints coming down . . .

I hesitated. Sure, all this was probably someone's idea of a joke. He'd be there in the dome, ready to jump out at me, but I couldn't see the fun in it.

Slowly I went on up. The stairs emerge on one side of the large, round, sheet-iron dome that crowns the old courthouse. There are small windows around the dome, caked with the grime of years, and now these admitted just enough light to make out an elongated figure suspended from one of the central beams that supported the roof—the figure of a hanging man!

I could feel sweat popping out on my face, and the hairs bristling on the back of my neck. I told myself firmly that it was a joke. The jokester, remembering the old story of the county official who had hanged himself here, had now hung a lifelike dummy in the same spot. Very funny.

I walked toward the dangling figure. It swayed gently in the vagrant puffs of wind that found their way through the cracks and crevices of the ancient dome. I shivered and told myself it was because of the chill and the damp.

Then lightning glared at the windows.

I jumped back and yelled. In the brief flicker of light, I saw the face of the hanging figure. It was a man's face—swollen, congested, and very dead. I forgot all about jokes. I forced myself to walk to the dead man. I squinted up through the gloom, waiting for the next bolt of lightning so that I could see the face suspended above me. From the corner of my eye I noted a ladder propped against the beam, some feet to my right.

It all made a pretty clear picture. Suicide. But, who . . . ? Another sheet of lightning, and I saw who. It was like a kick in the stomach. "Oh, no," I breathed.

Turning away, I stumbled back to the stairs and down them to my office. I fumbled for the phone, dropped it, picked it up again. I called the sheriff's office. In a moment Ed Carson's familiar drawl came on the line.

"Ed, this is Lon Gates. Come up to my office. Quick!"

The sheriff of Pokochobee County didn't waste words. "Be there in a minute."

He was, in less than a minute. I was glad to see him. He ran a handkerchief over his craggy face and panted, "Now what is it? You sounded like a dead man on the phone."

"Leland Russel," I said. "He's up in the dome. . . . Dead."

The sheriff stared.

I took a long drag at a cigarette. "Yeah. It looks like the old codger went up there and— and hanged himself. Suicide."

Carson tugged fiercely at a corner of his pepper-and-salt mustache. Then his suddenly icy gaze hit me. "Let's hear about it."

I told him about the phone call, the single trail of footsteps leading up the spiral stairs into the dome—and none coming down. I mentioned the ladder propped against the beam, and the old man's body, at the end of a seven-foot length of rope.

The sheriff's big, rawboned frame seemed to shrink into itself. Lines of pain appeared in his face, and then lines of bitter anger. He didn't speak. He didn't have to; I knew what he was thinking.

Now he whirled around, picked up the phone. He called his office and snapped an order to the deputy on duty. He broke the connection, immediately called another number—that of Dr. James Conley who served as county coroner.

When he'd finished, he put down the phone. He kept his back to me. Leland Russel had been one of his oldest and best friends. Now I heard quick footsteps in the corridor outside the office. Carson turned.

"It wasn't enough you took his job away," he said. "You had to take his life, too."

The sheriff was gone before I could reply. I started to follow him, the hot words rising in my throat, but I didn't. I stopped in the doorway and watched Carson and his deputy pound along the corridor toward the door that led to the dome. The deputy, Wally Hooper, was carrying a battery-powered floodlight and other equipment.

I turned back into my office. I went to my desk, sat down in the swivel chair. I'd never felt so sick in my life.

Leland Russel . . . a dry, straight, white-maned old man who had been Pokochobee county attorney for twenty years, even longer than Ed Carson had been sheriff.

Last year, I'd been brash enough to run against Russel, and I'd beaten him. The campaign had been rough, even brutal, in its final stages. Pokochobee County politics is no place for the faint of heart.

I'd thought Russel's ideas of justice, and the administration of the county attorney's office were strictly nineteenth century, and he himself little more than a relic. And I didn't hesitate to say so. Enough of the new generation of voters had agreed with me to put me in office.

But it had destroyed Leland Russel. He was like a man who has seen a beloved father turn on him and kick his teeth out. After the election, the old man had withdrawn almost completely from life. Callers were not welcome at his home, and the few who did get in to see him wished they hadn't. They found a gray-lipped, vacant-eyed shell.

He was seldom seen in downtown Monroe, and never seen at the courthouse, though he had many old friends there. He had crumbled away without even the solace of booze; he was a strict teetotaler. Now, a little over a year later, he'd come to this: the sick gesture of making himself the second "disgraced" county official to hang himself in the ancient dome of the courthouse.

But what about the phone call?

The cobwebs of shock and remorse began to lift from my mind. I sat forward in my chair. Yeah, and what about a couple of other things—like a man Russel's age carrying a heavy, twenty-foot ladder up that steep and winding staircase?

"Like hell," I said, and jumped up and left the office. In the gloomy corridor I bumped into the just-arriving Dr. Conley. We went on up to the dome together. There we found that Carson and Deputy Hooper had set up the floodlight.

The dangling body was bathed in the floodlight's hard white glare. Hooper was up on the beam, examining the rope. " . . . It's just looped around a couple of times and tied in a plain old hard-knot," Hooper was saying when the doctor and I arrived.

Dr. Conley brisked forward. He spoke to the sheriff. He eyed the body from several angles. He whistled tunelessly between his teeth. Then he said, "All right, let him down."

While Carson held the body, Hooper undid the knot that held the rope to the beam. Carson lowered the slack body to the floor and

stepped back. Then the sheriff came over to stand beside me near
the mouth of the staircase.

"Sorry about what I said a while ago," he muttered. "I was
just—well, anyhow, I had no business poppin' off. Even if old Leland
had killed himself . . . which he didn't."

I blinked. "That's what I was thinking. The phone call, the ladder—"

"Well, sure, that too," Carson said, "but the main thing is, his
neck ain't broken, which it sure as heck would be if he'd got up on
that beam, tied the rope around his neck and jumped off. Just look
at the poor old fellow. He died of strangulation."

A moment later Dr. Conley rose from his examination. He dusted
absently at the knees of his trousers and said, "I don't know what
kind of wild theory you men have, but I'll tell you right now, Mr.
Russel did not commit suicide."

No one spoke. Outside, the rain still pattered down. A burst of
thunder made the iron dome tremble. Wally Hooper asked, "Then
what did happen?"

"How should I know?" Dr. Conley complained. "The body has a
bruise on the point of the jaw. At a guess, I'd say the blow that made
the bruise was struck not long before death. That's all I'm saying.
You want detective work out of me, you can ask the county com-
missioners to raise my salary."

Ed Carson snorted. Then his hawk-nosed face sobered. "How about
this, doc? He was slugged, and his unconscious body was hoisted up
on the end of the rope so that he died of strangulation."

The pigeon-chested, fussy-mannered little doctor grimaced. "Could
be," he nodded. "Whatever, this man certainly didn't hang himself.
The fall from that beam to the point where the rope became taut
would have snapped his neck like a toothpick," the doctor added,
repeating what Carson had said a few moments ago.

There was a sudden clatter of footsteps on the spiral staircase.
Then the familiar rotund figure of Jeremiah Walton, editor of the
semi-weekly Monroe *Dispatch,* panted into view. Walton surveyed
the scene. His small, puffy eyes fastened on the corpse. "Ah," he
wheezed happily.

Ed Carson exclaimed in annoyance. "How did you get word of this
so quick, Walton?"

The editor waddled forward to peer down at the body. Then he
whirled and aimed a forefinger at me. "So. How do you feel now,

Gates? Now that you've driven this poor old man to take his own life—"

"Oh, shut up, you fat jackass," Ed Carson growled. "Mr. Russel didn't kill himself. He was murdered."

That stopped Walton for a few seconds. His tiny eyes flickered toward Deputy Wally Hooper. "But, I thought . . ."

"The last thought you had was thirty years ago," I said. Needless to say, the *Dispatch* and I are on opposite sides of the political fence. During last year's campaign, Walton had done everything from questioning my ancestry to accusing me of being a card-carrying communist.

He blinked a couple of times, nibbling at his small, pursed lips. Again his eyes flickered toward Hooper. The deputy was bending over the corpse, carefully keeping his broad back turned to the rest of us.

Sheriff Carson said softly, "Wally?"

Hooper turned. His face was a study in innocence.

"Wally, did you call Mr. Walton here? After I called you from Mr. Gates's office?"

The big deputy ran a finger around the open collar of his khaki shirt. He swallowed. Then he blurted, "Well, it wasn't supposed to be a secret, was it?"

Carson squeezed his eyes shut. He opened them again. "All right, Wally." There was something very final in the way he said the two words. Like, "You're through."

Even in the grim circumstances I couldn't help smiling to myself. I'd never liked Wally Hooper, and the feeling was mutual. He was a big, muscular towheaded guy a couple of years younger than me. This past spring he'd gotten his law degree from the state university. During the last two or three summer vacations, and now full time, he'd worked as a deputy to Ed Carson.

Which all sounds very fine and industrious, but not the way Hooper played it. Actually, his one purpose in serving as a deputy sheriff was to make political contacts. He had been a strong worker for Leland Russel last year, no doubt with the agreement that, if Russel were reelected, Wally Hooper would become the assistant county attorney, with every prospect of taking over the office when the old man retired. After the election, Hooper had the nerve to come to me and ask for the assistant's job. I took a good deal of pleasure in laughing in his "boyish" face.

No, Wally Hooper and I didn't care for each other.

But now Jeremiah Walton was thrusting his paunch forward, tilting his head back, and peering down his broad nose at the sheriff. He had recovered his composure. "Are you trying to tell me this was murder?" he sneered.

Carson's Adam's apple bobbed up and down his neck as he swallowed a mouthful of angry words. After a moment he said mildly, "It looks that way to me. Mr. Russel didn't die of a broken neck; he was strangled to death."

"So what?" Walton argued. His eyes darted about the dome, up to the beams that crisscrossed overhead, to the ladder leaning against the beam from which the body had been suspended. "Why, it's obvious what happened. Russel attached the rope to the beam, then he descended the ladder. He had a chair or something placed directly beneath the dangling rope. He then put the noose around his neck and stepped off the chair. Hah! Therefore, he did not drop a sufficient distance to break his neck. He simply strangled."

The editor luxuriously scratched his chins.

I said sardonically, "Where's the chair?" I paused, then added, "Or something?"

The editor again peered about him. There was nothing in the dome but the dust and grime of years. Walton shrugged fat shoulders. "Obvious. Someone carried away the object upon which Russel stood . . ."

"Oh, for God's sake," Dr. Conley barked. The little doctor waved his stubby-fingered hands in disgust. "Politics—politics. You people would debate over the ravished body of your own mother. I'm resigning as county coroner tomorrow."

The doctor stumped toward the stairs. I said, "Doc, could Mr. Russel have packed that ladder up here from the janitor's closet on the third floor?"

Conley paused. "Oh, yes. As far as that goes, Lon, when a man sincerely wants to do something, there's very little he can't do. Long as he don't care what it costs. But in this particular case, I'm here to tell you, Leland Russel didn't. Now I'm going to call the meat-wagon."

"Use the phone in my office," I called, as the doctor bustled down the steps.

An outraged cry responded. "I'll use the phone booth in the hall, thank you!"

After that, no one spoke again for a long moment, while the wind and rain howled outside the shuddering dome.

The glaring white circle of light illuminated the sprawled body on the floor. Walton drew Hooper off to the other side of the dome, and the pair were soon deeply engaged in a whispered conversation.

Carson muttered wryly, "Looks like the end of a beautiful friendship there."

I gave him an absent nod. I was staring at the corpse, particularly the dust-coated shoes on the small slim feet. "Those footprints on the stairs," I said, "there really was just the one set, leading up."

"Yeah," Carson grimaced. "No good to us now. What with all the trampin' up and down since you first saw them."

The sheriff lit a cigarette. I lit one of my own.

"Not that there's any problem about how they were made," the sheriff went on. "The killer was just careful to place his own feet in the prints old Leland made—you can be sure he had Leland in front of him, comin' up the stairs. And the same thing in reverse, when the killer went down, alone."

Carson sighed, rubbed his eyes. "Course I ought to be doin' a dozen things, but I feel like I've been clubbed. I don't care how long you're in this lousy business, or how hardened you think you've become. When it hits close to home . . ." He broke off, ended with a weary shrug.

By now the newspaper editor and Wally Hooper had finished their talk. They moved over to join us. Hooper looked chastened. Jeremiah Walton, as usual, looked like a pompous bullfrog, but he tried to sound friendly even though it was obviously a strain on him.

"Boys, I want to apologize for my somewhat rude language a while ago. But you understand that Mr. Russel was an old and dear friend, and I'd been given to understand he had killed himself."

"Yeah," I broke in, "and if he had, you would have a field day tearing me to pieces in your paper. 'The young upstart who drove the old and honored public servant to a disgraceful death.' I wouldn't be able to get elected dog catcher by the time you got through spraying your venom all over the county."

As I spoke, I took a few steps toward the editor. He quickly backed away, waving his hands before him. "Now, now. Nothing of the sort. I . . ."

A sudden yelp of pain interrupted us. We turned to find Wally Hooper crouched above the body. He had a finger in his mouth. Carson asked, "What's the matter with you?"

Hooper took his finger from his mouth and frowned at it. "I was just going through the old man's pockets again to see if we missed anything. I caught my finger on the point of a stickpin here, on the lapel of his jacket."

Carson snorted. "Too bad you didn't sit down on it."

By now Jeremiah Walton was at the top of the staircase. He passed and backed out of the way as Dr. Conley appeared. The doctor came on up the last few steps and brushed by Walton.

"The wagon will be here in a few minutes," Conley said. The little pigeon-chested doctor's face looked drawn and tired. I remembered that he too had been a close friend of Leland Russel's.

There wasn't anything to do right now but wait for the arrival of the ambulance. My burst of anger towards Jeremiah Walton was gone; this was hardly the time or the place.

The five of us milled slowly around the dome, not speaking. For something to do, I climbed the ladder that was propped against the beam overhead. At the top, I looked along the length of the massive, worm-holed oaken beam.

I sighed and started down. Then I stopped. I bent my face closer to the point where the ladder rested against the beam. There was a fur of undisturbed dust there. Even a cobweb draped from the beam to the side piece of the ladder.

Quite obviously, this ladder had rested in this position for months—maybe years. It was not, as I had thought, the ladder that was kept in the janitor's closet on the third floor. I backed down slowly to the floor of the dome. As I did, a lot of little things that hadn't seemed important began to come together and form a picture.

Maybe I was crazy. But—

I caught Ed Carson's eye, beckoned him over to the side of the dome, away from the others. "Listen," I asked softly, "when's the last time you talked to Russel?"

Ed blinked at me. "Why, I talked to him a couple of minutes on the phone, this noon. Tried to get him to come downtown and have lunch with me. Course, he wouldn't do it."

I swallowed. "Did you happen to mention to him that I'd be working this afternoon?"

"Why—I might have. Think I did. In connection with what a lousy day it is, something like that. Too bad for even you to get out on the golf course. But what the . . . ?"

"Tell you in a minute," I said. I ran down the twisting staircase to the narrow, long room at the bottom. I fumbled along the wall near the corridor door, found a light switch, flicked it on.

A single dusty bulb shed a dim glow over the room. Stacked along the walls and at the far end were a jumble of old packing crates, broken office equipment, a few discarded desks and chairs.

Almost at once I spotted what I wanted. On top of a pile of wooden chairs was a chair like the rest—only the dust on it was smudged in many places and the seat was clean, as if it had been wiped off recently.

Leaving the dingy light on, I went back upstairs.

I remembered certain ugly rumors I'd heard, but hadn't been able to substantiate. Back in the dome again, I went across to Carson.

He looked at me like he wondered if I'd lost a few more of my marbles, I was wondering myself, but it all made a weird kind of sense—up to a point.

"I was right the first time," I told him.

"What are you talking about?"

I didn't answer just then. I walked over to the edge of the glaring circle of light that centered on the dead man. I said, "Listen, would you all come over here a minute?"

The four men sauntered across the dome to form a little knot around me; Ed Carson, puzzled and worried; Dr. Conley, tired and irritable; Wally Hooper, looking as if he wished he were somewhere else; and the editor, Walton, who was very, very nervous, and stayed several feet distant from me.

"Just take a minute to tell," I said casually, though I was feeling far from casual. "Maybe I'm as crazy as Walton there thinks. It's this. I believe a sick, weary old man came up here this afternoon, sometime shortly before two. He knew the courthouse would be deserted practically—especially on a day like this. He also knew I was in my office. From one of the phone booths somewhere in the building, he called—a friend—and told the friend what he intended to do. He asked the friend to wait a few minutes, then call me. See? He wanted me to find his body."

The sheriff exploded, "Are you trying to say now that Russel really did commit suicide?"

"Exactly."

"But that's nonsense," Dr. Conley cried.

There was a confused babble of talk. Finally I shouted, "Shut up, and let me finish."

When they were quiet again except for an occasional mumble, I went on. "So then Russel came on up here. He brought a length of rope with him, and he stopped in the room at the bottom of the stairs long enough to pick up a straight-back wooden chair. Up here, he climbed the ladder to the beam, attached the rope, then climbed down. He placed the chair under the noose in the free end of the rope. He put the rope around his neck, and kicked the chair out from under him."

In the dead silence, I turned slowly to face Jeremiah Walton. "Just as you said, Mr. Editor, the drop wasn't far enough to break his neck. So he strangled to death."

Walton licked ashen lips. "But . . . I was just guessing."

"Good guessing," I said. I looked around at the pale, strained faces. "But then Russel's 'friend' entered the picture. Soon as he got Russel's call, he rushed over here. He was just too late. He was careful to step in Russel's footprints on his way up and down the stairs. He found Russel . . . dead. Pinned to the lapel of his jacket was a note. Remember, Wally? You stuck your finger on the pin a few minutes ago."

The big deputy mopped his face on his sleeve.

"Not much more," I said. "The friend couldn't afford to have Russel found a suicide. Certainly not with that note on his lapel, and probably a sheaf of very revealing documents in his pocket. So he took the note and the papers, and the chair. He left, again being careful to stay in the footprints made by Russel. Down in the anteroom he put the chair back on a pile of similar chairs. He hurried out of the building, noticing that my lights were on. He went across the square to his office. He called me—"

Suddenly everything happened at once. The floodlight smashed over on its face, breaking the lens and the bulb, plunging the dome into near darkness. Startled yells. Vague figures shifting about, silhouetted against the brief flares of lightning at the windows.

I was nearest the staircase so I blundered toward it. At the top, I turned back, meaning to block the way. But before I could set myself a pair of open palms plowed into my chest. I sprawled back and down, windmilling my arms. My flailing hands smacked into the iron railing at the first turn. I grabbed the rail with all my strength.

I was on my back, my head and shoulders hanging over into empty space. A dark figure loomed above me. I cried out, "Stop! Look out!"

Too late, the man tripped over my body. He went over the railing and emitted a grunt that turned into a brief scream. Then he hit the floor thirty feet below.

He was still alive when the rest of us got down there. He was looking up blankly at the dingy bulb that gave the only light. As we gathered around, his lips formed a wry smile. Blood seeped from a corner of his mouth and from his nose.

Ed Carson knelt down by him. He asked "Why?"

The dying man coughed. "Couldn't be—suicide. Be too much—searching—into past. Someone sure to find evidence, sooner or later—deals Russel and I made. But if it was murder—then —then—search would be for killer. I'd be safe." He struggled for his breath.

Dr. James Conley rose up on his elbows, his eyes glaring. "Safe," he repeated. He fell back. He was gone.

For a long moment no one spoke. Wally Hooper was bent over an empty box. Jeremiah Walton backed away, toward the door at the other end of the room. Suddenly he turned and ran. Ed Carson and I exchanged glances. Ed shook his head, got to his feet.

I said, "I heard, here and there, rumors that Russel and Conley had pulled some shady deals—payoffs to call murder suicide—that kind of thing. I never believed it."

Carson scrubbed his hands over his face. "I heard that, too, but I never for a minute . . ."

"Yeah, I know." I wanted to get out of there. "Listen. Let's leave Hooper here. You and me, let's go along to my office. I got a bottle there."

I had to take Carson's arm, lead him away.

At the door, he turned. He spat, "Politics!"

Then we left.

The Beast Within

by Margaret B. Maron

Early summer twilight had begun to soften the harsh outlines of the city when Tessa pushed open the sliding glass doors and stepped out onto the terrace. Dusk blurred away the grime and ugliness of surrounding buildings and even brought a kind of eerie beauty to the skeletal girders of the new skyscraper going up next door.

Gray haired, middle-aged and now drained of all emotion, Tessa leaned heavily-fleshed arms on the railing of the penthouse terrace and let the night enfold her.

From the street far below, the muffled sounds of evening traffic floated up to her, and for a moment she considered jumping—to end it all in one brief instant of broken flesh and screaming ambulances while the curious stared. What real difference would it make to her, to anyone, if she lived another day or year, or twenty years?

Still, the habit of life was too deeply in her. With a few cruel and indifferent words, Clarence had destroyed her world; but he had not destroyed her will to live. Not yet.

She glanced across the narrow space to the uncompleted building. The workmen who filled the daylight hours with a cacophony of rivets and protesting winches were gone now, leaving behind, for safety, hundreds of tiny bare light bulbs. In the warm breeze, they swung on their wires like chained fireflies in the dusk.

Tessa smiled at the thought. How long had it been since she had seen real fireflies drift through summer twilight? Surely not more than half a dozen times since marrying Clarence. She no longer hated the city, but she had never forgiven it for not having fireflies—or for blocking out the Milky Way with its star-quenching skyscrapers.

Even thirty years ago, when he had married her and brought her away from the country, Clarence had not understood her unease at living in a place so eternally and brilliantly lit. When his friends complimented them on the penthouse and marveled at the size of their terrace (enormous even by those booming wartime standards of the Forties), he would laugh and say, "I bought it for Tessa. Can't fence in a country girl, you know; they need 'land, lots of land 'neath the starry skies above!' "

It hadn't taken her long to realize that the penthouse was more a gift to his vanity than to still her unspoken needs. After a while, she stopped caring.

If the building weren't high enough above the neon glare of the streets to see her favorite stars, it at least provided as much quiet as one could expect in a city. She could always lie back on one of the cushioned chaises and remember how the Milky Way swirled in and out of the constellations; remember the dainty charm of the Pleiades tucked away in Taurus the Bull.

But not tonight. Instead of star-studded skies, memory forced her to relive the past hour.

She was long since reconciled to the fact that Clarence did not love her; but after years of trying to fit his standards, she had thought that he was comfortable with her and that she was necessary to him in all the other spheres which hold a marriage together after passion is gone.

Tonight, Clarence had made it brutally clear that not only was she unnecessary, but that the woman she had become, to please him, was the antithesis of the woman he'd chosen to replace her.

In a daze, Tessa had followed him through their apartment as he packed his suitcases. Mechanically, she had handed him clean shirts and underwear; and, seeing what a mess he was making of his perfectly tailored suits, she had taken over the actual packing as she always did when he had to go away on business trips. Only this time, he was going to a hotel and would not be back.

"But why?" she asked, smoothing a crease in his gray slacks.

They had met Lynn Herrick at one of Alison's parties. Aggressive and uninhibited, she wore the latest mod clothes and let her straight black hair swing longer than a teenager's although she was probably past thirty. Tessa thought her brittle and obvious, hardly Clarence's type, and she had been amused by the girl's blatantly flirtatious approach.

"Why?" she demanded again and was amazed at the fatuous expression which spread across Clarence's face: a blend of pride, sheepishness and defiance.

"Because she's going to bear my child," he said pompously, striking a pose of chivalrous manhood.

It was the ultimate blow. For years Tessa had pleaded for a child, only to have Clarence take every precaution to prevent one.

"You always loathed children. You said they were encumbrances—whining, slobbering nuisances!"

"It wasn't my fault," Clarence protested. "Accidents happen."

"I'll bet!" Tessa muttered crudely, knowing that nothing accidental ever happens to the Lynn Herricks of this world; but Clarence chose to ignore her remark.

"Now that it has happened, Lynn has made me see how much I owe it to myself and to the company. A 'pledge to posterity' she calls it, since it doesn't look as if Richard and Alison are going to produce an heir, as you know," Clarence said.

Richard Loughlin was Clarence's much younger brother. Together, they had inherited control of a prosperous chain of department stores. Although Tessa had heard Richard remark wistfully that a child might be fun, his wife Alison shared Clarence's previous attitude toward offspring; and her distaste was strengthened by the fear of what a child might do to her size eight figure.

With Clarence reveling in the newfound joys of prospective fatherhood, Tessa had straightened from his packing and snapped shut the final suitcase. Still in a daze, she stared at her reflection in the mirror over his dresser and was appalled.

In her conscious mind, she had known that she would soon be fifty, that her hair was gray, her figure no longer slim; and she had known that Clarence would never let her have children—but deep inside, she felt the young, half-wild girl she had been cry out in protest at this ultimate denial, at this old and barren woman she had become.

The siren of a fire engine on the street below drew Tessa to the edge of the terrace again. Night had fallen completely and traffic was thin now. The sidewalks were nearly deserted.

She still felt outraged at being cast aside so summarily—as if a pat on the shoulder, the promise of lavish alimony, and an "I told Lynn you'd be sensible about everything" were enough to compensate for thirty years of her life—but at least her brief urge toward self-destruction had dissipated.

She stared again at the bobbing safety lights of the uncompleted building and remembered that the last time she had seen fireflies had been four years ago, after Richard and Alison returned from their honeymoon. She and Clarence had gone down to Pennsylvania with them to help warm the old farm Richard had just bought as a wedding surprise for Alison.

The hundred and thirty acres of overgrown fields and virgin woodlands had indeed been a surprise to Alison. Her idea of a suitable weekend retreat was a modern beach house on Martha's Vineyard.

Tessa had loved it and had tramped the woods with Richard, wind-blown and exhilarated, while Alison and Clarence complained about the bugs and dredged up pressing reasons for cutting short their stay. Although Alison had been charming, and had assured Richard that she was delighted with the farm, she found excellent excuses for not accompanying him on his infrequent trips to the country.

Remembering the farm's isolation, Tessa wondered if Richard would mind if she buried herself there for a while. Perhaps in the country she could sort things out and grope her way back to the wild freedom she had known thirty years ago, before Clarence took her away and "housebroke her"—as he'd expressed it in the early years of their marriage.

A cat's terrified yowl caught her attention. She looked up and saw it running along one of the steel girders which stuck out several feet from a higher level of the new building. The cat raced out on it as if pursued by the three-headed hound of Hell, and its momentum was too great to stop when it realized the danger.

It soared off the end of the girder and landed with a sickening thump on the terrace awning. Awkwardly writhing off the awning, the cat leaped to the terrace floor and cowered under one of the chaises, quivering with panic.

Tessa watched the end of the girder, expecting to see a battle-scarred tomcat spoiling for a fight. Although cats seldom came up this high, it was not unusual to see one taking a shortcut across her terrace from one rooftop to another, up and down fire escapes. But no other cat appeared.

The night air had roused that touch of arthritis which had begun to bother Tessa lately, and it was an effort to bend down beside the lounge chair. She tried to coax the cat out, but it shrank away from her hand. "Here, kitty," she murmured, "it's all right. There's no one chasing you now."

She had always liked cats and, for that reason, refused to own one, knowing how easy it would be to let a small animal become a proxy child. She sensed Richard's antipathy and sympathized with him whenever Alison referred to Liebchen, their dachshund, as "baby."

Patiently, she waited for the cat to stop trembling and sniff her outstretched hand. She kept her tone low and soothing, but it would not abandon its shelter. Careful to make no sudden moves, Tessa stood up and stepped back a few feet.

The cat edged out then, suspiciously poised for flight, and the light from the living room beyond the glass doors fell across it. It was a young female with crisp black and gray markings and white paws; and judging by its leggy thinness, it hadn't eaten in some time.

"Poor thing," Tessa said, moved by its uneasy trust. "Wait right there, kitty—I'll get you something to eat." As if it understood she meant no harm, the cat did not skitter aside when she moved past it into the apartment.

In a few minutes, Tessa returned, carrying a saucer of warm milk and a generous chunk of rare beef which she'd recklessly cut from the heart of their untouched dinner roast. "You might as well have it, kitty. No one else will be eating it."

Stiff-legged and wary, the young cat approached the food and sniffed; then, clumsily, it tore at the meat, almost choking in its haste.

"Slow down!" Tessa warned, and knelt beside the cat to pull the meat into smaller pieces. "You're an odd one. Didn't you ever eat meat before?" She tried to stroke its thin back, but the cat quivered and slipped away beneath her plump hand. "Sorry, cat. I was just being friendly."

She sat down heavily on one of the chaises and watched the animal finish its meal. When the meat was gone, it turned to the saucer of milk and drank messily with much sneezing and shaking of its small head as it inadvertently got milk in its nose.

Tessa was amused and a bit puzzled. She'd never seen a cat so graceless and awkward. It was almost like a young, untutored kitten; and when it finished eating and sat staring at her, Tessa couldn't help laughing aloud. "Didn't your mother teach you *any*thing, silly? You're supposed to wash your paws and whiskers now."

The cat moved from the patch of light where it had sat silhouetted, its face in darkness. With purposeful caution, it circled the chaise until Tessa was between the cat and the terrace doors. Light from the living room fell full in its eyes there and was caught and reflected with an eerie intensity.

Uneasily, Tessa shivered as the cat's eyes met her own with un-wavering steadiness. "Now I understand why cats are always linked with the supernatu—"

The cat's eyes seemed to bore into her brain. There was a spiraling vortex of blinding light. Her mind was assaulted—mauled and dragged down and under and through it, existence without shape. She was held by a roaring numbness which lasted forever and was over instantly, and she was conscious of another's existence, mingling and passing—a being who was terrified, panic-stricken, and yet fiercely exultant.

There was a brief, weird sensation of being unbearably compacted and compressed; the universe seemed to tilt and swirl; then it was over. The light faded to normal city darkness, the roaring ceased and she knew that she was sprawled upon the cool flagstones of the terrace.

She tried to push herself up, but her body would not respond normally. Dazed, she looked around and screamed at the madness of a world suddenly magnified in size—a scream which choked off as she caught sight of someone enormous sitting on the now-huge chaise.

A plump, middle-aged woman held her face between trembling hands and moaned, "Thank God! Thank God!"

With a shock, Tessa realized she was seeing her own face for the first time, without the reversing effect of a mirror. The shock intensified as she looked down through slitted eyes and saw neat white paws instead of her own hands. With alien instinct, she felt the ridge of her spine quiver as fur stood on end. She tried to speak and was horrified to hear a feline yowl emerge.

The woman on the chaise—Tessa could no longer think of that body as herself—stopped moaning then and watched her warily. "You're not mad, if that's what you're wondering. Not yet, anyhow. Though you'll go mad if you don't get out of that skin in time."

Snatching up one of the cushions, she flung it at Tessa. "Shoo! G'wan, scat!" she gibbered. "You can't make me look in your eyes. I'll never get caught again. Scat, damn you!"

Startled, Tessa sprang to the railing of the terrace and teetered there awkwardly. The body responded now, but she didn't know how well she could control it, and twenty-eight stories above street level was too high to allow for much error.

The woman who had stolen her body seemed afraid to come closer. "You might as well go!" she snarled at Tessa. She threw a calculating glance at the luxurious interior beyond the glass doors. In the lamp lights, the rooms looked comfortable and secure. "It's a lousy body—too old and too fat—but it seems to be a rich one and it's human and I'm keeping it, so *scat!*"

Her new reflexes were quicker than those of her old body; and

before the slipper left the woman's hand, Tessa had dropped to the
narrow ledge circling the outside of her apartment. Residual instinct
made her footing firm as she followed the ledge around the corner
of the building to the fire escape, where it was an easy climb to the
roof. There, in comparative safety from flying shoes and incipient
plunges to the street, Tessa drew up to consider the situation.

Cat's body or not, she thought wryly, *it's still my mind.* She ex-
plored the sensations of her new body, absentmindedly licking away
the dried milk which stuck to her whiskers, and discovered that
vestigial traces of former identities clung to the brain. Mere wisps
they were, like perfume hanging in a closed room, but enough to
piece together a picture of what had happened to her on the terrace
below.

The one who had just stolen her body had been young and sly, but
not overly bright. Judging from the terror and panic so freshly im-
printed, she had fled through the city and had taken the first body
she could.

Behind those raw emotions lay a cooler, more calculating undertone and Tessa knew *that* one had been more mature, had chosen
the girl's body deliberately and after much thought. Not for her the
hasty grabbing of the first opportunity; instead, she had stalked her
prey with care, taking a body that was pretty, healthy, and, above
all, young.

Beyond those two, Tessa could not sort out the other personalities
whose lingering traces she felt. Nor could she know who had been
the first, or how it all had started. Probing too deeply, she recoiled
from the touch of a totally alien animal essence struggling for consciousness—the underlying basic *catness* of this creature whose body
she now inhabited.

Tessa clamped down ruthlessly on these primeval stirrings, forcing them back under. This must be what the girl meant about going
mad. How long could a person stay in control?

The answer, of course, was to get back into a human body. Tessa
pattered softly to the edge of the roof and peered down at the terrace.
Below, the girl in her body still cowered on the chaise longue as if
unable to walk into the apartment and assume possession. She sat
slumped and looked old and defeated.

She was right, thought Tessa, *it is a lousy body. She's welcome to
the joys of being Mrs. Clarence Loughlin.*

Her spirits soaring, Tessa danced across the black-tarred roof on
nimble paws. Joyfully, she experimented with her new body and

essayed small leaps into the night air. No more arthritis, no excess flab to make her gasp for breath. What bliss to think a motion and have lithe muscles respond!

Drunk with her new physical prowess, she raced to the fire escape, leaped to the railing and recklessly threw herself out into space. There was one sickening moment when she felt she must have misjudged, then she caught herself on a jutting scaffold and scrambled onto it.

Memories it had taken thirty years to bury were uncovered as Tessa prowled through the night and rediscovered things forgotten in the air-conditioned, temperature-controlled, insulated environment which had been her life with Clarence.

Freed of her old woman's body, she felt a oneness again with—what? The world? Nature? God? The name didn't matter, only the feeling. Even here in the city, in the heart of man's farthest retreat into artifice, she felt it.

What it must be like to have a cat's body in the country! Tessa thought, and then shivered as she realized that it would be too much. To be in this body with grass and dirt underneath, surrounded by trees and bushes alive with small rustlings, and uncluttered sky overhead—a human mind would go mad with so much sensory stimulation.

No, better the city with its concrete and cars and crush of people to remind her that she was human, that this body was only temporary.

Still, she thought, descending gracefully from the new building, *there can be no harm in just a taste.*

She ran west along half-deserted streets, heading for the park.

On the cross-town streets, traffic was light; but crossing the avenues terrified her. The rumble and throb of all those engines, the glaring lights and impatient horns kept her fur on end. She had to force herself to step off the curb at Fifth Avenue; and as she darted across its wide expanse, she half-expected to be crushed beneath a taxi.

The park was a haven now. Gratefully, she dived between its fence railings and melted into the dark safety of its jumble of bushes.

In the next few hours, Tessa shed all the discipline of thirty years with Clarence, her years of thinking "What will Clarence say?" when she gave way to an impulsive act; the fear of being called "quaint" by his friends if she spoke her inmost thoughts.

If Pan were a god, she truly worshiped him that night! Abandoning herself to instinctual joys, she raced headlong down grassy hills, rolled paws over tail-tip in the moonlight; chased a sleepy, crotchety squirrel through the treetops, then skimmed down to the duck pond to lap daintily at the water and dabble at goldfish turned silver in the moonbeams.

As the moon slid below the tall buildings west of the park, she ate flesh of her own killing; and later—behind the Mad Hatter's bronze toadstool—she allowed the huge ginger male who had stalked her for an hour to approach her, to circle ever nearer . . .

What followed next had been out of her control as the alien animal consciousness below surged into dominance. Only when it was over and the ginger tom gone, was she able to reassert her will and force that embryonic consciousness back to submission.

Just before dawn, her neat feline head poked through the railing at Fifth and East 64th Street and hesitated as she surveyed the deserted avenue, emptied of all traffic save an occasional green and white bus.

Reassured, Tessa stepped out onto the sidewalk and sat on narrow haunches to smooth and groom her ruffled striped fur. She was shaken by the night's experiences, but complacently unrepentant. No matter what lay ahead, this night was now part of her past and worth any price she might yet have to pay.

Nevertheless, Tessa knew that the strength of this body's true owner was growing and that another night would be a dangerous risk. She had to find another body, and soon.

Whose?

Lynn Herrick flashed to mind. How wickedly poetic it would be to take her rival's body, bear Clarence's child, and stick Lynn with a body which quite probably, after last night, would soon be producing offspring of its own! But she knew too little about Miss Herrick to feel confident in that role.

No, she was limited to somone familiar; someone young and financially comfortable; someone unpleasantly deserving; and, above all, someone *close*. She must be within transferring distance before the city's morning rush hour forced her back into the park until dark—an unthinkable risk.

As Tessa formulated these conditions, the logical candidate came into focus. *Of course!* She grinned. *Keep it in the family.* Angling across Fifth Avenue, she trotted uptown toward the luxurious building which housed the younger Loughlins.

Her tail twitched jauntily as she scampered along the sidewalk and elation grew as she considered the potentials of Alison's body, which was almost twenty-five years younger than her old body had been.

It might be tricky at first, but she had met all of Alison's few near relatives; and as for the surface friends who filled the aimless rounds of her sister-in-law's social life, Tessa knew they could be dropped without causing a ripple of curiosity. Especially if her life became filled with babies. That should please Richard.

Dear Richard! Tessa was surprised at the warmth of her feelings for her brother-in-law. She had always labeled her emotions as frustrated maternalism, for Richard had been a mere child when she and Clarence married.

Since then, somewhere along the line, maternalism seemed to have transmuted into something stronger. Wistful might-have-beens were now exciting possibilities.

Behind the heavy bronze and glass doors of Richard's building, a sleepy doorman nodded on his feet. The sun was not yet high enough to lighten the doorway under its pink and gray striped awning, and the deep shadows camouflaged her gray fur.

Keeping a low silhouette, she crouched beside the brass doors. As the doorman pushed it open for an early-rising tenant, she darted inside and streaked across the lobby to hide behind a large marble ash stand beside the elevator.

The rest would be simple as the elevator was large, dimly lit, and paneled in dark mahogany. She had but to conceal herself under one of the pink velvet benches which lined its sides and wait until it should stop at Alison's floor.

Her tail twitched with impatience. When the elevator finally descended, she poised ready to spring as the door slid back.

Bedlam broke loose in a welter of shrill barks, tangled leash and startled, angry exclamations. The dog was upon her, front and back, yipping and snapping before she knew what was happening.

Automatically, she spat and raked the dog's nose with her sharp claws, which set him into a frenzy of jumping and straining against the leash and sent his master sprawling.

Tessa only had time to recognize that it was Richard, taking Liebchen out for a pre-breakfast walk, before she felt herself being whacked by the elevator boy's newspaper.

All avenues of escape were closed to her and she was given no time to think, to gather her wits, before the street doors were flung open and she was harried out onto the sidewalk.

Angry and disgusted with herself and the dog, Tessa checked her headlong flight some yards down the sidewalk and glared back at the entrance of the building where Liebchen smugly waddled down the shallow steps and pulled Richard off in the opposite direction.

So the front is out, thought Tessa. *I wonder if their flank is so well-guarded?*

It pleased her to discover that those years of easy compliance with Clarence's wishes had not blunted her initiative. She could not be thwarted now by a Wiener schnitzel of a dog.

Halfway around the block, she located a driveway leading to the small courtyard which serviced the complex of apartment buildings. From the top of a rubbish barrel, she managed to spring to the first rung of a fire escape and scramble up.

As she climbed, the night's physical exertion began to make itself felt. Paw over paw, up and up, while every muscle begged for rest and her mind became a foggy treadmill able to hold only the single thought: paw in front of paw.

It seemed to take hours. Up thirteen steps to the landing, right turn; up thirteen steps to the landing, left turn, with such regular monotony that her mind became stupid with the endless repetition of black metal steps.

At the top landing, a ten-rung steel ladder rose straight to the roof. Her body responded sluggishly to this final effort and she sank down upon the tarred rooftop in utter exhaustion. The sun was high in the sky now; and with the last dregs of energy, Tessa crept into the shade of an overhanging ledge and was instantly asleep.

When she awoke in the late afternoon, the last rays of sunlight were slanting across the city. Hunger and thirst she could ignore for the time, but what of the quickening excitement which twilight was bringing?

She crept to the roof's edge and peered down at the empty terrace overlooking the park. An ivied trellis offered easy descent and she crouched behind a potted shrub to look through the doors. On such a mild day, the glass doors of the apartment had been left open behind their fine-meshed screens.

Inside, beyond the elegant living room, Alison's housekeeper set the table in the connecting dining room. There was no sign of Alison or Richard—or of Liebchen. Cautiously, Tessa pattered along the terrace to the screened doors of their bedroom, but it too was empty.

As she waited, darkness fell completely. From deep within, she felt the impatient tail-flick of awareness. She felt it respond to a cat's gutteral cry two rooftops away, felt it surfacing against her will, pulled by the promise of another night of dark paths and wild ecstasy.

Desperately, she struggled with that other ego, fought it blindly and knew that soon her strength would not be enough.

Suddenly the terrace was flooded with light as all the lamps inside the apartment were switched on. Startled, the other self retreated; and Tessa heard Alison's light voice tell the housekeeper, "Just leave dinner on the stove, Mitchum. You can clear away in the morning."

"Yes, Mrs. Loughlin, and I want you and Mr. Loughlin to know how sorry I was to hear about—"

"Thank you, Mitchum," came Richard's voice, cutting her off.

Tessa sat motionless in the shadows outside as Liebchen trotted across the room and scrambled onto a low chair, unmindful of a feline.

As Richard mixed drinks, Alison said, "The dreadful thing about all this is Tessa. Those delusions that she's really a young girl—that she'd never met Clarence—or either of us. Do you suppose she's clever enough to fake a mental breakdown?"

"Stop it, Alison! How can you have watched her wretchedness and think that she's pretending?"

"But, Richard—"

"What a shock it must have been to have Clarence ask for a divorce after all these years. Did you know about Clarence and Lynn?" His voice was harsh with emotion. "You introduced them. Did you encourage it?"

"Really, darling! You sound as if Tessa were the injured party." Alison's tone held scornful irony.

"Well, really, she is!" Richard cried. "If you could have seen her, Alison, when Clarence first married her—so fresh and open and full of laughter. I was just a child, but I remember. I'd never met an adult like her. I thought she was like an April breeze blowing through this family; but everyone else was appalled that Clarence had married someone so unsuitable. I remember her face when Clarence lectured her for laughing too loudly."

Richard gazed bleakly into his glass. "After Father died, it was years before I saw her again. I couldn't believe the change; all the laughter gone, her guarded words. Clarence did a thorough job of making her into a suitable wife. He killed her spirit and then complained that she was dull! No wonder she's retreated into her past, to a time before she knew him. You heard the psychiatrist. He said it often happens."

"Nevertheless," Alison said coolly, "you seem to forget that while Clarence may have killed her spirit, he's the one who is actually dead."

In the shadows outside the screen, Tessa quivered. So they had found Clarence's body! That poor thieving child! At the sight of Clarence lying on the bedroom floor with his head crushed in, she must have panicked again.

"I haven't forgotten," Richard said quietly, "and I haven't forgotten Lynn Herrick either. If what Clarence told me yesterday is true, she's in an awkward position. I suppose I should make some sort of arrangement for her out of Clarence's estate."

"Don't be naive, Richard," Alison laughed. "She merely let Clarence believe what he wanted. Lynn is far too clever to get caught without a wedding ring."

"Then Clarence's request for the divorce, his death, Tessa's insanity—all this was predicated on a lie? And you knew it? You *did!* I can see it in your face!"

"You're being unfair," Alison said. "I didn't encourage his affair with Lynn. I introduced them, yes; but if it hadn't been Lynn, it would have been someone else. Clarence wanted a change and he always took what he wanted."

As she spoke, Alison moved between the kitchen and living room, arranging their dinner on a low table in front of the couch. Liebchen put interested paws on the edge of the table, but Richard shoved him aside roughly.

"There's no need to take it out on Liebchen," she said angrily. "Come along, baby, I have something nice for you in the kitchen."

On little short legs, the dachshund trotted after Alison and disappeared into the kitchen. Relieved, Tessa moved closer to the screen.

When Alison returned from the kitchen, her flash of anger had been replaced by a mask of solicitude. "Must you go out tonight, darling? Can't the lawyers wait until morning?"

She sat close to Richard on the couch and tried to interest him in food, but he pushed the plate away wearily.

"You know lawyers," he sighed. "Clarence's will can't be probated as written, so everything's complicated. There are papers to sign, technicalities to clear up."

"That's right," Alison said thoughtfully. "Murderers can't inherit from their victims, can they? Oh, Richard, don't pull away from me like that. I'm not being callous, darling. I feel just as badly about all this as you do, but we have to face the facts. Like it or not, Tessa did kill Clarence."

"Sorry," he said, standing up and reaching for his jacket. "I guess I just can't take it all in yet."

Alison remained on the couch with her back to him. As Richard took papers from his desk and put them in his briefcase, she said with careful casualness, "If they decide poor Tessa killed him in a fit of insanity and she later snaps out of it, would she then be able to inherit?"

"Probably not, legally," he said absently, his mind on sorting the papers. "Wouldn't matter though, since we'd give it back to her, of course."

"Oh, of course," Alison agreed brightly; but her eyes narrowed.

Richard leaned over the couch and kissed her cheek. "I don't know how long this will take. If you're tired, don't bother to wait up."

"Good night, darling. Try not to be too late." She smiled at him as he left the apartment; but when the door had latched behind him, her smile clicked off to be replaced by a grim look of serious calculation.

Lost in thought, she gazed blindly at the dark square of the screened doorway and was unaware when Tessa slowly eased up on narrow haunches to let the lamplight hit her eyes—eyes that glowed with abnormal intensity . . .

It was after midnight before Richard's key turned in the lock. Lying awake on their wide bed, she heard him drop his briefcase on the desk and open the bedroom door to whisper, "Alison?"

"I'm awake, darling," she said throatily and switched on a lamp. "Oh, Richard you look so tired. Come to bed."

When at last he lay beside her in the darkness, she said shyly, "All evening I've been thinking about Tessa and Clarence—about their life together. I've been a rotten wife to you, Richard."

He made a sound of protest, but she placed slim young fingers against his lips. "No, darling, let me say it. I've been thinking how empty their marriage was and how ours would be the same if I didn't change. Richard, let's pretend we just met and that we know nothing about each other! Let's completely forget about everything that's happened before now and start anew. As soon as the funeral is over and we've settled Tessa in the best rest home we can find, let's go away together to the farm for a few weeks."

Incredulous, Richard propped himself on one elbow and peered into her face. "Do you really mean that?"

She nodded solemnly and he gathered her in his arms, but before he could kiss her properly, the night was broken by an angry, hissing cry.

"What the devil is that?" Richard asked, sitting up in bed.

"Just a stray cat. It was on the terrace this evening and seemed hungry, so I gave it your dinner." With one shapely arm, she pulled Richard back down to her and then pitched her voice just loud enough to carry through the screen to the terrace. "If it's still there in the morning, I'll call the ASPCA and have them take it away."

Where Have You Been, Ross Ivy?
by Pauline C. Smith

Ross Ivy, on his way home as usual after a day's work at the office, swung his car into the driveway and noticed, with vague surprise, the size of the tree that overhung his garage. Funny; he guessed he must not have really looked at that tree for a long, long time. He switched off the ignition, separated his house key from the others on the ring, picked up his briefcase from the seat, and loped across the wide lawn to his front door.

It was deep twilight of a late summer day, the broad street quiet, soft light shining from the windows of the homes. His own picture windows were shadowed sheets of plate glass.

He rammed the key into the lock. It stuck. He pushed on it, bent over to squint at it in the purple dusk. He worked it out of the keyhole, felt its familiar shape and size. It was the front door key, all right. He started it into the keyhole again, carefully, twisting it slightly. It entered just so far and jammed. "Crazy," he said, yanking the key out of the keyhole. He leaned on the bell button.

He could hear the triple-noted chime from within. He stepped to the edge of the porch and leaned over the wrought iron banister to peer through the window and see Gwen emerging into light that spilled from the master bedroom into the hallway. She was tying the belt of her dressing gown, hurrying. She must be dressing for something. Were they invited out tonight and had he forgotten?

"Damn!" he exclaimed under his breath, wanting only a drink and the opportunity to relax.

"Darling," he heard through the door as Gwen fumbled with the lock. The porch light startled him. "Darling." She threw open the door. "You're so early . . . " she began, and clapped a hand over her mouth.

"Early?" Yes, perhaps this was early for him, he'd been working late hours for so long, working like a dog . . . Incidentally, where *was* the dog? He should be barking up a storm, beginning back at the moment Ross drove the car into the driveway, and now he should be leaping wildly, shrieking in loyal hysteria.

Ross closed the door and asked his wife, "Where is Fritz?"

She backed off, the hand still covering her mouth, her eyes wide and staring.

"My key didn't work. Funny thing." He dropped his briefcase to a hall table and looked at his house key, still separated from the others on the ring. "Can't understand it. Maybe I put it in upside down." He tucked the keys into his pocket, turned, and switched on the lights as he entered the living room.

He was momentarily chilled by the cold formality of cool satin and silver. What did he expect? A sudden thought startled him: he had expected warmth and the glow of color. The bewildering expectation faded abruptly to leave him petulant.

"Well, where *is* Fritz?" He strode across the length of the room to the bar alcove beyond, stepped behind the bar, and ran his hand over the deep-grained, polished wood. It felt good and warmly welcome. He looked across the bar from the alcove, out along the length of the room and into the hall where Gwen still stood, spread-eagled now against the wall like some dramatic diva.

"Are we going somewhere? Did I forget about it?"

He reached under the bar for his familiar bottle of bourbon in its accustomed place and came up with scotch. He stooped then, to search with his eyes, knowing that he was the only one who drank bourbon. Gwen, as well as their friends, drank everything from scotch to vodka; he alone preferred the good, rich, colorful flavor of bourbon, and his bottle always stood in that one place. Now there was no bourbon there, none at all. Yet it was here only yesterday. And so was the dog, frisking about his legs, the long body stretching an exclamation mark of sheer joy at having him home.

"Where is the dog?" Ross shouted suddenly, wanting to weep.

Gwen, the impaled impresario, pushed herself away from the wall at last, and whispered, "Ross?" incredulously, as if she could not believe it was he standing there behind his own bar, in his own home, but without his own drink and without his dog so that he felt excluded, disoriented, canceled out of the world in which he stood.

It was then that he had the vision and the impression of warmth and laughter; a vision not upon the retina of his eye, an impression not upon the nerve endings of his touch, but somewhere deep between memory and prognostication, that the woman moving toward him now was not Gwen, beautifully perfect, but another who was perfectly beautiful.

She became Gwen again, cold and stiffly silken, approaching him slowly as if she were a toy drawn on a string—his string, pulled by his unwilling hand. Then he said, "Hell," and poured himself the drink of scotch he hated and asked once more, "Where is Fritz?"

"He's dead," she said, her eyes big and scared.

Ross thumped the bottle to the bar and his hand trembled on the glass.

"He died almost seven years ago," she whimpered.

Ross shook his head with the impact of the absurdity and stared at her, his wife, who seemed to be playing tricks with her face as she was attempting to do with her tongue. She was Gwen and someone else . . . a montage, a superimposed someone, someone he loved dearly and should phone. Yes, he had promised to place a phone call the minute he arrived—but arrived from where? And a call to what other place? "You're lying," he declared flatly, and tipped the glass to let the liquid fall down his throat and thump and splash in his stomach.

"Ross?" Why did she always speak his name with a question mark? Gwen, or this woman who was not Gwen, held up her hand as if she were refuting him or blocking him off.

Ross clicked his mind into logical action and came up with a grabber. "He couldn't have died almost seven years ago. He wasn't even seven years old," and analyzed his analysis to find it lacking in any kind of reason. "I mean," he said and groped reluctantly, "I mean, he was here yesterday so how could he have died almost seven years ago?" *There* was the grabber, a real clincher. He had this woman hanging on the ropes. Then Ross felt faint. He downed his drink and swayed. Something was wrong here. Where in hell was he and to whom was he talking?

"He died after you left," she said, "and *you* have been gone seven years."

The words were thrust from her as if she had a slingshot somewhere inside her voice box that plucked forth these meaningless pebbles of crazy sound. The dog flew gracefully from Ross's memory, on wings he had never possessed, big feet spread . . . and Ross felt lost.

"We thought you were dead," Gwen said, her arms folded tight across her breast as if in protection. "Ross?" with that rising inflection.

"Who's we?" he asked abruptly, just before the impact of her statement struck him. "Dead?"

She bent, with her arms clasped about her as if she were in pain, or as if, it seemed to Ross, the pain of *him* had suddenly assailed her. His mind gathered fuzzy facts, backing up to her first words begun before she had opened the door to see him and clapped a hand over her mouth, shutting out the "darlings" and the "early" routine. He leaned against the bar, allowing it to support him.

"Why was I early?" he asked softly, itemizing her words. "Early for what? And was it *I* who was early?"

Almost crouched, she held herself tight in her own private agony while he reached out with his mind in an effort to tabulate the hints, clues she had so sparsely indicated.

"You thought I was someone else," he said slowly, "someone too early. Who was that someone?"

"We were sure you were dead," she repeated, stooped and frightened. "There was no body, but we were so sure. Seven years!"

He shook his head with bewilderment, seven years being a long time from yesterday! Then he remembered again that he was to call someone before he had stopped for the night. Call whom? Stop where? And after what? He was bone tired—his exhaustion caused by long-distance driving, he realized now, recognizing the shoulder pain, the leg ache—so he must have been at it all day, going from somewhere to somewhere else.

He leaned heavily against the bar and reached for the bottle of scotch again and splashed a drink into the glass. "Where is my bourbon?" he asked petulantly. "Where is my dog?"

Gwen straightened. "You don't know. You don't remember. You come back, after all these years, to this house . . . "

He thought of the key and snatched the ring from his pocket separating from the others the key that could not unlock the door of this house.

"Where have you been if you haven't been dead?" she cried.

He streaked across the long living room and into the hall, opening the front door and, holding it wedged with his knee, tried the key that did not belong there. He shut the door, catching a fleeting glimpse again of warmth, laughter and color—another house, another place, and a phone call to be made.

"Ross," said Gwen, stiffly straight now and becoming sure of herself. "Ross," the name no longer a question but a declaration on her lips. "You don't remember?"

He moved cautiously back into the living room from the hallway, with a strange feeling that they were jockeying for a position of knowledge and that she had the upper hand. He felt like an animal circling her, never taking his eyes off her. Now it was he who questioned the name, this place and time. "What am I supposed to remember?" he asked warily.

"Well—you disappeared . . ." She eyed him as if to test his reactions and her voice became stronger. "You disappeared and now you're back, asking for your dog as if it were yesterday instead of seven years ago."

It was not a direct answer, and Ross said, "So you thought I was dead."

"Naturally we thought you were dead."

"Who's we?"

"Well, Arthur, of course . . ." The name caught in her throat, causing her to swallow as if she would erase it. So was Arthur the "darling" at the front door? Ross wondered. She attempted a desperate depersonalization. "We all thought you were dead, our friends, your business associates . . . everybody," waving her arms as if to include the entire population of Gannet Falls.

Of course, Gannet Falls. He knew now why he had broken his journey from someplace he could not now remember to someplace else he had forgotten about when he saw the sign, "Gannet Falls, the Superb Suburb," and turned off the main drag to drive to this house like a homing pigeon.

He caught his head in his hands and pressed his temples with his fingers as if he would rechannel his mind, gathering up the bits and tag ends of memory along the way to fit them into all the empty spaces. He wanted to question her, this Gwen who was familiar yet was not, and cry out for help—*Help me to remember*—but he studied her, distant and secretive, and knew that he could not, for that would give her the advantage of knowing what he did not know and of telling or not telling it to him, and she was danger, he was sure of that.

Ross walked to the bar and moved behind it, feeling the need of good solid substance between himself and this wife he did, yet did not, know. He surveyed her across the bar, a pretty woman, her eyes enlarged, enhanced and upturned through sheer artistry, her cheekbones fashionably high and prominent, her lips seductively curved—but fierce.

He recoiled from the fierceness . . . here was a woman who knew what she wanted and got it—some way, any way—and she did not want him. He knew this with chilling certainty.

The lips smiled and moved and spoke of shock. "Of course it was a shock to see you here tonight . . . " Smiling, she was, rocking back from the shock. Retreating, building her fences? "After all these years of loss and grief," she added, with her eyes cold, the mouth softly fierce. "Ross, you are home . . . " she advanced, arms extended, not in a gesture of loving welcome, but as if she would strangle him, it seemed.

He splashed some of the scotch into the glass and downed it, coughed, almost choked, and felt as if he were drowning. He looked at Gwen over his hand covering his mouth and felt himself borne down, sucked under water, and thought of the river as her arms fell and her hands, palms down, caressed the bar. The falls from which the suburban town had derived its name . . . the falls, an affectation only, caused by a minor drop in the riverbed so that the water tumbled over the rocky ledge. He stood rigid, his hand still over his mouth, beginning to remember at least the falls that were not falls but only a name, when Gwen interrupted, causing the falls to drip away just as the dog had flown.

"You don't remember?" she asked, leaning against the bar now, not reaching out to touch him as he looked at her blankly, dropping his hand and flattening his face with purpose. "You don't remember anything. Of course not."

"I remember the cabin," he said, so startling himself with the abrupt, fragmentary recollection that he failed to notice Gwen's look of alarm. "A cabin somewhere by a lake—no, a river . . . " The memory was elusive, untrustworthy. "Do we still have the cabin?" he asked her directly, and caught the look of terror in the beautiful, staring eyes. "The cabin," he repeated, probing, wanting to know, the cabin becoming less clear with the roar of the river and the falls beyond sounding deafeningly in his ears.

Gwen's softly fierce mouth became thinly fierce as she said, without expression, "What cabin?"

Ross knew then that there was a cabin by a river's edge, and if he could remember the cabin and that river clearly enough, he would know why it was he stood here in this faintly familiar house with a faintly familiar wife, and who awaited his phone call. "Then there is no cabin I should remember?" he baited her.

Gwen's face relaxed with relief. She fluttered her hands and positioned her mouth into gentle sympathy. "Not that I know of," she said. Then placatingly, "Perhaps it's a later memory." Her eyes became decisive and her lips more fiercely demanding. "You must have lived *somewhere* after you disappeared—had some kind of life.

Do you remember that? Where did you come from, Ross? And where have you been for the last seven years?"

Becoming the inquisitor, she put him on the defensive. His mind was a blank. He felt a screaming need for identity.

She leaned against the bar, her hands clenching its edge. "Does anyone know you are here?" she asked softly, and he thought of the phone call he was to make without knowing to whom he was to make it. "No, you don't remember. You don't remember anything, do you, Ross? So no one remembers you. Well, you're home again and I remember you." She changed, like quicksilver, to smiling welcome. "You're home again and that's all that matters."

It wasn't all that mattered. It was only a little that mattered. What mattered was the big gap in his life with these fleeting tag ends of memory—the frisking, happy dog, the bourbon in its place, a cabin on the river . . . the cabin on the river, the rocky falls . . . a rock . . . he felt pain explode in his head—a rock! Water closing him in, cold water that took his breath and gave it back to him . . .

"You drove here?" asked Gwen. "Well, of course you did," and she stepped to the side window to locate the shadow of a car in the driveway.

"My car," said Ross. "Where did you find my car?"

She turned, her face empty.

"I must have been in a car," he said impatiently, "seven years ago when I disappeared. So, what about the car? Where did you find it?" Now, he had the upper hand. He leaned on the bar and watched her face wrestle with the question, and remembered a long green car, his, parked next to the cabin, and another parked alongside it. He heard the falls. The falls drowned out the memory and also Gwen's trumped-up explanation—it had to be trumped-up since she denied the river and the cabin.

"All that is over," he heard her finale, "and now it is enough that you are here." She had made up her mind about something. He could see the decision in her eyes, the fierce resolution on her lips. "You are alive," she said, "and that is enough, at least for the present."

Enough for what? Ross wondered, watching her eyes, studying her lips, feeling the quick and powerful recall of warm eyes and loving lips to overwhelm him for an instant before both were gone to leave only the chill of this woman.

He shuddered and began to remember . . . or was it *this* woman he was remembering from *that* life, who spoke lies with decision in her eyes and resolution on her carefully smiling lips? As she was doing now in a falsely welcoming speech, her words rambling, her hands fluttering a distraction that allowed her brain to plan furiously.

She was edging away from the bar with a nervous laugh, saying that she must dress—my goodness! At his question, yes, she had planned on going out, but now she wouldn't leave—my goodness, no! They would, instead, celebrate his return to life.

That was an interesting choice of words. He widened his eyes and stared at Gwen without seeing, without hearing her, involved only with the certain knowledge that he had indeed returned to that past life, for he was beginning to remember his murder. He felt again the impact of a rock against his skull—stunning him this time as it had the other so that the room turned black and he clung to the edge of the bar to keep from slipping, as he had long ago, into the water to sink and rise and flounder, searching for a handhold, to find it on the rocky ledge of the diminutive falls . . .

Who had done that to him?

"Gwen!" She had started from the room. She halted and turned, her eyes guarded, her face impassive. She would tell him nothing but lies. He would have to remember it for himself. "Gwen! What was I like?"

"What were you like?" Her face was expressionless.

"When you knew me. Seven years ago." He clutched at the desperate hope that could he learn what kind of man he had been, he would also learn the reason for someone's wanting him out of the way. "What was my business? What did I do for a living?"

"What is your business now?" she asked.

He did not know! Just as he didn't know whom he was to phone once he reached some unknown destination for some unknown reason. He did not know the name he used, where he lived, or what friends he had, what family.

The floor rocked under his feet as the boat had rocked seven years before, and his head ached as if it had been dealt a crushing blow. *Gannet Falls is mine,* he heard from the boat and the past, *and so is Gwen.* Ross swayed and caught hold of the edge of the bar, these bits of past knowledge paining him as if they were being forced into his brain, jagged piece by jagged piece.

Gannet Falls had been his, a tract of houses set in a hilly nowhere because of the river and the river site he owned. So he must have been a builder, broker or promoter—something in real estate—with a business and a wife that someone else wanted. He felt like laughing because he certainly didn't want the business nor did he want the wife.

He looked at her, dazed.

"Well, never mind," she said, "you don't have to remember. Everything will be all right. Really it will."

He watched her leave the room, hips moving smoothly under the silk of her dressing gown, her step confident. "Where are you going?" he called after her childishly, afraid of losing, even for a moment, this only link he had with an identity.

"Just to get dressed," she smiled. "That's all. I'll be back and then we'll talk. I will help you remember." The last words sounded ominous. *How* would she help him to remember when she had hindered him thus far? "Darling," she added as she left the living room and started down the hall.

He wasn't her *darling,* someone else was, someone she had thought to be early, someone who wasn't there when she clapped a hand over her mouth and fell back in shock, someone she must notify . . . Of course, just as he must phone someone that he had arrived and was safe, so must she phone someone that he had arrived and she was not safe.

Ross grabbed the edge of the bar and swung around it, raced across the living room, looking for a phone—a second phone, or a third one. Hell, he'd built this house, lived in it—where were the phones?

His eyes swept the hall—no phone—no light either from the master bedroom beyond, so the door was closed and she was probably on the bedroom phone. He crossed the hall, reached around the doorway and switched on the lights of a kitchen. He remembered it. He was beginning to remember now, to move in familiar surroundings, and there was the wall phone.

He strode across the kitchen tile, placed a careful forefinger on the edge of the cradle, raised the instrument, let his finger lift gently, and heard Gwen say, in a frantic whisper, "Arthur . . . " There it was, *Arthur* again—so Arthur was her darling. "Arthur, he's here . . . " and the answering voice. Ross recognized it, not knowing to whom it belonged. He recognized the voice, by its timbre and intensity, to be one that could say, *Gannet Falls is mine, and so is Gwen.*

The voice was light now, questioning, almost playful, feeling good—and the reason it was feeling good, Ross knew, was that he had been dead for seven years now and the voice could claim Gannet Falls and Gwen. That is why, he concluded with sudden inspiration, the late date—a celebration . . . He felt sick and swallowed, holding his hand over the mouthpiece, sure that the sound was audible and filled with anguish.

She had come through to Arthur-the-voice at last. He was protesting, "I don't believe it." He repeated his protest over and over, not believing he had killed without killing.

Gwen was feeling the strain and the danger. "Dammit," she cried in a shrill whisper. "I tell you, he's here. He's in the bar, drinking the scotch and complaining about it. He doesn't know anything. Doesn't remember anything. Get over here, Arthur, and do the job right!"

Arthur whimpered audibly, and Ross Ivy, no longer Ross Ivy but a dead man inexpertly killed, whimpered inaudibly.

"I don't *care* how you do it," whispered Gwen fiercely, "just do it. He's got a car here. You can put him in his car and leave it out on a road somewhere. Don't you *understand?* He's someone else now. Get over here, Arthur. I can't *talk* any longer."

Ross heard a click, and replaced the phone.

He stood there in the brightly lighted kitchen, swallowing his sickness, then walked across the tile and switched the room to darkness.

His footsteps were muffled down the hall and he made no sound as he opened the door to the master bedroom.

She stood with her back to him, the dressing gown a circle of silk around her feet. She was reaching up into the open wardrobe for something off a hanger, her breath heavy in her throat, almost sobbing.

On the bedside table, at what had once been his side of the bed, he saw the photograph in an easel frame—a photograph of Arthur Gordon. He had never thought of him as Arthur, always Gordon, partner, associate, whatever—press agent with a personality, the one who had added the Falls to Gannet and coined the Superb Suburb bit.

As if he were going down for the third time, Ross saw his past life with these two, Gwen his wife, and Gordon her darling, like rapidly flipped pictures on the retina of his mind. He remembered his suspicions, buried like an iceberg in his work, just as all his worth was buried in the opening of this small, select tract called Gannet Falls.

The pictures flipped at a breathtaking pace, showing him the cabin, the river, the boat, and Gordon's surprise visit . . . Ross pressed his fingers hard against his temples to slow down the pace—but the pictures, as if they had been held in the darkroom of his brain too long, raced by, filling him with forgotten memory.

Just as the blackout pain of the final blow struck him again, the long-buried, seven-year-old sound track gave him once more Gordon's words, *Gannet Falls is mine and so is Gwen.*

"My God!" he breathed aloud and Gwen whirled in the circle of her dressing gown, one hand clutching the dress she had selected, the other raised and spread as if to ward off disaster.

As they stared at each other, she whimpered, "You don't know. You don't remember," her voice rising to a shrill note. "Ross, you *said* you didn't know . . . "

"My God," he repeated, stunned by the agony of knowing too much and remembering it all.

"That's what you said," she cried. "You said you didn't know. Didn't remember . . . "

"And now I do," he answered her.

She dropped the dress and started toward him, arms outstretched. Stumbling within the circle of the dressing gown, she tripped at its edge and pitched forward.

He reached and caught her before she fell.

Holding her upright, his hands firmly but gently grasping her bare shoulders, he remembered what she had once been to him: his love and his life. Then he remembered how she had taken from him her love and his life, and his grasp tightened, embedding his fingers in the warm and wicked flesh.

He let her go so abruptly that she swayed.

He stepped away, drew back his arm, and swung, striking her with the flat of his hand that sent her in a spin and sprawled her on the bed.

She lay there, wide-eyed, making small plaintive sounds, one cheek brightly crimson, the other paper-pale. Ross stared down at her, hating her with a violence he didn't know he was capable of—yet how could he know the capabilities of the man who was left once Ross Ivy was dead?

He wanted to weep and cringe, as she wept and cringed on the bed. Instead, he leaned over her and slapped the other cheek scarlet.

This man who had been Ross Ivy was appalled and joyful. He was going to kill her, slowly and with vengeance, and with great happiness.

She must have seen the compulsion in his eyes when she cried out, and she must have known what it meant when she made the attempt to roll free of him. She was awkward and not fast enough. He yanked her back, straddled her, both knees on the bed, and placed his hands around her neck.

She tried to speak, to plead. Each time her throat moved, he pressed his thumbs against the movement and pushed back the sound.

With his hands on her throat, he thought of the beauty of his crime, its perfection—the dead killing the killer to bring ultimate justice to the guilty.

He pressed gently. Gwen gagged. When he loosened his hold, she struggled weakly, forcing him to press less gently, and relish his act a little more hurriedly. Once she was gone, all he had to do was call the police from the phone that Gwen had used to order his second death, walk out of the house, step into his car, and drive away, leaving Gordon to arrive and explain.

Perfect. Absolutely perfect.

Gwen was making strange sounds under his fingers and her face was darkening. He lessened the pressure, reminding himself not to forget his briefcase—the briefcase that would give him away.

The briefcase! That would tell him who he was! And whom it was he was supposed to phone! He jerked his hands from the now-bruised throat, swung his leg over the body onto the floor, and leaned close, looking at her, still hating her, but not wanting her to die, not by his hands. He held them, trembling, out before him, aghast.

Her lashes fluttered, and he sighed in relief.

Time was growing short now. He didn't know where Gordon was coming from or how long it would take him to get here. He leaned over, a hand pressing the mattress on each side of her, caging her in. "Look," he said, "can you hear me and do you understand?"

She held her head very still and snapped her eyes tight.

"I know about myself now. And I know about you and Gordon. Listen to me and remember this, now that I can remember." He allowed himself a small smile of triumph. "If you declare me dead, I shall rise up and call you a murderer. Understand?"

She understood and she would remember; he could tell by the way her eyes flew open and how they clouded.

He straightened. "That's all," he said.

That was indeed all. Out of fear, she could never declare him dead and since she could not declare him dead, Gannet Falls did not belong to Gordon, nor did Gwen.

He walked down the hall of the house he now remembered clearly and without nostalgia. He picked up his briefcase, stepped through the door his key would not open, crossed the lawn, looked at the tree that was seven years taller than he remembered, stepped into his car, leaving the door ajar so that he could see by the dome light, opened his briefcase, discovered his name to be Robert Jones—what imagination!—and that he was a hardware sales representative.

He sat there, laughing.

Holding the car door open a moment, he looked back at the house he once lived in and at the life he once lived, said, "The hell with *that*," slammed the door, turned the ignition key, and backed into the broad street. He rounded the corner just as headlights slowed, parked in front of the house, and blacked out.

That would be Gordon, and those two, instead of celebrating the end of his seven-year death tonight, would be holding a wake over his live body—a comforting thought.

He drove into the city and parked in front of a drugstore. He broke a bill at the counter and took the change to a phone booth at the rear. He fed the coins into the box, dialed his area code, the prefix and number. "Vicki . . . "

With the sound of her voice, his world rocked back into position, filled with warmth and laughter. "How are the twins?" he asked, and listened.

"Vicki, I miss you. Know what? Think I'll bed down in a motel here and head on back home first thing in the morning. I've got something to tell you."

He hung up and pushed through the doors, smiling.

Did he plan to tell Vicki who he really was and what they had tried to do to him?

Never.

What he planned to tell Vicki was that the company could shove this territory—he didn't like the atmosphere and he didn't like the people. He wanted his old territory back.

Bronze Resting

by Arthur Moore

I have bet half the rent money, which is my limit, on a long shot in the eighth. This hayburner has become hypnotized by the sight of other horses' tails, so I pay off like usual. After it gets dark I am on the way home when I meet Banty.

Banty is a short, flat-faced type who has got scars where most folks have got freckles and moles, and he is retired from the mobs. I am sure he is retired because he informs me of this each time I see him, which is mostly once a week.

"Dubois," he says, running a finger through the buttonhole on my lapel, "it is lucky I meet you." His voice is also scarred. It is like he is speaking and clearing his throat at the same time. "Since I ain't runnin' wit de boys no longer, there is occasions w'en dey up an' gits me down."

"I am loaded with markers," I tell him, "which is only good to start fires with, if I can borrow a match."

"Nix, Dubois. Dis is Banty. W'en did I hit you for a mooch?" He tightens the finger in my lapel. "I am laying on you a sure t'ing," he glances around, "on account of I like you."

"A sure thing?"

"Lissen," he pulls at the lapel. "C'mere, we shouldn't get overhoid." I am almost standing on his toes now, and if I get closer I will be in his pocket. He glances the other way. "I got one left, Dubois, just one."

"That's great, Banty." I always agree with him.

"Yeah, it's de right one, Dubois, an' it's yours."

"It is?" I am hoping it ain't a whap in the teeth, and I am thinking back quick, wondering what I have said to anybody about Banty since I seen him last.

"De reg'ler price," he said, "is two clams." He pulls a little card from his pocket and holds it in front of my eyes so it is real blurred. "But for you, I am knockin' it down t'one. For one frogskin you is winnin' this special raffle."

I let my breath out. "Raffle?"

He grins at me, which wrinkles the scars on his cheeks. "You're smart, Dubois. I figgered you was hepped up. Who tole ya? Never min', I ain't da kind t'ask questions. Anyways, gimme da simoleon, but don't squeal t' nobody I cut da price. De bums what lose, dey won't like it." He grins some more and shakes me a little, so I grin, too.

I am glad that Banty is still going straight. I ask him politely to let me go, so I can reach in my pocket. He does this and I am separated from one more plaster of the rent scratch. He gives me the ticket, but it is too dark to read it.

"De raffle is tomorra," he says. "I dunno where yet, but I will try t' let you know in time." He claps me on the back, and when I finish choking he is out of sight.

I take the ticket to the nearest street lamp and read it. It is hand printed in ink, between two pencil lines, and says: RAFFLE. TICKET NO. 109. BRONZE: RESTING.

That's all. I put the ticket in my pocket and hustle the two blocks to my room, wondering what a Resting Bronze is. I don't find out till the next day.

My landlady, Mrs. Sherpy, is pounding on the door, which wakes me up early. I look at the clock; it is only eleven thirty, and I am afraid to say anything for a minute till I realize that rent day is a week off.

"Outa the sack, Dubois!" she is yelling. "There's guys outside who's got somethin' for you."

I have forgot about the raffle, and it isn't till I put on my pants and go downstairs that it comes to me. There are two large furniture-moving types in the lower hallway, and they are both panting. They are wearing overalls and greasy caps, and they are leaning on a large chunk of metal.

"Dis t'ing is heavier'n da State of Joisey," one of them says. "You Dubois?"

I nod, wondering why they are carrying around a blob of iron.

"Sign here," he says and shoves a clipboard at me. "It's yours."

"Is it paid for?" I ask. He nods, so I sign, and Mrs. Sherpy pushes them away to get a better look at the thing.

"It's a goat," she says. "Dubois, you gone off your rocker—buyin' iron goats?"

"I didn't buy it. I won it—in a raffle." There is a little plate under the front feet of whatever the thing is, and it reads BRONZE: RESTING.

It takes the two large types about a half hour to drag the statue up to my room. The steps is creaking, and Mrs. Sherpy is screaming at them not to scrape the walls. They put it in the middle of the room on top of a little black base, which one of the types brings from the truck outside, and leave it there. Mrs. Sherpy is still wailing about a dope, she means me, which will buy raffle tickets on cast iron goats instead of paying the rent. So I don't notice that the statue is in the middle of the room until the muscles have gone. Then it is impossible to move it; and I have to leave it there. It makes the floor sag towards the middle, and the cantaloupes I have stashed under the bed all roll out.

But the thing is mine. I have won the raffle like Banty said, and it is something to know that a man which has always been a grifter has kept his word. I study the chunk from all angles. It is an animal of some sort, and it has a very sad expression. It has a long head, two ears and four legs, and is sitting down like it is tired. I am positive it is not a goat. It is the feet which finally convinces me. The thing is a sitting horse.

There are no chairs in the room. I have to sit on the bed. The big trouble is that when I sit down the horse is staring at me. It faces the bed, and with it there, I can't move the bed. Finally I have to go sit on the floor and look out the window at the brick wall next door. I have never seen such a sad sitting horse.

When I go out, I check the mailbox like usual, and there is a note from Banty. The note wishes me congratulations, on account of I have won the raffle, which I already know. The note also says that this is a horse, cast from bronze, and is the work of a Coming Primitive Sculptor; he don't say who.

It is the word *primitive* which gets me, and I show the note to Albert in Katzie's Saloon. He reads it; then he reads it again, and ask me what it is all about. When I tell him, he buys me a beer.

"You have got depth, Dubois," he says, making wrinkles in his forehead. "I see Banty has noticed this trait."

"I'm also lucky," I say, and he nods very fast.

"I been wonderin' about Banty," he muses. "I heard he left town this mornin'."

"It must have been after the raffle."

"Oh, yes. It musta been." Albert waves to Jonesy for two more beers, and he signs me to clam up till Jonesy gets behind the bar again. "You bought the ticket las' night, huh?"

"On the way home."

He nods and stares out of the window, tapping his lower lip with his finger like he is handicapping a horse. "That payroll heist was jus' last week—"

"Banty is goin' straight," I protest.

"I forgot," Albert says. "You're right, Dubois. What say we go look at that there horse?"

I can see Albert is took with it right away. He even takes off his hat. He examines the statue from every angle, just like I done when I was trying to figure out what it was. He taps it and raps it with his knuckles, and then just sits for a long time and sort of smiles at it. I don't say nothing then to break the mood, on account of I have seen them signs in the museums which say SILENCE, and like that. Naturally I am surprised that Albert has turned out to be fascinated with horse sculpture, but then, he has always been a horse player and I guess there is a connection.

Finally he says, "Dubois, it is a beauty. I'll give you five clams for it."

"Five?" I am surprised because I have told him what I paid for the raffle ticket.

"All right. Dubois, I am not gonna insult you. You know this here is a genuine Primitive statue, so I am goin' to offer the tops. I'll slip you ten fish, how's that?"

"You got to pay for gettin' it outa here—"

"I know," he says. "And I ain't deductin' it from your ten. Is it a deal?"

"No," I say. It is still a week from rent day, and I have never owned a genuine Primitive statue before. I ain't really had no statues. "It ain't for sale. Thanks anyway, Albert."

He argues a polite bit with me, and he even goes up to twenty clams. But I get real set then because I am sure he ain't got that kind of moo. I have never seen Albert with twenty Irish flags. I begin to wonder if he is putting me on. But he don't look like it. He looks as sad as the horse; and when he leaves, he tells me that he is awful fond of it.

This is a side of Albert I have never seen before, and I am proud that I know guys what appreciate Primitive stuff.

About an hour after Albert leaves, there is a knock at the door and when I open it, Faceless Robert pushes me into the room.

"Where is it?" he says, and then he zeroes in on the statue.

"You dig sculpture?" I ask, astonished. Faceless is a tall, skinny, pinstripe type with connections; and he motions me to shut the door.

"I ain't been able to kick the habit," he says when the door is closed. "Don't let it get aroun'." He raps the statue like Albert done and he frowns at it a very great deal. "How much that bugger weigh?"

"I dunno," I tell him. "It sags the floor."

"It sure does. I can see that thing is worth plenty, pal. Maybe as high as fifteen smackeroonies." He comes over close to me and gives me the beady eye. "You sure this is the Banty Bronze, huh?"

"That's it." I appreciate that Faceless wants to be sure. He has got a reputation for not believing nothing. He is very large in the horse-playing dodge. But he don't take any chances with that, either; mostly he bets right after the race is over. This is not really called horse playing; this is called collecting.

"All right," he says. "We got us a deal. Fifteen green ones, minus the moving tab. Dubois, don't sell me nothin' more, you drive a hard bargain."

"It ain't for sale, Faceless." I back up, and he follows me till I reach the horse and have to stop. He towers over me and starts chewing a matchstick.

"Ever'thing's for sale, Dubois. When I like a thing, I like it good. Right now, I like you. That's why I am offerin' you so much."

"But—"

He lowers his voice. "Somethin' come over me when I seen that there—horse," he says. "There's things a man's just got to have; you know that, huh, pal?"

"But I like it, too—I—"

"That's good. You wouldn't want nothin' to happen to that there statue, huh?"

"But, Faceless, what could happen? That thing's a solid chunk. It's insurance proof."

His eyes go funny at that, and he backs off and stares at the statue again for a while. If he don't look puzzled, he is close to it. When he goes out he don't even slam the door. After that I have got the horse to myself for about a whole day.

There is a little private party after closing time at Katzie's, and Albert invites me as his guest. He lets me drink all the beer I want. When I get home it is about three in the morning. I am so fuzzy that I don't notice the horse is missing till I try to climb over it to get into bed.

That sobers me up pretty good and I turn on the light. But it ain't anywhere in the room. There are some chunks knocked out of the windowsill, and after a bit I figure that maybe it has been pushed out the window.

I rush downstairs then and look in the alley. Right under my window there is a hole in the asphalt about a foot and half deep. I light matches and look around the alley, but the statue ain't there either.

The next morning Mrs. Sherpy meets me in the hallway. "You feel the earthquake las' night?"

I tell her no and scram out. The hole is still in the alley, and in the daylight I can see skid marks. Then I know that I have been robbed. Somebody has took the statue away in a car.

I start toward Katzie's and I am feeling real sad. It is funny how a person can get attached to a sitting horse statue. But I am still lucky. Only half a block away is a beat-up car at the curb. It has got two flat tires and is leaning sideways like it is going around a curve at ninety miles an hour, except the engine part is almost off the ground. The trunk lid is half up and in the back is the statue. There is a little dirt on it, but otherwise it is perfect.

I am looking at it, and thinking it will cost me ten clams to get it back upstairs, when Albert comes along.

"What you doin' here, Dubois?" he asks me, like we have just met in front of a pyramid.

I am about to tell him I live on this street, but I reflect that he knows it and had just forgot. Then he sees the car.

"Hmmm, the axle is broke," he says. "Some poor guy is outa luck."

Albert is very sharp. I never even thought about the axle, but he spots it right off. Then he notices the horse and gets real excited.

"Hey, Dubois, that's your sitting statue!"

"I know it, Albert. It was heisted las' night durin' your party."

"It was?" He is relieved. "It's sure good you found it again. What you goin' do now?"

"I dunno. I ain't got the moo t'get it took back upstairs. Maybe I'll just give it to one of them museums."

"No, I wouldn't do that."

"Why not?"

"Nobody could get it out—" He takes a breath. "Dubois, we're pals, huh, you an' me? This here horse was a present. You ain't goin' to give away a present?"

I shake my head. "I can't afford it, Albert. Besides, it ain't right for me t'have a genuine Primitive thing like this in my room all to myself. I am gonna give it—"

Albert takes my arm and drags me toward the rooming house. "Dubois, we got to have a talk."

"But, Albert, I can't leave that statue out here."

He looks exasperated. "Who's gonna walk off with a million pound chunk of iron? C'mon."

He is right; so we go up to my room. I don't know what he wants to talk about, but I am willing to listen. He don't come right to the point, but after a while he gets around to it. "You are too smart, Dubois. There is no use me tryin' to outfox you, so I will put all my cards on the table. I will even cut you in."

"Cut me in on what?"

"The sittin' horse," he says.

He is confusing me. Maybe he guesses it, because he sits on the bed and takes a deep breath.

"Look, Dubois, you got that statue from Banty, right?"

"Sure, I won it."

"All right, you won it, in the only ticket—never mind. You won it. Now, Banty is outa town on account of the heat. Ain't that right?"

I shrug. "He don't say nothin' to me."

"He is. Take my word for it. Banty is a mobster, ever'body knows that." He holds up his hand to stop me from talking and goes on. "Okay, Banty don't believe in banks, so when he is loaded he has got to have some place to stash the loot. Right?"

"How come if he's loaded he is sellin' raffle tickets?"

Albert sighs. "Forget the raffle. I'm handin you the straight. Banty has got loot wadded up inside that horse statue."

I am astonished. "Inside the statue?"

"Of course. And he seen that you won it. Dubois, you have got a reputation aroun' town." He nods as I lower my eyes. It is nice to hear them things. "Ever'body knows what kind of a guy you are, Dubois. Where could Banty get a better type to guard his loot?"

"But the statue's mine."

"Sure," he says, "and, not knowin' about the loot, you'd give it back to Banty if he ast you, huh? You're that kind of guy."

I nod. He is right. Albert has got me figured out.

"But," he says, a gleam in his eye, "that's what makes it so legal. The statue is yours—and everything in it. Dubois, we'll take the thing to Jersey; I know a ex-safecracker; and I'm cuttin' you in on half what we find."

Albert is a right gee. He goes out, and in no time he is back with a rented truck which has got a winch on the back. It takes us a while, but we get the statue heaved up on the truck bed and we go tootling off to Jersey.

The ex-safe man is a little wizened-up guy named Blooie. Albert explains to me that this is a trade nickname. Blooie runs a junkyard, and we drive the truck around back of his shack. In about ten minutes Albert fills him in on the fix we are in. Blooie climbs up on the truck and looks over the horse with a professional eye. When he gets down he is shaking his head.

"I ain't gonna guarantee t'blow that thing," he says.

Albert wrings his hands. "But it ain't no different than a safe."

Blooie looks at him with disgust. "No dice. If I blow it open, I blow up what's in it. I ain't cuttin' me in on that kinda deal. You need a saw."

"A saw," Albert says. "Yeah!" He pushes me into the truck and we scram out of there. We stop at a hardware store, and Albert buys two hacksaws and a handful of spare blades.

We spend the rest of the afternoon growing blisters on our hands. About the time it gets dark we are both tired and sore. We have made a half dozen little scratches on the horse, most of which seem to improve his looks.

When we get back to the rooming house, Albert helps me dump off the statue in the alley. He is in a bad mood.

"Leave the damn thing there till morning," he growls. "Nobody in his right mind is gonna bother it. Maybe I'll figger out somethin'."

After he takes off, I sit on the horse for a while, but nothing comes to me. So I go upstairs. That is when I am surprised.

Banty is in my room, and he looks happy as a oiled lark. "You're a pal, Dubois," he says. "You got conned out of dat horse, huh? I figgered da news would get aroun'."

"It's down—what you doin'?" Banty is hammering the black base of the statue which I have pushed over into a corner out of the way. He busts it all up with a piece of iron pipe, and inside is a tin box.

"You're a good bank," he says. He takes out a ten spot and hands it to me. "Here's yer interest."

Actually, I made nine clams on the deal.

Dead End

by Stephen Wasylyk

The ringing of the phone drove deeply into my dream. I rolled over in protest, pulling the covers tight around my head in a futile gesture of defiance that dulled the shrill bell but did nothing to stop it.

I lowered the covers reluctantly and sat up, fumbling for the dimly glowing cube of my alarm clock. It was one in the morning. I groaned. My flight had been delayed, putting me into the city only a few hours ago, and it had been well after midnight before I went to bed. Supposedly no one from the office knew I was home again. The insistent phone said otherwise.

I switched on my bedside lamp and reached for the receiver.

"Cochrane? This is Ross."

I swung my feet to the floor. "I'm listening."

"Joe DiMarco was killed tonight." The voice was flat, emotion held in check.

I felt my stomach muscles tense. "How?"

"I had a call five minutes ago. He skidded and smashed through the retaining wall on West River Drive and went down the embankment about eleven o'clock. They say he was killed instantly."

"Weaver goes before the grand jury tomorrow," I said slowly. "It looks like he's lucky."

"Too lucky," snapped Ross. "That's why I want you to look into it."

"You think it might not be an accident?"

"I want to be certain that it was. A sergeant named Beckett from Accident Investigation is at the scene, recovering the car. Go over there and stay with him until the cause of the accident is determined."

"DiMarco was working late. Maybe he fell asleep at the wheel."

Controlled fury was in the voice now. "Dammit, I don't want maybes! Get over there and get the facts!"

The telephone slammed down.

I replaced the receiver slowly. Three years ago, Kirby Ross had run for district attorney on a reform ticket and, through some minor miracle, had won. Maybe it was because the people believed what he said, maybe it was because Ross had charisma. Tall, handsome, with a touch of gray at the temples, articulate and photogenic, he really looked like a crusader. That was the public image. Once you knew him, you forgot appearances and found he was a very vain and arrogant man, an ambitious man who used people as he saw fit. He'd be a crusader as long as there was something in it for him.

I didn't hold that against him. He made an honest attempt at cleaning up the city by filling the D.A.'s office with men he could trust. DiMarco had been the first, as assistant D.A., a darkhaired, bouncing bundle of energy with all the talent in the world. Ross may have had the title, but DiMarco had been the mover and shaker. Then Ross had pulled me from Homicide to be his chief investigator, and for the past three years DiMarco and I had a ball.

We hadn't cleaned up the city yet. No one could do that in three years, especially since the entire administration refused to cooperate. There were quite a few big men left, among them the mayor, who had suddenly graduated into an enviable life style shortly after he was elected; several councilmen who could be counted on to in troduce and vote for any special interest legislation for any special interest group for a given price; and quite a few department heads who awarded lucrative contracts without regard for anything except the size of their share. Sometimes I doubted there was an honest man in the administration. Money was easy and hard to resist, especially when you knew everyone about you had no qualms in taking it.

We also had to contend with several outside powers, the biggest of whom was Carleton Weaver. He had an excellent front as one of the largest contractors in town, but he made his real money in negotiating crooked contracts while heading up the drug traffic, prostitution, and gambling empire it had taken him years to build before he supposedly turned legitimate.

It looked now as if DiMarco had nailed him, not for any of those things but for a technicality. Called as a witness in a multimillion dollar building fraud, he'd naturally refused to testify. DiMarco immediately offered him freedom from prosecution. Again he refused, which was what DiMarco wanted. Weaver was held in contempt of court. He was to have been offered one more chance to testify. If he refused, the judge was prepared to give him the maximum two years in prison. It wasn't much, considering who Weaver was, but it was something. The trouble was, DiMarco had handled the whole thing and now that he was dead, there was no one prepared to step into his shoes except Ross.

Even so, the case would have to be postponed, perhaps not to be revived.

I fingered through my wardrobe for the warmest clothes I could find. A northeast snowstorm had hit the city a few days before, followed by the inevitable cold wave, and the streets were still full of slush during the day and ice at night. It would be bitter along the river at this hour of the morning and I was neither young enough nor my body upholstered enough to ignore the cold.

The spot along the Drive was easy to find. Barriers and blinking yellow caution lights funneled traffic into one lane around several parked police cars and a huge tow truck, the scene lit by portable floodlights. If it had been anyone except DiMarco, the operation would have waited until morning.

I pulled my parka hood up over my ears, flashed my identification at a patrolman on guard, and slid down the embankment to where some men were working around the wreck.

DiMarco's car had been a popular sports model, and even though the front was pushed in and the roof flattened, it still retained its racy lines.

I worked my way to a short, overcoated man watching the operation. "It's been a few years, Beckett," I said.

Becket smiled. "I knew you'd be here, Jack, since he was one of your boys. Ross get you out of bed?"

"That's why the man pays me. What do you know?"

Beckett's shoulders moved under his heavy coat. "He came around the curve, seemed to lose control, hit the wall, and flipped over. We know because there's a witness, a guy who was heading in the opposite direction. DiMarco almost hit him. He said it was weird, so that gives you an idea of the kind of witness he is. There was one other car following DiMarco, an Olds or a Caddy, the witness isn't sure except he says it was a dark color. That guy never stopped. Didn't want to get involved, I suppose."

One of the crew shouted and waved. The whine of the truck engine grew louder, the steel cable stretching down the embankment grew taut, and the smashed car began to move. It rolled onto its wheels and began to climb the slope; a harshly shadowed, misshapen, battered monster struggling upward toward sanctuary across the torn snow.

"Lucky it can be towed," Beckett said. "They'll have that thing in the garage in half an hour where we can really go over it. You want to meet me there?"

"You couldn't keep me away," I said.

The police garage was tucked away in a corner of the city that consisted of flat river land occupied by an almost endless succession of automobile graveyards. I pulled up behind Beckett and followed him into the warmth of the office, slipped out of my parka and stretched, my face tingling from the warmth after being chilled by the river wind.

Beckett was pulling his third sweater over his head. He grinned. "I've been on so many of these things I know how to dress. You want some coffee?"

"I never refuse."

Beckett poured two cups, black and hot.

"Who replaces DiMarco?"

"No one," I said. I meant it. Ross was the front man. DiMarco and I had done all the work.

A sudden flurry of noise from the garage showed that the tow truck had arrived. Beckett downed his coffee. "I'd better help them get it on the lift. Not going to find anything, but I'll look because Ross insists."

I sipped my coffee slowly, thinking of DiMarco, Ross, and Weaver and how our lives had become so entangled that even the death of one of us did nothing to loosen the cords. If anything, they had become tighter.

I finished my coffee and followed Beckett.

He had slipped into white coveralls and was probing the under part of the car, a powerful extension light in one hand, a screwdriver in the other.

"I thought that was a mechanic's job," I said.

"Usually is, but not this time. I don't want Ross to hit me with any unexpected questions." He stepped back. "Just as I thought. There is nothing wrong with the car. Front suspension, brakes, exhaust system, the works. All clear."

"You're certain?"

"I'll swear to it, which means there had to be something wrong with the driver. DiMarco was no teetotaler, it was late, and he could have had a few and been tired to boot. The autopsy will settle it."

I wasn't going to argue the point. "Have you checked inside the car?"

"Not yet." He pushed the button that lowered the lift, pried open the door on the passenger side, thrust the light inside, and followed it, squeezing beneath the flattened roof. I did the same from the driver's side.

The interior of the car was littered with flaked and powdered glass from the now nonexistent windows. Beckett played the light around carefully, front and rear. There seemed to be nothing.

The flood of light caught and was reflected by something on the floor of the front compartment rug, a beacon in a sea of broken glass. I picked it up carefully and held it under Beckett's light, rotating it slowly. It was a clear piece of glass, thin and curved.

"That isn't window glass," Beckett said. "Looks like it's from a small bottle of some sort."

"There must be more," I said.

We searched the floor, finding several more pieces, lining them up on the bloodied seat. It was obvious they were part of a small vial, perhaps a half inch in diameter and more than two inches long.

"You tell me," I said. "Where does it fit?"

Beckett grunted. "Not part of the car."

"Maybe DiMarco was carrying it."

"I think not. Something that small would have been in his pocket."

Beckett thrust his light under the dashboard and peered after it. He grunted again. "There's a wire to the heater where there should be no wire." He probed with the screwdriver. I heard something fall. Beckett pushed aside a rectangular black fiberboard box, about nine inches wide and two inches deep, that I recognized as the deflector at the end of the heater vent. Connected to the wire, a small transistorized circuit board about three by four inches had fallen out of the deflector. It looked like a radio but I knew it wasn't made for listening to music.

Beckett examined it carefully without touching it, poking it gently with the screwdriver.

"Now you know how DiMarco died," he said.

"I know nothing," I said.

He pointed with the screwdriver. "The vial fitted into these brackets. The upper half is still intact." The screwdriver moved. "This plunger at the bottom is held back by a solenoid. They tapped in on the battery side of the ignition so that they had plenty of current. When the current was turned on, the solenoid moved and the rod snapped forward, breaking the vial. The rest of the circuit exists for just that purpose, to move that solenoid when it receives a signal from a transmitter."

"What transmitter?"

"It would have to be close, maybe a couple of hundred yards."

"Like in a car following DiMarco," I suggested.

"It could be."

"So the vial breaks and the vial holds something that kills DiMarco."

"Didn't have to kill him, just knock him out so he loses control on the curve. Something that vaporizes in the hot airstream because it's a cold night and DiMarco is sure to have the heater on."

"An anesthetic agent. Maybe a nerve gas."

"Take your choice. The lab will have to come up with something." Beckett slid out of the car. "We'll leave things just as they are for Homicide. It's as far as I go and I'm happy about that. This is a far-out way to kill a guy. I'm used to dynamite under the hood or the brake lines cut, but this thing belongs in a spy story somewhere. It really took a lot of brains and money to figure this out."

"It looks a little complicated," I said.

"Not complicated at all when you think of what they can do these days. You have voice-activated switches. You can send things to the moon or to space and turn them on and off at will. You can even get a little transmitter that will make your garage door go up or down without your leaving the car. Breaking a little vial at the proper time is no trick at all. Whoever did it is really clever. He wanted DiMarco dead with no trace and it almost worked. I don't normally bother too much with the inside of the car except to look for whisky bottles." He shook his head. "It seems like there are an awful lot of ways to kill a guy."

He was right. It would take a special kind of person to conceive the idea; someone like Weaver, who would have those kinds of re-sources at hand. All he would have needed was someone to execute it.

Weaver might be behind it, Weaver *had* to be behind it, but there couldn't be too many men in the city who could build such a device and be trusted to keep quiet.

I followed Beckett into the office.

"You want to call Ross?" he asked.

I looked at my watch. It was five thirty. "Not yet. Let him sleep a few hours. This is going to hit him right between the eyes and he'll need all the rest he can get. I have something to check on first."

"Can I help?"

I slipped into my parka. "You give Homicide the details and tell them I'll be in touch."

The predawn darkness was cold and still, the wind gone. The inside of my car felt like a refrigerator. I raced the engine to force hot air through the heating system, my breath steaming the windows.

I swung the car around and headed for town. Beckett's technical knowledge could tell him how the device worked, but my background gave me the name of the man who could either build it or name those who could: Clint Brazil. It would be smart to check on him before Homicide did.

He was an old man now, but still young when it came to ideas, specializing in electronics surveillance devices for anyone who had the money to pay. He worked for every law enforcement agency in the city, for all the private investigators and, although no one ever did anything about it, for anyone on the other side of the law who had the price. If Brazil didn't have in stock a bug that would do the job, he'd invent one.

The device that had killed DiMarco was right down his alley.

Driving slowly because of the ice, it took me almost an hour to reach Brazil's street. I turned the corner and slammed on the brakes.

Brazil had a shop on the ground floor where he sold the installation and service of electronic alarm systems which, as thriving as it was, only fronted for his real business.

The street should have been deserted, so the police cruisers and an ambulance parked before the shop at that hour were a surprise. I pulled up and headed for the door. A uniformed man held up a hand. I flashed my badge. "What's it all about?"

"Someone killed the old man who owned the shop," he said. "Sergeant Solkowsky is inside. He can tell you about it."

Solkowsky and I had attended the Police Academy together and had once worked out of the same precinct. I found him inside the shop supervising the intern who was supervising the ambulance attendants. Solkowsky was a crewcut bull of a man whose chief virtue as a detective was his lack of imagination. Solkowsky never guessed; Solkowsky always knew before he moved or he wouldn't move.

The shop he was standing in was small, a plush reception area separated from the rest of the room by a waist-high glass counter. Behind the counter were a pair of desks backed by wall shelves lined with small, brightly colored boxes and beyond them an open door that showed a work area that contained benches, tools, and complicated-looking test equipment.

"Can I move him?" asked the intern.

"Can he move him?" Solkowsky asked the photographer.

The photographer nodded.

"You can move him," said Solkowsky. He spotted me. "You stop in to get warm?"

"Just checking on something."

"No lines of communication to where Brazil is now. Someone pressed a .38 to his chest and pulled the trigger twice, about twelve, which is the nearest we can figure at this point."

"Who found the man?" I asked.

"A patrol car went by the place a couple of times, the boys noticed the light was on, and so they stopped to investigate. They found the door open, walked in and found the old man. Otherwise, he would be still lying here growing stiff without nobody knowing nothing."

It was obvious the man for whom Brazil had built the device had returned to keep him from talking—but why not kill Brazil when the device had been delivered?

That was obvious, too. Brazil wasn't to be paid unless the device worked. Instead of money, the old man had collected two slugs.

"You have anything else?" I asked.

"We've just started. Now just what brings you here?"

I drew him aside and explained about DiMarco. Solkowsky raised his chin and scratched his neck thoughtfully. "You know how crazy this sounds?"

"It may sound crazy but it makes sense to me. That's why I want you to seal this place up tight until we establish a connection between the device and the shop. That's why I want you to bear down on this. Whoever killed DiMarco killed Brazil, and right now the number one candidate is Weaver."

"You figure on picking up Weaver?"

"That's up to Ross. I'm going to see him now. He'll be in touch. Just concentrate on what you have here. Hell, I don't have to tell you what to do."

"I'll have to check with the captain. Beckett probably called about DiMarco."

"He should let you handle both cases. Tell him Ross will be taking a personal interest."

"Where will you be?"

"In the office later. I'll call you. It's time I wake Ross and tell him what's been going on."

Outside, a gray dawn had arrived to reveal the streets filling with people whose jobs demanded that they get to work early and open the city for business each morning.

Ross lived in a fashionable townhouse across the street from a park, his three story brownstone overshadowed by expensive apartment houses and condominiums. I often wondered how he afforded it. The district attorney didn't draw that much salary, but Ross had once had a lucrative practice and his wife came from one of the oldest families in the city.

I slid into the reserved parking spot at the curb, mounted the marble steps, and rang the bell.

Ross himself opened the door in his shirtsleeves, no tie and the morning paper in his hand. "I've been expecting you to call," he said. He ushered me into the dining room. "Would you like breakfast?"

I shook my head. My appetite wouldn't be back until this thing was settled. "You'd better sit down," I said. "You're not going to believe what I tell you."

"DiMarco was killed?"

"It isn't only that. It's how he was killed." I went through it all for him while he sipped his coffee.

"How did you find the device?"

"It's hard to slip something by Beckett." I didn't tell him it had been my idea to look inside the car.

"You were fortunate. I would think something like that couldn't be tracked down at all. Where is the device now?"

"Probably at the lab."

"I'll want complete photos and a detailed analysis. To my recollection, nothing like it has ever been used. We shall have a difficult time explaining to a jury if we ever get that far."

"The man who planted it knew that."

"I'll leave everything in your hands," he said. "You'll coordinate the investigation with Homicide."

"This may be the break we needed to get Weaver."

He shook his head. "I doubt it. He will have covered his tracks well."

His sudden uninterest in Weaver puzzled me. It was almost as though he had dismissed the killings; as if he expected nothing further to be learned. He might be right. The killings could easily be a dead end. Ross was very good at analyzing that sort of thing very quickly and going on to whatever seemed more important. He lifted his head to say something, but the entrance of his wife cut him off.

I stood up.

Harriet Ross, at least fifteen years younger than her husband, was tall and graceful, a natural blonde with fair, glowing skin, slightly slanted dark eyes, and an oval face that broke into a thin smile when she saw me. The frilly pink housecoat she was wearing covered her from chin to toe, effectively hiding what I knew was a figure most women envied.

Always pleasant and polite, she nevertheless acted as if it were difficult to admit I existed.

"You are up early, Mr. Cochrane," she said. She made the words sound like a reprimand.

"It isn't a nine-to-five job," I said. I saw no reason to remain. "I'll see you in the office," I said to Ross.

"Just stay with it," he said. "There is no need to tell you how I feel about DiMarco. I want the man who killed him."

"I suppose you'll issue a statement. The newsmen will be at the office early."

He shook his head. "I'll have no comment. What we know we'll keep to ourselves. I'll see that Homicide issues no details."

That's the smart way to handle it, I thought as I walked out into the cold morning, even if it was unusual for Ross. Ordinarily, he would jump on something like the way DiMarco was killed to get more publicity.

There was no one in the office when I arrived. I busied myself for a few moments before dialing Solkowsky.

"Anything develop?" I asked.

"Give us time," he said. "We're just starting to coordinate. Beckett is here and we're expecting you. The heater of the car and the device have been dusted for prints and we've turned up nothing, but the lab fitted the broken pieces of glass together and we lifted a latent. Not good enough for court, but we think we can identify it. Doesn't seem to fit anything in our criminal files so far. We'll probably have to send it to the FBI."

"Has the lab tied in the device with anything in Brazil's shop?"

"They're working on it now. It seems that all of the components are common and available anywhere."

"Does the lab have any idea of what was in the vial?"

"Not enough residue. Right now they're sitting there surrounded by all sorts of medical books, trying to figure out what could be used. Do you know how many anesthetics there are?"

"I don't have the faintest idea."

"They tell me dozens. I doubt if they'll come up with anything."

"I'm sure they won't," I said.

I cradled the phone. A print on the vial didn't make sense, not in an operation as clever as this. Someone had made a mistake.

The people who worked in the office began to drift in: the typists, the secretaries, the legal assistants, the other assistant D.A.'s, their faces mirroring shock because they had all heard about DiMarco. They gathered in little groups, questioning me, believing that DiMarco had died in an accident. I wasn't going to tell them anything different.

They pressed in on me, their questions rasping my nerves, and the thought uppermost in my mind was that things weren't going well at all. I had to get out of there, to walk alone for a while.

I fled into the bitter wind sweeping across City Hall Plaza just as the clock in the tower sounded with measured beats. It was nine o'clock.

I started across the plaza in the face of the wind, past the cab stand at the corner.

A horn blew in short, sharp blasts. A cabbie waved at me, swung the door open, and came around the front of his cab, walking carefully across the ice at the curb, his thin face frowning.

"I'm glad I ran into you, Cochrane," he said. "I'm sorry about DiMarco."

I nodded. One of the reasons for our success had been the help of the Lennie Breckers, the people who saw almost everything that went on in the city but whom no one ever noticed because they blended into the background. Lennie could be depended on for a variety of information he constantly picked up cruising around town.

"I wanted to ask DiMarco if what I told him the other day meant anything, but now I'll never know," he said.

"Suppose you tell me and let me decide."

Lennie cupped his hands and breathed into them, rubbing them briskly. "Listen, Cochrane," he said, "let's get in the cab. This cold does my arthritis no good at all."

I climbed into the rear seat. He slid behind the wheel and turned to face me, draping one arm over the back of the seat. Lennie was small and thin, with lenses on his glasses so thick I often wondered how he passed a driver's examination.

"Listen," he said. "About three or four days ago, I picked up a fare in front of the building where Weaver has his contracting offices, one of those muscle men Weaver passes off as businessmen. I know he works for Weaver because I've seen him around and I'm always glad to pick up one of these guys because they tip good. Where do you think he wants to go?"

"I couldn't guess."

"He tells me to take him to the Japanese pagoda in the park. You know that *nobody* goes there in the winter. I'm surprised, but it's his money. I take him. The only people there are a couple of tourists who don't know no better and a darkhaired broad. She seems to be waiting for my fare. He tells me to wait and walks up to her. They talk for a minute, he hands her an envelope and comes back to the cab. I take him back to town. The woman looks familiar but I just can't place her." He touched his glasses apologetically. "Maybe it's these. Anyway, about an hour later, I'm cruising down Chestnut Street when I see this same broad come out of the bank at Ninth. This time I'm a lot closer and I recognize her. It looks like the D.A.'s wife, except I'm still not a hundred percent sure because I thought she was a blonde. A couple of hours after that, DiMarco flags me down in front of City Hall, so I tell him about it. He tells me not to mention it to anyone, that he'll be back to me. Next thing I know, he's dead."

Lennie's long story boiled down to one thing. What he had seen sounded suspiciously like a payoff.

"You got a funny expression on your face, Cochrane," Lennie said.

Lennie was an unexpected development but a lucky one. I could use what he told me. "I'll tell you what we'll do, Lennie," I said. "We'll check it out now. Suppose you take me to the newspaper office."

It took only a half hour at the photo morgue to find a picture of Harriet Ross sent in for use on the society page. It was a good portrait, with her hair drawn severely back, so that whether she was blonde or brunette didn't matter at all.

I showed it to Lennie. "Is this the woman you saw?"

"I would swear to it."

"Okay," I said. "Let's go to the bank."

I had no success with the first few people I checked. They didn't know her and it wasn't until I worked my way into the safe deposit vault section that I had any luck.

The elderly, fleshy guard named Gordon took one look at the picture. "That's Mrs. Pierce," he said.

"You're sure of the name?"

"Of course I'm sure. She comes in here often. At least once a month. I can check her card."

"Do that," I said.

The card showed visits shortly after the first of the month for the last six months, the signature *H. Pierce* firm and flowing and definitely feminine.

"I'd like a copy of this card," I told Gordon.

"I'm not sure that's allowed."

"I am, and I want it kept between us. If anyone asks, I was never here."

He waddled over to a copying machine and gave me a copy which I tucked away with the photo.

"This is official business, I suppose," he said.

"You can bet on it," I told him.

Things were moving now the way I wanted them to move. I went back to Lennie's cab, which was double-parked and the object of an impatient glare from the traffic cop on the corner.

"What's it all about?" asked Lennie. "The D.A.'s wife . . . "

"Just forget the whole thing, Lennie," I said. "Unless I personally tell you to remember."

"If you say so. Where to now?"

"Police headquarters."

Lennie dropped me in front of the headquarters building and I took the elevator to the third floor fingerprint lab. Humphrey, the man in charge, wasn't too happy to see me.

"I suppose you came about that print," he said.

"You guessed it. Have you identified it yet?"

"It isn't that good and it takes time."

"Suppose I gave you a lead. Would that help?"

"You know it would."

I leaned over his desk and wrote *Ross* on a notepad.

He was just extracting a cigarette from a pack when he saw the name. The pack slipped from his hand as if he had suddenly lost control. "You're kidding."

"Not about something like this."

"It will take a few minutes." He rescued his cigarettes and fumbled one out, his hands still not quite steady.

"I'll wait."

"I suppose you know what you're doing."

"I never know," I said. "I only do things and sometimes they turn out right."

I put my feet up on his desk and relaxed, not feeling tired in spite of having no sleep the night before. Maybe the adrenalin flow was increased as I worked the thing out and got closer to the showdown. I had to admit that things were going well now.

Humphrey came back. "It isn't too clear."

"What does that mean?"

"It means I don't have a perfect print to work with. It could be or it couldn't be. I'm not committing myself."

"It won't hold up in court?"

"Not even with a dumb attorney on the defense."

"It probably will never come to that," I said. "If anyone asks, you never saw me. This is between us unless I tell you otherwise."

"I should tell Solkowsky you were here."

"Why get him all excited? If it works out, I'll tell him myself. In the meantime, earn your salary by going through your print file. Maybe you'll find another that you like better, and that will keep Solkowsky busy."

I left him fumbling for another cigarette. I had found out that the print couldn't be identified and I had started Humphrey thinking about Ross, both of which seemed like good ideas.

On the street, I turned my parka hood up and headed for the municipal garage a block away. The place was as cold as a tomb, my breath steaming in the damp stillness as I walked down the ramp to the official parking places.

Ross's Cadillac was in its reserved slot, the keys in it. I searched the interior perfunctorily and found nothing. I took the keys and opened the trunk.

It had to be there and it was. The box was about eight inches high and six inches square, painted black with a telescoping antenna on top and a dial and some knobs on the front. It looked like an innocent piece of electronics test equipment like those I had seen in Brazil's shop, but I knew this was no tool for a technician. It was the transmitter that had been used to set off the device in DiMarco's car. I closed the trunk lid. It was time now to see Ross.

He was in his office, having just come from the courtroom where he had the Weaver case postponed. He looked up in annoyance. "I don't have time for you now, Jack."

I don't think I ever disliked him more than at that moment. I closed the door and crossed to the window next to him, half sitting on the broad sill, the gray light behind me flooding his face and shadowing mine. He was forced to look up at me, placing him in an awkward position and giving me a definite advantage. "You'll have to take time," I said. "I know who killed DiMarco."

He sat up straighter. "You're certain?"

"A conviction would be no problem."

"Let me decide that. What do you have?"

I handed him the photocopy of the safe deposit vault record card. He glanced at it and dropped it on his desk. "What exactly is this?"

"A record of your wife's visit to a safe deposit box each month after accepting an envelope from one of Weaver's men. She rents the box under her maiden name and wears a dark wig. I'm sure a court order will open the box to find it filled with cash."

His face was blank. He leaned back in his chair and crossed his arms. "I know nothing of any safe deposit box."

"There's more," I said. "I also have a print on the vial that was used in the device that killed DiMarco. It could be yours."

"That's impossible," he said coldly.

I pressed on. "I do have the transmitter that was used to set off the device. It's in the trunk of your car. The witness to the accident said the car following DiMarco was dark. Yours is dark brown."

"Just what does all of this mean?"

"It means you sold out to Weaver. Your wife took the payoff. DiMarco found out, so you had to get rid of him. You would have had to get rid of him in any event because he was getting too close to Weaver, and Weaver was paying you to get DiMarco off his back."

"I suppose you can prove I killed Brazil, too."

"There's a .38 in your desk drawer I would like to have checked by ballistics."

He never showed more cool than he did then. "It's all a frame, of course. A good one, but still a frame."

I studied him closely. I hated to admit it, but I was inclined to agree. Ross was no murderer. He could conspire to commit a crime, but he would consider himself above executing it. He would leave that to others. "Anything is possible except your wife being seen with Weaver's man," I said. "That was no frame."

"No," he said. "That can't be faked." He looked more concerned than worried.

"All right," I said. "I'll buy the frame. Anyone could have left the transmitter in your car, but you'll have to come up with a good explanation for your wife."

"She's the only one who can do that."

"I could go out there and bring her in, but it would be simpler for you to call and ask her to come here."

"No," he said. "You and I will go talk to her."

I didn't quite see it that way. There was something about being questioned in the D.A.'s office that kept people off balance. Talking to her in her own home put her on familiar ground, put her more at ease.

"All right," I said. "Let's get it over with."

We left by the side door, to avoid reporters who might be waiting in the anteroom, and picked up Ross's car. Neither of us said a word about the device still in the trunk, but I knew he was thinking of it and so was I. I wanted that little box along so I could keep an eye on the thing.

At the house, he led the way, stepping aside as he ushered me into the study.

I took one step and my head exploded. I didn't know what he hit me with, but my legs went out from under me and I went down while the stars that burst suddenly before my eyes faded before they really had a chance to form.

I came to with the rug rough against my face, pain radiating from somewhere in the back of my head. Ross's well-polished shoes, magnified by their closeness, were inches from my face. I rolled over painfully. He was standing above me, my gun in his hand. I blinked at the weird perspective. Ross seemed enormously tall.

"I'm sorry I had to do that," he said.

I sat up slowly, hoping my head wouldn't come loose. From this angle, Ross looked less omnipotent. "So it was no frame," I said thickly. "You really did kill DiMarco."

"No," he said. "I didn't kill DiMarco. Weaver had that done and obviously the Brazil job, too. I have no idea who he hired."

"Where do you fit in?"

"Weaver *has* been paying me for months to take it easy on his operations. I did what I could, but I couldn't control DiMarco. Then DiMarco found out about the payoff and came to me. I stalled him. Weaver wanted to kill DiMarco because if he talked, it would be bad for both of us. I balked. Killing DiMarco would cause a great many questions to be asked by the newspapers, perhaps even bring in the state crime commission. Weaver said not to worry about it. No one was supposed to know DiMarco had been murdered, but you and Beckett broke the whole thing open. I didn't expect that when I went through the motions of having you investigate."

"Why would Weaver have the device placed in your car?"

"I can guess at two reasons. My job would be to keep the investigation away from it if necessary. You jumped the gun. It may also be Weaver's subtle way of telling me I am as vulnerable as DiMarco."

I tried to stand.

Ross pushed me down with one hand. "Stay where you are. I feel safer with you on the floor."

"What now?" I asked.

"You're a menace, Cochrane. You have to be eliminated. I called Weaver while you were out and he's sending someone over to do just that."

My head was spinning and not just because he had hit me. It was going around with thoughts of DiMarco and Ross and Weaver and the way DiMarco had died in a high-powered professional killing. Now it was my turn. Power and money . . . I wondered if there were anything Weaver couldn't buy.

What I needed at that moment was some help. "Your wife might walk in," I said, hoping that she would.

"Not likely. Her activities will keep her out all day. I knew that when I suggested coming here."

"If I turn up dead, you'll have a great deal of talking to do."

"You're a man with many enemies. I think I can cover up quite satisfactorily since I can steer the investigation."

There was no doubt of that. My trouble was my own fault. Instead of going to Solkowsky, I'd gone directly to Ross, trying to do it all myself, trying to be a hero. Now I had no one to back me up. The people who devised departmental procedures were no fools, and I had been around long enough to know there was a reason for everything—particularly for not working alone. I was on my own and I had to do something before Weaver's men got there.

Mrs. Ross had decorated the house in excellent taste, her preference running to highly polished floors with small braided rugs protecting the high traffic areas. Ross was standing on one of those rugs now.

Without thinking, without wanting to think, I thrust out a hand, grabbed a handful of rug and jerked hard.

Ross didn't go down—that sort of thing happens only in films—but he did totter off balance long enough for the gun to waver. I threw myself at his legs and he went over, the gun going off above me. Aching head and all, I handled him easily from that point, almost breaking his fingers as I tore the gun away from him and struggled to my feet.

I leaned against the wall weakly, my head pounding, staring down at him. He wasn't looking at me. The quick struggle had taken us out into the hall and his eyes were fixed on the front door behind me.

The chill that went down my spine didn't come entirely from the cold draft.

A voice said, "Drop it, Cochrane."

I let the gun slip to the floor.

"Into the room," the voice said. I stepped into the study.

"You, too," the voice said to Ross.

Ross's lips narrowed in surprise but he rose to his feet and followed me without saying a word.

I turned and studied the two men who came into the room. They were typical Weaver men, molded in crime's new image. Well dressed, carrying attaché cases, they looked more like aggressive young businessmen than hoods until you examined the faces closely and realized that few young businessmen came equipped with that flat, dead look.

"Take him out and get it done," Ross said.

One of the men was wearing a heavy, fur collared tan coat; the other a well-fitted dark blue cashmere. The one in the fur collar held my gun, the other a silenced pistol.

The one in the cashmere coat said, "Shut up," to Ross.

"Don't talk like that to me," snapped Ross. "Weaver wouldn't like it."

The man grinned coldly. "Weaver doesn't give a damn. You're through. He said to tell you that you've become more trouble than you're worth." He jerked a thumb at me. "Cochrane isn't the only one who gets it. So do you. Weaver figures this is too good an opportunity to miss. We make it look like you and Cochrane had a little disagreement and shot each other. It will be quite a puzzle for the crime boys to work on. Should keep them busy all winter."

Ross stood stunned. I measured the man in the fur collar, wondering how far I could get before he gunned me down, thinking that I wasn't going to stand there and take it.

Ross forced the issue. It had taken a great deal of raw guts to get to where he was, and he had counted on that courage to take him even further, to the governor's chair and perhaps to the U.S. Senate. No one was going to take that away without a fight.

He stepped forward, jaw thrust out, fist doubled, swinging at the man in the cashmere coat.

Cashmere Coat had no choice. He shot him before Ross's fist was halfway around, the sound of soft popping, Ross's coat jumping a little as the slug hit.

It distracted the other man long enough for me to make my move. I was a little more scientific than Ross. With one hand I grabbed the gun, chopping down on his forearm with the other.

The gun came loose in my hand just as Cashmere Coat turned and fired at me. The slug tore through my left arm but I had my gun pointed by then, its weight and balance welcome and familiar. I squeezed the trigger.

The cashmere fabric jumped a little just as Ross's had. He went down.

Before I could recover, Fur Collar fled down the hall and out into the street, not taking time to close the door.

I sank into a chair as the bitter cold filled the room, driving out the pungent smell of cordite. Ross and the man in the cashmere coat had fallen close to each other like long-lost brothers embracing in death.

I looked at Ross. He had died well. Somehow the fact that he had been corrupted by Weaver no longer seemed important. If he hadn't moved toward that gun, I would probably be dead and I owed him something for that, even if he hadn't really done it for me. One thing I could do was preserve the thing he had valued above anything else. His reputation. There was no point in making him look bad, not now.

I would say nothing about the money in the safe deposit box. If I knew Mrs. Ross, she would be far from willing to testify as to its source. Let her have it. She could snuggle up to it these cold winter nights in place of her husband.

I would turn the transmitter over to Solkowsky, telling him Ross himself had discovered it in his car. The unimaginative Solkowsky would accept the implication of a frame without too many questions. It was something he could easily understand.

The transmitter would lead us nowhere, except to go down in the books as a bizarre new way to commit murder and make life a little more difficult for every investigating officer in the country.

For the time being, Weaver would get away with DiMarco's murder and with that of Brazil and of Ross. It was simply too difficult to connect him with any of them.

Right now I needed a story to cover Ross's death. I put my head down between my knees and tried to think above the pain now flooding from my bleeding arm.

ASSASSIN KILLS D.A.
AND WOUNDS AIDE

The words came from nowhere and sounded good. I would say that the gunman had burst into Ross's home while he and I were having a conference and shot us both before I killed him. There would be a great many questions, but I would hold them off until I could think more clearly.

I sighed, heaved myself to my feet, and wove my way to the phone.

Intrigue. Conspiracy. Corruption. That was the city and Ross had been part of it and it had killed him.

Beckett had said there were an awful lot of ways to kill a man. There were also a great many roads a man could take toward death.

Someone as smart as Ross should have thought of that before he made his deal with Weaver.

The Trouble Was

by Ron Goulart

It happened on an awful day—cold, with snow and wind. The trouble was, they'd been arguing again, mostly about this Jerry and a little about money. He'd slapped her a couple of times. She threw the phone at him and the part you talk into cracked across the bridge of his nose. This Jerry had *four* phones in his big house up on Mountain Road, in colors that matched the decor, and he didn't have to worry about a few long-distance calls.

After she threw the phone, she heaved one of the bricks out of their makeshift bookcase. Seeing all his paperbacks and old college outlines go tumbling helter-skelter onto their secondhand rug made him somehow angrier than usual. He grabbed up the gray construction brick, which had crashed into the wicker magazine basket after missing him, and threw it straight back at her—something he didn't usually do.

The heavy gray brick knocked her in the head and she fell back, pushed by the force of the thrown brick, and smashed right on through the window. Wind and snow forged into their recreation room as she collapsed out on the snow-covered patio.

One of the troubles with living in the East was snow. He hated snow and the muddy slush that filled their hill-facing patio, so he didn't go out to see how she was. He figured she'd sulk out there for a while and then go off and spend the evening with this Jerry. The trouble was, he hadn't been able to stop that, not in all the past five months. She liked to tell him about it, this Jerry and his four bedroom house up on Mountain Road, his income in six figures, his connections with people in local government and maybe even with some syndicate people. No, that wasn't maybe—that was for sure. She'd said just tonight that this Jerry was worried about being subpoenaed to testify at an upcoming hearing on organized crime.

He left her alone out there. In half an hour it was too cold in the rec room, even with the thermostat set at eighty and the portable heater on. He went to the broken window and called out to his wife. One of the few good things about their house was its distance from any neighbors. The main trouble with their old apartment in Brooklyn Heights had been that somebody always pounded on the floor or ceiling when they had one of their quarrels. Out here in this part of Connecticut there was nobody near enough to hear or care. "Come on in and help me rig up some way to patch this window," he shouted. "The whole house is freezing and there's all kinds of snow on the rug here."

He squinted out and saw her still sprawled in the drift, whiter than the snow and freckled all over with it. The overhead lighting that splashed out on her made her look like a flash photo. Then he realized she was dead.

He stayed at the broken window, vaguely bothered by the cold wind, watching her. He tried to make himself feel sorry or guilty, or even pitying. Instead, he felt relieved. She'd often said that was the trouble with him. No sympathy, no empathy. This Jerry was not like him. Maybe he did deal with the syndicate and with hoods, but he was a sympathetic person. Handsome, too, and not overweight. One of his own troubles was his weight, and the fact he wasn't handsome enough. She reminded him of it many times, telling him he was, according to some chart she'd seen in a women's magazine, twenty-six pounds too heavy and not handsome. Probably that was why he let her go off and spend time with this Jerry, and then come back late at night, or even not until the next morning, and tell him all about it. One of his troubles was he couldn't stop her from going and he couldn't even stop her from rubbing it in.

He watched the snow falling on her body and he decided he didn't want to go to prison over this. He didn't actually want to get into any trouble. He smiled. Another thing wrong with him, she'd said, was smiling at the wrong times. He kept smiling, thinking of a way to get out of this. He knew that often completely unpremeditated crimes were the easiest to cover up. Extemporizing on the spot, thieves and murderers had been able to fake something, some clever coverup, which allowed them to go completely free.

Turning, not wanting to catch cold, he went into their kitchen and reached under the sink. He tugged out a pair of black rubber gloves from among boxes of detergent and put them on. Then he knelt and pulled out two big, folded, plastic garbage bags. The main trouble was getting rid of the body, but he'd figured that out in an instant while walking from the chilly rec room into the kitchen. He'd use this Jerry.

With the plastic garbage bags under his arm, he went into their bedroom and took his .32 revolver from the secret drawer in the night table. The trouble was, he wasn't sure if real hoods would use a gun of this caliber. Didn't they go in more for .38s and .45s? No matter. He had to use what was at hand. The gun was European, smuggled in when he came back from the service in 1959. There was no way to trace it.

Out on the patio he unfurled the plastic bags and put them over her body. There shouldn't be any snow on her if he was going to bring off what he had in mind. He picked up the brick and looked at it carefully. It would have to be cleaned later tonight. Out in the garage he had a sheet of glass and from that he could cut a new pane to replace the one she'd fallen through. Yes, and he'd have to pick up all the fragments of glass, inside and out here in the snow, and brush away the indentations made by her body. No use worrying about these details yet. The only trouble was, he'd probably be up all night straightening things out. Whenever he was up all night, as he was when they had a particularly bad quarrel, he was irritable at work the next day.

He got her body into the big plastic sacks, one over her feet and legs, and one over her head and torso. He got some plastic tape and sealed the bags where they joined at her waist. He carried her into the garage and put her into the trunk of their car, first spreading out newspapers. Then he went back into the house and got one of her winter coats and her purse, the one she would have taken with her tonight to go and see this Jerry. He left the lights on in the house and turned on the television set. He opened the garage, took off the gloves, and stuffed them into a pocket of the warm mackinaw he'd put on. His prints should be on the steering wheel of his own car and he didn't want to smear any of hers. He backed the car out of the garage and drove on up their road. He gunned the motor too much on the curves, the way she always did. The few neighbors he passed would remember hearing that. The trouble was, how was he going to get this Jerry to let him in?

By the time he reached Mountain Road he'd figured a way. He parked beyond this Jerry's long, low, lighted house, on a narrow dirt road under some dark dead trees—the same place she'd park, probably, out of sight but not too far from the house. The house was wood and glass, a sprawling, California sort of place, really. There was only one other house on this stretch of the road and it was dark.

He took the plastic bags off her, folded them up, and shoved them under his coat. He put his rubber gloves back on, hung her coat and purse over one arm, then lifted her body out and carried it along the snow-banked mountain roadway to this Jerry's house. He knew he'd probably leave footprints in the snow and that they might not be covered by morning, so he was wearing an old pair of rubber boots left behind by the previous tenant of their house. The only trouble with them was, they were three sizes too big. They gave a lopsided wobble to his walk as he carried his dead wife straight up to this Jerry's front door. The snow was falling hard, swirling hundreds of prickly flakes around him.

He marched up the red stone stairs and elbowed the buzzer. Chimes sounded deep inside and then the door opened a slit, held with a bright brass chain. This was the first time he had seen this Jerry up close. A tall man, broad in the shoulders, tan. Not really that handsome though, eyes a little too small and nose a little too big.

"What in the hell is this?" asked Jerry.

"Are you alone?" He knew he must be if he were expecting her. Still, it paid to be cautious.

"Yes. I just got home." Jerry opened the door wider. "What's wrong with her?"

"There's been an accident. A serious accident, and she's badly hurt," he told this Jerry. "I'm her husband."

"I know."

"Listen, we've got to call an ambulance right away. The accident happened right up the road."

Jerry hesitated. "Well, bring her in. I don't want a big frumus going on. I can call a doctor I know. What kind of accident, and why are you with her?"

Inside, in the beam-ceilinged living room, he kicked the door shut behind him. Then he dropped her on the thick white rug in front of him.

This Jerry had been walking thoughtfully, toward a tan phone. He turned now and started to ask an angry question.

He shot him three times with the revolver, carefully, not shaking, doing it quite calmly. The trouble with something like this was you could very easily get nervous and rattled. Two of the shots hit this Jerry in his chest and one got him in the shoulder. The man fell back and down sideways, blood growing all over the front of his blue chambray shirt. He hit the rug in an odd, soft way and his legs kicked out and one of his fleecelined brown slippers flipped off. It skidded along the pale rug, leaving a faint line of red. Then this Jerry was dead.

He now dragged his wife closer to the man and then carefully shot her twice, to cover up what the brick had done. He stepped away from the two of them and looked around the big room. This had to look like a hood killing, quick and efficient, so there was no need to make it look as though there was much of a struggle. Still, if she died first, this Jerry might have had time to put up a little fight.

He walked over to a teakwood table and knocked over a big buff-colored ceramic lamp. Then, after that had crashed and the three-way bulb had popped, he decided to shove the low sofa out of line. For good measure he tore one tan drape partly down—not one that anybody would notice from the road.

This Jerry wouldn't have let a killer in the front door. No, that wasn't the way a gangland killing went. He stomped through the expensive house and into the large white kitchen. Copper cookware hung from racks above the built-in stove and there was a butcher's block with a cleaver and an electric knife atop it. She'd told him about these things. The trouble with this job he had now, well, *one* of the troubles, was the salary. Working right in Connecticut had its advantages but you couldn't draw the kind of salary you could in New York City. He'd explained that to her often enough.

He went out the kitchen door and into a yard thick with snow. He made sure there was no car passing on the road, nothing around. He crept up to a kitchen window, reached up and smashed it in with a gloved fist. Maybe real hoods wouldn't be that flamboyant, but then again they might. Anyway, this Jerry had said he'd only just come home, so a real hood could have broken in as noisily as he wanted after making certain no one was home. Sure, and then waited quietly.

As soon as this Jerry walked in, the real hood would have done it. But noticing the woman he would have decided to kill her too. Her first and then this Jerry. That was certainly plausible. A real hood might well do it that way, to be nasty maybe—to let this Jerry see her die.

To make things completely realistic, he actually climbed through the kitchen window, crunching a boot right into the sink, and smashing a brandy glass. He walked into the livingroom and checked it once more. He was still carrying the revolver in his hand. What would a real hood do? Leave the gun or take it? Take it, probably. The trouble was, he had to make this look completely like a real hood killing. From what she'd told him about this Jerry, the man was really involved with the rackets. If this Jerry was going to be questioned by a commission on organized crime, the police would know about it. When the police found the two of them dead here they'd conclude it was a gang killing. This Jerry was killed to keep him quiet and the woman because she had the bad luck to be with him. It all sounded plausible.

What he had to do now was get back home and clean up everything there. When the police discovered the bodies and contacted him, there should be no trace of any quarrel. They'd probably get in touch with him while he was at work and the only trouble there was to look surprised in front of everybody. That shouldn't be too hard. He'd look shocked, stunned, maybe cry a little. No, don't cry. Men don't like to see another man cry. Show shock, pain, and, yes, admit that he knew his wife had been seeing another man. Other people must know about her, too; friends of this Jerry's. They'd back up that part.

He took one final look around and walked to the front door. Then he stopped, snapped his fingers. The car. He'd have to leave their car here. He'd made it look as though she were driving, so the car would have to stay. That would work out, because she really had spent nights here before, so the police wouldn't expect him to report the fact that she hadn't come home. The little Penn Central train station was only over the hill from their house. He walked there every morning.

The trouble was, if he walked all the way home now it would take a lot of time. He needed time to clean up there. Maybe he could take Jerry's car. Would a real hood do that? Not likely. No, but suppose this Jerry had driven over to somewhere near their house and met his wife there. That was logical. Parked his car someplace, possibly down in the train station lot, and then rendezvoused with her. He'd come over to Mountain Road in her car. Yes, that was the sort of thing a couple of people meeting on the sly might well do.

He walked back to the dead man's body, bent and poked at his pockets with the barrel of the revolver. No keys jingled. He frowned, then spotted a ring of keys on the floor against the wall. They must have been on the teakwood table and fallen from there. He scooped them up in his gloved hands. Yes, these were the car keys. This Jerry had two cars, it looked like, one domestic and one foreign sports car. He smiled to himself.

He went cautiously out of the big house and walked around to the garage. The snow was still falling, straight down now through the cold darkness. He listened, heard nothing unusual, and opened the garage. There was a blue station wagon, still warm, in the shadowy garage, and a new sports car, low and gray. He looked at both cars and jingled the key ring on his gloved palm.

Might as well travel first class and take the sports car. He smiled again and got in. He put the key in the ignition and turned it.

The trouble was that this was the car the real hoods had wired with dynamite that afternoon.

The Grapevine Harvest
by Ed Dumonte

The guard called, "Stand away from the doors!" and threw the switch that electrically opened the half dozen doors of the cell block. The boy standing outside the cell at the end of the block stepped inside the cage and the door slid into place behind him. Inside the cell, the boy watched the barred door roll across the opening he had come through and heard a note of finality in the snap of the electric lock.

The cell, nine feet wide by twelve feet deep, contained four bunks. The boy threw the roll of bedclothes he carried up to the top bunk on the right side, the only unoccupied one. Stepping on the foot of the bunk, he swung himself up and straightened out the bedding as best he could.

The three men in the cell had pointedly ignored the boy's entrance and continued their conversation. The man on the top bunk on the left side of the room was telling a story that seemed to involve considerable quantities of girls and booze, an interruption by a police patrol car, and a good deal of violence. A skinny, sandy-haired man in the lower bunk had stories that matched or excelled each of the other's exploits, while a man wearing glasses in the lower right bunk read a paperback novel and looked up only for an occasional halfhearted jibe at the other two.

After a few minutes the lights in the cells went out, leaving only the inspection lights in the corridor burning, and the conversation continued in semi-darkness. Gradually the silences between the stories became longer than the stories, and soon the men were asleep. If anyone heard a slight sniffling sound from the upper right bunk, it wasn't mentioned.

In the morning, Don was awakened by a rough hand on his shoulder.

"Hey there, boy, it's chow time," Charlie said. Don opened his eyes slowly and stared into the man's broad, dark face. "It ain't much, but it's all we got to offer."

"Hey, Charlie," the skinny man said, "I'll trade you my bowl of cereal for whatever fruit we get this morning. Sight unseen."

"Not me you won't, Red," Charlie said as the two left the cell. "I wouldn't trade you rocks for diamonds without knowing what your angle was. You have a dishonest face."

When Don sat up on his bunk, the cell was empty. He stared blindly at the wall of bars that formed one side of the cell, and a wave of nameless terror swept over him. Fighting back a sensation of choking or suffocating, Don jumped down from the bunk and hurried out into the corridor.

The corridor, too, had a wall of bars. On the other side—the outside—a group of a half dozen trusties filled metal trays with food and passed them through a narrow slot in the bars of the room that served the prisoners as a dayroom.

Don fell into the chow line and accepted one of the trays. Some of the men stayed in the dayroom to eat at the single, long table that ran almost the entire length of the room. Others drifted away to their cells.

Don went back to his cell and sat on the edge of one of the lower bunks. He put the tray on his lap and stared at the bowl of cereal, the two pieces of cold toast, the orange, and the tin cup of coffee as though he didn't know what they were for.

After a moment the man with glasses came in with a tray and sat down to eat. Between bites he looked up from his food to study Don's face.

"The food's lousy, as usual," he said at last, "but you might as well eat it, kid. It's the only way to get rid of the stuff."

Don looked blankly at the other man, his mind still dazed by the things that had happened to him.

"Name's Wilson," the man muttered, turning away from the pain and bewilderment in the boy's face. "First day's always the worst. Get used to it after a while."

"Seems like our roommate ain't much of a talkin' man," Charlie said, leaning against the door frame of the cell. Red stood behind the big man, peering at the boy through the bars. "But he don't need to be. Grapevine's got the word on him."

"His name's Markham," Red said. "Don Markham, nineteen. Waiting trial for grand theft. Seems like he copped a big rock from a jewelry store where he worked."

"First fall, too," Charlie went on. "Nothing on his record at all. He never even stole an apple from a peddler's cart. That's what comes of trying to get a home run off the first ball that's pitched you."

"I didn't do it," Don said quietly. When no one paid any attention to him, he raised his voice. "I said, I didn't do it! I never stole a thing from ole man Clemson. And he knows it."

"Sure you didn't, kid," Red said, his voice reeking with sympathy. "Just like Charlie here didn't stomp up those two cops, and Wilson didn't pigeon-drop that old lady out of her bankroll. And I certainly never forged those lousy five checks."

"You're only charged with forging three checks," Charlie pointed out.

"Well, I didn't forge five of them!"

"But I didn't," Don said. "I didn't even know the store had been robbed until the police arrested me. I'm innocent."

"So are we all, so are we all," Wilson murmured.

"I'm not," Charlie told them. He added, with a touch of pride, "I'm a victim of my environment."

"What's the story?" Wilson asked. "Stickup?"

"Not on your life," Red told him. "A real pro-type job. A fake break-in, a torch job on the safe, and one helluva good 'Who, me?' act."

"According to the police report," Charlie continued, "a squad car was sent to the jewelry store of Rudolph Clemson at 7:04 A.M. yesterday. The rear door had been jimmied open and the safe cracked. All that was missing was an unset five carat diamond valued at twenty-five thousand dollars."

"Twenty-five grand for a five carat rock?" Wilson seemed incredulous.

"It's not a real big stone," Don put in, "but it's perfect. I've examined it with a loupe, a beautiful emerald-cut, blue-white diamond without a flaw."

"A couple of detectives arrived after the cops radioed in the story," Red picked up the narrative. "When the kid came to work they put the arm on him. He was indicted yesterday afternoon, his trial comes up next month."

"So what tripped him up?"

Charlie said, "First, the detectives found that the door wasn't really forced. Somebody put a few jimmy marks on the outside, then opened the door with a key or picked the lock, and there was something funny about the safe. The combination had been worked on the outside door, but an inside compartment had the lock burned out. According to the old man, the kid knew the combination but didn't have a key for the inside door, where the more valuable stuff was kept. Then, too, he didn't have an alibi. Gave 'em the 'home-in-bed' routine."

Wilson was silent a moment, looking Don over. Something like amusement touched the corners of his mouth, then became a grimace.

"Looks like they got you pretty well fitted for that suit you'll be wearing for the next ten to twenty years," he said, "but I must admit it was a pretty good try for a beginner. You start big."

"I tell you I didn't take it," Don pleaded. "I wouldn't even know what to do with a twenty-five thousand dollar jewel."

"I bet I could think of a couple of interesting things," Red said wistfully.

Charlie was more helpful. "Why didn't you take it to the guy you sold hubcaps to as a kid? He might know somebody who could handle something that big."

"Hubcaps?" Don asked in bewilderment.

Charlie threw up his hands in despair.

"You know, the kid has a point," Wilson said thoughtfully. "After all, a diamond is no more use to you than a piece of glass unless you know how to peddle it. You say nothing else was taken, Charlie?"

"Only the big rock."

"Red, if you were in that safe what would you take?"

"Everything I could carry."

"Yeah, so would I. Once you've gone to the trouble of getting the box open, why not take all you can get away with? Did the fuzz find the rock?"

"Not a smell," Charlie said. "The kid didn't tip a thing; played clam all day yesterday. This Clemson bird even said he wouldn't press charges if the stone is returned."

"He just said that to impress Carrie," Don said. "He doesn't want her to know we had that fight last week."

"Who is Carrie?" Wilson asked.

"Carrie's his daughter. Last week I told him I wanted to marry her and she wanted to marry me. He said he wasn't going to let his daughter marry any wet-nosed, uneducated, talentless punk. But I'm not talentless; I'm a good jewelry designer, and I'll get better. I could support Carrie on what I make working at designing, and go to school nights. But Mr. Clemson wouldn't listen to me and pretty soon we were hollering at each other."

"So the way it looks," Wilson said, "the kid and the old man fight over the girl. In a few days, to get even, the kid breaks into the store to steal something—not a lot of little stuff he could get rid of at any hock shop, but a pretty good-sized stone that even a reputable fence might balk at handling.

"Because he's ignorant, he pulls the job so everything points right to him. He doesn't even bother to arrange an alibi for himself. Then he hides the diamond so well that even the cops can't find it, and he doesn't crack under a full day of interrogation. When the old man offers to let him go if he'll return the stone, the kid refuses and decides to take what will almost certainly be a long prison term.

"Does anybody else notice a strong aroma of fish?"

"Long dead and not buried deep," Charlie agreed.

"Oh, I don't know." Red wasn't convinced. "Maybe that baby face conceals a wealth of criminal cunning."

Three heads turned to scrutinize Don carefully. Three heads turned away, shaking slowly in disbelief. That baby face didn't conceal a wealth of anything.

"You know what that means, don't you?" Wilson asked, as wheels in his head meshed into gear and began spinning rapidly.

"It means the kid was framed," Charlie said.

"Yeah, that too, but I had something more important in mind."

"Like what?"

"Like the fact that there is a twenty-five thousand dollar diamond floating around unaccounted for. Think about it."

All through lunch they thought about the twenty-five thousand dollar diamond. When the metal trays were returned to the dayroom and the men came back to their bunks for afternoon naps, they dreamed about the twenty-five thousand dollar diamond. It was a pleasant thought and it inspired sweet dreams.

After the evening meal had been served and the men had returned to the cell, they again began to talk about the twenty-five thousand dollar diamond.

"I think," Wilson said, "we're all agreed that the kid was framed." He waited for affirmative nods from the others before continuing. "And it doesn't have the mark of a professional job." More agreement. "Our logical conclusion, therefore, is that the old man did it himself to get the kid out of his hair."

"But that's silly," Don protested. "Why would he want to steal something so valuable from himself?"

"Forget it, son," Charlie said. "We'll explain it all to you later."

"All of which seems to indicate," Wilson went on, "that this Clemson bird has a good healthy instinct for larceny. That's good. That's the kind of man I like to work with, and I have an idea we maybe able to transact a little business with Mr. Clemson."

"How can we do anything from in here?" Don asked.

"Well, there are ways, and there are ways," Wilson told him. "I have a few friends on the outside and some of them owe me favors."

"I have a few friends," Red said, "that I can buy favors from."

"I have a few friends," Charlie said, "who'll do me favors . . . or else."

"And I have a scheme," Wilson concluded, "that is going to lose us all one friend."

Wilson outlined the scheme to the others, and the men spent the rest of the night making and coordinating their plans.

In the morning, after breakfast, there was a note concealed beneath Charlie's hand when he passed his tray through the bars to the trusty. The trusty took the note down to the ground floor kitchen where the trays were washed and slipped it to a cook's helper, also a trusty, who got it out of the building by pushing it through the heavy mesh covering a storeroom window.

Red asked for and received permission to make a phone call to his sister to have her bring some things he needed.

Wilson made arrangements to meet with his lawyer.

Don spent the day drawing. First, he sketched the Clemson diamond, then he designed a pendant incorporating two five carat diamonds. Red, too, was busy with pen and paper that day. The first document he created was an ownership history of the Clemson diamond. The second, with the help of notes and other handwriting samples found in Don's wallet, was a bill of sale in the amount of twenty-five thousand dollars, signed by "Rudolph Clemson."

When the lawyer arrived later that day, Wilson was taken from the cell and led to a conference room. Under the desultory eye of a guard, Wilson and his lawyer, a tall, heavyset man with thinning hair and clear, grey eyes, were able to discuss Wilson's forthcoming trial. To make himself clear, Wilson made notes of significant points on the back of several sheets of paper he had. The lawyer glanced at the notes, placed the papers carefully in his briefcase and soon thereafter left the prison.

Back in the cell, Wilson was exultant. "The job is under way, boys. The seed is sown and soon the harvest shall be reaped."

"I don't see how anything can come of all this," Don said. "Old man Clemson will never admit he took the diamond, and unless he does, I'll never get out of here."

"Then let me try to explain it to you," Wilson said patiently. "We're pretty sure Clemson stole the diamond in order to collect the insurance and did it in such a way as to make you appear guilty. We want to get our hands on that stone—to steal it, you understand?—but we don't know where Clemson may have put it. To find out, we have given a man a description and your sketch of the diamond so he can get a synthetic stone that closely resembles it. Then . . . "

The tall, heavyset man with thinning hair and clear, grey eyes gave Mr. Clemson his card. ALAN ROLAND, INVESTMENT CONSULTANT.

"I do hope you'll be able to help me, Mr. Clemson. I've been to practically every jeweler in town without success."

"I'm sure I'll be able to help you, Mr. Roland," Clemson said, rubbing his fat hands together and beaming confidently. "My shop may not be large, but it has a wide variety of quality merchandise."

"Yes, but my problem is somewhat unusual, I'm afraid. You see, I must duplicate a particular diamond—a rather large diamond."

Roland removed a small velvet packet from his coat and slowly unfolded the cloth. In his hand he held what appeared to be a five carat, emerald-cut diamond. He held it out for display briefly, then folded the cloth and replaced it in his pocket.

The smile left Clemson's face at the sight of the stone, and his eyes bugged in astonishment.

"Why, what's the matter, Mr. Clemson? Are you ill?"

"No . . . no," Clemson stammered. "It's just that . . . For a moment I thought I recognized the stone."

"No, Mr. Clemson, you must be mistaken. A man of your reputation would have no knowledge of this particular stone. It was, umm . . . imported into this country only last week."

"You mean it was . . . "

"I didn't say that," Roland said quickly. "It was merely that when I was offered the stone I recognized it immediately as something I've wanted a long time, and asked no questions. Well, what do you say, Mr. Clemson? Can you find me a mate for this little beauty?"

"No, I cannot," Clemson said in a voice meant to end the interview. "As you say, it is a difficult jewel to match. I don't know where such a diamond might be found."

"I was afraid not," Roland sighed, his face downfallen. "I need that particular stone very badly. You see, it is to be a part of . . . Here, let me show you." Roland took a sketch from an inside pocket and spread it on the desk between them. "The pendant is a part of a jewel collection that was in my mother's family for generations. The collection is still complete, except for this one piece which was stolen long ago and presumably broken up by the thieves for easier resale. I have been hoping to reconstruct the pendant and give it to my mother for her birthday this year. When I found the first stone, I thought I had a chance, but now I see I'm no closer than I ever was."

Roland looked across the desk at the other man, his face a mask of despair, his voice filled with tears. "I tell you, Clemson, I'm a desperate man. I'd pay forty thousand dollars to have such a stone. But it must be soon."

"Forty—" Clemson's ruddy face paled slightly, his fingers gripped the edge of the desk. "Forty thousand. Wait, don't leave, Mr. Roland! Ordinarily I would not do such a thing, but for a man in your desperate circumstances, perhaps—just perhaps—I may know of such a diamond."

"I would be eternally grateful to you."

"This must be done in the strictest confidence, you understand?"

"Confidence is precisely what I had in mind, Mr. Clemson."

"The stone is, as you say, of uncertain origin. It must be a cash transaction, and I can guarantee you nothing except that the stone is genuine."

"Yes, of course, I understand."

"It might be best to conduct our business someplace other than my store. My home, perhaps. Would that suit you?"

"Your home? Certainly," Roland said, "but it must be quickly. Would tomorrow morning be too soon?"

"I think it can be arranged. Tomorrow morning, then, at my home."

"Once we have an idea of where the diamond will be, it's easy," Wilson said. "With the layouts you've given us of Clemson's store and home, it'll be a simple matter for Charlie's men."

In the dark of night, three men stealthily approached the back door of the house. One of the men crouched over the door lock with a flexible wire pick and a penlight. Soon, all three disappeared into the house.

They walked quickly through the house to the study, entered it and closed the door behind them. They pulled a picture aside to reveal a recessed safe. The man who had opened the door started to work again.

When the safe was open, they removed a small, black leather box and opened it to reveal an emerald-cut diamond cushioned in a nest of purple velvet. In the pale glow of the penlight, the stone sparkled brilliantly. They removed the stone and replaced it with another that was almost identical, then put the box back in the safe, and left the house.

"With the synthetic diamond in place of the real one," Wilson said, "and nothing to indicate he's been robbed, Clemson will never know what happened. With the bill of sale Red made out, our man will be able to sell that stone for almost full market value. And when the insurance investigators turn up the diamond and the bill of sale—and you may be sure they will—they'll know Clemson was pulling a fast one and trying to frame you, and they'll set you free. Now, do you understand?"

"Yeah, I guess so," Don said glumly. "But it all sounds so—criminal."

Wilson and Red and Charlie looked at each other in amazement. It had never been presented to them in quite that way before.

A couple of days later, a trusty who worked in the garage servicing the city's squad cars removed a rear hubcap from one of the cars. From inside the hubcap he took a small, oilskin wrapped package that had been taped there. When he was returned to his cell for lunch he gave the package to one of the sweepers.

Somewhere in the course of the sweeper's regular rounds, the package slipped from his pocket and an accidental bump of the broom pushed it through the bars from the corridor to the cell block.

Charlie, who happened to be sitting with his back against the bars, laid his hand over the package and casually got up to walk to the back of the cell. The men gloated silently as Wilson riffled through a stack of bills.

That evening the grapevine brought the news that Don was going to be released. He rolled up his bedding and placed it on the floor in front of the door. Wilson caught his shoulder and turned him around to talk to him.

"Hey, kid, I've got something to tell you," he began. "I was supposed to . . . That is, the boys told me to say . . . Well, it's a wedding present for Carrie."

He thrust a small roll of bills into the boy's hand and walked back to his bunk.

The guard called, "Stand away from the doors!" and threw the switch that electrically opened the half dozen doors of the cell block.

Don stepped outside the cage, and the door slid into place behind him.

The guard led Don to the end of the corridor and unlocked the solid steel door leading out of the cell block. Don looked back, but the men in the cell at the end of the block were paying no more attention to his departure than they had to his arrival. He walked out of the cell block, and the huge door clanged shut behind him, and was locked.

Final Acquittal

by Edward Wellen

Sweat shone like gilt on Byrne's brow. Without moving his head he kenw the sudden stir and hush in the courtroom meant the jury was returning from its long deliberation. He tried to maintain his air of impassiveness, but as the jurors filed in he was stiff with willing them to look at him. Somwhere he had heard that when a returning jury avoided looking at the defendant it was because the jury had made up its collective mind to convict.

Now, however, when members of the jury did in fact eye Byrne it gave him no comfort. He still could not tell. He was unable to read the eyes behind the glittering glasses on the grave face of the butcher who was the foreman. The fixed faint smile on the face of the woman smoothing her skirt beside the foreman might be a smile she meant to be reassuring, then again it might be a smile of gloating.

Byrne looked no further. In any case, the judge's gavel was drowning out his heartbeat. Hogan, his defense attorney, nudged him to stand and face the jury.

The judge leaned forward slowly. "Ladies and gentlemen of the jury, have you reached a verdict?"

The foreman balanced himself by pressing his thumb on the railing. "We have, your Honor."

"What is your verdict?"

The foreman hammily let a pause weight the air. "We find the defendant not guilty."

Newsmen charged out. Byrne's knees gave, but he held himself up. The prosecuting attorney, voice trembling with anger, demanded a poll. The judge gaveled down a babble, permitted the polling, discharged Byrne, rather coldly thanked the jurors and discharged them—but that was all a blur to Byrne.

He sat down heavily. For a moment he had a job focusing, then he turned to his lawyer. He took Hogan's hand in both of his, thanking him silently. Hogan freed himself and began stuffing papers into his battered briefcase.

The courtroom was emptying except for a few friends making their way toward Byrne. His late wife's aunts had stopped by the door.

Meed was with them, looking embarrassed because he was a friend of Byrne's and yet a second cousin, or something of the kind, and business associate, of the women.

"Justice!" the tall thin one said, looking right at Byrne.

"A mockery!" the other said.

They wheeled and stalked out. Meed awkwardly followed them, throwing back a don't-get-me-wrong look of appeal at Byrne.

Byrne smiled wryly. The smile faded as he caught Lieutenant Harris of Homicide watching him. Lieutenant Harris, the man who had arrested him and testified against him, stood leaning against a pillar, a twisted smile on his face. Then people were between them, blocking Harris from Byrne's view, friends coming with uncertain eagerness through the gate from the spectator's section.

Byrne stood up. His legs were still weak but he knew he was able to proceed under his own motive power. A surge of need told him to get far from this place and its sickening associations. Yet now that he could leave, could step outside and breathe the sooty air of freedom, he hesitated.

His friends were crowding around uncomfortably, trying to keep out of their eyes that they were wondering how to word their congratulations.

"I knew you had to get off."

"Of course. Absurd to think you could ever have . . ."

"We all know you loved Madelon too much to . . ."

Byrne found his voice. "You stood by me, that's what counts. I can't thank you enough." His face twisted, but in a smile. "Don't worry, I'm not going to get sloppy. Except maybe sloppy drunk."

They laughed, but their laughter had a forced, hollow sound in the courtroom, where so many voices had wrung the most out of rhetoric throughout the trial.

He saw Meed returning. He looked down at Hogan pounding the briefcase on the table to settle the papers and make room for more to be placed crosswise on top. Then Meed was at his elbow.

Keeping his eyes on Byrne, almost defensively, Meed nodded toward the outside, where he had gone with the aunts. "I was just seeing them to a taxi. I had to come back to tell you I never for a moment believed you murdered Madelon."

"Thanks." Byrne glanced around at his friends hovering in an uneasy arc. Abruptly he took a step toward the door. "How about all of you coming up to our—to my apartment for a few drinks. Say in an hour; give me a chance to get ready."

All but Hogan accepted, nodding almost too eagerly.

Byrne eyed Hogan. "How about it?"

Hogan snapped his briefcase shut. "I don't make a practice of socializing with my clients." Then he seemed to come to a decision. "But I'll be there." He smiled a rare smile that transformed his gray face. He said for Byrne's ears alone, "Frankly, Byrne, you puzzle me." His smile widened. "I can afford to say that now."

A court attendant, eyeing Byrne with curiosity, showed him out through a side entrance. The door closed. No one passing paid Byrne any mind. He breathed deep—it was fine to be alone, unwatched, free. Then farther along the block he saw a weary-looking Lieutenant Harris getting into a police car. Byrne quickened his step, came alongside just as the door slammed.

"Hello, Lieutenant."

Harris eyed him bleakly.

Byrne received heartier greetings when his friends showed up. They were almost too hearty. To do them justice, they were trying hard to be cheerful and nonchalant, to accept him unquestioningly, to pretend the death and the trial had never been.

Hogan sat quietly to one side, his eyes never leaving Byrne's face, trying to strike through the mask of flesh. Meed, too, sat apart, eyes for the most part on the drink in his hands, like a man watching a gauge. The others milled around.

Their keynote was gaiety, but there were warning looks from one to another, irrelevant comments on innocuous topics, sudden silences and sudden spates of talk, and much reaching for glasses. They watched Byrne out of eyecorners, plainly thinking, *the man's been through a great nervous ordeal; he won't want to talk about it, at least not right now.*

Yet he did talk about it. He had been upending his glass, seemingly without stop, and now began commenting mockingly on the judge, prosecuting attorney, and jurors.

They eyed him in polite puzzlement, as though witnessing a stranger. They had never known him to drink like this or talk like this; but then, hadn't his ordeal earned him a measure of forbearance? Hadn't it warranted a certain amount of license? They tried to relax understandingly, but they fell silent.

Byrne's nostrils whitened. He looked around. He was holding himself in but it was like holding in a steel spring. "Come on, this isn't a wake. It's a reawakening. Let's celebrate."

They laughed uneasily.

Byrne lifted his glass. "To my loyal friends." He tossed it off, then grinned suddenly. "People usually suspend judgment—like a sword." This won him a round of unsure smiles and nods.

Byrne refilled his glass sloppily. "There'll always be suspicion in the minds of some." He swayed slightly. "Let me put *your* minds at rest."

They tried to wave him down deprecatingly, but he seemed blind to them. He gazed past them, through the French doors which opened on the balcony, at the night and at the dim reflections of all of them in the room.

He said almost casually, but pronouncing the words with care, "I got away with murder." A bright, wild look flared in his eyes as though he knew he was overdoing it but didn't know when or how to stop. He said into the silence, "I killed Madelon."

They sat in shock, wanting to disbelieve, but believing.

He started to go on. "I can speak freely, without fear of further prosecution . . ."

Rising almost as a jury about to retire, they drew back from Byrne, set down the drinks with great care, and fumbled getting their coats and hats, their faces saying they were already gone.

Hogan was first to the door. He stopped and faced Byrne, examining him crossly. "I knew I shouldn't have come. I suppose this was the very thing I was afraid of." He left without pausing to put on his hat and coat, his face set, it seemed, more in anger at himself than at Byrne.

The others left silently, in various degrees of disgust. Everyone left but Meed.

Meed sat twirling his glass and gauging it with an odd smile.

Byrne turned on him challengingly. "How come you didn't pull out with the rest?"

Meed looked up with a sorrowful, understanding smile. "Because I know it isn't true." He put up a forestalling hand. "Oh, I know why you said that. Not to shock us; not to get back at society that put you on trial for something you didn't do."

"No? Then why?"

"Because you *feel* guilty. It's only human. All of us have at one time wished someone else dead. And if that person dies we feel—even if we had nothing to do with the death—a kind of guilt."

Byrne eyed him mockingly. "Oh? You think that? Well, think again. I murdered Madelon—really murdered her. And I got away with it."

Meed eyed him narrowly, with a thin smile. "Either the strain you've been under has cracked you or . . ."

Byrne leaned back easily, something between a sneer and a smirk on his face. "Or what?"

Meed shook his head. "No, I think that's it. You're just giving way to aftershock and alcohol. You've been under too much tension and you've had release."

Byrne grinned crookedly. "Meed, you're wasting your breath playing psychoanalyst. Murdering Madelon put no strain at all on my conscience."

Meed gazed into his glass. "Go right ahead. But when you're cold-shivering sober you'll wish you hadn't shot off your mouth."

"Speaking of shots—" Byrne downed his drink and reached for a refill. "That one was for Madelon. Poor Madelon. I done her wrong."

Meed said very quietly, "You'd better lay off the drink and that kind of talk. How do you expect to pick up the pieces of your life here?" He looked thoughtful. "Maybe it's too late already. You saw how the others took it."

"Maybe I just don't give a damn about anything, now that I've got away with murder. After all, you can't do much more than that in life, can you? You're right about one thing: I've a great feeling of release."

Meed gave a short explosive laugh. "I can understand how you might've been driven to feeling like murdering Madelon. I'll admit the woman could be trying. But that doesn't excuse your empty bragging."

Byrne raised an eyebrow in a leer. "Empty bragging? Shouldn't what I say loosely here be more credible than what I said under oath for my life?" He smiled smugly.

A shadow crossed Meed's face. He breathed hard, then he smiled. "What do you think you're proving? Only that you're irrational."

Byrne took a sizable swallow and came up looking sly. "You're trying too hard to be broadminded. But I think down deep you're taking it like the others. What you're really angry at is not my guilt but my bad taste. Here I am boasting of my guilt just after a jury of my so-called peers has found me guiltless. Come on, confess. Isn't that it?"

Meed stood up abruptly, his eyes hostile. "You're damn right it's bad taste." He set down his glass savagely. "I should've left with the others." He snatched up his coat and rammed his arms into the sleeves. "I don't know why I stayed, except to see how much of a fool you'd prove yourself to be."

"Fool enough to get away with murder." Byrne eyed Meed disdainfully, turned and walked with great precision to the French doors, flung them open, and took a deep breath. He turned back with an evil smile.

Meed's eyes glittered. "I don't know why I should be so angry. I know you're not responsible. You're foolish drunk."

Byrne laughed. "I know what I know. I got away with murder."

Meed swelled with fury. "You damn blowhard, they let you go because they couldn't find the weapon. They never found it because I threw it in the quarry just outside town."

He stared in amazement as Byrne turned again to the night, moved nearer to the balcony railing, and took a deep breath.

"Didn't you hear me, Byrne? I'm saying *I'm* the one who murdered Madelon." He came up behind Byrne. "You poor drunken fool, you won't know what hit you either. I'm telling you because they're going to say you couldn't live with the guilt you admitted here tonight. Listen to me, damn you. I'm saying *I* did it. I was tired of her, but she threatened to make the end of the affair messy, and so—" Hands drawing back to push, he advanced on Byrne, watching him intently.

Lieutenant Harris stepped between them out of the darkness on the balcony, handcuffs gleaming. Meed froze till too late; the cuffs clicked fast.

Byrne turned slowly and saw the gleams as webbed blurs, like stars burning in mist. His vision cleared and he saw Lieutenant Harris eyeing him with a twisted smile.

"So I was wrong. I still don't know why I went along with you on this. I thought sure you did it—even up to just now." He shoved Meed toward the door. "Good night, Mr. Byrne."

"Good night, Lieutenant." He turned again to the night. He heard the door close. He took a deep drink of night. Night would soon fade. He would take a deep, deep drink of dawn.

Mousetrap

by Edwin P. Hicks

There was a pounding on his front door. Joe Chaviski turned on the light. It was two A.M. by his bedside clock, a full hour before the alarm was set to go off, rousing him to go fishing. The pounding continued. Who the devil would be wanting him at this hour?

"All right! All right!" Joe shouted, as his two hundred and sixty pounds suddenly came alive. His great feet hit the floor lightly. He looked like a king-sized teddy bear as he switched on the overhead light and started toward the front door. After turning on the porch light he peered through the glass of the door into the frightened face of Frank Waverly, Fort Sanders's leading contractor.

Joe threw open the door. "Come in, Frank. What the hell—"

Waverly pushed through the door as if demons were clutching at his coattails.

"What's wrong, Frank?"

"I'm in trouble, Joe!"

"What kind of trouble?"

"Murder!" Waverly was shaking violently, his black eyes staring wildly. His suntanned face was three shades lighter than usual.

"Sit down." Joe said. Waverly sank into the leather divan. "Here, light up a cigarette, and tell me what this is all about."

"Joe, I came to you for advice—and help. The police will be after me tomorrow as soon as the murder is discovered."

"Whose murder, Frank?"

"Sally Caviness," Waverly said. He took out his handkerchief and wiped his eyes.

"Sally Caviness?" Joe knew plenty about Sally Caviness. She was a pretty redhaired divorcee, and Frank Waverly's mistress. "Let me make some coffee," Joe said. "We'll both feel better."

While the coffee was perking Waverly would have time to pull himself together. This was going to be a mess. He and Frank Waverly had always been good friends. What a man does in his private life is his own business, and Joe had never mentioned Sally to Frank. Yet Joe and Wanda Waverly were good friends, too, and Wanda was

315

Frank's wife. Wanda had the money in the family, an inheritance, and she had financed Frank's early construction work until he had reached his present status as an extremely successful contractor, the builder of buildings, bridges and highways.

Frank was about forty-five, and Wanda was seven years younger. They had been married fifteen years, and there were no children. Sally Caviness? Joe shook his head. It was the old, old story of a well-to-do businessman making a fool of himself over a much younger woman. Sally wasn't yet thirty, and she was beautiful, extremely beautiful, with a figure that caused men to turn and watch when she passed on the street.

Joe turned off the three o'clock alarm on the bedstand clock. There went his fishing trip to Cove Lake. It was the tenth of October, the time of year when they hit on the surface.

He took the coffee into the living room. Frank Waverly was sitting there with his face buried in his hands. He looked weary, like an old man.

"Here, get some of this hot coffee in you," Joe said.

Slowly, sentence by sentence, Frank told his story. He had left Sally's apartment in the Superior Arms at nine thirty that night. She was happy when he left because, he said, he had told her that as soon as he obtained his divorce from Wanda, they would be married. After a long pause, Waverly continued. "When I returned sometime after midnight with some good news, she was dead—she was lying on the floor on her back. And she had been shot!"

Joe put down his empty cup. "Did anyone see you go to, or leave, her apartment?"

"The elevator operator, in the early part of the night. He took me up about eight o'clock, but he was gone when I left at nine thirty."

"What about the second time?"

"No one saw me. It is an automatic elevator, and the operator goes off duty at nine o'clock."

"You say you returned after midnight with good news. What was the good news?"

"I think it was a quarter after midnight. I went there to tell her we had caught Wanda—my wife, you know—in a compromising situation and that now Wanda could not possibly contest our divorce."

"What do you mean by 'compromising situation'?" Joe asked, bristling. He had known Wanda Waverly since she was a little girl. A police officer for thirty years knows pretty well what goes on in his hometown—both on the surface and beneath. Wanda had a temper, all right, no question about that, but never had he heard the slightest word against Wanda's character.

"Just what I told you," Waverly said. "We found her in a compromising situation. I want you to keep this in confidence, Joe. We trailed her to the Picardy hotel. She was there with a man."

"What man?" Joe said coldly.

"Harry Vallery."

"That son— You framed her, Frank. I *know* you framed her!"

"Yes, I framed her. She refused to give me a divorce so I could marry Sally."

"And now what do you want me to do?" Joe asked sharply.

"Joe, I haven't anybody to turn to now."

"How about Wanda?"

"Joe, man, I didn't kill Sally! I swear I didn't. But as soon as she's discovered, the police will be after me. They'll question the elevator operator and find out I was there last night. This whole town knows about Sally and me."

"Who else would be interested in killing Sally except you—or Wanda?"

"That's just it!" Waverly moaned. "And Wanda has a perfect alibi. She checked in at the hotel sometime shortly after nine, was there all the time until we caught her there with Vallery, sometime between ten thirty and ten forty-five. Then after we left, Vallery rode around with her for about thirty minutes. She seemed pretty much upset."

"Who's 'we'?" asked Joe.

"My private detective, Choc Churchill. And there was a photographer, Jim Durnell, and the hotel manager, and I."

"Then what?"

"I was waiting for Vallery in front of the Superior Arms, as planned. We sat in the car and talked and checked scores, to be together in the divorce proceedings if Wanda contested it. Then I went up to see Sally."

"Did you see anyone enter or leave the Superior Arms while you waited outside?"

"No."

"Where's Sally's divorced husband?"

"In Leavenworth prison, on a Dyer Act violation. He was a repeater and still has a year to serve."

"Why did you come to me?"

"Joe, you and I have been friends for a long time. You know I'm no saint, but I wouldn't kill anybody. I watched you for years on the police force. You're level-headed. The boys there will be hard on me, but they respect you. You've got influence there. Please, Joe."

"The first thing I'm going to do," Joe said, "is call the police and tell them Sally's been murdered."

"Wait, Joe. You can tell them, all right, but I want you to go to the apartment and look the place over. See if you can dig out anything that points to the killer—and it's not me. You're the best detective they ever had. Those cubs they've got there now don't know what to look for."

"Go home, Frank."

"Go home? I haven't any home to go to after tonight."

"Then go to your hotel."

"I'll be at the Wardlow."

"Okay. You be there when we want you." Joe reached for the telephone.

Chief Detective Marty Sauer and Detective Frank Hopp were waiting in front of the Superior Arms when Joe drove up. Johnnie Brooksher, identification officer, got out of a parked car, carrying his camera and fingerprint kit.

"Sally Caviness was Frank Waverly's girl, wasn't she?" Sauer said.

Joe grinned. He had trained Sauer. He hadn't told headquarters who his informant was, and already Sauer was connecting Waverly with the crime.

Brooksher powdered the doorknob to Sally's apartment, then swore. "Nothing; clean," he said.

Joe opened the door with Waverly's key. They entered—and there was Sally lying in the middle of the floor in front of a divan. She was wearing a sheer blue nightgown and transparent negligee. There were three bullet holes in her chest.

"Twenty-five caliber automatic," said Brooksher, pouncing on three empty brass cartridges on the floor. An expensive stereophonic phonograph was playing a thunderous Beethoven sonata.

"Stop that racket," Sauer said. "It gives me the creeps."

"Would rock and roll sound any better at a time like this?" Joe growled. He turned off the stereo.

"Somebody must have been planning a celebration," Sauer said,

"but if they were all that happy, why did he have to kill her? Somebody throw a sprag in the wheel?"

Again Joe was pleased. Let the boy's mind work. Ten years ago
when Sauer moved up from car officer, the last thing anyone would
have accused Sauer of was thinking.

Now Hopp was examining a framed photograph which he had
found on Sally's dressing table in the bedroom. It was a recent photograph of Frank Waverly, and at the bottom was written, "To my
darling Sally."

"A shame for a man like Frank Waverly to lose his head over a
girl like this," Hopp said. "But she sure was a pretty one—and built!"

They let Brooksher photograph the body and the room, the glasses
on the table, the bottle of champagne in the ice bucket. Then they
began digging into things. Beneath a ruffled pillow on the divan
Sauer found an ivory-handled .25 caliber automatic.

Brooksher examined it, then shook his head disgustedly. "Wiped
clean."

"All right," Sauer said, "tell us what you haven't told us, Joe.
What do you know?"

Joe told them about Waverly's coming to see him.

"All right, let's go pick him up," said Sauer. "He's bound to have
done it—or if he didn't he knows something about it."

"Sure," said Joe, "only there's one thing I don't understand. If
Frank Waverly had a quarrel with Sally and shot her, why would
he leave the murder weapon, assuming that's the gun that killed
her? And if he was fool enough to leave the gun here, because of
some subconscious psychological quirk demanding that he be
caught, why did he so carefully wipe the fingerprints off the gun?"

"Let's go ask Frank Waverly," Sauer said.

"You go ahead," said Joe. "He's at the Wardlow Hotel. Here's the
key to Sally's apartment. I'm going home."

At home, all up in the air, Joe cooked breakfast. He was thinking
about Frank Waverly and the pitiful sight of gorgeous Sally Caviness lying dead on the floor of her apartment, but most of all he was
thinking of Wanda Waverly.

He knew Wanda as one of the finest women in the city of Fort
Sanders. She was wealthy. She could be hard. She had a reputation
of ruling women's organizations to which she belonged with a firm
hand. But as far as anyone knew she was a faithful and devoted
wife. There hadn't been a breath of scandal about her, even when

the town was buzzing about Frank and Sally. Frank had been seeing
Sally now for two years—just another damn fool man and a pretty
golddigger of a girl.

Say that Frank and Sally had had a quarrel—maybe Sally had
threatened to blackmail him. Few men ever shot a woman black-
mailer. He might slap her around or beat her up or, in a rage, even
strangle her. Yet if Waverly had done the unusual and shot Sally,
why had he carefully wiped his fingerprints off the gun and left it
where it would be found?

Another thing, too—that little ivory-handled .25 caliber pistol was
a woman's choice of weapons. A man would use a larger gun, a .32
or a .38 at least. That ivory handle also pointed to a woman's touch.
Yet what woman? The only two women so far in the case were poor
dead Sally, and Wanda Waverly. Yet Wanda had been in the Picardy
hotel at the time the murder must have occurred, and she had witnesses to prove it—the very best of witnesses—her husband, a private detective, a photographer, the hotel manager, and Vallery.

Joe Chaviski decided to go fishing anyway. He wanted to hit Cove
Lake right at sunup. He was leaving an hour later than he'd planned,
but by driving fast he still might make it.

The car, boat, and trailer moved at seventy miles an hour along
Highway 22, then south from Paris, around the winding hill road
at a slower pace. The top of Mount Magazine was wreathed in a fog,
but the eastern sky was all ablaze and the water of the lake was
still cloaked in shadow as he backed his trailer down the launching
ramp. He loaded the boat, *Lucy*, with his rods, his tackle box, his
water jug and lunchbox, and two life preservers. He put in his gas-
oline tank and attached it to the motor, then he threw in a paddle.

Joe moved to various hotspots about the lake casting diligently.
On this date for the last two years he had caught big bass, but Old
John Bass was not at home this morning. At times Joe sat back and
just enjoyed being out. There was a ripple on the surface as the sun
moved over the hill and transformed the opposite shore into a ka-
leidoscope of color—the red of sumac, persimmon, sweetgum, and
water oak, the green of cedar and pine, intermingling with shadowing blue haze and gray crags.

Joe fished until noon, catching a few small ones and releasing
them as fast as he caught them. He devoured his lunch hungrily,
topping it off with a quart of sweet milk he had kept in the icebox.
Then he turned his boat back toward the landing and soon had it
on the trailer and heading home. His trip had been a disappointment,

but he had done a powerful lot of thinking—going over all the angles of the Caviness murder.

As soon as he had unloaded his boat at home and changed clothes, he drove to the police station. Brooksher had news for him. The bullets removed from Sally's body in the autopsy had been fired from the little automatic found beneath the pillow, and Frank Waverly had admitted buying the gun three years before. The prosecuting attorney would file a murder charge against him in the morning.

"Has Waverly cracked yet?" Joe asked.

"No," Brooksher said. "We advised him of his rights not to answer questions, but he waived everything. We grilled him then for several hours. He swears he knew nothing of Sally's death until he walked into her apartment and found her lying on the floor. Then, he said, he beat it to you, hoping you could help him."

Joe went to Waverly's cell and sat down with him on the cot. "What about the gun, Frank? They say it's yours."

"Sure it's mine. I told them I bought it at the Star Hardware Store three years ago."

"How do you explain its being the murder weapon?"

"I can't explain it—except it was taken from my cottage on Sugar Loaf Lake in a break-in a little over a week ago. The sheriff has a report on the burglary."

"What was it doing at the cottage?"

Waverly hesitated before he answered. "It was Wanda's. I bought it for her three years ago."

"How did they gain entrance?"

"Broke out the window with a rock, then climbed through it."

"You still sticking to your guns, you didn't kill Sally?"

"Joe, you know I didn't. I'm innocent. I'm asking you to help me."

Joe waddled out of the cell. At the door of the corridor he came face to face with Frazier Amanda, one of the city's best criminal lawyers. Amanda nodded and walked on toward Waverly's cell. Well, there went ten thousand dollars of Waverly's money at the very least, Joe said to himself.

As Joe drove up in front of the Waverly home, the woman who came out and got into a taxicab seemed disturbed, and didn't speak to him, although he knew her well. It was Elizabeth Andrews, the last survivor of one of the oldest families in Fort Sanders, and a friend of Wanda Waverly's since childhood. Perhaps she had stopped in to offer her sympathy to Wanda. The story of Sally's murder and

of Frank Waverly's being picked up had been on television throughout the day.

A maid answered the doorbell. Wanda Waverly came into the
living room almost immediately.

"I'm glad to see you, Joe," she said.

"Wanda, what's all this nonsense about your going to the Picardy
with Harry Vallery?"

She colored, but quickly recovered her composure. "Joe, my husband, Frank—he has not—Mr. Vallery is a charming man."

"And you are a charming liar," said Joe. "Come on, help me out,
Wanda. You're a smart woman, and I know you better than that."

She laughed. "Who are you working for—for Frank?"

"Yes, for Frank, but not for money. He came to see me last night
after he found Miss Caviness's body."

"Yes, I know. It has been on television all day. The police came
to see me this morning, but of course I knew nothing about it. Poor
Frank. I was afraid he would wind up in a mess with that Sally
Caviness."

"Frank told me that he framed you last night, set up a little deal
with Harry Vallery."

Again she laughed, but she said nothing.

"Wanda, I came to you first. If you don't play ball with me, I'm
going to Harry Vallery. A man has a way of getting a rat like Vallery
to talk, and legally. Frank admitted he framed you. I know darn
well you weren't infatuated with Harry Vallery. You're too sensible
a woman. And I know you didn't go there to make Frank jealous.
You had always opposed giving him his freedom to marry Sally. It
just doesn't add up, your suddenly going to the hotel with Harry
Vallery."

Wanda studied Joe for several seconds. Then she smiled. "All
right, Joe. I knew when I first walked into this room that you would
keep after it until you got the truth. I wasn't seduced by that gallant
young Casanova, Harry Vallery. He's ten years younger than I—and
I'm a married woman and—well, I'm not that kind of a gal."

"Then why—"

"It was obvious from the first that Frank had hired Harry to make
up to me. Frank was making out of town trips more often than
usual—to give Harry every opportunity of seeing me. Harry took
me out to dinner several times, became very ardent, finally propo-
sitioned me—in a gentlemanly manner of course—and let it slip

that Frank was playing around with Sally, something I had known
for a long time.

"I forced his hand, bribed him with a little money, and learned
Frank was paying him a thousand dollars to get me to go to a hotel
with him. He was doing this, of course, to compromise me so I would
be easy pickings in the divorce suit which he would file."

"So you played right into his hands?"

"Yes, but for a purpose. By matching Frank's money, I got Harry's
promise to tell the whole drab story when the case came up in divorce
court. I was confident that when the whole picture went before the
judge, my lawyer and I could make Frank Waverly hate the day he
had ever seen Harry Vallery—or Sally Caviness."

Joe whistled. "I would hate to play poker with you, Wanda."

She laughed. "I'm no angel, Joe. My father didn't leave his money
to me to have a man like Frank Waverly take it away—nor a Sally
Caviness either. When it comes to fighting dirty, I can get just as
dirty as they can—or a little dirtier. I've always been able to hate,
Joe. I never forget, never forgive."

"Okay," said Joe. "I was going to ask what you wanted me to do
about Frank. After all, you must have some affection for him after
fifteen years of marriage."

For a moment the poise and bravado left Wanda. "I loved Frank
dearly, Joe, gave him everything. I was entirely faithful to him in
thought as well as deed. Then this hussy, Sally Caviness, came into
his life. All he has wanted for the past two years was a divorce, and
that hurt, Joe. But, in addition, he wanted the lion's share of our
joint holdings—for Sally, understand—for Sally!"

Now she was laughing again. Joe thought she was near hysteria.

"I wish," she said, "I wish I could have seen his face when he
walked into her apartment and found her lying dead, *dead* on the
floor!"

That evening Joe cornered Harry Vallery. Within five minutes,
Harry was spilling everything he knew—how Frank Waverly indeed
had hired him to seduce his wife and how Wanda had suspected
what he was up to and had induced him with more money to betray
Waverly.

"When did she agree to play along?" Joe asked.

"About two weeks ago. Let's see, it was the night her husband
was supposed to be in St. Louis. Yes, it was two weeks ago last night.
She said she would go along on a fake date to the hotel—and a fake
was all it was."

That night, after Joe had finished his supper, he walked the floor for more than an hour, pounding his fist at intervals, and scrubbing at his grizzled, short-cropped hair.

"Dammit!" he said. "Dammit!"

He reasoned there had to be a fourth party in the murder case. It couldn't be Harry Vallery, for Vallery's movements were accounted for every second the night Sally Caviness was murdered. He was with Wanda Waverly, or at his apartment waiting for a call from Wanda, or with Frank Waverly, every minute between the time Frank had left Sally's apartment and had returned there to find her body. It couldn't be Wanda, although he knew now, from the moment she had lost her poise, of the agony that Frank and Sally had caused her—and of her bitterness and hatred not only for Sally but perhaps for Frank as well. He knew that she was woman enough to kill Sally, had the opportunity presented itself, but Wanda's alibi was Harry Vallery and the hotel. Hopp and Sauer had checked at the hotel, and she had been there from nine fifteen on. She'd had coffee sent up to her room at nine thirty, had returned the tray at ten.

It most surely was not Frank Waverly—that is, there was no reason for it before the raid on Wanda and Harry at the hotel. All this was being done so that Frank and Sally could marry—by compromising Wanda into giving him a divorce. Yet if Frank had killed Sally when he went to her apartment the second time, what was the reason? Why had he carefully wiped his fingerprints off the murder weapon and then left it at the scene of the crime, carefully placed beneath a pillow on the divan? No, it wasn't plausible that he had done it. The bottle of champagne in the bucket of ice was mute testimony that Frank and Sally had planned to celebrate if everything went well in framing Wanda at the Picardy hotel.

There just had to be somebody else, some fourth party involved in all this mess, who hated Sally Caviness. Could it have been a discarded lover? You never could tell when a jealous man was going to get violent. If so, how did the Waverly gun figure in it? A coincidence? Had the discarded lover broken into the Waverly cottage, stolen the gun, and then shot Sally? The odds against such a coincidence were too great to consider.

Definitely someone was out to get Frank Waverly—to mousetrap him. *Mousetrap?* Joe stopped short in his pacing and stood there scratching his head.

Mousetrap—in competitive business, Joe knew, a firm might try to make the opposition think they were going to do one thing, and then do another, as a clever criminal might bait a trap, then clobber the victim who walked into it. But in the killing of Sally Caviness? What about a clever amateur—how would he or she operate? Joe felt there was something phony about this Sally Caviness murder, yet for the life of him he couldn't fit all the pieces together. He decided to fall back on regulation police routine.

He rechecked the hotel, backtracking Sauer and Hopp. Their report on Wanda Waverly's stay there—the time of registering, the time she called room service, the time she sent back the tray—was entirely accurate. Next, Joe drove by the Black and White Cab Company headquarters. Had Wanda driven to the Picardy in her own car or had she called a cab? Waverly had told him that Vallery and Wanda had driven around for about thirty minutes after the raid on the hotel room, but he hadn't said whether Vallery had taken her directly home or back to the hotel where Wanda would have left her car—perhaps parked on the street.

There was no record of a call to the Waverly address. Joe began checking the calls the cabs had made to the Picardy that night. There had been eight. Five of them had been in the early part of the evening between six and nine o'clock, one had been at ten ten, two had been around midnight.

The ten ten call was interesting. It had been made by cab No. 150, and Chuck Frambers was the driver. The dispatcher's assistant located him at home. Sure, he remembered the call. It was a good-looking dame about forty years old. She had been wearing something blue. He had taken her from the hotel to her home at 201 North Sixteenth Street. He ought to know her name, but couldn't think of it right off. No, she wasn't drinking, wasn't a hustler or anything like that; a nice woman. She was blonde and "real pretty" in his estimation.

A check of the calls between eight thirty and nine fifteen that night showed none to 201 North Sixteenth Street, but that didn't mean anything. The woman could have gone to the hotel with a friend and then come home by cab. Or she could have walked the short distance over to Main Street and been picked up there by a cab. Or, she could have dined at a restaurant somewhere and gone to the hotel from there.

In the old days Joe could pretty well have named every person living on North Sixteenth. It was in the better section of the older part of Fort Sanders. He would drive past 201 North Sixteenth

Street. This "nice" attractive lady going home alone from the Picardy
at ten ten o'clock at night—no women's party or anything like
that—intrigued him.

First, Joe drove by the other cab company, the Checkered Cab.
He was lucky immediately. Their call records showed No. 235 had
made a call to 201 North Sixteenth at eight past nine. The driver,
Lem Johnson, was called to the office.

"Let's see," he said. "Sure, that was a snappy looking lady I picked
up at the old brick house. Sure, I remember her—dressed in a light
blue suit. No spring chicken, but a real dazzler. Kinda tall but good
shape. Dark hair. Never seen her before, but I'm new in this town.
I took her to the Picardy hotel. Seemed kinda excited. No floozie—a
real nice lady. That's all I can tell you."

Blonde . . . brunette! A brunette going to the hotel, a blonde coming from the hotel! Otherwise identical description. One of these
guys must be color blind. Joe headed for 201 North Sixteenth. Then,
on the way, it hit him—he knew who lived there. He headed for the
police station.

Marty Sauer was just getting into his car. He was calling it a day.

Joe drove up beside him. "Come on, get in the car," he said.

"What for?"

"Going to talk to someone."

"What about?"

"You coming, or do I get the sheriff?" Joe asked.

Sauer piled in beside Joe. "Where we going?"

"We're going to have a little chat with Miss Elizabeth Andrews
about the Sally Caviness case."

Sauer whistled. "I never heard Waverly was fooling around with
her, Joe."

"Neither did I," Joe said.

They parked in front of an aging brick house with white columns,
apparently in need of repair. Two giant magnolia trees stood in
front, and the yard was covered with dead leaves. It was nearing
sunset, and a mockingbird was trilling from one of the magnolias.
A faded sign above the door read "School of the Drama."

Joe gave a twist to the old fashioned doorbell. Elizabeth Andrews
came to the door wearing a blue housecoat. She was a woman of
impressive beauty, and the styling of her platinum blonde hair was
a work of art.

"Why, Mr. Chaviski—I hardly recognized you. I'm so excited I
hardly know what I'm doing. I'm closing my school, Mr. Chaviski."

"Closing your school!"

Elizabeth's eyes were red; she had been crying. She led them to the living room. "Yes, closing it. There will be an announcement in Sunday's paper. I'm returning to Hollywood. But be seated, gentlemen. What can I do for you?"

"Returning?" Joe said.

"Why, yes. I'm sure you remember. I was out there years ago—it's been too long. It's wonderful to be going back."

"Signed up for another picture?"

"Well, not exactly. I'm going out there to spend the winter, and confer with my agent. I'd like to get in television. But, Mr. Chaviski, this is—"

"Marty Sauer. Detective Marty Sauer of the police department."

"Police department! Goodness! I've been rattling along. Why have you come to see *me*?"

"It's about this Frank Waverly case," Joe said bluntly.

Elizabeth's face suddenly went white—then very red.

"You are a good friend of Wanda Waverly, aren't you? I saw you leaving her house yesterday afternoon."

"A very, very dear friend, Mr. Chaviski. I was so grieved when I heard on television about Sally Caviness, and Frank Waverly being held, I went right over to see Wanda. Wanda didn't deserve this. She made Frank what he is today. He wasn't anything until he got her."

"Yes, yes—I know." Chaviski's eyes swept about the room. A bit of plaster the size of his hand was missing near one corner of the ceiling. There were cracks in the plaster on the opposite wall. The covering on the arms of his chair was frayed. The carpet had been worn through in front of the door and in front of the chairs. "We've come to take you over to Wanda's," Joe said.

"But Wanda doesn't want to see me again. I've done all I can do."

"I don't think so," said Joe. He smiled without mirth.

She studied him. "All right," she said quietly. "Let me get something on."

Elizabeth was silent all the way to the Waverly house. When Wanda appeared she looked pale, but she still carried her head high.

"You again, Joe? And you, Liz?"

Joe came directly to the point. "This is Detective Marty Sauer of the police department. We have been checking Miss Andrews' movements the night Sally Caviness was killed."

Elizabeth half rose from her chair, her hands going quickly to her mouth. "Wanda, I haven't told them a thing!"

"Don't you want to tell us all about it, Wanda?" Joe said.

"Tell you about what, Joe?"

"Just how deeply is Miss Andrews involved in this thing with you, Wanda? It would be a shame if she missed the chance to go back to Hollywood."

For the first time, Wanda dropped her head. She began speaking in a voice hardly audible. "It's no use—no use denying it. You wouldn't be here if you hadn't figured it out. And I thought I was being so clever!" Then she raised her head, and her old voice came out defiantly: "Elizabeth is entirely innocent, Joe, damn you." She softened the oath with a smile. "She put two and two together when she heard about Sally on television yesterday, and came over here to have it out with me. I told her to keep her mouth shut, forget what she didn't know and merely suspected—and I would pay her expenses in Hollywood for at least six months."

"I haven't told them a thing!" Elizabeth repeated.

Wanda smiled. "Don't worry, Elizabeth. The deal still stands. You see, up until yesterday all Elizabeth had done for me was to spend an hour or so in the role of Wanda Waverly at the Picardy. I knew she needed money desperately, and I told her I would pay her two hundred dollars if she would register in my name at the hotel. I told her that Frank was trying to frame me, and that it was necessary for me to be in two places at once that night. She agreed. She went to the hotel early, made up like me—same clothes, same accessories, and a dark wig matching my natural hair. She called room service in twenty-odd minutes, as I had directed, and had them send up something. This was to establish proof that 'I' was in the room all the time. Then after a time she sent the empty plates back down again, tipping the waiter very well so he'd remember. The desk clerk knew neither one of us. That's all in the world Elizabeth knew or did."

"We won't press charges against Miss Andrews," Joe said, but he knew she'd be a key witness in the event of a trial.

Wanda continued: "When hate takes a person over she becomes blind to reason. Frank became contemptible in my eyes. I actually began to hate him more than I did Sally. It wasn't just a case of protecting my own money, the money my father left me. I wanted to hurt Frank in the worst way."

"So you mousetrapped him," Joe said. "You agreed to the deal with Harry Vallery, in this way setting up a perfect alibi. You had Miss Andrews, impersonating you, register in your name at the Picardy. The arrangement was that when you were ready you would call Vallery at his apartment, and he would come to your hotel room—to be followed fifteen minutes later by your husband, the photographer, and other witnesses."

"Yes, Joe. While Elizabeth was registered in my name at the hotel, I waited half a block down the street from the Superior Arms until Frank left Sally's apartment. Of course I had known for months where the love-nest was located. I had the little automatic with me, the one reported stolen from the lakeside cottage. Frank came out about nine thirty, got in his car and drove off to meet with Harry at his apartment. I entered the Superior Arms immediately, wearing a blonde wig in case I should meet someone, which I didn't. Sally didn't recognize me in the wig when she opened the door a crack. I whispered to her that I had a message from Harry Vallery, and she let me in. I removed my wig then, so she would know who I was, turned up the stereo—and shot her three times as she whined for mercy. You know the rest."

Joe nodded. "You went to the hotel then, relieved Miss Andrews, and made your call to Harry Vallery at his apartment. You figured you had the perfect alibi—'you' had been at the hotel all evening, now you were meeting Harry Vallery there—and your husband and his raiders would be witnesses to the fact that you couldn't possibly have murdered Sally Caviness."

Wanda lifted her head regally. "Eliminating Sally gave me more satisfaction than anything I have ever done," she said.

The Adventure of the Haunted Library

by August Derleth

When I opened the door of our lodgings one summer day during the third year of our joint tenancy of No. 7B, Praed Street, I found my friend Solar Pons standing with one arm on the mantel, waiting with a thin edge of impatience either upon my arrival, or that of someone else, and ready to go out, for his deerstalker lay close by.

"You're just in time, Parker," he said, "—if the inclination moves you—to join me in another of my little inquiries. This time, evidently into the supernatural."

"The supernatural!" I exclaimed, depositing my bag.

"So it would seem." He pointed to a letter thrown carelessly upon the table.

I picked it up and was immediately aware of the fine quality of the paper and the embossed name: Mrs. Margaret Ashcroft. Her communication was brief.

"Dear Mr. Pons,

I should be extremely obliged if you could see your way clear to call upon me some time later today or tomorrow, at your convenience, to investigate a troublesome matter which hardly seems to be within the jurisdiction of the metropolitan police. I do believe the library is haunted. Mr. Carnacki says it is not, but I can hardly doubt the evidence of my own senses."

Her signature was followed by a Sydenham address.

"I've sent for a cab," said Pons.

"Who is Mr. Carnacki?" I asked.

"A self-styled psychic investigator. He lives in Chelsea, and has had some considerable success, I am told."

"A charlatan!"

"If he were, he would hardly have turned down our client. What do you make of it, Parker? You know my methods."

I studied the letter which I still held, while Pons waited to hear how much I had learned from his spontaneous and frequent lectures in ratiocination. "If the quality of the paper is any indication, the lady is not without means," I said.

"Capital!"

"Unless she is an heiress, she is probably of middle age or over."

"Go on," urged Pons, smiling.

"She is upset because, though she begins well, she rapidly becomes very unclear."

"And provocative," said Pons. "Who could resist a ghost in a library, eh?"

"But what do you make of it?" I pressed him.

"Well, much the same as you," he said generously. "But I rather think the lady is not a young heiress. She would hardly be living in Sydenham, if she were. No, I think we shall find that she recently acquired a house there and has not been in residence very long. Something is wrong with the library."

"Pons, you don't seriously think it's haunted?"

"Do you believe in ghosts, Parker?"

"Certainly not!"

"Do I detect the slightest hesitation in your answer?" He chuckled. "Ought we not to say, rather, we believe there are certain phenomena which science as yet has not correctly explained or interpreted?" He raised his head suddenly, listening. "I believe that is our cab drawing to the curb."

A moment later, the sound of a horn from below verified Pons's deduction.

Pons clapped his deerstalker to his head and we were off.

Our client's house was built of brick, two and a half stories in height, with dormers on the gable floor. It was large and spreading, and built on a knoll, partly into the slope of the earth, though it seemed at first glance to crown the rise there. It was plainly of late Victorian construction, and, while it was not shabby, it just escaped looking quite genteel. Adjacent houses were not quite far enough away from it to give the lawn and garden the kind of spaciousness required to set the house off to its best advantage in a neighborhood which was slowly declining from its former status.

Our client received us in the library. Mrs. Ashcroft was a slender, diminutive woman with flashing blue eyes and whitening hair. She wore an air of fixed determination which her smile at sight of Pons did not diminish.

"Mr. Pons, I was confident that you would come," she greeted us.

She acknowledged Pons's introduction of me courteously, and went on, "This is the haunted room."

"Let us just hear your account of what has happened from the beginning, Mrs. Ashcroft," suggested Pons.

"Very well." She sat for a moment trying to decide where to begin her narrative. "I suppose, Mr. Pons, it began about a month ago. Mrs. Jenkins, a housekeeper I had hired, was cleaning late in the library when she heard someone singing. It seemed to come, she said, 'from the books.' Something about a 'dead man.' It faded away. Two nights later she woke after a dream and went downstairs to get a sedative from the medicine cabinet. She heard something in the library. She thought perhaps I was indisposed, and went to the library. But the library, of course, was dark. However, there was a shaft of moonlight in the room—it was bright outside, and therefore a kind of illumination was in the library, too—and in that shaft, Mr. Pons, Mrs. Jenkins believed she saw the bearded face of an old man that seemed to glare fiercely at her. It was only for a moment. Then Mrs. Jenkins found the switch and turned up the light. Of course, there was no one in the library but herself. It was enough for her; she was so sure that she had seen a ghost, that next morning, after all the windows and doors were found locked and bolted, she gave notice. I was not entirely sorry to see them go—her husband worked as caretaker of the grounds—because I suspected Jenkins of taking food from the cellars and the refrigerator for their married daughter. That is not an uncommon problem with servants in England, I am told."

"I should have thought you a native, Mrs. Ashcroft," said Pons. "You've been in the colonies?"

"Kenya, yes. But I was born here. It was for reasons of sentiment that I took this house. I should have taken a better location. But I was little more than a street waif in Syndenham as a child, and somehow the houses here represented the epitome of splendor. When the agent notified me that this one was to be let, I couldn't resist taking it. But the tables turned—the houses have come down in the world and I have come up, and there are so many things I miss—the hawkers and the carts, for which cars are no substitute, the rumble of the underground since the Nunhead-Crystal Palace Line has been discontinued, and all in all, I fear my sentiments have led me to make an ill-advised choice. The ghost, of course, is only the crowning touch."

"You believe in him then, Mrs. Ashcroft?"

"I've seen him, Mr. Pons." She spoke as matter-of-factly as if she were speaking of some casual natural phenomenon. "It was a week ago. I wasn't entirely satisfied that Mrs. Jenkins had not seen something. It could have been an hallucination. If she had started awake from a dream and fancied she saw something in their room why, yes, I could easily have believed it a transitory hallucination, which might occur commonly enough after a dream. But Mrs. Jenkins had been awake enough to walk downstairs, take a sedative, and start back up when she heard something in the library. So the dream had had time enough in which to wear off. I am myself not easily flightened. My late husband and I lived in border country in Kenya, and some of the Kikuyu are unfriendly.

"Mr. Pons, I examined the library carefully. As you see, shelving covers most of the walls. I had very few personal books to add—the rest were here. I bought the house fully furnished, as the former owner had died and there were no near heirs. That is, there was a brother, I understand, but he was in Rhodesia, and had no intention of returning to England. He put the house up for sale, and my agents, Messrs. Harwell and Chamberlain, in Lordship Lane, secured it for me. The books are therefore the property of the former owner, a Mr. Howard Brensham, who appears to have been very widely read, for there are collections ranging from early British poetry to crime and detective fiction. But that is hardly pertinent. My own books occupy scarcely two shelves over there—all but a few are jacketed, as you see, Mr. Pons. Well, my examination of the library indicated that the position of these books as I had placed them had been altered. It seemed to me that they had been handled, perhaps even read. They are not of any great consequence—recent novels, some work by M. Proust and M. Mauriac in French editions, an account of Kenya, and the like. It was possible that one of the servants had become interested in them; I did not inquire. Nevertheless, I became very sensitive and alert about the library. One night last week—Thursday, I believe—while I lay reading, late, in my room, I distinctly heard a book or some such object fall in this room.

"I got out of bed, took my flashlight, and crept down the stairs in the dark. Mr. Pons, I sensed someone or something moving about below. I could feel the disturbance of the air at the foot of the stairs where something had passed. I went directly to the library and from the threshold of that door over there I turned my flashlight into the room and put on its light. Mr. Pons, I saw a horrifying thing. I saw the face of an old man, matted with beard, with wild unkempt hair

raying outward from his head; it glared fiercely, menacingly at me.
I admit that I faltered and fell back; the flashlight almost fell from
my hands. Nevertheless, I summoned enough courage to snap on
the overhead light. Mr. Pons—there was no one in the room beside
myself. I stood in the doorway. No one had passed me. Yet, I swear
it, I had seen precisely the same apparition that Mrs. Jenkins had
described! It was there for one second—in the next it was gone—as
if the very books had swallowed it up.

"Mr. Pons, I am not an imaginative woman, and I am not given
to hallucinations. I saw what I had seen; there was no question of
that. I went around at once to make certain that the windows and
doors were locked; all were; nothing had been tampered with. I had
seen something, and everything about it suggested a supernatural
apparition. I applied to Mr. Harwell. He told me that Mr. Brensham
had never made any reference to anything out of the ordinary about
the house. He had personally known Mr. Brensham's old uncle,
Captain Jason Brensham, from whom he had inherited the house,
and the captain had never once complained of the house. He admitted
that it did not seem to be a matter for the regular police, and mentioned Mr. Carnacki as well as yourself. I'm sure you know Mr.
Carnacki, whose forte is psychic investigation. He came—and as
nearly as I can describe it, he *felt* the library, and assured me that
there were no supernatural forces at work here. So I applied to you,
Mr. Pons, and I do hope you will lay the ghost for me."

Pons smiled almost benignly, which lent his handsome, feral face
a briefly gargoylesque expression. "My modest powers, I fear, do not
permit me to feel the presence of the supernatural, but I must admit
to some interest in your little problem," he said thoughtfully. "Let
me ask you, on the occasion on which you saw the apparition—last
Thursday—were you aware of anyone's breathing?"

"No, Mr. Pons. I don't believe ghosts are held to breathe."

"Ah, Mrs. Ashcroft, in such matters I must defer to your judgment—you appear to have seen a ghost; I have not seen one." His
eyes danced. "Let us concentrate for a moment on its disappearance.
Was it accompanied by any sound?"

Our client sat for a long moment in deep thought. "I believe it
was, Mr. Pons," she said at last. "Now that I think of it."

"Can you describe it?"

"As best I can recall, it was something like the sound a book
dropped on the carpet might make."

"But there was no book on the floor when you turned the light on?"

"I do not remember that there was."

"Will you show me approximately where the spectre stood when you saw it?"

She got up with alacrity, crossed to her right, and stood next to the shelving there. She was in a position almost directly across from the entrance to the library from the adjacent room; a light flashed on from the threshold would almost certainly strike the shelving there.

"You see, Mr. Pons—there isn't even a window in this wall through which someone could have escaped if it were unlocked."

"Yes, yes," said Pons with an absent air. "Some ghosts vanish without sound, we are told, and some in a thunderclap. And this one with the sound of a book dropped upon the carpet!" He sat for a few moments, eyes closed, his long, tapering fingers tented before him, touching his chin occasionally. He opened his eyes again and asked, "Has anything in the house—other than your books—been disturbed, Mrs. Ashcroft?"

"If you mean my jewelry or the silver—no, Mr. Pons."

"A ghost with a taste for literature! There are indeed all things under the sun. The library has, of course, been cleaned since the visitation?"

"Every Saturday, Mr. Pons."

"Today is Thursday—a week since your experience. Has anything taken place since then, Mrs. Ashcroft?"

"Nothing, Mr. Pons."

"If you will excuse me," he said, coming to his feet, "I would like to examine the room."

Thereupon he began that process of intensive examination which never ceased to amaze and amuse me. He took the position that our client had just left to return to her chair, and stood, I guessed, fixing directions. He gazed at the high windows along the south wall; I concluded that he was estimating the angle of a shaft of moonlight and deducing that the ghost, as seen by Mrs. Jenkins, had been standing at or near the same place when it was observed. Having satisfied himself, he gave his attention to the floor, first squatting there, then coming to his knees and crawling about. Now and then he picked something off the carpet and put it into one of the tiny envelopes he habitually carried. He crept all along the east wall, went around the north and circled the room in this fashion, while our client watched him with singular interest, saying nothing and making no attempt to conceal her astonishment. He finished at last, and got to his feet once more, rubbing his hands together.

"Pray tell me, Mrs. Ashcroft, can you supply a length of thread of a kind that is not too tensile, that will break readily?"

"What color, Mr. Pons?"

"Trust a lady to think of that!" he said, smiling. "Color is of no object, but if you offer a choice, I prefer black."

"I believe so. Wait here."

Our client rose and left the library.

"Are you expecting to catch a ghost with thread, Pons?" I asked.

"Say rather I expect to test a phenomenon."

"That is one of the simplest devices I have ever known you to use."

"Is it not?" he agreed, nodding. "I submit, however, that the simple is always preferable to the complex."

Mrs. Ashcroft returned, holding out a spool of black thread. "Will this do, Mr. Pons?"

Pons took it, unwound a little of thread, and pulled it apart readily. "Capital!" he answered. "This is adequately soft."

He walked swiftly over to the north wall, took a book off the third shelf, which was at slightly over two feet from the floor, and tied the thread around it. Then he restored the book to its place, setting it down carefully. After he restored the book to its place, he walked away, unwinding the spool, until he reached the south wall, where he tautened the thread and tied the end around a book there. He now had an almost invisible thread that reached from north to south across the library at a distance of about six feet from the east wall, and within the line of the windows.

He returned the spool of thread to our client. "Now, then, can we be assured that no one will enter the library for a day or two? Perhaps the Saturday cleaning can be dispensed with?"

"Of course it can, Mr. Pons," said Mrs. Ashcroft, clearly mystified.

"Very well, Mrs. Ashcroft. I trust you will notify me at once if the thread is broken—or if any other untoward event occurs. In the meantime, there are a few little inquiries I want to make."

Our client bade us farewell with considerably more perplexity than she had displayed in her recital of the curious events which had befallen her.

Once outside, Pons looked at his watch. "I fancy we may just have time to catch Mr. Harwell at his office, which is just down Sydenham

Hill and so within walking distance." He gazed at me, his eyes twinkling. "Coming, Parker?"

I fell into step at his side, and for a few moments we walked in silence, Pons striding along with his long arms swinging loosely at his sides, his keen eye darting here and there, as if in perpetual and merciless search of facts with which to substantiate his deductions.

I broke the silence between us. "Pons, you surely don't believe in Mrs. Ashcroft's ghost?"

"What is a ghost?" he replied. "Something seen. Not necessarily supernatural. Agreed?"

"Agreed," I said. "It may be hallucination, illusion, some natural phenomenon misinterpreted."

"So the question is not about the reality of ghosts, but, did our client see a ghost or did she not? She believes she did. We are willing to believe that she saw something. Now, it was either a ghost or it was not a ghost."

"Pure logic."

"Let us fall back upon it. Ghost or no ghost, what is its motivation?"

"I thought that plain as a pikestaff," I said dryly. "The purpose is to frighten Mrs. Ashcroft away from the house."

"I submit few such matters are plain as a pikestaff. Why?"

"Someone wishes to gain possession of Mrs. Ashcroft's house."

"Anyone wishing to do so could surely have bought it from the agents before Mrs. Ashcroft did. But, let us for the moment assume that you are correct. How then did he get in?"

"That remains to be determined."

"Quite right. And we shall determine it. But one other little matter perplexes me in relation to your theory. That is this—if someone were bent upon frightening Mrs. Ashcroft from the house, does it not seem to you singular that we have no evidence that he initiated any of those little scenes where he was observed?"

"I should say it was deuced clever of him."

"It does not seem strange to you that if someone intended to frighten our client from the house, he should permit himself to be seen only by accident? And that after but the briefest of appearances, he should vanish before the full effectiveness of the apparition could be felt?"

"When you put it that way, of course, it is a little far-fetched."

"I fear we must abandon your theory, Parker, sound as it is in every other respect."

He stopped suddenly. "I believe this is the address we want. Ah, yes—here we are. Harwell & Chamberlain, 221B."

We mounted the stairs of the ancient but durable building and found ourselves presently in mid-nineteenth century quarters. A clerk came forward at our entrance.

"Good day, gentlemen. Can we be of service?"

"I am interested in seeing Mr. Roderic Harwell," said Pons.

"I'm sorry, sir, but Mr. Harwell has just left the office for the rest of the day. Would you care to make an appointment?"

"No, thank you. My business is of some considerable urgency, and I shall have to follow him home."

The clerk hesitated momentarily, then said, "I should not think that necessary, sir. You could find him around the corner at the Green Horse. He likes to spend an hour or so at the pub with an old friend or two before going home. Look for a short, ruddy gentleman, with bushy white sideburns."

Pons thanked him again, and we made our way back down the stairs and out to the street. In only a few minutes we were entering the Green Horse. Despite the crowd in the pub, Pons's quick eyes immediately found the object of our search, sitting at a round table near one wall, in desultory conversation with another gentleman of similar age, close to sixty, wearing, unless I were sadly mistaken, the air of one practicing my own profession.

We made our way to the table.

"Mr. Roderic Harwell?" asked Pons.

"That infernal clerk has given me away again!" cried Harwell, but with such a jovial smile that it was clear he did not mind. "What can I do for you?"

"Sir, you were kind enough to recommend me to Mrs. Margaret Ashcroft."

"Ah, it's Solar Pons, is it? I thought you looked familiar. Sit down, sit down."

His companion hastily rose and excused himself.

"Pray do not leave, doctor," said Pons. "This matter is not of such a nature that you need to disturb your meeting."

Harwell introduced us all around. His companion was Dr. Horace Weston, an old friend he was in the habit of meeting at the Green Horse at the end of the day. We sat between them.

"Now, then," said Harwell when we had made ourselves comfortable. "What'll you have to drink? Some ale? Bitters?"

"Nothing at all, if you please," said Pons.

"As you like. You've been to see Mrs. Ashcroft and heard her story?"

"We have just come from there."

"Well, Mr. Pons, I never knew of anything wrong with the house," said Harwell. "We sold some land in the country for Captain Brensham when he began selling off his property so that he could live as he was accustomed to live. He was a bibliophile of a sort—books about the sea were his specialty—and he lived well. But a recluse in his last years. He timed his life right—died just about the time his funds ran out."

"And Howard Brensham?" asked Pons.

"Different sort of fellow altogether. Quiet, too, but you'd find him in the pubs, and at the cinema sometimes watching a stage show. He gambled a little, but carefully. I gather he surprised his uncle by turning out well. He had done a turn in Borstal as a boy. And I suppose he was just as surprised when his uncle asked him to live with him his last years and left everything to him, including the generous insurance he carried."

"I wasn't sure, from what Mrs. Ashcroft said, when Howard Brensham died."

Harwell flashed a glance at his companion. "About seven weeks ago or so, eh?" To Pons, he added, "Dr. Weston was called."

"He had a cerebral thrombosis on the street, Mr. Pons," explained Dr. Weston. "Died in three hours. Very fast. Only forty-seven, and no previous history. But then, Captain Brensham died of a heart attack."

"Ah, you attended the captain, too?"

"Well, not exactly. I had attended him for some bronchial ailments. He took good care of his voice. He liked to sing. But when he had his heart attack and died I was in France on holiday. I had a young *locum* in and he was called."

"Mrs. Ashcroft's ghost sang," said Harwell thoughtfully. "Something about a 'dead man.'"

"I would not be surprised if it were an old sea chantey," said Pons.

"You don't mean you think it may actually be the captain's ghost, Mr. Pons?"

"Say, rather, we may be meant to think it is," answered Pons. "How old was he when he died?"

"Sixty-eight or sixty-seven—something like that," said Dr. Weston.

"How long ago?"

"Oh, only two years."

"His nephew hadn't lived with him very long, then, before the old man died?"

"No. Only a year or so," said Harwell. His sudden grin gave him a Dickensian look. "But it was long enough to give him at least one of his uncle's enthusiasms—the sea. He's kept up all the captain's newspapers and magazines, and was still buying books about the sea when he died. Like his uncle, he read very little else. I suppose a turn he had done as a seaman bent him that way. But they were a sea faring family. The captain's father had been a seaman, too, and Richard—the brother in Rhodesia who inherited the property and sold it through us to Mrs. Ashcroft—had served six years in the India trade."

Pons sat for a few minutes in thoughtful silence. Then he said, "The property has little value."

Harwell looked suddenly unhappy. "Mr. Pons, we tried to dissuade Mrs. Ashcroft. But these colonials have sentimental impulses no one can curb. Home to Mrs. Ashcroft meant not London, not England, but Sydenham. What could we do? The house was the best we could obtain for her in Sydenham. But it's in a declining neighborhood, and no matter how she refurbishes it, its value is bound to go down."

Pons came abruptly to his feet. "Thank you, Mr. Harwell. And you, Dr. Weston."

We bade them goodbye and went out to find a cab.

Back in our quarters, Pons ignored the supper Mrs. Johnson had laid for us, and went directly to the corner where he kept his chemical apparatus. There he emptied his pockets of the envelope he had filled in Mrs. Ashcroft's library, tossed his deerstalker to the top of the bookcase nearby, and began to subject his findings to chemical analysis. I ate supper by myself, knowing that it would be fruitless to urge Pons to join me. After supper I had a patient to look in on. I doubt that Pons heard me leave the room.

On my return in mid-evening, Pons was just finishing.

"Ah, Parker," he greeted me, "I see by the sour expression you're wearing you've been out calling on your crotchety Mr. Barnes."

"While you, I suppose, have been tracking down the identity of Mrs. Ashcroft's ghost?"

"I have turned up indisputable evidence that her visitant is from the nethermost regions," he said triumphantly, and laid before me a tiny fragment of cinder. "Do you suppose we dare conclude that coal is burned in hell?"

I gazed at him in open-mouthed astonishment. His eyes were dancing merrily. He was expecting an outburst of protest from me. I choked it back deliberately; I was becoming familiar indeed with all the little games he played. I said, "Have you determined his identity and his motive?"

"Oh, there's not much mystery in that," he said almost contemptuously. "It's the background in which I am interested."

"Not much mystery in it!" I cried.

"No, no," he answered testily. "The trappings may be a trifle bizarre, but don't let them blind you to the facts, all the essentials of which have been laid before us."

I sat down, determined to expose his trickery. "Pons, it is either a ghost or it is not a ghost."

"I can see no way of disputing that position."

"Then it is not a ghost."

"On what grounds do you say so?"

"Because there is no such thing as a ghost."

"Proof?"

"Proof to the contrary?"

"The premise is yours, not mine. But let us accept it for the nonce. Pray go on."

"Therefore it is a sentient being."

"Ah, that is certainly being cagey," he said, smiling provocatively. "Have you decided what his motive might be?"

"To frighten Mrs. Ashcroft from the house."

"Why? We've been told it's not worth much and will decline in value with every year to come."

"Very well, then. To get his hands on something valuable concealed in the house. Mrs. Ashcroft took it furnished—as it was, you'll remember."

"I remember it very well. I am also aware that the house stood empty for some weeks and anyone who wanted to lay hands on something in it would have had far more opportunity to do so then than he would after tenancy was resumed."

I threw up my hands. "I give up."

"Come, come, Parker. You are looking too deep. Think on it soberly for a while and the facts will rearrange themselves so as to make for but one, and only one, correct solution."

So saying, he turned to the telephone and rang up Inspector Jamison at his home to request him to make a discreet application for exhumation of the remains of Captain Jason Brensham and the examination of those remains by Bernard Spilsbury.

"Would you mind telling me what all that has to do with our client?" I asked, when he had finished.

"I submit it is too fine a coincidence to dismiss that a heavily insured old man should conveniently die after he has made a will leaving everything to the nephew he has asked to come live with him," said Pons. "There we have a concrete motive, with nothing ephemeral about it."

"But what's to be gained by an exhumation now? If what you suspect is true, the murderer is already dead, beyond punishment."

Pons smiled enigmatically. "Ah, Parker, I am not so much a seeker after punishment as a seeker after truth. I want the facts. I mean to have them. I shall be spending considerable time tomorrow at the British Museum in search of them."

"Well, you'll find ghosts of another kind there," I said dryly.

"Old maps and newspapers abound with them," he answered agreeably, but said no word in that annoyingly typical fashion of his about what he sought.

I would not ask, only to be told again, "Facts!"

When I walked into our quarters early in the evening of the following Monday, I found Pons standing at the windows, his face aglow with eager anticipation.

"I was afraid you might not get here in time to help lay Mrs. Ashcroft's ghost," he said, without turning.

"But you weren't watching for me," I said, "or you wouldn't still be standing there."

"Ah, I am delighted to note such growth in your deductive faculty," he replied. "I'm waiting for Jamison and Constable Mecker. We may need their help tonight if we are to trap this elusive apparition. Mrs. Ashcroft has sent word that the string across the library was broken last night.—Ah, here they come now."

He turned. "You've had supper, Parker?"

"I dined at the Diogenes Club."

"Come then. The game's afoot."

He led the way down the stairs and out into Praed Street, where a police car had just drawn up to the curb. The door of the car sprang open at our approach, and Constable Mecker got out. He was a fresh-faced young man whose work Pons had come to regard as very promising, and he greeted us with anticipatory pleasure, stepping aside so that we could enter the car. Inspector Seymour Jamison, a bluff, square-faced man wearing a clipped mustache, occupied the far corner of the seat.

Inspector Jamison spared no words in formal greeting. "How in the devil did you get on to Captain Brensham's poisoning?" he asked gruffly.

"Spilsbury found poison, then?"

"Arsenic. A massive dose. Brensham couldn't have lived much over twelve hours after taking it. How did you know?"

"I had only a very strong assumption," said Pons.

The car was rolling forward now through streets hazed with a light mist and beginning to glow with the yellow lights of the shops, blunting the harsh realities of daylight and lending to London a kind of enchantment I loved. Mecker was at the wheel, which he handled with great skill in the often crowded streets.

Inspector Jamison was persistent. "I hope you haven't got us out on a wild goose chase," he went on. "I have some doubts about following your lead in such matters, Pons."

"When I've misled you, they'll be justified. Not until then. Now, another matter—if related. You'll recall a disappearance in Dulwich two years ago? Elderly man named Ian Narth?"

Jamison sat for a few moments in silence. Then he said. "Man of seventy. Retired seaman. Indigent. No family. Last seen on a tube train near the Crystal Palace. Vanished without trace. Presumed drowned in the Thames and carried out to sea."

"I believe I can find him for you, Jamison."

Jamison snorted. "Now, then, Pons—give it to me short. What's all this about?"

Pons summed up the story of our client's haunted library, while Jamison sat in thoughtful silence.

"Laying ghosts is hardly in my line," he said when Pons had finished.

"Can you find your way to the Sydenham entrance of the abandoned old Nunhead-Crystal Palace High Level Railway Line?" asked Pons.

"Of course."

"If not, I have a map with me. Two, in fact. If you and Mecker will conceal yourself near that entrance, ready to arrest anyone coming out of it, we'll meet you there in from two to three hours' time."

"I hope you know what you're doing, Pons," growled Jamison.

"I share that hope, Jamison." He turned to Mecker and gave him Mrs. Ashcroft's address. "Parker and I will leave you there, Jamison. You'll have plenty of time to reach the tunnel entrance before we begin our exploration at the other end."

"It's murder then, Pons?"

"I should hardly think that anyone would willingly take so much arsenic unless he meant to commit suicide. No such intention was manifest in Captain Brensham's life—indeed, quite the contrary. He loved the life he led, and would not willingly have given it up."

"You're postulating that Ian Narth knew Captain Brensham and his nephew?"

"I am convinced inquiry will prove that to be the case."

Mecker let us out of the police car before Mrs Ashcroft's house, which loomed with an almost forbiddingly sinister air into the gathering darkness. Light shone wanly from but one window; curtains were drawn over the rest of them at the front of the house, and the entire dwelling seemed to be waiting upon its foredoomed decay.

Mrs. Ashcroft herself answered our ring.

"Oh, Mr. Pons!" she cried at sight of us, "you *did* get my message."

"Indeed, I did, Mrs. Ashcroft. Dr. Parker and I have now come to make an attempt to lay your ghost."

Mrs. Ashcroft paled a little and stepped back to permit us entrance.

"You'll want to see the broken thread, Mr. Pons," she said after she had closed the door.

"If you please."

She swept past us and led us to the library, where she turned up all the lights. The black thread could be seen lying on the carpet, broken through about midway, and away from the east wall.

"Nothing has been disturbed, Mrs. Ashcroft?"

"Nothing. No one has come into this room but me—at my strict order. Except, of course, whoever broke the thread." She shuddered. "It appears to have been broken by something coming out of the wall!"

"Does it not?" agreed Pons.

"No ghost could break that thread," I said.

"There are such phenomena as *poltergeists* which are said to make all kinds of mischief, including the breaking of dishes," said Pons dryly. "If we had that to deal with, the mere breaking of a thread would offer it no problem. You heard nothing, Mrs. Ashcroft?"

"Nothing."

"No rattling of chains, no hollow groans?"

"Nothing, Mr. Pons."

"And not even the sound of a book falling?"

"Such a sound an old house might make at any time, I suppose, Mr. Pons."

He cocked his head suddenly; a glint came into his eyes. "And not, I suppose, a sound like that? Do you hear it?"

"Oh, Mr. Pons," cried Mrs. Ashcroft in a low voice. "That is the sound Mrs. Jenkins heard."

It was the sound of someone singing—singing boisterously. It seemed to come as from a great distance, out of the very books on the walls.

"Fifteen men on a dead man's chest," murmured Pons. "I can barely make out the words. Captain Brensham's collection of sea lore is shelved along this wall, too! A coincidence."

"Mr. Pons! What is it?" asked our client.

"Pray do not disturb yourself, Mrs. Ashcroft. That is hardly a voice from the other side. It has too much body. But we are delaying unnecessarily. Allow me."

So saying, he crossed to the book shelves, at the approximate place where she had reported seeing the apparition that haunted the library. He lifted a dozen books off a shelf and put them to one side. Then he knocked upon the wall behind. It gave back a muffled, hollow sound. He nodded in satisfaction, and then gave the entire section of shelving the closest scrutiny.

Presently he found what he sought—after having removed half the books from the shelving there—a small lever concealed behind a row of books. He depressed it. Instantly there was a soft thud—like the sound a book might make when it struck the carpet—and the section sagged forward, opening into the room like a door ajar. Mrs. Ashcroft gasped sharply.

"What on earth is that, Mr. Pons?"

"Unless I am very much mistaken, it is a passage to the abandoned right-of-way of the Nunhead-Crystal Palace Line—and the temporary refuge of your library ghost."

He pulled the shelving farther into the room, exposing a gaping aperture which led into the high bank behind that wall of the house, and down into the earth beneath. Out of the aperture came a voice which was certainly that of an inebriated man, raucously singing. The voice echoed and reverberated as in a cavern below.

"Pray excuse us, Mrs. Ashcroft," said Pons. "Come, Parker."

Pons took a flashlight from his pocket and, crouching, crept into the tunnel. I followed him. The earth was shored up for a little way beyond the opening, then the walls were bare, and here and there I found them narrow for me, though Pons, being slender, managed to slip through with less difficulty. The aperture was not high enough for some distance to enable one to do more than crawl, and it was a descending passage almost from the opening in Mrs. Ashcroft's library.

Ahead of us, the singing had stopped suddenly.

"Hist!" warned Pons abruptly.

There was a sound of hurried movement up ahead.

"I fear he has heard us," Pons whispered.

He moved forward again, and abruptly stood up. I crowded out to join him. We stood on the right-of-way of the abandoned Nunhead-Crystal Palace Line. The rails were still in place, and the railbed was clearly the source of the cinder Pons had produced for my edification. Far ahead of us on the line someone was running.

"No matter," said Pons. "There is only one way for him to go. He could hardly risk going out to where the main line passes. He must go out by way of the Sydenham entrance."

We pressed forward, and soon the light revealed a niche hollowed out of the the wall. It contained bedding, a half eaten loaf of bread, candles, a lantern, books. Outside the opening were dozens of empty wine and brandy bottles.

Pons examined the bedding.

"Just as I thought," he said, straightening up. "This has not been here very long—certainly not longer than two months."

"The time since the younger Brensham's death," I cried.

"You advance, Parker, indeed!"

"Then he and Narth were in it together!"

"Of necessity," said Pons. "Come."

He ran rapidly down the line, I after him.

Up ahead there was a sudden burst of shouting. "Aha!" cried Pons. "They have him!"

After minutes of hard running, we burst out of the tunnel at the entrance where Inspector Jamison and Constable Mecker waited—the constable manacled to a wild-looking old man, whose fierce glare was indeed alarming. Greying hair stood out from his head, and his unkempt beard completed a frame of hair around a grimy face out of which blazed two eyes fiery with rage.

"He gave us quite a struggle, Pons," said Jamison, still breathing heavily.

"Capital! Capital!" cried Pons, rubbing his hands together delightedly. "Gentlemen, let me introduce you to as wily an old scoundrel as we've had the pleasure of meeting in a long time. Captain Jason Brensham, swindler of insurance companies and, I regret to say, murderer."

"Narth!" exclaimed Jamison.

"Ah, Jamison, you had your hands on him. But I fear you lost him when you gave him to Spilsbury."

"The problem was elementary enough," said Pons, as he filled his pipe with the abominable shag he habitually smoked, and leaned up against the mantel in our quarters later that night. "Mrs. Ashcroft told us everything essential to its solution, and Harwell only confirmed it. The unsolved question was the identity of the victim, and the files of the metropolitan papers gave me a presumptive answer to that in the disappearance of Ian Narth, a man of similar build and age to Captain Brensham.

"Of course, it was manifest at the outset that this motiveless spectre was chancing discovery for survival. It was not Jenkins but the captain who was raiding the food and liquor stocks at his house. The cave, of course, was never intended as a permanent hiding place, but only as a refuge to seek when strangers came to the house, or whenever his nephew had some of his friends in. He lived in the house; he had always been reclusive, and he changed his way of life but little. His nephew, you will recall Harwell's telling us, continued to subscribe to his magazines and buy the books he wanted, apparently for himself, but obviously for his uncle. The bedding and supplies were obviously moved into the tunnel after the younger Brensham's death.

"The manner and place of the ghost's appearance suggested the opening in the wall. The cinder in the carpet cried aloud of the abandoned Nunhead-Crystal Palace Line which the maps I studied in the British Museum confirmed ran almost under the house. The captain actually had more freedom than most dead men, for he could wander out along the line by night, if he wished.

"Harwell clearly set forth the motive. The captain had sold off everything he had to enable him to continue his way of living. He needed money. His insurance policies promised to supply it. He and his nephew together hatched up the plot. Narth was picked as victim, probably out of a circle of acquaintances because, as newspaper descriptions made clear, he had a certain resemblance to the captain and was, like him, a retired seaman with somewhat parallel tastes.

"They waited until the auspicious occasion when Dr. Weston, who knew the captain too well to be taken in, was off on a prolonged holiday, lured Narth to the house, killed him with a lethal dose of arsenic, after which they cleaned up the place to eliminate all external trace of poison and its effects, and called in Dr. Weston's *locum* to witness the dying man's last minutes. The captain was by this time in his cave, and the young doctor took Howard Brensham's word for the symptoms and signed the death certificate, after which the Brenshams had ample funds on which to live as the captain liked."

"And how close they came to getting away with it!" I cried.

"Indeed! Howard Brensham's unforeseen death—ironically, of a genuine heart attack—was the little detail they had never dreamed of. On similar turns of fate empires have fallen!"